CLASH OF KINGDOMS

DIRTY BLOOD
BOOK 6

PENELOPE BARSETTI

HARTWICK PUBLISHING

Hartwick Publishing

Clash of Kingdoms

Copyright © 2024 by Penelope Barsetti

All rights reserved.

No part of this book may be reproduced in any form or by any electronic or mechanical means, including information storage and retrieval systems, without written permission from the author, except for the use of brief quotations in a book review.

CONTENTS

1. Aurelias — 1
2. Harlow — 29
3. Aurelias — 51
4. Harlow — 95
5. Vine — 107
6. Aurelias — 111
7. Aurelias — 135
8. Harlow — 147
9. Aurelias — 155
10. Vine — 171
11. Harlow — 175
12. Huntley — 181
13. Huntley — 203
14. Harlow — 215
15. Aurelias — 229
16. Harlow — 245
17. Huntley — 253
18. Aurelias — 267
19. Harlow — 301
20. Aurelias — 309
21. Harlow — 337
22. Aurelias — 355
23. Huntley — 363
24. Aurelias — 375
25. Aurelias — 397
26. Harlow — 409
27. Harlow — 419
28. Aurelias — 425
29. Aurelias — 449

30. Harlow	453
31. Aurelias	465
32. Harlow	469
Epilogue	477

ONE
AURELIAS

When I opened my eyes, it was morning.

Light came through the part in the curtains, not the golden light of Delacroix, but the murky gray kind from the overcast sky. It reminded me of home, so I preferred it over the constant sunshine of Harlow's home.

I looked at her beside me, the sheets to her shoulder, her naked body tucked underneath and pressed against me. My shoulder was her pillow. Her hand stretched out to my other arm, her hand cupping the bicep. She slept soundly, her breathing like a gentle lullaby.

I pressed a soft kiss to her hairline before I gently rolled her away to hug a pillow instead of me. She was so out of it after our long night that she grabbed on to that right away and continued to sleep without interruption. Her beautiful hair spread out behind her, like my cape in battle.

Duty was the only thing strong enough to get me out of that bed. If I had nowhere else to be, I would wait for her to wake up so I could take her again, so I could feel the fire when our bodies connected.

When I was dressed and armed, I left the bedroom, walked past the guards in the hallway, and then moved up the stairs to the great room, the place where their deliberation and meals took place.

Ivory sat at the table alone, drinking a cup of coffee, wearing a uniform and armor similar to Huntley's but far less heavy. If she wore something identical to his, she probably wouldn't be able to stand.

When I approached the table, she didn't acknowledge me. Emptiness burned in her eyes.

I approached the window and looked out, the landscape cold and dry. Darker clouds were on the horizon and headed this way. It would probably snow sometime today. I could see the trails of smoke coming from all the cottages, everyone trying to stay warm in the chill. I turned back to her, standing behind her so I looked at the back of her head. "Is there anything I can do for you, Your Highness?" It was weird to call anyone that, because I didn't even refer to my own father that way. I was used to being referred to as such, being revered as one of the deadliest vampires to have ever lived.

She said nothing for a while. "No."

I looked out the window again for a moment before I approached the table and took a seat on her right. "He'll return."

She brought the mug to her lips and took a drink, her eyes still devoid of emotion. "Ever since I met my mother-in-law, she's been alone. A widow. Taking care of her children even when they had their own children. I never pitied her before, but now I do. To live the rest of your life without your husband to share it with. I don't think I can bear it..."

"You won't have to."

"We survived many wars together, but even with that hardship, I realize I never truly appreciated the peace that came afterward. I took it for granted. I didn't cherish it nearly as much as I should have."

My gaze shifted back to the window because looking directly at her felt like an invasion of privacy.

"And now we may never have that again. My husband may never return. And I'll fail to protect our children and our Kingdoms. And then we'll all die...or worse."

"You have my sword," I said gently. "So you'll never fail."

She stared into her coffee.

I could feel her despair. It was potent, stronger than the black coffee she'd just brewed. The dark clouds in the distance now appeared over her head—and she suffocated in the snow that buried her underneath. "We both know that humankind is powerless against these demons."

Her eyes shifted back to me.

"But you and your husband are exceptional people, and I believe you'll find a way."

Her eyes remained on mine, like she could see straight through me.

I never would have fallen in love again if Harlow weren't the most exceptional woman I'd ever met. And now I knew exactly where she'd gotten the traits that had made me fall headfirst the moment I kissed her. "He'll return."

She looked down into her coffee again.

"Let me know how I can be of service to you, Your Highness."

A gentle smile moved over her lips. "Please don't call me that. Ivory is fine."

"Very well," I said. "How can I be of service to you, Ivory?"

"I've moped around since my husband left because his absence is all I can think about. But I know my time is better spent preparing for war. We need to prepare HeartHolme for the influx of citizens about to join us—and we also need to strengthen our fortifications to prepare the field for battle."

"I agree."

"I have some ideas."

"I'm listening."

"Since they come from underneath the ground...what if we covered the field with stone? The same stone we use to create our streets. I realize that's labor-intensive and a waste of resources, but it may prevent them from rising and getting too close to the wall."

I nodded in agreement, impressed by the suggestion. "That's a good idea."

"Our ground is much denser and colder, so I hope that's enough to prevent them from coming altogether. Delacroix is full of fertile soil and sand, much easier to penetrate than the hard earth we have here."

"That's true."

"Perhaps they'll only be able to rise farther south, and we'll have some warning they're coming."

She really was Huntley's equal. "That means we should prepare an attack farther south as well."

"But all those soldiers will die..."

"Then we do something with the dragons. Have them drop boulders the way Harlow did in Delacroix."

She nodded in agreement. "I can have the miners harvest the largest stones they can find. Put them in a location for the dragons."

"Good idea," I said as I rose to my feet. "I'll speak with General Macabre, and we'll begin preparations."

"Thank you, Aurelias."

I turned away to get to work.

"Aurelias?"

I turned back to her, waiting for further orders.

"I'm sorry my husband was so unkind to you."

I wasn't resentful then, and I wasn't resentful now. "If I had a daughter, I would have done the same thing."

It grew dark earlier here than it did in Delacroix, so the daylight was gone quicker than I wished. The temperature dropped further, and that's when I felt the cold pierce my gloves and numb my knuckles. I returned to the castle after a long day spent working with General Macabre and the men who owed me no loyalty. It was hard to believe I was there to *help* humans, when all I'd done before was kill them. My father and I had intended to defeat the Ethereal then take the kingdom of men for ourselves, to subjugate them to be what they were meant to be—food and labor.

Before I stepped into the bedchambers, I knew Harlow was inside. I'd known she was inside when I was down the hallway. Her mind was like a low-burning fire, her heat felt in every corner of the room—except, in her case, her mind was felt in every corner of the world.

I stepped inside and found her sitting on the couch in front of the fire, wearing a nightdress because I'd been gone from dawn till dusk. She'd showered and combed her hair, and in that white dress, she looked fucking stunning.

Her eyes found mine, and there was the identical flash of desire that I felt. She always felt it when she saw me, whether I was buck naked or fully armed. My appearance provoked the same longing that hers did for me. Whenever we were in a room together, it was a blaze of fire.

I turned away to undress, to remove all the pieces of armor and the weapons that weighed down my body. But even then, I was uncomfortable after a long day working at the wall, giving orders and watching men practically run off to fulfill them because they were terrified I would bite them. "I'm going to shower." I knew she wanted me, but she would have to wait.

"Hurry."

I clenched my eyes as I walked away, feeling a rush of light-headedness because my dick got so hard so fast. A shiver slid down my spine because she turned me on so damn much, the way she wasn't afraid to beg.

I took a quick shower, my dick hard the entire time, letting the heat warm my skin and release the dirt and sweat. I did a quick towel-dry before I walked back into the room and froze when I spotted her on the bed.

Naked.

Sitting on the bed with her perfect tits exposed. Her long hair down along her arms. Confidence burning in her eyes, along with desire. Her arousal was so intense that I could actually feel the wetness between her legs without touching her. "I told you to hurry."

Holy fuck. I moved onto the bed and quickly got on top of her, her head hitting the pillow, all the sheets and covers kicked to the side so it was just the two of us on the mattress. Her soft thighs gripped my hips, and her palms moved up my chest as she tilted her head back to receive my kiss.

I wanted to kiss her hard, but it came out soft, because every time I touched her, my heart ached. Everything was different now. The moment I'd given in to my weakness and said those three little words, my life had changed. I could have lied to myself forever—but I couldn't lie to her.

So now everything was slow and purposeful. Instead of fucking her until those sparkling tears streaked down her cheeks, I wanted to touch her heart with mine, wanted to savor every kiss and every touch, to make every moment feel like an eternity.

Her fingers moved into my damp hair, and she kissed me, squeezing me anxiously with her thighs, desperate to feel me inside her.

I guided myself into her, and my tip instantly felt just how soaked she was, like she'd been thinking about me long before I'd walked through the door. I pushed inside, the tight fit easy when she was wet like this. I sank all the way, losing my breath for a second because it felt so damn good.

Her mouth ravaged mine as she started to rock her hips with me, her nails slicing down my back.

I moved with her, our quiet breaths accompanied by the sound of the crackling fire. It'd been so long since I'd done this with someone I cared about that I'd forgotten how it felt, how vulnerable it forced me to be. I couldn't hide behind my anger or my coldness. It was all there for her to see. It was also easier to keep control over my body, because whenever we fucked, I just wanted to come the entire time. But when we made love…it was different. My mind and body didn't want it to end. Wanted it to last forever.

She came right away, moaning against my lips, her hand gripping my ass and tugging me hard inside her.

I ended our kiss to watch, watch her hit her high and get stars in her eyes. The tears came a second later, beautiful diamonds that reflected the firelight before they fell down her cheeks.

I caught each of them with my lips and kissed her, wanting her to taste the salt of her desire. Sweat drenched my body and the muscles in my body ached, but I couldn't feel either of those things when I was locked in this embrace.

We hadn't spoken since our conversation by the fire, when I'd explained to her exactly why this would end. Instead of getting angry with me for not sacrificing my immortality, she calmly accepted it and then dragged me to bed, asking me to make love to her…as if that would make us both forget.

There was no hesitation before I spoke, the walls of my restraint crumbled. I'd dedicated my life to this woman, but now I dedicated my heart. "I love you, baby." I fisted her hair and kissed her hard, falling deeper into the cocoon we made together. "I love you so fucking much."

She squeezed my hips as she dug her hand into my hair. She said it breathlessly, her nails sharp on my flesh, her hips anxious to take more of me. "I love you too."

I lay with her, her thigh hiked over my hip, her lips swollen from my kiss, her eyes heavy with exhaustion.

Her hair stuck to her neck because of the sweat, even though I'd done all the work. No complaints.

Her fingers played with my jawline, feeling the coarse hair of my stubble, moving against the growth so she could feel the sharpness against her fingertips. She liked to touch me, always had her hands on me whenever we were in the same room together.

I watched her stare at my jawline, looking at her stunning blue eyes. I'd never appreciated a woman's eye color before, but hers...I could look at them forever. Their depths were endless. Her kindness had its own light. And her soul...I could see that too. I could see what she couldn't see in me.

"You were gone all day." Her hand moved to my chest.

"I did some things for your mother."

She nodded slightly.

"What did you do?"

"I never left the room." Her eyes weren't on mine as she said that, like she wanted to hide from me.

I knew she was depressed for a lot of reasons. She feared her father wouldn't return, and she knew we would never be more than what we were right now. Combined, it was enough to keep her in bed all day. Her mother had been at the table this morning, but it was clear she didn't want to be there, that her life was on hold until her husband returned.

"It was just one of those days, you know."

The last time I'd had a day like that was a long time ago, and it had been more than a couple of days.

Her eyes eventually came back to me. "It feels like the first time I actually get to be with you." Her blue eyes were emotional, shining with her love for me. "I get to sleep with you. You come home to me at the end of a long day. It's nice."

It was nice. I'd never been so happy and so sad simultaneously.

She continued to rub my hard chest. "Can I ask you something?"

I knew what her question was because I could feel it, feel the curiosity that had never waned. "Just because I love you and we're in domestic bliss doesn't mean I ever want to discuss what you're about to ask me. Don't take it personally—and don't ask me again."

She had no reaction, but inside, I could feel her jerk away. "May I ask why?"

I restrained my anger because the last time I'd failed to do so, she'd stormed out into the cold and cried...and that made me feel like shit. She was in my arms that very moment, our lives at peace, and the last thing I wanted to do was ruin that. "Because it hurts."

Her eyes softened, and then her heart clenched. "How long ago was this?"

"Five hundred and thirteen years ago."

Surprise moved onto her face. She couldn't understand time the way I could. To her, that may as well have been forever. For me, it felt like a couple of decades. "And it still hurts...?"

I could feel her unease, feel the roar of jealousy that my heart had ever belonged to another. I knew I would feel the same way, that Ethan's unrequited obsession was enough to piss me off. But I wouldn't lie to her. "It'll always hurt."

She paused, my words causing her pain in several different ways. "So...you were married?"

"No."

"Were you—"

"I'm here with you, baby. Leave my past where it belongs—in the past."

Her eyes flicked away.

"Don't pull away from me." My hand grabbed her chin and forced her stare back on me. "I want you here with me—always." I kissed her, kissed her hard on the mouth, showing her the depth of my love because my words weren't enough. I might have loved another woman in my life, but she'd been gone a long time, and now my heart was occupied by a single woman, a single name.

Her kiss was hesitant in the beginning, but it turned fiery within seconds, her hand in my hair, her thigh squeezing my side.

I rolled her onto her back and buried myself inside her like I hadn't already made love to her twice. But that was how much I wanted this woman—always.

A knock sounded on the door.

It was the middle of the night. The fire was almost extinguished. The candles had burned out. I'd been dead asleep a second ago, but I was on my feet with my sword in my hand instantly.

Harlow jerked up and gave a quiet yelp in surprise.

"What is it?" I said through the closed door.

"Riders approach the gate," the guard said. "Queen Rolfe has been notified."

"How many?" I asked.

"Four."

I quickly dressed and donned my armor and weapons.

Harlow threw on whatever she could find. "Who are the riders?"

"I don't know."

"Could it be *them*?"

"They don't strike me as the diplomatic type." I walked out, and she followed me, wearing a sweater and trousers, her hair a mess from the hours of rolling around in the sheets.

I made it to the great room, Queen Rolfe already there, dressed in armor like she was ready for battle.

"The guards said they're unable to identify the riders because of the snow."

I glanced out the window and saw it falling, so much of it that it was difficult to make out the torches in the distance. "I'll go to the gate," I said. "I'll report back what I discover."

"I'm not staying here," Queen Rolfe said. "If someone enters my gates in times of war, I want to know who it is."

"I think that's unwise—"

"Your job is to protect me," she snapped. "So when I go down there, you protect me." She turned away. "Let's go."

Harlow watched her mother walk away before she turned back to me. "Now you know where I get it from."

There wasn't an opportunity to crack a smile, not in the seriousness of the moment, so I walked behind Queen Rolfe down the hallway, out of the castle, and into the cold, and followed the torches down to the gate.

I stayed behind her, acting as her guard rather than her equal.

We eventually made it to the gate, which was still closed and locked since General Henry and the soldiers would arrive sometime in the morning.

"What do you see?" I called to the archers on top.

They stared through the darkness and the snow, taking a moment to identify the travelers who approached without invitation. "Two of the riders bear black-and-red armor. The other two...I think I see gold."

My heart gave a burst at the information. "My brothers."

Queen Rolfe turned to me. "You're certain?"

"Yes."

She turned to the guard. "Open the gate."

We stepped back, and slowly, the enormous doors began to swing open, the gears in the mechanism creaking from the weight. They parted wide enough for the four riders to come through, and then minutes later, they arrived, their horses' hooves loud against the earth.

They tugged on the reins and brought the horses to a standstill.

Up close, I could see the details of their armor, the snakes engraved on their chests, the serpents on their blades. I went to Larisa and gave her my hand to help her down from the horse. "What are you doing here?"

"It's a loooooooong story," she said. "And we're fucking freezing." She unhooked a bucket made of sheep's wool and handed it to me. "Fang needs to get warm. Even in that bucket, he's turning solid."

Kingsnake came to me next and pulled back his hood. There was no smartass comment from him because the cold and the famine had exhausted him too. "Of course, when we get here, there's a blizzard..."

Queen Rolfe came to my side and regarded them, focusing on their eyes where their pupils were slitted.

"This is Queen Rolfe," I said in introduction. "I don't think you met previously."

Kingsnake gave a slight bow. "Your Highness."

Cobra and the others did the same. Cobra and Kingsnake wouldn't have made that gesture in another scenario, but because they knew these people were important to me, they sucked it up.

I was quiet, letting Queen Rolfe take the lead because she was the ruler and I was the servant.

"Join us in the castle," she said. "Any guest of Aurelias's is a guest of mine."

We walked the long path to the castle in the freezing snow, no one speaking because everyone was too cold to say anything. Once we entered the castle and the doors shut behind us, there was a sigh of relief from all of them. We traveled upstairs and entered the great room. Harlow sat in one of the chairs, and a fire had been made in the grand fireplace to light up the room.

Larisa placed the wool bucket in front of the fireplace so Fang could warm himself near the flames. He slowly poked his head out, his tongue slipping in and out, and then he slithered closer to the flames, curling up into a ball like a dog on the rug.

Thisss isss much better.

Harlow stared at the snake with wide eyes. "Is that…a pet?"

"Not a pet," Larisa said. "More of a companion."

More of a ruthlesss killing machine…

I always found Fang's words refreshing. *It's nice to see you again.*

And you.

I moved to Kingsnake and embraced him. I did the same with Cobra and Larisa. With Clara, I didn't know her very well, and I still felt uncomfortable knowing she used to be an Ethereal, so I regarded her with a nod.

"Take a seat," Queen Rolfe said. "You must be tired. Refreshments will be provided momentarily."

I knew what they really wanted was blood, but they couldn't have that.

We all sat at the table, and for a moment, all was quiet, as if my brothers didn't know how to speak candidly in front of Queen Rolfe, a stranger.

The staff brought rounds of ale and scotch, and my brothers immediately went for the good stuff. Harlow had a hot chocolate, and I found that cute for some reason. I wasn't sitting close to her at the table. I was on Queen Rolfe's right, while Harlow was down at the other end, closer to Fang. She continued to glance at him, like she found him fascinating.

I spoke first. "I guess Father said no, then?" It was a defeat, a terrible one.

Kingsnake threw back his head as he took a drink, treating it like a shot rather than a beverage meant to be savored. "We were just victorious in the battle against the werewolves, and now he's busy structuring his new rulership over the humans." His tone implied all his disapproval for that. "Another war is deeply inconvenient."

"I guess I'm not the favorite after all."

"He said he needed more time to think about it."

I was shocked once again. "Yes, because wars only happen on his timetable." My father was a fucking prick. "Then why are you here?"

Kingsnake exchanged a look with Cobra. "You thought we'd abandon you?"

"Abandon isn't an appropriate description," I said. "I can leave anytime I want, but I've chosen to stay here. My decisions should have no bearing on yours."

Cobra rolled his eyes before he took a drink. "He's stiffer than this drink."

Larisa gave a quiet chuckle.

I didn't find it the least bit funny, and my look made that pretty clear. "Just because it's my decision to fight this war doesn't mean it needs to be your decision too. I appreciate the fact that you came all the way over here—"

"In the freezing cold," Cobra said. "And our boat almost capsized... But glad you *appreciate* it."

I ignored the sarcasm. "I appreciate your loyalty, but I don't want you to die for me."

"And we don't want you to die alone," Larisa said.

I looked at her, the only member of the family I actually liked at the moment.

"There's more to our decision," Kingsnake said, capturing my attention. "We know Father will feel a greater urgency when three of his sons are at risk. Now that we've left, he'll worry, and then he'll send that army quicker than he would have otherwise."

"Sounds like a risky plan," I said.

"We've done it before," Cobra said. "When he rode to Evanguard to burn it to the ground, we stood in his way until he was forced to change his mind. It worked."

Evanguard should have burned to the ground as far as I was concerned. But I held my tongue in the presence of my new sister-in-law.

"I think Father would have come instantly if he weren't preoccupied with so many other things," Kingsnake said. "And I know he's perplexed that you've chosen to give your sword to humans." Kingsnake said nothing else on the topic, but his stare implied all the things he chose to conceal from the humans sitting with me, that my usual ruthless politics weren't in their favor. "He is worried about you. Deeply."

"You're still the favorite," Cobra said coldly. "Don't worry about that."

Harlow gave a chuckle from where she sat at the table.

We all turned to look, seeing Fang perch up to look at her, his tongue sliding in and out.

She rubbed his chin, grinning as she watched him regard her with those luminous eyes.

I like her.

"He likes it when you rub his head too," Larisa said. "Especially if you have sharp nails."

"I bet she has sharp nails…" Cobra said to himself before he took a drink.

I glared at him, Harlow's mother sitting right there.

He grinned and took another drink.

Harlow scratched Fang's head, and he immediately closed his eyes in pleasure.

Yaaasssssss.

Ivory regained control of the conversation. "A lot has happened since your last visit to our lands. My brother-in-law traveled to the east to discover everything he could about our enemy, against my husband's orders, and now my husband has gone to rescue him from his captivity." She spoke with a strong voice despite the terror in our hearts. "He should return soon—and hopefully with the knowledge we need to destroy these fiends."

"So at this moment in time, you know nothing new about them?" Kingsnake asked.

I shook my head. "We're preparing HeartHolme for the assault. All the Kingdoms are traveling here for the battle. It's the only place that can contain all of humankind. We may not be able to match their strength, but perhaps our numbers will greatly exceed theirs."

"Yes," Kingsnake said, staring at me. "Hopefully…"

We sat in silence for a few minutes. Ivory continued to stare at my kin, and Harlow continued to give Fang a rubdown, not the least bit afraid of his size and strength. She treated him like a puppy dog.

Ivory cleared her throat. "My servants will prepare your accommodations in the castle. If there's anything you need, let them know." She rose from her seat. "Once my husband returns, we'll have another discussion."

We all stood when she stood, giving her the respect that others gave to us in our lands.

She nodded before she walked away.

Harlow remained, hypnotized by the beauty of Fang's scales. "You're cute."

I know.

When Harlow felt the intensity rise, she knew she didn't belong in this conversation. She patted him on the head before she rose from her chair. "It's nice to see you again. Goodnight." She left the room and stepped into the hallway.

My back was to her so I couldn't watch her go, but I wanted to crane my neck to see her walk away. My attention returned to my brothers across from me.

"Now that they're gone..." Cobra grabbed the bottle and refilled his glass until it nearly spilled over the top. He did the same for Kingsnake, filling it like it was water after a trek across a desert. "So when did you become such a little bitch?" He drank from his glass as he stared me down. "You said you wanted to protect your woman, but from what I can see, you're the queen's guard."

I would have denied that statement before, but that's exactly what Harlow was...my woman. "When her father left, he asked me to protect his family like they're my own."

"But they aren't your own," Cobra said. "*We are*. And we sailed across the world for you."

"I didn't ask you to do that—"

"When it comes to family, you never have to ask." He slammed his drink down. "Aurelias, what the fuck?"

I turned to Kingsnake. "Let's ignore the child."

"Actually..." Kingsnake pulled his drink toward him. "I'm with our brother on this one. You're making an immense sacrifice for these people. I don't even recognize you with the way you're behaving. You said you wanted to protect your woman, but you've *become* one of them."

"I will never be one of them." Even though Harlow had asked me to.

"If you want to protect the girl, just bring her back with you," Kingsnake suggested. "Live in Crescent Falls with her—"

"She would never abandon her family."

"Well, if you want her to survive, that might be your only option," Kingsnake said. "Because these humans are far too weak to face these demons."

I stared at my glass for a moment, the past flashing across my eyes. The way Harlow's mother stood her ground against those monsters. The way I could *feel* Huntley's love for his family every time we were in the same room together. The way his own son risked his life for his people rather than hiding behind the castle doors. "They're stronger than you realize."

Kingsnake continued to stare at me, his head cocked slightly. His ruthless stare continued, and the anger and resentment slowly faded into something else. "You love her."

My eyes went back to my glass.

The others stared at me too, waiting for me to vehemently deny it.

I didn't. "Her family...they're good people." They're different from the humans in our world. They aren't weak and submissive. They are strong and brave. "They serve their people...rather than expect to be served. I've grown to respect them, especially her father."

Kingsnake had nothing to say.

Cobra didn't either, surprisingly.

"They don't deserve this," I whispered. "They don't deserve to be wiped from existence just because the Teeth betrayed them."

"You can't betray someone who was never your ally," Kingsnake said. "The Teeth were conquered then subjugated. It was foolish for the king to assume there would be no repercussions for that, even twenty years later. You may respect him, but he sounds arrogant to me."

"He's just," I said coldly. "He doesn't order an execution unless he intends to fulfill it himself. He doesn't order his general and soldiers into battle while he sits on his throne in the safety of his castle. He's on the front lines. He went to save his brother himself rather than leaving him to his fate. He's a brave man, which is more than I can say about our own father..."

"Why don't you just turn her?" Cobra said. "She's far more likely to survive as a vampire."

I shook my head. "No."

"If you want to be with her, it's going to happen anyway—"

"*I said no.*" Just the thought made me sick to my stomach.

Kingsnake's stare hardened, like he understood perfectly. "One of us can do it, Aurelias—"

"No." If I chose to spend my life with one woman, I wouldn't let another man turn her, regardless of the circumstances. "I promised her father I would never do that."

"Then what's your plan?" Cobra snapped. "How is this going to work—"

"*It's not.*" I took a drink of my scotch, the heat numbing the pain.

"What are you saying?" Kingsnake asked. "That you love this woman, but you aren't going to commit to her?"

"Commitment isn't the issue." If she were already a vampire, everything would be different.

Kingsnake seemed to understand. "Aurelias, I know this is a touchy subject—"

"*Then don't touch it,*" I said coldly. "Even if I were willing to do that, which I never will be, she said that's not the life she wants. She wants to join the afterlife with her family. She wants to have children of her own. She's not willing to give that up for me—and I respect her for it. There's only one other option, and I told her I'm unwilling to do it."

They were all quiet, the revelation soaking into their bones.

"Even if this is a brief moment in my very long life, and probably not worth the heartache, I will fight for her. I want her to live a long, happy life, even if it's with someone else, even if it's over in the blink of an eye."

They remained quiet, staring at me across the table.

I looked into my glass to dodge their gazes.

"Aurelias." Larisa was the one to speak. "You're putting your life and, therefore, your immortality, on the line for her. She's worth it to you?"

My eyes lifted to look at hers. "Yes."

"Then why are you unwilling to give up your immortality to be with her?"

I remained quiet as I held her gaze, confronted with a question I couldn't answer. I felt the stares of my brothers, both thinking the same thing. But I kept my silence, not having a single word to say.

TWO
HARLOW

"Stay." I grabbed his arm and pulled him back toward me when I felt his body move. It was early, so early there was barely any light outside, but I woke up because I didn't want to wake up later and not see his face.

"Baby, I have work to do."

I tugged him anyway, drawing him back toward me. "I don't care." My hand slid into his hair, and I kissed him, doing my best to entice him to stay, to move between my thighs and claim my flesh as his.

He kissed me back, his mouth opening to take my tongue, and slowly he started to move on top of me, his dick obeying my silent orders.

My thighs squeezed his hips, and I brought him toward me, wanting that dick buried inside me.

He smiled against my lips. "You win."

"I always win."

He guided himself inside me and sank in, giving a moan when he realized I was this wet first thing in the morning. Once he was fully sheathed inside my warmth, he paused to savor it, the muscles in his ass tightening.

After a pause, he started to thrust, his strong body positioned above mine, his abs firm and powerful, his chest like a mountain looming over me. He was sexy no matter what he did, whether he sat in front of the fire or he carried himself with confidence as he wore his armor, but he looked the sexiest like this...when he fucked me.

My arms circled his neck as I kissed him, as I felt him breathe into my mouth while he rocked into me. His breathing quickened in desire, not exertion, and I felt the way he thickened inside me, like he wanted to come the second he felt me.

Every time we were together, I loved him more, loved him deeper than I thought was possible. When I grabbed on to him, I never wanted to let go. This man had conquered my heart and left a permanent flag that would continue to flap in the wind even when he was long gone. It was hard to imagine myself in a wedding gown about to marry someone else, not when these memories would haunt me forever. Maybe I would never marry, not when I couldn't have the love of my life.

His hand dug into my hair as his face pressed into my neck, giving me deep thrusts that rubbed against my clit perfectly. Every time he moved, it was ecstasy, the pressure just right. He rarely did this, only when he needed me to come so he wouldn't have to edge himself.

"Can you feel me come?" I said into his ear, my nails digging deep into his back.

He released a heavy moan.

"Can you?" I whispered.

He lifted himself again, his face above mine, his eyes dark and intense, almost scary. "Yes."

"How does it feel?"

He gave another moan, his thrusts slowing down because the sensations became harder to resist. "Oh fuck."

I pulled my legs closer to my chest, folding myself underneath him so he could deepen the angle. My hand grabbed his ass, and I tugged him into me. "Here it comes..." I felt the fire between my legs, flames that burned my stomach and extremities, a sweat so hot it felt good. And then I hit the precipice and fell, moaning loudly as my toes curled and cramped, my eyes watering because of the sting of pleasure.

His intensity had deepened, his hard face tight in pleasure and concentration. His pumps quickened out of control, and he thrust into me harder before he gave a loud moan, releasing inside me as I crested the high he gave me.

He was the best sex of my life. And he was the sexiest man in my life.

I clung to him as I finished, as I received his seed. "Aurelias…" I loved saying his name. Loved saying it more than any other name I'd ever said in bed. I slowly came down from the high as I felt him soften inside me, but the tendrils of pleasure were still anchored deep in my flesh. My ankles crossed against his ass so he couldn't pull away. "Don't ever leave me without saying goodbye." I'd rather wake up at the crack of dawn to him between my legs than wake up hours later with him gone. "Alright?"

He dipped his head and kissed me hard, like he wanted to leave me even less now. "Yes, baby." He pulled away and moved off me, standing naked beside the bed, tall and muscular, his back carved with endless muscles.

The bedroom door cracked open, but there was no one there.

I looked at the crack, refusing to believe it was the draft that had pushed it open.

Aurelias didn't look alarmed. "You have a visitor."

Fang slithered up the bed then slid toward me, his powerful body gliding through the covers as he approached me. When the bottom half of his body appeared, he was holding a deck of cards in his coiled tail.

"Hey, Fang." I sat up to pet his head, letting my naked body be fully exposed to him.

He closed his eyes as he enjoyed my sharp nails against his hard scales.

Aurelias got dressed, pulling on his articles of clothing as he watched us. "He wants to play cards."

Fang brought his tail close and set the cards in front of me.

"He plays cards?" I asked with a laugh.

Aurelias gave a slight grin. "He more than plays cards. He's undefeated."

Fang slipped his tongue in and out as he stared at me.

"Wow," I said. "That's pretty impressive."

"He's not exactly humble about it. Larisa thinks he cheats."

Fang turned to Aurelias and hissed, exposing his razor-sharp fangs.

"As fun as that sounds, I don't know how to play," I said.

Aurelias finished piecing his armor together before he took a seat at the edge of the bed. "I'll give you a short rundown." He shuffled the cards quickly then showed me the different kinds of cards, the dragons, the types of fangs, the swords, and the poisons. "Each combination of cards creates a unique number. Whoever has the higher number wins." He showed me the rules for trading out the cards and the strategy behind it.

"I've never heard of this game."

"Good luck." He prepared to move away.

I grabbed him by the vambrace and tugged him back toward me, forcing his mouth to mine for a hard kiss.

His hand automatically dug into my hair, and he deepened a kiss that was already hard, like if he had it his way, he would be back in that bed with me…and Fang would be kicked out.

"I love you." I said it against his mouth, treasuring the fact that I got to say it at all. I didn't have to hide my feelings. I didn't have to sheathe my emotions. I could be myself, completely and utterly, and I wanted to embrace every moment before there were no more moments.

He said it back, his eyes locked on mine. "I love you too."

I sat across from Lila at the bar, her eyes dimmed in darkness. She brought the glass of wine to her lips and took a drink before she swirled it once more.

"My father will bring him back."

She continued to stare at the glass.

"You know he will."

Her eyes lifted again, and she released a sigh. "I didn't even get to say goodbye."

"You can say hello when you see him."

"You aren't terrified for your father?"

Oh, I was fucking terrified. "I know he'll be back." Aurelias had faith in him, and I needed to share that faith as well.

"I feel so guilty for the way I treated him."

"It was a complicated situation."

"We both know I was a bitch." She took another drink.

"Well, I had no idea all this was going on in the first place."

"I always looked at my father as a hero. A man who could do no wrong. Who had so much integrity and honesty, but he's human like the rest of us. I guess that was the hardest part, picturing my father as one of the sleazebags I've come across."

My mother had told me what happened. "He wasn't a sleazebag."

"I know that now...since I actually listened to him. I apologized. But I lost all that time with him because of my behavior."

"He doesn't hold it against you, Lila." My father adored me, no matter what. There was nothing I could do or say to change his love. Uncle Ian was the same way. "When he comes back, he can tell you himself."

She drank from her glass then asked the barmaiden to get her another. "What's new with you? Other than demons and evacuations."

Her mother had been so focused on Uncle Ian that she probably didn't know about Aurelias at all. "Well...I'm kinda with someone."

"Ethan?"

"Gods, no," I said quickly, knowing I hadn't thought of him once since the last time we'd spoken. "His name is Aurelias."

"Never heard a name like that."

"And you've never seen a man like this..."

"Ooooh, you gotta tell me everything."

So I did. Told her every last detail.

She leaned forward as she listened to it all, her fingers around her wineglass without taking a drink. Completely engrossed, she didn't interrupt me once. "Girl, I've never been so jealous in my life."

"Well, you won't be jealous when this is all over."

"Why not?"

I told her the truth, that this would end when the war was over.

"Why does it have to end?" she asked. "I don't understand. Don't let this man go, Harlow."

"It's complicated."

"Complicated, how?"

"Well, he's an immortal vampire, and the only way I can join him is if I forsake my soul...and my ability to have children."

She turned quiet, the light dimming in her eyes again. "Oh..."

"So, I asked him if he would be willing to be human...and he said no."

Her body slumped a little farther. "Oh."

"Yeah..."

She looked down, at a loss for words.

"So don't be too jealous. He's the man I've always wanted, and I'd marry him tomorrow if he asked me. But it's all going to fall apart and wreck my soul. I'll have to watch him sail from these shores, knowing I'll never see him again. He'll bed a line of beautiful women until he forgets me, and then I'll marry someone whom I love...but not quite as much."

Lila reached her hand for mine. "I'm sorry, girl."

My fingers squeezed hers. "Thanks."

"Maybe he'll change his mind about being human."

I shook my head. "He's lived over fifteen hundred years. He's not going to give that up to live one life with me—

and I don't blame him."

"If the situations were reversed, you wouldn't do the same?"

"I don't know..." If my family were immortal, I wasn't sure if I could leave them, if I could put them through that pain to spend one life with a single person, especially across the sea where they would hardly ever see me. "It's hard to say."

"Then maybe it's better to end it now before you get in deeper."

I released a chuckle. "I don't think I can get in any deeper, Lila."

"And I guess he wouldn't protect you anymore."

I pictured his face, those intense eyes that rivaled the violence of a hurricane. "He would."

Her eyes softened before she pulled her hand away and grabbed her glass again. "Then enjoy every moment while you can...and toughen your heart for the end."

No matter how tough my heart was, I would never be prepared for that agony. To release his hand and watch him walk out of my life forever. It would be unbearable. It would be unbearable for him too, but I knew he would handle it much better.

The door to the pub opened, and Aurelias appeared, scanning the crowd in search of me.

It took me a second to understand it was him, because I'd never told him where I was going. "Speaking of which..."

Her eyes followed mine to the door before they jerked back to me. *"That's him?"*

I nodded.

"Oh my mama..."

"What?" I asked.

"I don't even know how to talk right now."

Aurelias locked eyes with me then approached our table.

"Please tell me he has a brother," she said quickly before he arrived.

"I've seen two, but they're both married."

"Ugh..."

Aurelias ignored Lila and only stared at me. "Dragons have been sighted from the east."

I stilled at that revelation, picturing my father on Nightshade. "Have you seen my father?"

"It's too dark to tell. But all the dragons are accounted for, so I'd say that's a good sign."

Lila got to her feet. "Let's go."

I got to my feet too, forgetting about the tab. "Lila, this is Aurelias—"

"I'll meet your hot boyfriend later." She was the first one out the door. "Let's hurry."

We reached the field where the dragons would land, and dusk had settled into a deeper shade of night. Dragons could see in the dark, but torches lit the kingdom and the field to make it easier for them to spot their landing place.

My mother was already there when I arrived, stone-faced and silent, holding her breath in anticipation of my father's return. Aunt Avice was also there, and Lila immediately went to her mother's side.

Aurelias stood beside me, close enough that his arm touched mine, but he didn't offer me any substantial affection. If we were alone, his chest would be pressed to my back with his arms crossed over my body, keeping me warm and making me feel safe.

Nightshade was hard to see because he was as dark as the night, but I heard him land hard on the ground and reflect the flames with his brilliant scales.

I couldn't see who was in the saddle. "Father?"

"Huntley?" Mother moved forward, anxious to see, her voice breaking in desperation.

His deep voice reassured us all. "I'm here, baby."

I gasped when I heard his strong voice, the voice of the man who brought me so much protection during my greatest insecurities.

One of the guards approached with a torch, bringing light to the darkness.

And that was when I saw my mother and father making out right in front of everyone.

If I weren't so happy to see him, I'd run off in disgust.

Mother broke apart, her hands cupping his cheeks. "What about Ian?"

Father looked behind him. "Hurry your ass up."

"My leg got stuck in the strap." Uncle Ian climbed down and landed beside my father.

Mother rushed to him next and gave him a hard hug.

Uncle Ian patted her on the back and quickly moved away. "Where's my baby?"

Aunt Avice ran straight into him, hitting him so hard he stumbled back slightly. Her lips were locked on his, and they had a greater kissing session than my parents just had.

Father moved to me next, his eyes set on me with that subtle look of adoration.

"Father." I ran into his chest and felt the hard impact of his solid armor, but I didn't care.

His strong arms enveloped me, and he kissed me on the forehead like he always did. "I'm home, sweetheart."

Lila embraced her father next, and the two held each other the longest.

"We have much to discuss," Father said in the glow of the guard's torchlight. "Let's head to the castle."

Aurelias grabbed his family members, and they stood near the window. Kingsnake had Fang wrapped around his shoulders, as if the snake wanted to watch the proceedings as well.

The room had a table, but there were too many people for everyone to sit, and it seemed like all of us were too anxious to sit down anyway. Grandmother said nothing as she stood there, like all she could think about was her son walking into the room and seeing him with her own eyes.

Mother's shoulders weren't as stiff, but she was still plagued by stress.

My father had gone to his chambers first, eager to remove the heavy armor he'd worn for days since he'd left.

When Uncle Ian entered the room, he had Aunt Avice at his side, her hand grasped in his. His armor was gone, and now his uniform was visible, the muscles of his arms stretching the fabric. He stilled for a moment to look at the vampires who accompanied Aurelias, their appearances distinctive because of their paleness, their slitted eyes, and their unusual armor.

Grandmother went to Ian, squeezing him tightly before he even realized she was there. Aunt Avice was forced to let go as his mother embraced him like a child rather than a man. She rested her face on his chest and stood there for a while.

Uncle Ian let her hold him, his chin resting on her head.

She finally pulled away and gave him a gentle pat on the cheek.

When my father entered the room, the energy changed completely. It became charged with authority, a tension stronger than a taut rope keeping a galleon secured to the shore. The heavy armor was gone, replaced by a simple shirt and trousers, like he welcomed the cold rather than shied away from it.

The first thing he did was embrace Grandmother, the person who loved him the way he loved me. But then he looked at the vampires who stood beside Aurelias. His stare was a sea of stone, but his energy was subtly hostile. There had been very few times in my life when my father had been genuinely mad at me—and it was always terrifying.

Aurelias spoke. "King Rolfe, this is my family." He turned to the brother in red. "Kingsnake, King of

Vampires and Lord of Darkness, and his wife, Larisa, Queen of Vampires and Lady of Darkness."

Kingsnake gave a slight bow. So did Larisa.

Fang gave an angry hiss.

"And Fang," Aurelias said quickly, casting an annoyed stare in the snake's direction. "A companion of ours." He turned to his other brother. "And this is Cobra, King of the Cobra Vampires, and his wife Clara, Queen of the Cobra Vampires."

They also gave him subtle bows.

My father stared for a moment. "Your land has multiple kings?"

"Different factions, I would say," Aurelias said. "Because we are all different vampires."

"You look the same to me."

"Our abilities set us apart, and those are invisible to the eye."

Father gave a subtle sigh. "Don't expect me to be impressed by your titles, nor do I expect you to be impressed by mine. I'm Huntley from this moment forward, because all that *m'lord* and *Your Majesty* shit is a waste of time. Why are you here?"

Aurelias spoke. "While my father deliberates his decision to join our war, my brothers and sisters have returned to fight for us."

"Deliberates his decision?" Father asked coldly. "It's a yes or a no."

"Much has happened in our lands," Aurelias said. "He has several kingdoms to rule—"

"Four vampires won't turn the tide of this war," Father snapped. "I need an army of vampires if we have any chance of winning this."

My heart sank—because that meant whatever he'd discovered in the east was bad news.

Aurelias didn't flinch at my father's anger. "I didn't promise he would come. I promised I would ask."

"You said he would *probably* come—"

"And I still think he will. Now that my brothers are here, he's risking more than just his firstborn, but nearly all of his sons," Aurelias said calmly. "To orchestrate an exodus of that magnitude will take ample time and resources—"

"Both of which we don't have."

Now I understood why I'd never been part of my father's deliberations before. It was stressful, to hear him bark his orders and show his fear in the form of aggression.

"What happened, Huntley?" Mother asked, her voice gentle.

When he turned from Aurelias to my mother, he regarded her completely differently, with a hint of softness and respect. "Palladium is a kingdom that once flourished in those lands. When it was destroyed, there were survivors, and those survivors saved Ian before the demons could capture him. They have a stronghold in the mountain, but there are very few of them, maybe a hundred. They say there are more deeper in hiding, a few thousand."

Mother crossed her arms over her chest, her eyes hardening.

"Since they rescued Ian, they've asked to come here and be given a ship to sail for new lands. I'm not their king and can't order them to fight, so I agreed. In their opinion, these demons can't be defeated...because they're invincible."

"No one is invincible," Mother said. "Our soldiers defeated their army and protected Delacroix." A note of pride was in her voice, proud of her people and her son for defending our lands.

My father wore a hard stare, like he'd already spoken the truth. "Their magic is fueled by crystals, giving them a form of immortality. When they're killed in battle, they're reborn in the crystals. They wear the scars from their previous battles, but in every other way, they're brand-new."

The entire room was silent. I forgot to breathe, the horror so potent it collapsed my airway.

Aurelias must have felt my terror because his hand moved to my back, a gentle touch to remind me that he was there, that his sword would protect me from the beings that couldn't be killed.

"So even if we kill all of them in the battle to come, they'll come again...and again." My father never spoke with fear, always with a strong voice and a tinge of annoyance. "Fighting them is a pointless effort and a waste of energy and resources."

"So, what are we going to do?" Mother asked. "Flee?"

"I'm not going anywhere," Father said. "These are my lands. The blood of my ancestors feeds the crops we harvest. A great line of kings and queens fills the cemetery of Delacroix. My kingdom was taken from me before—and I won't let that happen again."

"But, Huntley—"

"I reminded the Exiles that their people are working their hands bloody in the labor camps in the east. That their husbands and wives, brothers and sisters, even their children, are subjected to cruelty on a daily basis. To abandon them is the greatest act of cowardice. I asked them to help us instead of taking the ship, and they've agreed. They know a path that leads to the demons' domain under the earth. I will travel down there and destroy those crystals."

Mother was dead silent, unable to react to that information.

No one else did either.

Father continued. "I believe they've left their domain because they're running low on the crystals that hold their magic. That's why they have prisoners mining for jewels in the earth. If we destroy the source of their power, when we kill them in battle, we will never have to kill them again."

"That still leaves the original problem," Grandmother said. "Defeating them in battle…"

"Aurelias and I have been preparing the kingdom for the siege," Mother said. "We've been laying foundation around the castle walls to prevent their penetration. Been doing other things to mitigate the damage."

"But what we really need are the vampires," Grandmother said. "We can't do this alone."

Father turned to look at Aurelias, like this was somehow his fault.

Aurelias spoke. "I disagree with your plan. Stepping into their domain without any knowledge of their world is foolish and will only get you killed—"

"Then what's your idea?" Father snapped.

"The Teeth."

Father's hostility slowly faded.

"They must have reached the east by now," Aurelias said. "They're the ones who forged an alliance with these demons. Perhaps we can convince them to sever the deal and spare the Kingdoms. If that partnership is successful, that eliminates all our problems."

Father continued his hard stare, not blinking once.

"That is a good plan," Uncle Ian said in agreement. "Far safer than entering their territory unannounced."

"I agree," Mother said.

When my father spoke, he said every word slowly, his anger seething. "You expect me to speak to the fiends who arranged my daughter's kidnapping? You expect me to look them in the eye...and not slaughter them all?"

"Then I will go," Uncle Ian said.

"No," Father said quickly. "I will go—because they know I'll look for any reason to kill them." He turned back to Aurelias. "Aurelias will join me—since he knows them *so* well." My father had respected Aurelias when he left, but the memory of what had happened to me infuriated him all over again.

Aurelias held my father's gaze before he turned to Kingsnake. They shared a look, a long one without words, but they seemed to come to an understanding. He looked at my father again. "I will join you, Huntley. Only because I know my brothers will protect Harlow in my absence."

THREE
AURELIAS

I stood with Kingsnake in his chambers, prepared to depart and leave my woman behind. Fang was wrapped around his shoulders, his tongue slipping in and out every few seconds, his eyes bright and fiery.

"You don't trust me?" Kingsnake crossed his arms over his chest.

My eyes lifted to his. "I thought I was the one who could read minds."

A subtle grin moved on to his lips. "Four vampires protecting Harlow is better than one. If anything, she'll be safer than if it were just you."

"Would you trust me to protect Larisa?"

His smile slowly faded as his gaze hardened. "Completely."

My eyes shifted to the window to avoid his look.

"She'll be alright, Aurelias," he said. "What are you afraid of?"

"That I won't return..." My eyes came back to him.

"I know you aren't afraid of dying."

"And you'd be right about that."

"I gave you my word that I wouldn't leave these lands until these demons were defeated and peace had returned to humankind."

"You have your own kingdom, Kingsnake."

He gave a slight shrug. "Viper is a great king, even if he refuses to believe it. And with the werewolves defeated and humankind enslaved by Father, the Kingdoms don't really mean much anymore..."

I will protect your mate, Aureliasss.

My eyes shifted to the snake. "Thank you, Fang."

I will crush bonesss. I will feassst on flesssh. I will kill them all.

I gave a nod. "Never doubted you."

And then I will—

"We got it," Kingsnake said quickly.

"I know you have your own wife to protect, Kingsnake," I said. "To ask you to look after another—"

"I know she would be your wife if circumstances were different, so I'll protect her like she's one of us. It's no burden."

I dropped into the armchair by the fireplace, my elbow curling so my fist could rest against my chin. "Thank you,"

"Hopefully, by the time you return, Father will have landed on these shores."

"Yes...hopefully."

Kingsnake moved to the other armchair, and that was when Fang slithered away to curl up in front of the fire like a faithful companion. My brother crossed his ankle over the opposite knee and stared at me. "You said her family were good people, but her father seems like an asshole."

"He's not."

"After you saved his wife and his kingdom, he should be kinder to you—"

"If someone had kidnapped Larisa, would you ever let it go?" I turned my head to look him directly in the eye. "Is there anything that person could ever do to make up for that monstrous terror?"

Kingsnake remained quiet.

"Now you understand..."

He stared ahead, massaging his bare knuckles because his gloves had been removed. "You can't expect us to stay strong for HeartHolme without adequate sustenance." His eyes remained on his hands. "We can wait until you return to discuss it, but we need to come to some sort of agreement."

"You can feed, but only if it's voluntary."

He turned to look at me.

"But keep it quiet. He doesn't want us to parade it around."

He cracked a subtle smile. "I thought you looked better than last time."

I avoided his gaze.

"But if you aren't feeding on Harlow, who are you feeding on?"

Huntley needed a night of rest after his arduous journey, so we planned to leave the following evening. I went to the bedchambers I shared with Harlow and grabbed my belongings.

"What are you doing?" She'd just stepped out of the shower, her hair damp, a thin towel barely covering her gorgeous curves.

I released an irritated sigh, dreading the fight Harlow was about to put up. "I can't stay here while your father is in the castle—"

"You aren't going anywhere, Aurelias." That fire burst from her eyes, incinerating everything around her. The bedchambers were immediately engulfed in flames. "We've already talked about this."

"It's disrespectful—"

"Says who?"

"I don't think your father would allow a suitor to stay in your bedroom—"

"We aren't living in normal times, and my father isn't like other men of this kingdom. He's chosen me to succeed him, which is something unheard of. My mother has told me stories about their relationship when they were young, and we aren't doing anything they didn't do themselves. It would be hypocritical for him to say a damn thing."

I stared at my bag where it sat on the bed. "Harlow—"

"No."

"Baby—"

"*I said no.*" Her eyes were formidable. "I'm not having this conversation again." She dropped her towel, showing her perky tits and her flat stomach, and looked at me triumphantly, like there was no way I'd walk away now.

And she was right.

She climbed up onto the bed with her ass in the air, showing off her sex to me. Then she sat back on her heels and looked at me over her shoulder, her long hair down her back, a sparkle in her eyes.

It was hard to resist.

Women had come and gone, all beautiful, all enthusiastic, but my desire had never sparked the way it did for her.

"Get over here." She shook her ass, enticing me further.

I should just grab my stuff and go, but fuck, I couldn't. My pants were down, my dick was out, and I was at the foot of the bed, holding on to her hips as I pushed myself deep inside the sexy slit that was slicker than it'd ever been.

She gave a sexy moan, arching her back deeper, taking all of my length without giving a wince.

My hand gripped her throat and squeezed to silence her, and then I thrust into her at a steady pace, making sure that the headboard didn't tap against the wall, that we were as quiet as we could be, even though her parents occupied the bedchambers upstairs.

I could feel her desire, crackling flames from a fire in the midst of winter. She enjoyed my dick as much as I enjoyed giving it to her. That made it even more enjoyable, feeling a woman on the brink of climax the second she had my cock between her legs.

When her moans grew louder, my fingers slipped into her mouth.

Her lips closed, and she sucked, using it as a way to drown out her moans.

"Fuck." I was already there, on the precipice of a climax, but I had to edge myself for her, to hold on a little bit longer to allow her to go first.

She moved her face to the bed, deepened the arch in her back, and pushed her ass even higher in the air. "Come inside me." Her hands reached down to grab my thighs. "And then fuck me again."

That was all it took to lose control. My hips bucked unnaturally, and I filled her with my seed, my hand moving to her lower back to keep her in position as I gave it all to her. It was a long one, the kind that stretched on forever, the pleasure so good that my body smoked in an invisible blaze.

I came to a stop, stilled my heavy breathing, staring at the perkiest ass I'd ever seen. And then I started to thrust again, this time harder, my fingers kneading her ass as I gripped those plump cheeks.

She started to come, her moans muffled by the sheets her face was pressed into, teardrops staining the bedding.

My hand snaked into her hair, and I pressed her face into the mattress harder. "Yes, baby..."

I spent my day executing Ivory's orders, fortifying HeartHolme against invasion, but I wished I were in Harlow's bedchambers instead, enjoying my last day with her before I had to depart at dusk.

At the end of the day, I returned to shower, and Harlow was there waiting for me, not naked this time—both to my relief and disappointment. Her eyes were heavy with the weight of my departure, with the weight of her father's departure. We exchanged a look instead of words, and then I showered alone.

Even in another room, I could feel her despair, feel the dread of goodbye.

I returned, my hair slightly damp and my body dry. Now it was time to put on my armor and meet Huntley where the dragons would be waiting for us. Harlow and I exchanged a look before I dressed, and she sat in front of the fire hopelessly, watching me.

When I was ready, she walked up to me. "I'm not worried about you, but I'm worried about him."

My hands cupped her face. "He has my sword."

"I know."

"Your father is a great swordsman—exceptional by human standards."

"But I know our enemy isn't human."

I pressed a kiss to her forehead. "Then you're lucky, because I'm not human."

Her face rested against the plate over my chest, and she closed her eyes, enveloped in my arms.

I held her that way, not wanting to let her go, not wanting to leave this bedroom that was warm with our memories. Whenever we were together, there was no past or future. There was just that moment…and it was easy.

I kissed her again. "It's time to go."

She pulled away and gave a nod.

We left the bedchambers and traveled the long road down to the field. The dragons were there, and one of them was Storm, Huntley's dragon. The other was the one that had flown Ivory to safety when she'd been burned, the one I'd ridden before.

Harlow rubbed his snout and pressed a kiss to his cheek. "He'll take care of you."

He pushed against her, wanting her to rub harder.

She chuckled before she gave him another kiss, loving him like he was the family dog.

I watched her be affectionate with the dragon while feeling a hard stare on the side of my face. Without turning to look, I knew the culprit. Her father had a distinct energy, and the emotions inside his chest burned hotter than the average man's. I met his gaze.

He didn't turn away, as if he didn't care whether I knew he'd been staring.

Someone clapped me on the back. "Tell Rancor I said hello."

I turned to see Kingsnake there, Fang around his shoulders.

"I'm sure there will be plenty of time for pleasantries." I wasn't sure if the Teeth would try to kill me on sight or if they would try to capture me to torture me. After all, I'd taken their prisoner immediately after I'd delivered her... and then had fallen in love with her.

Ivory gave Huntley a hug goodbye and then a kiss. Then he said goodbye to his brother.

I felt like that was all we ever did these days...say goodbye.

Harlow returned to me, her hair blowing in the breeze, her cheeks rosy from the cold. Every time I touched her, I was aware of the vitality in her veins, the pounding heart inside her little chest. She was strong and fearless, but so delicate. "Be careful."

"I will." I gave her a quick kiss on the lips, keeping the affection appropriate because of the audience gathered.

Her eyes filled with sadness as she let me go.

I walked away and secured my belongings to the dragon's saddle. Instead of bringing water, I brought blood, hidden deep inside my pack so no one would see.

Huntley came to my side, and with every step closer, his anger became more potent.

I turned to meet his gaze.

"How will they receive you?"

"Coldly," I said. "I did take their prisoner..."

There was a burst of anger inside him, but that rage didn't creep into his features. "Anything you can share with me?"

"They fear your dragons. The demons are invulnerable to their fire, but the Teeth are as susceptible as you or I."

"Then we'll take more. A few to circle in the air in case we need them to burn everything."

I nodded in agreement.

He walked to Storm wearing his bulky black armor, the kind he hadn't worn before. His back carried his blade as well as an axe. He grabbed on to the bindings and pulled himself up onto the mighty beast.

I did the same and grabbed on to the reins. I couldn't communicate with the dragons the way the Rolfes could, so I had to rely on Huntley communicating with him. There was barely any warning before we launched into the air, just the subtle dip of the creature's arms. The cold wind moved past my face as we soared into the sky in mere seconds. The world became a dot below. Harlow's mind became faint before it disappeared altogether. Then it was just Pyre and me, high in the sky, the dark world at our feet.

We crossed the mountains under the starlight, and once we made it to the other side, the sun crested the horizon. The world was a distant haze, the shadows from the mountains stretching far into the distance.

Huntley brought his dragon to a halt in midair.

Pyre knew to approach, so he came to Storm, their faces close together.

I looked at Huntley, feeling odd talking to him in the middle of the sky, the sound of flapping wings around us.

"Assuming the tunnel is linear, it should be half a day's ride north," Huntley said. "If we fly hard, we can cover more ground before there's too much light in the sky. As far as I can tell, there's no civilization this close to the mountains."

"Except the ring of fire." I could see it, and it was the most peculiar thing I'd ever observed in my fifteen hundred years. "I suspect that's where the Teeth are headed. Must be the front door to their domain."

Huntley stared at it, his mind incisive the way his daughter's was. He felt everything intensely because he was passionate and thoughtful at all times.

"We'll get as close as we can, but we may want to traverse on foot, just in case."

"I agree," he said. "Let's go." Storm turned away and flew off, his mighty wings creating a boom right in my ear.

Pyre immediately followed, and we continued our path along the mountains, the other dragons behind us.

When the light became too bright, we landed at the base of the mountains, the shrubbery thick and dense, perfect for hiding from prying eyes. Huntley dismounted and provided water for his dragon before he did the same for Pyre and the others.

I watched him care for the dragons like they were equals rather than merely animals. My father had a prized stallion that he rode into battle, but he didn't care whether the beast lived or died. Didn't groom him himself. Didn't show an ounce of affection, not the way Harlow did with Pyre.

Huntley returned, every footstep clear because his armor weighed him down into the dirt.

The sun was already painful on my skin, a dull burn that was constantly present until I stepped into the shade again. I could tolerate sunlight for an extended period of time, but the damage was irreversible, and once I received too much of it, I would perish. And I'd spent more time in the sunlight in this land than I ever had in my long life.

Wordlessly, we trekked forward, sticking to the shade of the trees.

I walked behind him, feeling the minds of the dragons become faint the farther we traveled.

My eyes examined the mountain, looking for signs of passage, of a heavy wall that would conceal the entrance from unwanted eyes, but there was never any indication of that. There was also a chance the Teeth moved underground until they entered the domain of the demons... and never came to the surface at all.

I kept all those thoughts to myself.

Hours passed and we continued forward, moving under the branches of the trees, searching for signs of the Teeth.

The sun was just starting to lower in the sky, making the shadows lengthen once more, and before long it would be dark.

Huntley came to a stop. "We're north of the Teeth's domain now."

"It's possible their path remains underground and connects to the demons."

He turned back around to face me, his eyes shifting in consideration. "Perhaps."

"The composition of the earth is more than just sand and rock. It's possible they had to make many detours to reach the other side. It could be farther north..."

Huntley moved to unfasten his chest piece, ready to take it off after carrying it for so many leagues. He leaned it against a log before he took a seat, opened his water canteen, and took a drink.

I remained standing, taking a long sweep of our surroundings, opening my mind further to detect another presence. But I saw nothing and felt nothing. I moved to the other log, keeping space between us because we might be allies, but we weren't friendly.

Time passed and sunset arrived. The colors of the sky began to deepen into shades of pink and purple. My arms rested on my knees, and I thought of the woman I'd left behind, the woman who would sleep alone while my brothers remained down the hallway.

Huntley's mind had been quiet at first, but then it started to deepen, with shards of anger and guilt, different shades of darkness. The weight of his people rested on his shoulders, and despite his strength, he struggled to carry it.

"We'll find them."

He slowly turned his head to look at me. Instead of being assuaged by my encouragement, he was pissed off. "You can read minds." His gaze hardened like the steel of his sword, and he looked at me like I was his enemy once more. "You know every move before I make it."

"That's inaccurate."

"Don't lie to me, *vampire*."

Now we were back to where we'd started—ground zero. "I understand your anger has been provoked, but let's not forget all the progress we've made. We're allies, and the Teeth are *our* enemy. Before you left, you entrusted your kingdom to me. I'm the one watching your back while we're out here."

He looked away, and there was another, more potent surge of anger.

I knew I was just making it worse. "And I need you to watch mine."

In silence, he seethed, looking at the shadows as they grew longer. It took him a few moments to respond, to wrestle his anger like a combative dog that wouldn't return to its cage. "You're right. Whenever I think about that time...I lose my mind."

"I understand—"

"Unless you're a father, you could never possibly understand." His look was back on me. "I know I should be grateful that it was you who was put in charge of her abduction, because if it had been someone else, the events that transpired would have unfolded very differently. She would probably be dead right now...and my kingdom gone."

"That didn't happen, so let's not entertain the fantasy." My dead heart had come back to life and pounded for a single woman. I didn't understand his grief as a father, but as a man who loved a woman...I understood a different kind of grief.

"You can read minds," he repeated, his eyes prodding for an explanation.

"I can't," I said. "But I can *feel* minds."

His eyes narrowed.

"I can feel the emotions of those around me. At first, I could only feel emotions when they were intense, but with more experience, I was able to pick up on more subtle ones. Now I can feel a lot more...even though it can be suffocating. So much experience has taught me to read intent in emotions, to anticipate where that emotion will drive someone next. So when you were striking me, I could feel where you would hit me next. When you grew frustrated, I knew there would be several blows in a row."

He listened, his eyes unblinking.

"Some people feel more deeply than others. Some more often. That's how you and your family are. You all feel things very intensely. Most people live a passionless existence." I could feel it in his mind at that very moment, and I missed the company of Harlow's intensity. "I'm not the type to condone an inconvenience. I'm not compassionate toward others. I rarely care about anyone but myself. I tolerate very little, and in another circumstance, I wouldn't tolerate you. But I've never met a man who cares so deeply for others, especially his family. I feel the way you love your children. I feel the loyalty you have for your wife. For your brother. It's hard not to respect a man who possesses so much integrity. You may not like me, but it's impossible for me not to like you."

His eyes remained on mine for a long while before he turned away and released a quiet sigh. "All vampires are capable of this?"

"No. Just the Originals."

He gave a slight nod. "What about the Teeth?"

"They're the dogs of our species. They have no abilities."

"So, when we approach the Teeth, you'll be able to perceive their intentions immediately?"

"Yes."

"Do they know you have this ability?"

"No." It wasn't something we shared outside our own. Larisa had the ability to feel minds, but her abilities were akin to a newborn's. She could only feel the most intense versions of emotions.

"That's a great advantage."

"The only reason I survived the demons."

"Then you must know how my daughter feels for you," he said quietly. "I see it on her face."

I stared at my hands, unsure how to respond.

"It's hard to stand there and let it happen, knowing what the aftermath will be."

I kept my eyes on my hands. "Just know that it'll hurt me a million times worse than it'll hurt her."

"I'd rather it not hurt her at all," he said quietly. "When she hurts, I hurt."

I'd grown to care for this man, and I knew my departure would wound more than just Harlow, but everyone who loved her. I hated myself for that. I would protect them from a massacre, but I would still leave behind destruction. "I'm sure you've been there…and you made it through."

He gave a subtle shake of his head. "I've only loved one woman—and I married her."

Hundreds of women had graced his bed, but only one graced his heart. My love was just as hard to earn because it had taken me five hundred years to love someone again.

"What about you?"

My thoughts shattered at the question, and then I felt his stare on me. "I loved someone a long time ago…but they died."

His stare remained hard, but inside, his body softened, his muscles relaxed, and the sadness poured in. "Were you married?"

"She was my fiancée." I told him more than I'd told Harlow, because somehow, it was easier to share this with him.

He didn't ask me how she'd died, exactly like I'd expected. "I'm sorry."

"It happened a long time ago." It had taken years before I could sleep with a woman again. There was too much guilt. Too much heartbreak. Decades passed, and I still mourned like it had happened the day before. At some point, it got easier, but it took a very long time, because when I felt something, I felt it intensely.

"How long ago?"

"Five hundred years."

The sadness was still in his chest, feeling empathy for me when he'd felt hatred a second ago.

"I didn't think I could ever love someone again, but then Harlow knocked the wind out of me." She was a fucking tornado of fire, passion, and bliss. I'd gotten swept up in the current, and she pulled me under. I hadn't taken a full breath since.

He was quiet, and then a different kind of sadness filled his chest. "You love my daughter?"

I hadn't realized what my words implied. When it came to my feelings, it was hard to mask them, because they were obvious in everything I did, every waking moment. There was no other reason I would be there, sitting in the fucking dirt in a land that wasn't home. "I thought that was obvious..." My eyes were on the mountains as I spoke, not expecting him to respond to a statement so profound. It was awkward for me and uncomfortable for him.

Anger and disappointment didn't emit from him. His mind seemed to be clear, his heart empty of anything at all. It was one of the rare times when I couldn't discern the emotions because they were too complicated to strip down. "I've seen the Bone Witch turn immortal beings human. Perhaps she could do the same for you."

I remembered how it felt to be human. To be weak and unremarkable. To feel vulnerable without the abilities I now possessed. That was probably the worst part...and mortality was the second. But I didn't tell him the truth, that I wouldn't make the sacrifice for her, no matter how much I loved her. No one was worth that existence, a life-span that passed in the blink of an eye. "Maybe..."

We traveled before dawn, the light so minimal it was practically dark.

"How are the dragons?" I asked from the rear.

"Bored." After our talk last night, he wasn't hostile anymore. Anger didn't burn in his chest like a lit pyre.

"Perhaps we should have them come closer—in case."

"I agree. Wasn't expecting to travel this far north. There's only one thing I like about the east—no yetis."

I nearly chuckled. "I second that."

"You've met one?"

"One almost killed me when I crossed your lands. My sister-in-law spared me."

He stopped then turned to look at me. "It was you who left those two yetis in the snow."

"Yes." Kingsnake took down one, and I'd nearly lost my head to the other. It had been dark, freezing cold, and an overall unpleasant experience.

The reminder would normally piss him off, but he turned forward and continued his trek.

I remained several feet behind.

Moments later, the sound of wings was audible overhead, and then the ground shook when they landed among the trees.

I turned back to look at them, but their only visible feature was the reflection of the moon off their scales.

Huntley and I continued forward, a long trek into the darkness, both of us fearing the daylight because of the scorching heat. I would take the blizzards of the west any day over the arid dryness. The soil was different, more like sand than earth, because there was little moisture. The trees weren't lush pines covered in snow, but trees with shriveled leaves. I was too proud to complain, and so was Huntley, even though he wore the heaviest armor I'd ever seen.

Hours passed—and then I *felt* something.

Emotions. Lots of emotions from several different sources.

I quickened my steps to catch up to him, and my hand moved to his shoulder to halt him in place. "We aren't alone." I kept my voice quiet, unsure how close or far these beings were. "I can feel their minds."

"Can you discern their identity?"

I shook my head.

"What do you feel?"

I felt various things, but only one was the most prominent. "Hunger."

Huntley's chest immediately filled with anger, his grudge against the Teeth a lightning storm. "Then we're close."

"Very."

He reached behind him and grabbed his axe instead of his sword because this wouldn't be a fight, but a massacre.

We made our way forward, the sun rose higher over the sky, light moving through the brittle leaves of the trees. When their emotions grew louder, I knew we were close. We approached the end of the trees and looked beyond—seeing the entrance to the tunnel. It was ten feet high and ten feet wide, large enough for carts and animals. Torches were lit on either side, even though the sunlight made the illumination unnecessary.

The Teeth were filing out, walking in several rows side by side, sometimes wagons appearing with live animals that they'd fed on along the way. They all look demoralized, like the extensive travel had exhausted every single one of them.

"We need to find Rancor."

"He would be somewhere in the lead."

"They must be traveling to the demons…since Rancor is their little bitch."

"Which means we need to get to Rancor first," I said. "What about the dragons?"

"I won't put them at risk unless it's absolutely necessary."

I moved to a different side of the tree line, trying to get a better understanding of their trajectory. "They're headed to the ring of fire. Their path heads east. The route through the mountain probably had many detours."

Huntley came to my side. "Then we travel back through the trees to get as close to the front of the line as possible. They're going to need to replenish their canteens after being under the mountains for so long, and there was that small river we passed."

I'd barely call it a river, it was so small. "You're right."

"It's still a long journey to the ring. They'll need to rest tonight. That's when we make our move."

"Agreed."

Just as Huntley predicted, they camped that night near the stream. Tents were erected in the dirt, but most of the Teeth slept in cots directly under the sky. Fires were lit around the camp, not to keep warm, but to see their surroundings.

"The demons know they're here," he said. "Otherwise, they would attack."

"Let's sneak to the front. Rancor will have the biggest tent—so he'll be easy to find."

We stayed on the opposite side of the stream and made our way forward, the camp quiet because most of them were dead asleep. In a land conquered by their allies, there was no reason to keep watch for enemies.

There was a long line of Teeth, so it took quite a while to reach the front, and across the stream we spotted it—a red tent. All the others were black, but this one stood out not just for its color, but also its size.

We were lucky we'd arrived when we did. If we'd gotten here a day later, we would have missed the chance altogether.

Huntley crossed the stream first, which only went to his knees, and I followed close behind, the water loud enough to cover our movement. We reached the opposite shore without arousing suspicion then hunched down behind another tent as we surveyed the situation.

There were two guards on duty, on either side of the tent flaps.

I couldn't speak, not when the occupants of the tent might hear me, so I gestured with my hand, slicing it across my throat.

Huntley nodded, understanding this had to be a stealth kill. He gestured for me to travel around the back of the tent to surprise the guard on the other side. Once the plan was made, we broke apart and made our move.

When I came around the side, Huntley emerged with his dagger and sliced it clean across the guard's neck.

I did the same, catching the body before it fell and made a loud thud.

We dragged both of the bodies away from the tent and into a pile of bushes. In daylight, they would be easy to see, but in the darkness, it was easy to overlook them completely.

Huntley took the lead for the tent, his shoulders swaying with adrenaline, the anger in his chest so potent, it seemed like he'd never been angrier.

I didn't have an opportunity to sheathe his anger, to tell him to be quiet—not when he was a man on a mission to exact revenge for his stolen daughter.

We entered through the flaps, and the inside of the tent was illuminated by a couple of candles. The tent was luxurious enough for a king, with a real mattress on a frame, rugs across the floor so Rancor wouldn't have to step on the bare dirt. There was a desk, and he sat there, paying more attention to the scroll in his hand than the visitors who'd just come into his tent.

"Yes?" he asked coldly, having no idea he spoke to Huntley, the King of Kingdoms, not the lowly guard positioned outside in the dark. When he didn't get a response, his eyes lifted in annoyance.

But in an instant, all the annoyance disappeared, replaced by the deepest plunge of terror I'd ever felt. He stilled at the desk and sucked in a quick breath in astonishment. His stare continued, like he couldn't believe his own eyes. He was about to scream out in fear...I could feel it.

I moved behind him and pressed my dagger right against his throat, close enough to prick the skin.

The words he was about to scream died on his tongue.

"Scream—and it's the last thing you'll ever do." I withdrew the knife then remained behind Rancor. My arms crossed over my chest, and my thumb played with the hilt of my dagger, slowly dragging it down to feel the cool metal. I wanted to kill him myself for taking Harlow, but that would be a bit hypocritical. If anything, I should thank Rancor. Otherwise, I wouldn't have her now. But once I returned to my lands with a broken heart, perhaps I'd wish I'd never met her.

Huntley pulled out the chair across from Rancor and took a seat.

Rancor immediately sat back and left the scroll on the desk, trying to get as far away from Huntley as possible without actually leaving the seat.

Huntley held up his bloody dagger for Rancor to see then placed it on the desk between them.

Rancor glanced down at it but didn't dare take it.

Huntley stared at him for a long time, his eyes wide open and unblinking, his stare so angry smoke practically came from his ears. His expression was formidable, but it was nothing compared to the rage that stormed inside his chest. "Did you really think I wouldn't hunt you down to the edges of the world?" For a man so angry, he spoke calmly, but that made the tension tauter. "That I wouldn't fantasize about this moment in my waking hours, dream about it in my deepest sleep, imagine your blood on my axe."

Rancor's back rose and fell with his labored breaths. His expression was hard with indifference, but his quick breathing gave away his terror.

"You thought I would kill you with my sword?" He cocked his head. "This little dagger between us? No, Rancor. I'm going to chop your head into little pieces the way my wife slices meat before she throws it in the frying pan."

Rancor glanced down at the dagger between them and swallowed.

Huntley leaned forward.

Rancor immediately jerked, his nerves wired.

The corner of Huntley's mouth rose in a smile as he rested his arms on the table. "I granted you mercy, Rancor. I could have massacred your entire race, but I let you be. In my attempt to be a just king, I became a stupid one. A hard lesson learned, a failure I'll never repeat."

Rancor stayed quiet.

"You've been plotting this a long time, haven't you?"

When Rancor couldn't take Huntley's stare anymore, he looked away.

Huntley reached across the table with the speed of a Golden Serpent and grabbed Rancor by the face, gripping his cheeks in his gloved hand and forcing his stare back where it should be. "Look. At. Me."

Rancor's terror rose to new levels. It was about to burst from his chest.

"That's better." Huntley returned to his relaxed position.

"Just get on with it and kill me—"

"Be patient," he said coldly. "Your time will come."

Rancor glanced at the dagger between them once more, and as soon as he realized his eyes were where they shouldn't be, he looked up again.

"You planned this moment for twenty years. That's a long time. A long time to dig through the mountain to the other side. A long time to forge an alliance with an enemy that will likely kill us all. All because I granted you mercy?"

"You took our lands and our food—"

"You mean I stopped allowing you to feast on my people like deer," he snapped. "And I took back the land you took from us. Get your facts straight."

"What do you want from me—"

"I want to know what I did to deserve that torture. For you to take my only daughter, my fucking pride and joy, my entire reason for living." His voice rose like he didn't give a damn if anyone heard him in the camp. "To break me down to tears...to kill my spirit...to make me look my wife dead in the eye and tell her everything would be okay when I wanted to slit my own throat to make the pain stop. *Tell me what I did to deserve that.*"

Rancor dropped his gaze.

"*Bitch, look at me.*" He slammed his fist down on the table.

Rancor obeyed.

Huntley raised his fist to his chest. "I did nothing to deserve that—because no one deserves that."

Rancor's expression hadn't changed, but inside his chest was a swirl of so many emotions that I couldn't tell them apart. It was a cloud of dread and terror mixed with regret, but I suspected he didn't regret taking Harlow... only getting caught.

"Answer me."

"As I already said, you took our food source—"

"*Then leave,*" he snapped. "Sail away to lands full of the blood you seek. But you decided to forge an alliance with an enemy so powerful they can destroy this world from the inside out. You would do that to your savior...for food?"

"I've been hungry for twenty years, Huntley—"

Huntley grabbed the dagger off the table and stabbed the point into the wood. "Call me that again and see what happens."

"My apologies...King Rolfe."

"You were hungry for twenty years, so you decided to kill my daughter and let these demons destroy all of humankind. Now, if this plan is successful and we're all dead, what will you eat then?"

Rancor kept his stare on Huntley, but it shifted slightly, as if to remain steady was too difficult.

"Am I missing something, or is this the stupidest plan ever?" he snapped. "I wouldn't put it past you, because you were stupid enough to think you could take my daughter and get away with it."

"*I* didn't take her." He turned to regard me. "He did. And yet, he stands here as your ally."

"Because he saved her from whatever cruelty you had planned. I owe Aurelias my life for what he did for my daughter. Don't change the subject—"

"He betrayed me. What makes you think he won't betray you?"

"Because I'm the hero trying to save my people and you're the villain trying to destroy them. Whatever hope you had that this plan would succeed is now gone. So, tell me what I want to know, or I'll slice you into pieces to get you talking."

"You're just going to kill me anyway—"

"Then give me a reason not to, Rancor. Save my people—and walk away with your life."

He shook his head. "I know how this ends. I took your daughter, so you'll kill me no matter what I offer you."

"I understand why that's hard for you to believe because I'm a man of my word and you aren't. Tell me everything about these demons, how we can defeat them, and I'll let you live."

Rancor remained quiet.

"*Or.*" He grabbed the dagger and pried it out of the wood. "I torture you until I get what I want—and then I'll kill you." He stabbed the dagger into the wood again, this time close to Rancor, an invitation to take the dagger and see what would happen.

Rancor must have realized there was no way out of this. He could scream, but then his throat would be slit, and being dead would get him nowhere. "I'll make a deal with you—"

Huntley chuckled. "That's cute, trying to cut a deal with the man whose daughter you kidnapped."

Rancor took a moment before he continued. "I'll tell you everything. But once this is over, you give us a fleet of ships to leave your lands and never return."

"That's quite the ask."

"We're both kings. Just as you strive to protect and provide for your people, I do the same. We can't live in these lands any longer, not without real sustenance. The existence is so unbearable that many of my people have taken their own lives."

"Oh, how sad..." Huntley sank back into the chair. "You need to offer more if you want me to accept that."

"I don't have anything else—"

"You fight for us. Not them."

Rancor released a heavy sigh.

"Tell me what you know, fight for us, and I'll give your people a ship to leave these shores. But I have one more addition."

Rancor stared.

"You call yourself a king and compare your stature to mine—so prove it. I will grant your people safe passage from my lands once the war is over, but you won't join them. You'll pay for your betrayal with blood. I will execute you once your people are gone, the last Teeth that will ever stand on my lands. That's my price."

I was acquainted with Huntley through his emotions. Knew the purity in his heart and the integrity in his veins. But now, I saw him in a whole new light, witnessed his strategy, witnessed his ferocity. He was a just king, but he was also formidable...and a bit terrifying.

"You said you would spare my life if I told you everything—"

"That was before you insulted my character by comparing it to yours."

A surge of anger moved through Rancor. "I'm sorry—"

"You're sorry?" Huntley asked blankly. "Is that supposed to mean something to me?"

"I'm sorry I took your daughter."

"I don't want your apology, Rancor. I want your blood. If you're such a servant to your people, then prove it. Make the ultimate sacrifice the way I would for mine—and then you can compare us."

"We didn't hurt Harlow—"

"I never want to hear my daughter's name come out of your mouth again," he snapped. "And she was only unharmed because Aurelias decided to return her home instead of letting her be a feast." Pain throbbed inside his chest when he said those things, but he gave no hint of weakness as he spoke.

"If I refuse to cooperate, the demons will defeat you. If I'm going to die either way, then I'd rather you die too."

"Then I guess you aren't sorry," Huntley said. "Because your remorse would drive you to a different decision. I granted you asylum, and you stabbed me in the back—but you feel *nothing*. I'll just kill you and extend the offer to your people instead. Perhaps they'll be smart and take it."

Rancor gave another sigh before he rubbed the back of his neck. "You don't kill me...but you can exact your revenge in whatever way you choose."

Huntley fell silent.

Rancor held his gaze and waited.

"Your daughter was unharmed, so that's far more reasonable."

"I will decide what's reasonable," Huntley said coldly. "You're lucky you aren't a father, because if you were, your child would be in my dungeon as we speak."

Rancor brushed off the statement. "Do we have a deal?"

I stared at Huntley, wondering if he would accept this revision. Choosing the method of torture for your enemy was more satisfying than a clean death—in my opinion.

Huntley lifted his hand across the table, ready to shake Rancor's hand.

Rancor released a sigh of relief then reached forward.

With unparalleled speed, Huntley grabbed the dagger and stabbed it straight into Rancor's palm, digging the tip into the wood and pinning him in place. Blood spilled everywhere, several shades darker than that of a human.

Rancor released a restrained scream, unable to move because the dagger was too deep.

"Yes," Huntley said. "We have a deal."

Rancor winced as he tightened the gauze around his bloody hand. It stained the white handkerchief as he continued to bleed, dyeing the cream color a ruby red. He kept his hand on his thigh, his eyes still hard in pain.

I pulled up a chair and sat between the two men.

"Let's hear it," Huntley said impatiently. "I've got demons to kill."

Rancor shifted his gaze to me, looking at me head on for the first time since I'd stepped into that tent. "You broke our alliance. Why?"

"This isn't a family reunion," Huntley snapped. "You're answering my questions, not asking any of your own."

Rancor kept his gaze on me.

"Kidnapping a princess is not equivalent to harvesting venom from a wild snake," I said. "It was an unfair trade from the beginning, and you know it. You took advantage of my situation to get what you wanted, so I don't feel bad for my betrayal. You also told me that you would only use her as leverage to draw out her father, that she would be returned unharmed, but when I arrived, you informed me your plans had changed." I could feel Huntley's anger suddenly explode inside his chest. "That wasn't the deal, so I couldn't leave her there. I'm not a good man, but I don't kill innocent women." Intentionally...at least. "I don't regret my decision, even if our relationship is irreparable."

Rancor narrowed his eyes, like he could make out something in the air between us. "I see it now."

I didn't ask for an elaboration, but I knew what he meant. He probably wanted to say more, but because her father sat right across the table, he was wise and kept those words to himself.

"Speak," Huntley ordered. "Before the sun rises."

Rancor turned to Huntley. "I only know what the demons have agreed to share with me, but I suspect they're hiding more than they show, like an iceberg that only reveals its tip. They've come to our lands in search of power, power that can only be harvested from a special type of crystal, which only exists beneath the surface of the earth."

"The Exiles of Palladium mentioned this," Huntley said. "Their loved ones are trapped in camps as they mine for what the demons seek."

"Their reserves have diminished, and they've grown desperate for a replacement. The yield of the camps is minimal, but it's better than nothing. The soil of the east is so dry and arid that crystals are unable to grow here. From what they said, it seems like the crystals are a solid form of water, but not cold like ice. It subdues their fires, fuels their magic, allows them to thrive. But as a consequence, the harvesting of the crystals kills the land where these stones resided. Without that form of water, the land goes barren and dead, and the effects are irreversible." Rancor adjusted his hand again, wincing when he moved his fingers. "I told them I knew where they could find more crystals…if they removed you from power."

My eyes shifted to Huntley's face, waiting for his reaction to this horrible news.

"Our lands are cold and wet, so they're an ideal place." He seemed to say it more to himself than anyone else. "And that's why this place is a barren desert, because they've already used up the crystals that were once here."

Rancor gave a nod. "The plan was to defeat you in Delacroix and then accept your surrender—"

"And put us to work like the other prisoners." A rage should be burning inside Huntley, but he digested all of this with a sense of calm. Or maybe it was defeat.

"Yes," Rancor said. "And then—"

"Once they've finished using all the crystals, they move on to the next place, our lands barren and dry just like the east, and you would rule over us the way a farmer rules over his flock of sheep." He stared at Rancor, giving him the harshest look of judgment I'd ever seen.

Rancor hesitated before he answered. "Yes..."

Huntley stared him down.

Rancor's hand was slightly exposed on the table, so he tucked it underneath because the bloody dagger was still sitting there.

Huntley was quiet for a long time. He didn't stare at Rancor, but *through* him. "You were wrong to assume we would ever surrender. We'll fight until every last one of us is dead, because we'd all rather be bones in the ground than prisoners to someone else. You underestimated your enemy, Rancor."

Rancor kept his gaze elsewhere.

"The Exiles of Palladium told us the crystals reincarnate them. When the demons are killed in battle, their bodies somehow return to their domain. They carry the scars from their wounds, but otherwise, they're exactly the same. As long as they have any crystals in their possession, they'll continue to be invulnerable."

Rancor slowly turned to look at Huntley, like that was news to him.

"You need to call off the deal."

Rancor blinked several times.

"You heard me."

"I don't think there's anything I can say or do to change what's going to happen," Rancor said. "I already told them your lands were probably a viable source of power. The damage has been done."

"Then you'll convince them to go elsewhere."

Rancor sighed. "They're not the kind to be reasoned with—"

"Nor am I."

If they went somewhere else, they could choose my homeland, and that thought terrified me. Everywhere they traveled, they wrought destruction. It was only a matter of time before the earth was completely destroyed.

Rancor was quiet for a while. "The only way I could get them to leave is if I had something better to offer. And since I've never left these lands, I have nothing up my sleeve. And I suspect they wouldn't take my offer even if I did...since your lands are so close."

"Why haven't they invaded us yet?"

"The earth is different under the mountains," Rancor said. "It's solid rock nearly all the way through. They penetrated Delacroix because the soil is different. They're also preoccupied by other things..."

So Ivory's assessment was correct. When they attacked HeartHolme, they would attack from the north. Evacuating the northern kingdoms had been a smart call.

"What things?" Huntley asked.

"I'm not sure why you think they share so much with me—"

"Then how do you know they're preoccupied?" he snapped.

"Because it's the only explanation that makes sense," Rancor said. "I don't know anything about their kingdom, their hierarchy, or their domain. I've only been there once..."

"But you do have a contact."

Rancor nodded. "Vine."

"Is he their king?"

"I'm not sure if they have a king...or kings."

"Where is their domain?"

"The ring of fire," Rancor said. "I'm sure you've seen it."

"But what is it?" Huntley asked. "Do they live in underground caves?"

"No," he said quickly. "Definitely not caves. Their kingdom is located deep in the earth, in the grand chasms below the surface, the crystals glowing with light like a sunrise. Torches light the rest of the way. It's something you have to see for yourself to understand. Their architecture rivals yours in every way. Think of a glorious kingdom, but instead of being underneath the sky, it's underneath the ground you walk on."

In my lands, vampires and the Ethereal were at the top of the hierarchy, and now that the Ethereal had been defeated, it was just us. It was hard to imagine a foe more formidable than our own kind.

Huntley was quiet, reflecting on everything we'd just learned about these beings. His arms were crossed, and he slouched in the chair. "I want you to take me to him."

Rancor looked at me, like he'd misheard what Huntley said.

I nearly did a double take.

"To Vine?" Rancor asked.

"It looks like that's where you were headed anyway," Huntley said.

"Yes," Rancor said. "But he's expecting me."

"Perfect."

I didn't want to undermine Huntley in front of his enemy, but I couldn't quiet my protests. "I think that's unwise. You haven't fought these demons in the flesh—"

"That's exactly why I should go." Huntley turned to me.

"If one of us goes, it should be me." I was related to the Teeth. And I could read their intentions. Huntley was utterly blind.

"Are you the King of Kingdoms?" Huntley asked coldly. Without waiting for an answer, he added, "No. That's why it needs to be me. Perhaps if we meet face-to-face, I can convince them to turn their destruction elsewhere."

"Like I said..." Rancor hesitated. "They aren't the type to be persuaded."

"Even if that's true, I could learn from their domain. I could learn their ways. I could figure out a weakness. It's better than staying in the dark and allowing you to do all the negotiation."

Rancor flicked his gaze to me, as if he expected me to say something else.

"You might get yourself killed, Huntley," I said. "Think of your family."

"I am thinking of my family," he said coldly. "And I have to do everything I can to protect them...even if it costs my life." He looked at Rancor again. "So you're taking us both with you—and I will speak to Vine."

FOUR
HARLOW

I sat at the table in the great room across from Fang. The game was new to me, so I was still learning the structure of the cards and the rules. Fang had clearly been playing a long time because he always seemed to know his next move long before he made it.

I looked at the options in my hand before I made my selection and put it down.

"*Hiiiissssssssss.*" He grabbed the cards with his tail and shuffled them into a pile so we could play again.

"How did you get so good at this?" I asked, even though I knew he wouldn't answer.

"*Hiiissssss.*" He continued to mix up the cards, his eyes on me because he could do two things at once.

"You should play for money. Now, that would be fun."

He nodded.

"I wish I could understand you like Aurelias does."

Kingsnake appeared in the room, his armor black and red, a snake on his chest that was identical to Fang. "You don't have to keep playing with him."

"I don't mind."

He took the seat at the head of the table, having similar features to Aurelias, midnight-dark hair and eyes the color of espresso. But their facial structures were a little different. Aurelias had a harder jawline and a naturally displeased-looking expression. Kingsnake seemed a little kinder.

"It's not like I have anything else to do." Aurelias and my father had left days ago. My mother woke up every day and worked to protect our kingdom in her queen's armor, but she was dead behind the eyes, strained with worry.

Atticus hadn't arrived with the people from the Kingdoms yet, and that had started to worry us as well. I told myself it was a heavy expedition and to prepare all the Kingdoms for evacuation would take a very long time. Just because Atticus hadn't been sighted in the distance didn't mean he wasn't coming.

"Do you ever play him for money?" I asked, trying to think about something other than my missing family members...and the love of my life.

Kingsnake shook his head. "Not anymore," he said with a chuckle. "Learned that lesson the hard way."

"*Hiiissssssss.*"

Kingsnake ignored him. "He's taken a liking to you."

"Because I'm an easy opponent."

He gave another subtle chuckle. "I think it's because my brother had a lot of nice things to say about you."

I looked down at the stack of cards that Fang had just shuffled. He started to deal, dealing Kingsnake into the game as well. My heart ached when I pictured Aurelias's face, when I considered the possibility he wouldn't return.

"Which is saying something," Kingsnake said. "He rarely has nice things to say about anyone, including me."

"He seems close to your wife."

"Well, she's the only person in the family he actually does like."

"You talk like you guys aren't close, but if you weren't close, you wouldn't be here right now." I looked at Kingsnake as Fang continued to deal the cards.

Kingsnake grabbed his hand and sorted through the cards. "It's complicated. Aurelias and I are closer now, but we didn't talk much the last couple centuries."

"Why?"

"He's close with my father, and I'm not his biggest fan."

"That's right... He's the favorite." I remembered that being mentioned before.

"We had different politics, which is clearly over now. But my father..." He shook his head. "He'll never change."

"Why do you think that is?"

He shrugged. "He thinks he's entitled to do whatever the fuck he wants because he lost my mother. That her death somehow justifies his cruelty and malice. He craves power the way he craves blood, and every time he gets it, he needs more. The satisfaction is only temporary, but he keeps going anyway."

"I'm sorry about your mother." Aurelias had never told me what happened.

Kingsnake turned quiet.

We started to play the game, Fang setting up his traps for us to walk right into.

"How long have you been married?" I asked.

"A couple months."

"Was she always a vampire?"

"She was human." His eyes remained on the cards.

"So, she chose to be with you?" She chose to give up her soul, the possibility of children.

"Not quite," he said with a sigh. "She nearly died in battle, so I turned her to save her."

I was quiet, unsure what to say to that.

"It was hard for her to accept at first, but then she embraced it."

"She could have changed back if she wanted to…right?"

"Technically," he said.

"And you could have changed too."

"Yes." His eyes were on his cards.

"Can I ask you something?"

He put down his cards, and of course, both of our hands were defeated by Fang's. "Always."

I knew Kingsnake's kindness and openness came from his love for his brother. He didn't strike me as the kind of man to make small talk with a human like me. He had a beautiful wife whose company he undoubtedly preferred to mine. "Would you be willing to be human for her?"

Fang hissed before he gathered the cards again, the victor in yet another match.

Kingsnake remained silent, as if he'd dismissed the question.

I didn't repeat it.

"I told her I would if I had no other choice, but I really didn't want to. Why would I want to live a single life with her when we could have forever? I understood her desire to have children, but life can be just as fulfilling without them. More so, if you ask me."

"But you would make that sacrifice?"

"Our love wouldn't be real if I weren't willing to make the same sacrifice that I asked her to make."

I wasn't willing to sacrifice my mortality for Aurelias, and he wasn't willing to make that sacrifice either. But our love felt so real, as real as the sunrise every morning and the rainfall on an autumn day.

"I understand your curiosity. Aurelias is one of the most hardheaded men I've ever known, and I can't see him choosing a mortal life for any reason. I don't say that to hurt you, but to prepare you."

Aurelias had already told me this, but it still hurt to hear it from another source.

"As much as I love my brother, I don't think you should make a sacrifice he's unwilling to make himself. It wouldn't be fair to you."

My eyes had drifted away, my heart heavy. "Does Larisa have any regrets?"

"It's been such a short amount of time that I don't think there's been an opportunity for regret. Maybe someday in the future she will. But I will make her so happy that she'll never have the chance to feel a moment of lament."

I sat in front of the warm fireplace with a book on my lap, reading the same sentence over and over because I couldn't focus. The sun had set, and the frost pressed against the windows. My bed was empty because Aurelias was still gone. I'd only slept beside him a couple nights, but without him there, I felt utterly lost.

The door cracked, and then Fang slithered across the floor, approaching the rug and then the couch. He climbed up then curled his body into a ball, his head perched on top.

The door opened wider, and Larisa entered, wearing an oversized shirt that obviously belonged to her husband and lounge trousers. "Fang wanted to keep you company. Is that okay?"

"Of course it is." I scratched my nails over the scales on his head, and he closed his eyes in relaxation. "I'm pretty lonely without Aurelias." He wasn't much of a talker, but his presence brought a sense of peace to my soul. He felt like...home. "But I don't want to take him from you." I looked at her.

"Honestly, he's been sleeping under the sheets right between us because it's cold, and it would be nice to have a break... He's kind of a cockblock."

I chuckled. "Well, there's no cock to block here, unfortunately."

She turned away. "Goodnight."

"Larisa?"

She looked at me again.

I was about to ask something that was personal, and then I realized I didn't know her very well. "Never mind."

"It's okay," she said. "Ask."

"How did you know I wanted to ask anything?"

She walked to the couch and sat down, Fang between us. "I have the same abilities as Aurelias. But he's much, much better at it than I am. Your unease is very potent right now."

I wasn't sure where to begin, how to explain this incessant need I felt. "I would never want a vampire to feed from me. The idea is just...barbaric. But with Aurelias...I want it to happen. I can't explain why."

She watched me, her eyes soft.

"But he won't."

Her stare continued in silence, so it was unclear if Aurelias had already told her this or if it was brand-new information.

"I don't know why it bothers me so much."

"It bothers you because it's a very intimate moment between two people. It's about trust and intimacy, about giving your partner pleasure and receiving it in return. I understand why it bothers you."

"So…Kingsnake fed from you?"

"That was the foundation of our relationship. I was his prey…and then I became something more."

"And you…let him?"

"Well, I didn't want to," she said. "I was repulsed by the idea. But we made an agreement. He gave me what I wanted if I gave him that in exchange. He told me it would feel good, and once I felt his bite, I knew it was true."

"How does it feel?"

"It's hard to describe…" She looked away as she considered her answer. "It's like being the most aroused you could be…but having no release. It's wanting more but never having it. It's like being in a haze that you want to stay in forever. Over time, it deepens, knowing I give Kingsnake something that makes him strong, something that no one else can give him. There was a time when I was angry with him and refused to let him feed, but the idea of him being with anyone else…made me sick to my stomach. I feared our relationship wouldn't be the same once I turned, but that hasn't happened."

I listened to all of that, disappointed I was denied a deeper connection with the man I loved. "Why doesn't Aurelias want that with me?"

She stared, her eyes full of empathy.

"You know…"

Her eyes shifted away.

"Why?"

"It's not my place to say."

I didn't want to put Larisa in a tough spot with Kingsnake, so I didn't press her on it further, but it still hurt me. "I love him. He loves me. Why isn't that enough?"

"I think his love for you is the very problem."

I wanted to know more, but I'd have to settle for less. "Aurelias and I agreed that when this is over…it's over. But now that he's gone and I'm distraught with fear and longing, I realize just how hard that separation will be. I'm terrified of it…utterly terrified."

Her eyes softened.

"So, do you have any regrets…about turning?"

She stared for a long time, her dark hair a curtain around her shoulders. "I don't think my answer will help you, Harlow. When Kingsnake turned me, my parents were already gone and I was alone in the world. And on top of that, our enemies were employing magic that used souls as power, so my parents weren't in the afterlife anyway. The only sacrifice I've had to make is bearing children."

"I'm sorry…about your parents."

"It's hard," she said. "I think about it every day. But there's nothing I can do about any of it."

My eyes dropped in sadness.

"That's how it would be if you turned."

My eyes moved up again.

"Knowing you would never see your parents again."

That was just as painful as losing Aurelias. Never seeing my father's face. Feeling my mother's spirit. Hearing my brother's laugh. Knowing I would live several lifetimes while they knew I would never cross into their eternal realm...was too hard to bear. My father would be distraught. My mother...she'd be devastated.

"I think you have your answer."

FIVE
VINE

I sat at my mahogany desk, the golden sconces along the walls lit with flames. It cast the room in a golden hue and pushed the shadows far toward the thirty-foot ceilings. My elbow was propped on the golden armrest, my fingertips against the bottom of my mouth. The schematics were before me, but my eyes were tired of staring at them.

The heavy doors far on the other side of the room opened, and then Rakier entered my chambers, his boots tapping against the gold-plated floor. It was a long walk, at least seventy feet to where my desk sat against the window overlooking the chasms.

The doors to my bedchambers were open, and he couldn't help but glance at the naked woman asleep in my bed. He focused his stare on me and pretended he hadn't looked. "The Teeth have left their passage and approach our domain."

All I did was give a slight nod.

He pounded his closed fist against his chest, gave a slight bow, and then departed my chambers.

A sleepy voice came from my bedchambers. "Come to bed…"

Like I hadn't heard her, I left the chambers and walked out.

This part of the city was quiet.

Braziers burned along the long walkways, the flames reflecting off the gold material. The sea of darkness far out into the distance was illuminated by the distant glow of crystals…crystals that were far less bright than they used to be. Some were along the ceiling, showing the surface of the earth that was leagues away. I passed guards on my way, and every time I passed, they saluted me in the same way, their fists banging against the steel plates that covered their chests.

It was a long walk that consisted of many different pathways. I finally reached a gate made of solid gold. Thirty feet high and impenetrable by any outside force. The guards silently opened the gate, not needing permission to allow me entry. Before I passed, they saluted me.

It was another eighty feet to the main doors, which the guards opened for me as well. Civilizations aboveground condensed their kingdoms into small plots of land because they were restricted by space. We had no such problem, so our kingdoms stretched for leagues and leagues, through the chasms that connected beneath the surface.

The doors shut behind me, and I entered the palace, stairs on either side leading to the second landing of doors. At the opposite end were three thrones, all at the same level, and the throne in the center was occupied.

My boots thudded against the floor as I approached, every step echoing off the gold that plated these halls. If humankind were to see our kingdom, they would see we were far richer than any king on the surface.

Lord Ashe sat upon the throne, his skin a mixture of black and gray, like the remains of a burned pyre. Flesh that should be bright and taut with youth looked faded and weak. There was a tear over his cheekbone, a pale bone visible. His hair was the color of midnight, black with an intense shine, long and well-maintained. He was both weak and strong, at the end of his life but also the beginning. He was outfitted in deep blue robes, his boots dark like his hair. He stared with eyes both intense and weary. "Vine." There was a strange vibration to his voice whenever he spoke, a bass that came from his entire body, not just his mouth. "Your presence shines like gold."

Lord Ashe was one of the Demon Lords, a being that had existed since the beginning of time, his mind greatly misunderstood because it had experienced not many lifetimes, but *all* the lifetimes. He was one of the servants of Velkum, the mortal enemy of the gods. And once the gods were brave enough to show their faces, Velkum would strike—and win dominion over the entire world.

None of us had seen Velkum in the flesh. That was a privilege only for the Demon Lords. With his magic, Velkum reincarnated us once our bodies were defeated, bringing us back to the pinnacle of our prime. "The Teeth have left the mountains and approach our domain."

Lord Ashe gave an empty stare, as if he hadn't heard what I said or didn't care about it.

But I knew that wasn't the case.

"Escort Rancor into our domain. Entertain the Teeth… until we're ready to put them to work." His voice reverberated against the gold-plated walls. His eyes were heavy, like the exhaustion of eternity had spoiled his energy. "The soil must be tilled. The crops must be watered. The harvest must be collected. That is their purpose—to put food on the table for us to eat."

But instead of crops, it was crystals. "It will be done, Lord Ashe."

"I know it will."

SIX
AURELIAS

The sunrise crested the horizon because we'd spent the entire night interrogating Rancor. Now we stood near the river, replenishing our canteens as we enjoyed the cool morning air. Huntley drank the entire contents before he refilled it and returned it to his pack.

"This isn't a good idea, Huntley."

He looked across the strange world, one that was mostly desert with dried shrubs and red dirt. "Then don't come."

"I can't let you go alone."

"Then silence your protests." He continued to look across the stream, his eyes squinting in the light.

"You're giving them your head on a silver platter."

"And what would you have me do?" He turned to regard me head on, his stare hard, his blue eyes identical to his daughter's…eyes that I loved. "Return home and sit on my ass and wait for them to march on our gates? That's no plan."

"The second we step into their territory, we're at their mercy."

"In case you haven't noticed," he said coldly, "we're *already* at their mercy." His stare was vicious. "The Exiles of Palladium know a path to their kingdom, but based on Rancor's information, their city is so vast that the odds of us finding what we seek are very unlikely—"

"Less unlikely than walking out of there with our heads still on," I retorted. "This is a bad idea."

"*Then don't come.*" He turned away.

"I can't fucking do that." I said it under my breath, doing my best to bottle my frustration.

He stilled and looked at me again.

"Harlow asked me to watch your back."

"I don't need your protection, Aurelias."

"Even I wouldn't dare walk into their domain alone. I understand you're scared and desperate, but throwing yourself into this isn't the answer."

Huntley marched back toward me. "Then what is?"

I held his stare.

"What is the answer, Aurelias?" he snapped. "We fight them when they arrive at our gates, and if we somehow succeed, we do it again...and *again*? Or do we take the passage into their domain blindly to try to find what we seek? If we walk in with Rancor, it will give us the only opportunity we're ever going to have to observe. To persuade them to turn their attention elsewhere. To glean whatever knowledge we can. That is the most effective plan—by far."

"And also the riskiest."

"The greatest risks yield the greatest rewards," he said. "I know that all too well."

I knew there was no way to convince him otherwise. His mind had been decided.

"I release you of any obligation." He prepared to turn away again.

"I'm not leaving you, Huntley."

He continued to walk away. "My daughter would prefer to lose only one of us—not both. I'll tell Pyre you're returning to HeartHolme with the others. Storm will remain behind and wait for me."

"I'm not leaving," I repeated. "And not just for her."

He stopped, his boot grinding into the red dirt beneath his feet. He slowly turned around, looking at me over his shoulder.

"But for me."

At nightfall, we began our procession, leaving the Teeth behind at the campsite as we trekked forward toward the ring of fire. As the night deepened, the fire became more visible, and the closer we approached, the bigger the flames became. They were stagnant, burning without fuel, lighting up the world around them.

Rancor took the lead, while Huntley and I trailed behind. The world was quiet, so quiet that the flames were audible as we drew close. The space didn't appear to be guarded until we came closer, until we approached the ring that was impossible to cross.

Then one of the demons stepped across the line of fire, and instantly, that section of the ring was snuffed out. The ground beneath it was charred and black, no sign of the red hue visible. Seven feet tall with veins of liquid fire on his muscular arms, he was built like the others, but also familiar…

It only took a few seconds for me to realize who he was. He'd led the charge against Delacroix—and burned Ivory's throat. I'd killed him myself, knew his body had been burned in the pyre on the field, but he was there again—as lively as the last time our paths had crossed.

I hoped he wouldn't recognize me—because then Huntley would try to kill him.

But he seemed more interested in Rancor. "He's expecting you." He gave a slight gesture with his arm, telling Rancor to move ahead.

Rancor passed over the line.

When Huntley tried, the demon held his hand to his chest. "And you are?"

Huntley said nothing, but there was a flourish of rage, probably because he wasn't used to being spoken to that way. And he wasn't used to holding his tongue either.

"He's with me," Rancor said. "My first general."

"What do you need a general for?" The demon turned to him. "You don't trust us?" Then he grinned—like we definitely shouldn't trust them.

Rancor shifted his gaze to Huntley in a subtle panic, but then he found his footing. "I'd rather not waste my time repeating the plan when they can hear it themselves. I brought my generals before, and it was no issue."

"But those were different Teeth." He looked at Huntley again. "This one looks strange..." He came closer, invading Huntley's space unnecessarily to examine him.

Huntley stepped into him, pushing against his chest to force him back. "Get a good enough look?"

The demon stayed back, but he grinned like this was all a game. Then his eyes flicked to me.

I kept my face hard, gave no hint of a reaction.

He continued his stare.

His emotions were quiet, so I was unable to determine his thoughts in that moment. If he recognized me but couldn't place me, he would feel confused, but that confusion wasn't deep enough for me to feel.

He finally moved to where Rancor stood. "Let's go, boys."

I closed my eyes in relief, knowing that could have been the end for all of us.

Stairs carved out of the earth took us deep underground. It was in a spiral that hugged the walls, taking us deeper and deeper beneath the surface, away from the flames that continued to burn on at the top.

It made me uneasy, because regardless of how fit Huntley and I were, there was no way we would be able to run up these stairs and evade our enemies if it came to that. I remained in the rear, and not a word was said as we approached the bottom.

There was a wall made of solid gold, and in the center were double doors constructed out of chrome. Sconces burned on either side, burning without a source of fuel just like above. These beings seemed to have the ability to control and manipulate fire, in addition to their reincarnation.

Every man claimed he was unafraid to die, but that wasn't true.

With the exception of these guys.

And that made them the most formidable opponents I'd ever encountered.

The demon pounded his fist against the chrome door, which had to be at least fifty feet tall, and solid, based on the way his fist sounded.

A second later, both doors swung inward, revealing a grand hallway lined with gold. Sconces were mounted down the walls, the fire making the golden color even brighter, like it was being struck with sunshine.

The demon led the way, his passing making the sconces flicker slightly.

In a single line behind Rancor, we passed through the hallway and into a large archway.

I nearly stopped at the sight of it.

We were leagues underground, a great expanse of space high above us, the scale so immense it was hard to discern the size of the buildings in comparison. There were sections of crystals in the cliffs that surrounded us, casting a dull light that provided some illumination in the darkness.

And it was quiet, so quiet.

Huntley seemed to have the same reaction because he stopped too.

A long pathway lay ahead, a bridge over the emptiness that led to a new section of buildings. The demon took us forward, and we continued to walk, passing through the silent city of gold.

Lit sconces were placed everywhere, reflecting in the shiny gold that plated nearly every surface. It was a display of wealth I'd never seen, not even back home, not even in the castle my father and I occupied. The scale of everything was remarkable, like it had been made for beasts four times their height.

It was a long walk, moving to one section of buildings and then across other bridges to get to the next sections. This was not a linear city, made in the chasms that were available. It wrapped around to the left, and the bridges continued like there was no end to this place. Their city was already built under the east, so that meant it had been here long before Huntley and Rancor were aware of it.

We finally stopped at a building that looked like all the others, double doors in the center. The demon gave a knock before he opened one of the doors and gestured for us to walk inside.

It was like all the other buildings, grand and beautiful, but with no unique ornamentation. The three of us stepped inside, and then the heavy door shut with a distinct thud.

The demon took the lead, and then we crossed the large room and approached a demon seated behind a large desk. It was a long walk like all the rest, an impressive room with no contents.

We stood feet away as the demon walked forward. "Rancor and some of his little friends." He gave a chuckle before he walked off, heading all the way back to the large door that we'd stepped through a minute ago.

The man I assumed to be Vine remained seated, slouched slightly in the chair with his elbow propped on the armrest. Unlike the other demons, he was dressed with greater elegance, adorned in a uniform made of black and gold. His arms were hidden underneath the material, but the cords up his neck showed the glow of fire in his veins. He had dark hair and a hard face, his eyes the color of ash. "Sit."

There were three high-backed armchairs in front of his desk, champagne gold with red cushions. He had exactly enough for the three of us, like they had a system to transfer messages quicker than hand-delivering them.

Rancor took the seat on the left, Huntley in the middle, and I took the seat on the right.

"You brought friends." Vine stared at Rancor. "How nice." He had a deep voice that sounded calm, but the hostility he emanated was clear as glass. It came from his eyes, smart and perceptive, the flames burning far underneath. "Who are they?"

When I'd asked Rancor for the Golden Serpents, he'd had the upper hand. As a result, he'd been confident and arrogant. But now that the tables had turned and he was the weakest being in the room, he was plagued by hesitancy. He behaved like an invisible knife was pressed to his throat. "This is—" He paused, realizing he couldn't use Huntley's name. "Mastodon...my first general."

If it was obvious to us that Rancor was riddled with discomfort, then it must be obvious to Vine too. I tried to pick up on his emotions, but the demon was a chasm of nothingness, just like the darkness that surrounded us that very moment.

"And this one?" He nodded to me at the end.

"My second general...Aurelias."

"Doesn't the general stay with the army?" Vine asked.

Now he was toying with us.

"I have many generals." Rancor rested his arms on the armrests and gripped the edges. "I've completed the task you've assigned me."

"Really?" Vine asked. "You said King Rolfe would be dead once he came for his daughter—*but here he sits.*" He shifted his gaze to Huntley and gave him a hard stare, the kind that could penetrate through solid rock.

If I'd had a heart, it would have been racing.

Vine regarded him impassively. "Walked right into our kingdom with nothing but his sword and an axe. I'm not sure whether I should admire you...or pity you."

Huntley was quiet, and despite the revelation, his heart didn't race in fear. He was as calm as he was when we'd walked in here.

That was impressive.

"For what it's worth," Vine said. "I prefer Mastodon to Huntley."

A heavy moment of silence stretched in the great room. It seemed to last forever, and it was only broken by the quiet chuckle of a woman from the other room. There was an open doorway on my side of the hall, but I didn't dare take a peek.

It was the two of us versus one of them—and I liked those odds.

But Huntley didn't move, so I stayed put.

Vine continued. "Rancor, your spine has shortened since the last time I saw you. You walk with a hunch like an old man, succumbed to the power of the man who overruled you with his axe and his dragons." His eyes stayed on Huntley as he said this. "I judge your weakness, but I'm grateful it happened, because otherwise, I wouldn't have the pleasure of staring my enemy right in the face. Was that your plan?"

Huntley remained quiet.

"To walk in here and earn my respect through your bravery? Or is it stupidity? I'm not sure yet."

Huntley still didn't speak.

Vine didn't seem remotely intimidated, not even when he was outnumbered by one Teeth, one vampire, and one king. That meant he knew something we didn't...or he had a better poker face than Fang. "You came here for a reason, Huntley. Now's your chance to tell me that reason—or try to kill me."

I still felt nothing from Vine.

Huntley was quiet a long time, trying to gather his thoughts before he spoke, knowing he only had one chance to get this right. "You've come to my lands out of necessity because these crystals fuel your power and immortality. I know you must have done this countless times before, destroyed kingdoms and all those who lived there. It would be easy to call you evil, but I know I would do anything to ensure my survival and the survival of those I love, so that would be hypocritical of me to say."

Vine listened, his chin propped on his closed knuckles.

"But we aren't like the kingdoms before us. We won't be conquered easily. There will be many battles, and we'll keep killing you over and over...draining the clock until you're out of time and resources and are forced to move on elsewhere. All of that could be avoided if you choose to move on."

"Pallidum was a mighty kingdom—and they were defeated in a single day."

"We're mightier." Huntley's voice suddenly rose, mixed with pride and offense, echoing off the walls slightly. "We will *not* stop. We will *not* give up. We will *not* surrender."

"Your dragons won't save you—"

"Our people will save us," he snapped. "But I would rather not waste lives in battle. I would rather not watch my people anguish over lost loved ones. Take your people elsewhere for what you seek. That is my request."

Vine remained still, his eyes transfixed on Huntley like he actually cared to listen. "I have a proposal for you. Allow us to dig in your lands for the crystals we seek. Once we get what we want, we'll leave you be."

"No."

Vine cocked his head slightly, as if he expected Huntley to say more.

"Without those crystals, our soil will become as barren as yours. Our crops will be destroyed. Our trees will die. Our game will disappear. It'll destroy our home, the land of my ancestors, the burial site of all previous generations of my people. I will not leave it."

"The land will wither, but it's temporary."

"It doesn't matter how temporary it is if we die before it can renew."

Vine dropped his knuckles from his chin. "That's the best I can offer you, Huntley, King of Kingdoms."

"Spare our lands and go elsewhere."

"Why?" he demanded. "In exchange for what?"

Huntley stared, having nothing to offer.

"You came all the way here to plead for your people, and while I admire that, that's not reason enough to inconvenience myself and everyone else in this kingdom."

"There are a million other crystals out there—"

"Yes, but there's one crystal we need above all else. We can't leave your lands without verifying it's there."

"The odds are slim to none—"

"*Even so.*" He stared Huntley down, his patience waning. "You've spoken and I listened. Now, go. And thank me for allowing you to leave with your head."

Huntley remained seated.

"Huntley." We shouldn't squander the generosity Vine had just offered. I moved to rise from the chair.

Vine's eyes shifted to me, examining me with that hard gaze. "I know your kind."

I said nothing.

"Vampire."

I didn't confirm or deny it.

Vine turned to Rancor. "You have more friends than you previously mentioned."

"He's not a friend," Rancor said.

"More like a cousin," I said, refusing to give more than that.

Vine kept his stare on Rancor. "Leave, and take these two with you. We'll give you our instructions shortly."

And then I felt it, a flickering candle, a light that had barely enough fuel to sustain it. It was merely a glimmer but still enough for me to absorb. Disgust and resentment...and vengeance.

I knew it would be unwise to overstay our welcome. "Huntley."

Vine's emotions intensified, turning from annoyance to full-blown anger. It was hard to understand what had provoked it, but now that little candle flame had turned into a forest fire.

Huntley remained in the chair for a moment, but then he stood up and approached Vine's desk. "Listen to me—"

I grabbed him by the arm. "*Huntley.*"

He stilled and slowly looked at me.

All I had was a stare, but I hoped that would be enough for him to understand the danger we were in.

He seemed to get it because he took a step back.

"Thank you for your time," I said diplomatically. "We'll leave now."

Vine's expression remained the same, but his insides boiled like a hot pot on the stove.

The three of us turned away and walked down the long rug to the opposite door that felt like a league into the distance. Our backs were turned to him, and I'd never felt more exposed in my life.

When we were out of earshot, Huntley spoke. "What is it?"

"He's angry," I said. "*Really angry.*"

"We're not getting out of here alive," Rancor said.

I had the same fear. "Be prepared to fight."

"There were so few of them on the way here," Huntley said. "Child's play."

We pushed open the doors and stepped onto the bridge that led back the way we'd come.

But the path was blocked…by a dozen armed demons.

My sword was in my hand instantly, and Rancor and Huntley followed suit. The demon in the lead was the one who had escorted us down here—and he wore the biggest grin. And to make matters worse...there was something else.

An enormous serpent.

Enormous wasn't even the right word. Fang was enormous. This thing was gargantuan, standing next to the bridge, its big body fading into the blackness of the chasm below. It had yellow eyes, and its mouth was already parted to show its exposed fangs.

"You should have taken my deal."

I turned to see Vine behind us, relaxed as if he didn't see us as a threat.

His eyes shifted to Rancor. "And you shouldn't have crossed me." He snapped his fingers. "Kill him."

The gigantic snake prepared to strike. His fangs dripped with venom, and his powerful body tightened as it prepared to drive forward and bite us in half.

I locked eyes with the serpent and held up my hand. *Stop.*

The snake remained still, but it issued a hiss so high, it hurt everyone's ears. The sound was so powerful, it seemed to make the earth shake around us.

Your venom runs in my veins.

Huntley looked at me, like he knew I was responsible for the snake's behavior.

We are the same. I slowly dropped my hand, knowing the snake was intrigued by my ability to speak with him, the fact that we were connected in a way he didn't understand.

Vine snapped his fingers again. "*I told you to kill them.*"

The snake continued to hesitate, my words enough for him to question his allegiance.

My hand moved to my chest, showing him the golden snake engraved in my armor. *To them, you're a slave. To me, you're an equal.* I kept my eyes locked on his yellow ones, feeling an undeniable warmth spread through his scales. The emotions of animals were different from humans, similar, but somehow more complex. And I could feel his hesitation once he realized we shared the same venom, that the power of the Golden Serpents was alive in my dead body.

He hissed, but this time, it was unclear who was the recipient of that threat.

"What the fuck is happening?" Vine unsheathed his own blade and moved to strike me down.

But I was too focused on the snake to keep up my guard. I moved for my sword, but I wasn't quick enough.

But Huntley was. His blade met Vine's, and he pushed him off me and spared my neck.

Please help us. I kept my eyes on the snake, our only way out of there. *Free us.*

The other demons rushed forward across the bridge to strike us down. Rancor prepared his blade, but he wouldn't be enough to stop the onslaught. I wouldn't be either, not even with my abilities.

I looked at the oncoming attack then back at the snake. *Please.*

His eyes remained on mine before a surge of anger rushed through him. Then he released a hiss greater than the previous one, a war cry. "*Hiiiiisssssssssssssssssssss!*" He struck, not at me or Huntley, but for the middle of the bridge. His powerful body launched at the stone, breaking it into pieces so the middle caved in. The vibrations were strong enough to knock nearly everyone to the ground. Stones crumbled and fell into the chasm below.

Now the army of demons were stuck on the other side, and all they could do was stare us down with potent rage. Some screamed. One grabbed his sword and chucked it across the opening to strike one of us.

Huntley looked at me in amazement, like I had personally destroyed that bridge. "What the fuck just happened?"

I saw Vine come from behind him, swinging a sword made of gold.

I shoved Huntley to the side and caught his blade with mine, stopping it before it came down on me and the others. Vine's rage was like wildfire, explosive and combative, uncontrollable. He came at me again with the strength of a mountain and the speed of a viper. I blocked his flurry of hits, but it took all my concentration.

He was different from the others.

He drove me back, sword striking me down, hitting my armor and leaving a mark. He pushed me to the edge of the bridge, his intention to push me over so I would fall into the abyss. Then Huntley stepped in, coming at him from the side with a blow to his neck.

He managed to duck it and turned his ire on Huntley.

It was two-on-one, but Vine could still handle us without a bead of sweat. His speed was unmatched. I blocked his hits because I knew when they would come, but even then, I struggled to keep up.

Huntley got hit a couple of times, but his armor was strong enough to protect him from serious injury.

"Rancor!" I spotted him off to the side, shrinking away because he didn't want to help us if Vine ended up as the victor. "Get your ass over here."

Rancor remained off to the side, leaving us to duel the demon that could handle both of our swords with a single one of his. Vine blocked Huntley's hit then slammed his fist hard into his face, making him fly back. With Huntley down, Vine turned his full wrath on me, coming at me with such ferocity, it was obvious he wanted me dead.

I knew Huntley and I were no match for this being. He was superior to the demons trapped on the other side, gifted with supernatural power and ability. For the first time, someone was making me feel inadequate. *Kill him.*

My ally listened and issued another cry. "*Hiiii-issssssssssss!*" The snake struck.

Vine smacked the sword out of my hand then faced the snake, staring him down with fire in his eyes. The veins up his neck suddenly burned a deeper shade of red. "*You wouldn't dare.*"

The snake hesitated then pulled back, like this demon somehow had enough power to make him cower in fear.

I reached down for my sword, and that brief instant was enough to lose sight of Huntley on the other side of Vine. Just as I grabbed the hilt and straightened, I heard him cry out in pain.

I turned frantically, seeing the demon shoving his blade straight through Huntley's shoulder, breaking through the thick armor that was sword-proof and fire-proof. Huntley had turned at the right time, protecting his heart and lungs from the tip of the golden blade.

"Motherfucker." I rushed to Vine and slammed my sword down.

He was turned the other way, but he met my blade like he knew it was coming. His immense strength drove me back because every hit had the force of a hurricane. "Submit."

I continued to fight, matching his ire because I had the strength of ferocity. I was fucking furious.

"*I said submit.*"

"And I say fuck off." I found an opening and kicked him hard in the chest, forcing him back to the ground.

The snake's deep voice entered my mind for the first time, sounding different from Fang's. ***Jump.***

I rushed to Huntley, who had already pushed himself to his feet but staggered slightly. "Come on."

He raised his sword to fight rather than flee.

"Jump," I said, grabbing his shoulder and guiding him toward the edge.

Blood oozed down the front of his armor and onto his gloved hand. It even dripped onto the hilt of his sword, making the grip slippery. He stood tall and proud, like the open wound wouldn't be enough to slow him down. "What?"

"Come on." I tugged him to the edge and forced him over. We were both in free fall for a second before hard scales cushioned our fall. There were grooves in every mark, so we had something to hold on to so we wouldn't slip away into the abyss below. Rancor landed on the snake a second later, on the other side of the bridge.

Thank you. I looked up to see Vine at the edge of the bridge, his sword gripped tightly in his fist, his face tinted red with the fire that burned inside him. His ire was reserved for the snake that had betrayed his loyalty. It looked like he might jump down and join us, stab his blade through the beautiful scales and pierce the flesh beneath. But he stayed, his anger so potent it gave my mind a headache.

The snake suddenly dove, and we were forced to grab on to whatever we could hold. He brought us deep into the darkness, away from the lit sconces along the bridge and the buildings. Deep down, we went...until we could no longer see anything.

SEVEN
AURELIAS

The snake moved through the dark chasm, taking us horizontal for a long time before he finally began to move up, making its way back to the surface.

"Wait." Huntley continued to ooze blood, which made his gloved hand slippery on the scales. "He probably knows where the crystals are."

"You're bleeding out, Huntley."

"Ask him."

"Huntley."

"Ask him."

I touched the snake's mind with mine. *My friend is bleeding, and I must attend to the wound. Is there a safe place to stop?*

There are many placesss in the underworld. He turned another direction, and then a moment later, he approached an isolated tower of stone, a sea of them in the distance, and propped himself high so we could move onto the ledge.

"Where are the crystals?" Huntley asked. Without the sconces, the world was dark. Distant clusters of crystals cast illumination along the ceiling and the sides of the stones.

"Take off your armor," I said. "We have to stop the bleeding."

Huntley groaned as he removed piece after piece, the armor heavy and locked together.

Rancor stood off to the side, staring into the endless abyss.

When we finally got his skin exposed, I saw the open wound, the blood that continued to pour out. "This is an unusual wound."

A wound that doesss not heal.

What do you mean?

The gold in their blade isss pure. It'sss much harder for flesssh to heal. He'sss doing better than most.

How do you stop it?

It wearsss off naturally. But the victim isss usssually dead before that happensss.

I ripped apart the fabric of my own clothing and secured it around Huntley's arm, applying as much pressure as I could to stop the bleeding. Harlow had told me their ancestors were powerful healers, and as a result, their afflictions healed quickly. I just hoped that would be enough in this case.

Huntley gave a grimace but didn't complain otherwise. "Did you ask him about the crystals?"

"I care more about you right now, Huntley." I ripped off another piece of my uniform and secured it around his shoulder.

"I will heal," he snapped. "Now, ask him."

I didn't want to tell him the truth, to worry him if there was nothing he could do. *There are crystals that grant the demons their immortality. Do you know where they are?* I looked up to see the golden eyes of the large serpent, its golden scales still brilliant in the darkness. *When they fall in battle, they return exactly as they were before. I need to destroy the source of their power.*

I know of which you speak. They are not called crystalsss...but Veinsss of Velkum.

I need to find them.

You can't go there.

But I need to go there.

You do not understand.

Destroying these crystals is the only way I can destroy them.

I underssstand. But you can't go there.

I grew frustrated by the snake, but I swallowed my annoyance because he'd saved our lives and was our ticket out of his dark grave. *I can go there if you take me.*

Not all crystalsss contain the sssame powersss. He lifted his head and looked up, seeing a blue one lodged in the crust of the ceiling. **Sssome emit light in dark places. Sssome are pretty to behold. The onesss that possess power are sacred…and guarded by the Demon Lordsss.**

"What is he saying?" Huntley asked, impatient.

I held up my hand to silence him. *How many Demon Lords are there?*

Three.

Are they like Vine?

No. They're beings that have always been… and will always be.

What does that mean?

"Does he know where they are or not?" Huntley snapped.

"Yes," I said. "But it's complicated."

"Complicated how?"

"I would know if you stopped interrupting me."

Huntley's eyes narrowed in anger, but he held his tongue.

I turned back to the snake. *What does that mean? They've always been...always will be?*

They're like time. No beginning—and no end.

Bumps suddenly formed on my arms, and I wasn't sure why. *What are their abilities?*

I don't know...but all demonsss fear them.

Does that include Vine?

Vine isss one of the few who ssspeaksss to them directly. The only one they allow near the crystals.

So the Demon Lords are the ones in charge...and Vine is their first general. Everyone else was simply foot soldiers.

That isss incorrect.

My eyes focused on the snake once more. *What do you mean?*

The Demon Lords are not in charge.

Then who is?

They call him Velkum.

And who is Velkum?

I don't know…no one hasss ever ssseen him.

How can someone maintain order and never show their face? I'd thought destroying the crystals was a straightforward plan, but now I realized this underworld was far more complicated than I'd realized. *Can you still take us there? Just so we can see?*

The snake stared at me for a while. **Only from a dissstance.**

What is your name?

Beassst.

It suits you.

I know.

I'm Aurelias. I turned back to Huntley.

Huntley moved to me, the impatience written across his face. "What's the plan?"

"Beast says the crystals are guarded—"

"Who's Beast?"

Beast gave a quiet hiss that echoed all around.

Huntley gave a nod in understanding. "Nice to meet you." He looked at me again. "How many guard the crystals?"

"Three—"

"*Three*? Then let's go now."

"It's not guarded by three demons, but the three Demon Lords. From what Beast described, we should fear them."

"I fear no one."

"Well, they're unlike anything living or dead. He described them as beings that have always existed...like time. No one is allowed to approach the crystals, except for Vine. Beast refused to take us there."

Huntley looked at the snake, pissed off. "It needs to be done."

"He also said their leader is Velkum, someone no one has ever seen."

Huntley's eyes narrowed.

"I want to destroy these crystals as much as you do, but I also want to live to tell the tale. I want to return to my—" I halted, catching myself before I said something I shouldn't. "We need a plan."

"We can't make a plan if we don't know what we're dealing with."

"Beast agreed to take us close enough to see, but not close enough to enter. Then he'll take us to the surface, and we'll return home to figure out a plan. I understand you want this done as quickly as possible, but we need to be smart about this."

Huntley continued to breathe hard, like it took all his strength not to scream.

"Let's go."

Beast lowered his head so we could jump onto the back of his neck. Rancor was the last one to join us, silent the whole time as if he was still in shock. Beast began his progression through the darkness, slithering through chasms left and right, even downward as his strong body gripped the jagged rocks to keep himself suspended.

After an hour of traveling, he stopped.

In the far distance was a crystal unlike all the others, brilliant blue, so bright it lit up the surrounding rock like sunshine. It protruded directly from the surface of the cavern, a tall prism that pointed downward directly on top of a fortress. A massive iron gate blocked entry to the estate.

We all stared at it in silence.

There were no guards at the gate. No one on the premises. It was silent.

They've expired their crystalsss…and that'sss the last one that remainsss.

That's why Vine refused to go elsewhere.

Yesss.

After minutes of silence, Huntley spoke. "It would take a thousand men to destroy that with pickaxes."

"We need explosives."

Huntley looked at me. "Explosives?"

"They're packed with powder and lit with fire. My brothers use them all the time."

Huntley continued to look confused.

"I'll show you when we return. If we have enough of those, we may be able to destroy it."

"Then we'll get these explosives and return," Huntley said. "That sounds like a simple plan."

They'll sssenssse you. You'll have only ssseconds.

"We'll have to do it fast," I said. "Beast says they can sense you."

"I don't give a shit if they sense me," Huntley snapped. "As long as that crystal is gone before they do."

Beast took us back to the surface, sliding along the different crevices and chasms, maneuvering in the dark when the rest of us were blind. He used his body to breach the surface, to break through the rock and sand at the top to poke his head out. ***It'sss clear.***

We climbed up through the hole, the world in darkness because it was sometime in the middle of the night.

"That's why the ground shakes…" Huntley said to himself more than anyone else. His bleeding seemed to have stopped, but he was still pale like he'd lost more blood than he should have.

The ring of fire was far in the distance, and the tents of the Teeth were visible in their bonfire.

"Thank you for your help, Beast," I said. "You really saved our asses back there."

I know. He stuck his head out farther, his massive head visible, his eyes like orbs in the darkness.

I grinned. "Will you be okay?"

There will be consequencesss, but that'sss my burden to bear.

"If we destroyed the crystals and killed the demons, would you be free?"

Yesss.

"That's why you helped us."

Yesss. But alssso…we're the sssame.

"Yes, we are the same," I said. "Come with us. You can meet us on the other side."

I cannot.

"Why?"

Beast stared at me for several long seconds. ***He'll hurt my hatchlingsss…***

"Oh…I'm sorry." And I was sorry, especially when I felt the emotional turmoil in his chest. "We'll defeat them so you can be free, Beast. So your family can be free."

I hope sssoo.

"How will I find you again?"

He perched up his head and turned to the mountains farther east, where the Exiles of Palladium were hidden. ***There's a passsage near the mountains. Follow it until you can go no farther. I will check the passsage every day until your return.***

"Then we shall meet again, Beast."

We ssshall.

Huntley came to my side. "Tell him I'm grateful for his aid—"

Beast suddenly hissed, opening his jaws wide and releasing a terrifying threat. ***I am no male.***

"Oh…I'm sorry."

"What did I say?" Huntley asked.

"Um, she's a girl."

"Oh…"

"When you said your name was Beast, I just assumed…"

She closed her jaws and released a threatening growl.

"But Beast is a very beautiful name…"

It'sss not beautiful. It'sss fersiousss, asss am I.

"Of course," I said quickly.

Beast disappeared into the hole and left us alone on the surface.

I ran my fingers through my hair. "Fang would love her."

EIGHT
HARLOW

I fell asleep on the couch in front of the fire, my book dropped to the rug, the blanket pulled over me. It was hard to sleep in the bed without Aurelias. Our time together had been so brief, but so permanent. It felt like we'd been married for twenty years, and whenever he didn't share our bed with me, I was beside myself.

A hand cupped my cheek, and then strands of my hair were pushed away.

I was dead tired from not sleeping well, so it was hard to stir, hard to believe the touch was real, not a vivid dream.

Then I heard his voice. "Baby."

My eyes cracked open, seeing his coffee-colored eyes with the glow of the fire behind him. His expression was hard and intense, but the longer he stared at me, the more it softened. Then a smile broke through. "Aurelias?" My voice was raspy, like nails against stone.

"I've returned."

Reality set in, that this was real and not a dream, and that was when my heart raced and my mind woke from its slumber. I sat up and hooked my arms around his shoulders, hugging him hard, my chest aching because it hurt so much. I'd missed him every moment he was away, worried he would never come back to me. His armor made the embrace uncomfortable, but I was so happy to have him in my arms that I didn't mind. My eyes closed and I stayed that way, completely still, letting him support my body. "My father?"

"He's okay."

He pulled back to look me in the face, and that was when I noticed how weak he appeared. His face was paler than usual, and his eyes didn't have the same shine. He looked hungry, like his journey had taken a serious toll.

"You look...tired."

The corner of his lip lifted in a smile. "I'll take that as a compliment. Because I'm fucking exhausted."

"You need to feed." I'd offered my blood before, but he'd viciously rejected the offer. I wanted to offer now, but I feared it would ruin the wonderful reunion we shared.

"I will." His hand cupped my face, and his thumb rested in the corner of my mouth. "But I wanted to see you first." He leaned in and pressed a soft kiss to my mouth, a small touch that lit a fire inside my belly. "I missed you."

"I fucking missed you."

When he got to his feet, he lifted me with him, bringing my body flush against his as he carried me to the bed with crumpled sheets. He dropped me on the bed before he loosened each piece of armor and dropped it onto the couch. His sword was against the wall, and then his uniform came off...but it was ripped in certain places. But I didn't have a chance to ask about it because I was too busy watching him get naked, muscles and flesh revealed, his big dick saved for last.

Then he was on top of me, my nightdress shoved to my waist while my straps were pulled down to reveal my tits. He folded my little body underneath him then found my entrance. He sank inside, nice and slow, his hand fisted deep in my hair the way he liked. "Baby..."

I was full of his dick and fully possessed by his grip. The love of my life had returned to me in the same condition as when he left. All the sadness in my chest was dispelled by his return. "Yes..."

I woke up before dawn, when the sky barely had a hint of light, but he was gone. My hand moved to the last place he'd been—and the sheets were ice-cold. I lay there for a moment, all my happiness from the night before gone with his absence.

I got out of bed and showered, getting ready for the day. When I was done, I walked down the hallway to the great room. My father was there with my mother, breakfast served on the table but untouched.

"Father."

He turned, and all the stress and anger in his face evaporated at the sight of me. "Sweetheart." His mouth lifted into a smile, and he came to me to embrace me in one of his big bear hugs. His lips brushed my hairline as he planted a kiss like he always did. But then he gave a wince, like I'd squeezed him just a little too hard.

"Are you okay?" I pulled away, and then I noticed the cloth secured over his shoulder underneath his shirt, a bit of the end sticking out. "What happened?"

"I'm fine," he said quickly. "It's just a little raw."

I'd never seen my father injured before. "What happened?"

He grabbed my shoulder, his smile still there because the sight of my face seemed to be all that mattered. "I heard you spent a lot of time with that snake while we were gone."

"Yeah, he's really cool."

"Never knew they were such fascinating creatures." He moved back to the head of the table. "Have some breakfast." He pulled out the chair for me.

I looked at the table, expecting to see Aurelias and the other vampires, but they were absent. I took a seat and kept my questions to myself. A bowl of oatmeal was brought to me topped with nuts, fruit, and honey.

My father's plate was full of his usual breakfast, twelve eggs and a steak.

Mother sat across from me, and instead of being dead behind the eyes like she had been lately, her features were soft, her eyes light. "We received a scroll from your brother this morning. He's begun the evacuation. It'll take a couple weeks, but they'll be here shortly."

"Oh good," I said. "I'd started to worry."

"Nothing our son can't handle."

We ate in silence for a while, but I was riddled with questions, questions I never asked Aurelias because we were occupied with other matters throughout the night. "So, what happened with Rancor?"

Father continued to scarf down his food as if I'd never asked a question. After a while, he provided an answer. "It's a very long tale. Ready to hear it all?"

"Yes."

My father told me how they'd forged a new alliance with the Teeth and ventured underground to confront the demon Vine, who turned on them and forced them to escape...and then they were aided by an unlikely ally.

"*A huge snake?*" I asked incredulously. "Seriously?"

My father nodded. "Her name is Beast."

"Wow..."

"She saved our lives. I've never cared for snakes, but now I have a new appreciation for them."

"You're lucky Aurelias can communicate with them," Mother said. "I'd say he's also a hero in this story."

Father didn't say anything to that.

"So, did you find where the crystals are?" I asked.

"It's one crystal," he said. "And yes. But getting to it will be complicated."

"But it can be done?" I asked hopefully.

He turned away from his food and looked at me directly. "Yes. It can be done."

I was in my bedchambers when Aurelias made his return. It was obvious that he had fed because he carried himself differently, had a more substantive vitality in his veins. There was more color to his face, and his eyes...they looked different.

"You've been gone a long time." He'd left in the middle of the night and had been gone for the first part of the morning. He fed when I wasn't around, did it in secret because

I was only aware it happened when I saw the change in his appearance. I noticed the other vampires had been missing from the castle as well, meaning that they must have gone together.

He turned his hard gaze on me, and he must have felt my disappointment because he was guarded. "Lost track of time."

"You were gone all night—"

"What do you want from me?" His stare was sharp as a dagger, aimed right between my eyes. All the bliss of our reunion had been stripped away the moment this subject was broached.

My arms crossed over my chest.

He stared back, waiting for me to say something.

I had a lot to say, but I was afraid to say it.

"I'm going to shower." He turned away to head to the bathroom.

"Larisa told me Kingsnake used to feed from her. She told me how it felt, that it brought them close together—"

"*What the fuck did I say?*" He turned back to me, his stare livid. "I warned you what would happen if you brought this up again—"

"Well, I'm calling your bluff—"

"*I will never feed from you.*" He got in my face, moving across the room in just a couple quick steps. He backed me up into the wall, right against the window, his hand on my throat like I was his enemy. "Do you understand? Beg. Plead. Do your worst. I will never change my damn mind." He didn't yell, but his tone was like claws scratching the side of my cheek. He forced my face away, his lips right against my cheek. "*Ever.*" He released me and stormed off, stepping into the bathroom and slamming the door shut. The lock clicked to make sure I wouldn't follow him.

NINE
AURELIAS

"I can't feel emotions, and I can still tell you're pissed off." Kingsnake sat in the armchair across from me. The chambers I shared with Harlow were one large room, with a sitting area at the end of the bed, but Kingsnake had an entire separate sitting room. He stared at me, a glass of scotch in his hand, Fang draped over the wooden beams of the four-poster bed, his eyes closed like he was asleep but he hung on every word we spoke.

"She asked me again."

"Asked you what?"

"To feed from her." Larisa was in the next room taking a shower, not privy to this conversation. I trusted her to keep my secrets, but I knew she liked Harlow...and so did Fang. "She has no idea what she's asking me."

"Then you should explain it to her."

I gave him a look so cold I felt the frost.

"She would stop asking. All I'm saying..."

I would never tell her. I would never tell anyone that story as long as I lived. "No."

"What if I told her—"

"*Fuck you, Kingsnake.*"

He raised both hands in surrender and slowly lowered them. "I apologize."

I stared at the bottle between us, ready to take it and drink straight from the top. "I guess your wife decided to tell her how it felt to be bitten by you…that it deepened your connection and led you to falling in love."

"Did you want Larisa to lie?"

"I wanted her to keep her mouth shut."

Kingsnake's anger immediately prickled. "Talk to me how you want—but not my wife. This warning is the only one you'll receive."

I didn't apologize, but I did feel somewhat bad for insulting the only person in the family I actually liked.

"Aurelias." My brother turned serious. "You need to tell Harlow the truth. Because if she finds out some other way…" He shook his head. "The damage could be irreparable."

"I can't protect her on animal blood. I can't protect her family and her kingdom on a poor substitute. I do it *for* her."

"Then you need to tell her that."

I inhaled a slow breath and let it seep out. "I know how she'll react."

"Then you *definitely* need to tell her."

I shook my head. "I can't."

"Aurelias—"

"Because she'll beg me to feed from her instead, and the only way I'll be able to deny her is by telling her the truth, and I'm not going to do that." I looked elsewhere. "I can't...I won't."

Kingsnake was quiet for a long time. "Then let's hope she never finds out."

"I know none of you would betray me."

"But she's a smart girl, Aurelias. She'll figure it out eventually."

"And hopefully that happens when the war is over...and it'll make it easier for her to watch me leave."

Too angry to look at her, I stayed out of the castle and avoided her. I'd been gone for days, almost died on that journey, and all I'd wanted was to come back to her in our warm bed… And now I didn't want her at all.

It was the kind of anger that had no respite. It burned inside me long and hard, a fire that had unlimited kindling, the kind with so much smoke, it polluted the air and burned the lungs. General Macabre came up to me at my post near the mountains, where the men were working with the dragons to organize the boulders. "King Rolfe requests your presence in the great hall."

I wanted to deny his request, because Harlow would probably be there, but our personal problems weren't his problems. In fact, he'd rather not know a damn thing about it. Without a word, I climbed onto the horse and rode back to HeartHolme and through the open gate. The city was being prepared for the exodus of the Kingdoms, living quarters rearranged to accommodate as many people as possible and protect them from the cold.

I rode up to the castle then dismounted before I entered the double doors and strode up the stairs. When I entered the great hall, it was just Huntley and his brother waiting for me. The gauze that padded his shoulder was visible under his clothing. Without his remarkable ability to heal, he probably would have bled out and died.

There was a bottle and three glasses on the table. He pushed one of the glasses toward me, an invitation.

I sat down.

Huntley uncapped the bottle and filled all our glasses.

I drank the whole thing in one go.

He eyed me but didn't comment.

Ian rested his fingertips on his glass, like he'd already had enough for the day.

Sunlight was slowly leaving the horizon, changing the sky from an ugly gray to hues of pink and purple.

I grabbed the bottle and refilled the glass.

Huntley gave a quiet sigh like he was exhausted, his fingers rubbing over the scruff of his jawline. "Rancor and the Teeth are making their return through the tunnel back to our lands. But in the meantime, I think our provocation with Vine will undoubtedly incite his rage. I think we can expect a siege."

Ian stared at the table. "I hope it doesn't happen before Atticus and the Kingdoms arrive…"

"So do I." Huntley sat back and took a drink. "We need to take out that crystal."

Despite our being at war with the Ethereal for over a century, this felt infinitely more complicated.

Huntley turned to me. "He got angry when he realized you were a vampire."

My eyes met his.

"That means he doesn't like you…or he fears you."

"Probably both," I said coldly.

Huntley continued his stare. "He said he's met your kind before. Who's he referring to?"

"I'm certain he's never been to my lands, so he must be referring to other vampires in some other part of this big world."

"Are all vampires like you?" he asked. "Sired by snake venom?"

"I have no idea." This was the only continent I'd ever traveled to. Everything else in the world was a mystery. "The vampires he met could be much more powerful than I am. But it's best if he doesn't know that."

"Or you're more powerful," Ian said.

"Perhaps," I said. "The Originals are quicker and stronger than our counterparts."

Ian stared at me, fingers still on the glass. "You can talk to snakes?"

"Telepathically," I answered.

"How?" he pressed.

I shook my head. "It has something to do with the venom. I'm as much human as I am serpent. That's why my brothers have slitted pupils."

"We should have asked Beast if there are others like her," Huntley said. "Enormous snakes that live underground. Because that could be the army we need to destroy their crystals...and them."

I nodded in agreement. "She said she had hatchlings."

"That means she had a mate," Ian said. "And maybe those hatchlings are smaller than her, but still enormous to us and the demons."

"Maybe," Huntley said in agreement. "I think a coordinated attack with Beast and others like her and the vampires would be our best chance to destroy that crystal. I don't know anything about the Three Demons, but perhaps a vampire would be enough to challenge them." He looked at me, putting me on the spot without words.

"I can ask my brothers to accompany me to the crystal and destroy it with our detonators. But if we have any hope of getting out of there, we're going to need backup." I wasn't sure whether my father was coming. It would have been a tremendous help if he were already present, because I could take other Original vampires with me to get the job done.

"Detonators?" Ian asked in confusion.

"It's an explosive," I said. "My brothers make them."

He continued to stare in confusion.

"I don't understand it either," Huntley said. "They'll have to show us."

"I think it'll be the only thing strong enough to destroy that crystal," I said. "Especially since we won't have the time to chip away at it with pickaxes and hammers."

"We need to do this as soon as possible," Ian said. "Because you're right, they're probably preparing for war as we speak."

"Then let me speak to my brothers," I said. "And see if we can figure out a way to create them in your lands."

"You're back." Kingsnake was shirtless when he opened his bedroom door, the fire burning in the hearth in the background.

"We need to speak."

My brother looked at me with annoyance before he gave a sigh. "We didn't talk enough earlier today?"

"I can give you five minutes to fuck your wife if that's what you want," I snapped. "I know that's all the time you need."

He gave me a cold stare before he shut the door in my face.

I cocked a smile before I stepped away, and a moment later, he emerged in his uniform without the armor. We moved to the main table, and Cobra joined us a moment later. It was late, and I still hadn't returned to our bedchambers. I wasn't sure if I'd be sleeping there tonight or crashing on a couch.

"What is it?" Cobra asked. "I'm a newlywed, you know…" He waggled his eyebrows.

Kingsnake helped himself to the bar against the wall, pouring three glasses of booze before he distributed them. "You aren't the only one, brother."

"Well, I need more than five minutes." Cobra smirked, having clearly heard our previous altercation.

Kingsnake set down his glass with a distinct thud, like he wanted to shatter it into pieces before he stabbed us with the shards. "Should I get my wife out here to prove how inaccurate that is?"

"Oooh." Cobra waggled his eyebrows again. "I'd love to watch that."

Kingsnake glared at Cobra across the table. "So she can *tell* you it's inaccurate."

"I prefer the first option," Cobra said.

"*It was never an option*," Kingsnake snapped.

"Okay." If I didn't intervene, this would go on all night. "We can't bicker like kids right now. We have matters to discuss."

"Such as?" Cobra turned to me.

"We need to make detonators to destroy the crystal," I said. "Either one of you know how to do that?"

"That's more of Viper's thing," Cobra said. "All he thinks about is war because he's not getting laid."

"I know the components," Kingsnake said. "I can figure it out. But the problem is, does this land have what we need?"

"What do you need?" I asked.

"Charcoal, saltpeter, and sulfur," Kingsnake said. "And I'll need a lot of it, based on your description of the crystal."

"If we have it back at home, I'm sure we have it here," I said. "I'll ask Huntley to dispatch some of his soldiers to find whatever quantity we need."

Cobra placed his feet on the table, crossing his ankles, getting comfortable. "Excellent."

"*Cobra*," I warned. "We aren't at home."

He rolled his eyes before he took his boots off the table.

I felt terrible for asking my brothers for anything when they'd already sacrificed so much, but I didn't know who else to ask. "Vine seemed to lose his temper when he realized I was a vampire and not one of the Teeth. That means he must regard our kind as an enemy, meaning—"

"We're a threat to them," Cobra said. "Good. He should feel threatened."

I continued. "Since Father isn't here...and I'm not sure if he's coming at all, I need company when I go back down there."

Kingsnake stared at me. "You don't need to ask us."

"We assumed we were coming," Cobra said.

"You think we'd let you risk your neck with nothing but humans to watch your back?" Kingsnake asked incredulously.

"I know you're hard for King Rolfe, but he's still an unremarkable human—"

"*Cobra.*"

"Just saying..." He grinned.

"We're with you on this," Kingsnake said. "Always."

My eyes shifted away, and I was unsure what to say. "This isn't your responsibility. I'm the one who decided to help these people, and it feels wrong to ask you guys to risk your lives...especially when we haven't been close these last few years."

Cobra dropped his smirk and turned serious. "It doesn't matter if we haven't been close. We're brothers."

"*Brothers,*" Kingsnake repeated. "And you aren't helping these people. You're protecting the woman you love. And if you love her, then we love her."

A wave of shame rushed over me. "I wasn't very accepting of Larisa..." Not at all. Not remotely. I called her a bitch. It was only when she saved my life that I gave her a chance. "And we all know I don't care for Clara."

Neither of them said anything for a while.

The silence made me feel worse.

"But you accept her now," Kingsnake said. "You love her now."

"And I understand you're intimidated by a strong, confident, sexy woman," Cobra said with a smirk. "My baby was a queen, for fuck's sake. It'll take some time for you to rise to her level, you know what I mean?"

I knew Cobra was just giving me a way out, even when I didn't deserve it. "Nonetheless, it feels wrong to ask you to do this. But I can't do it alone."

"You didn't ask," Kingsnake said. "We volunteered."

"What about Harlow?" Cobra asked. "If the three of us are gone, who will protect her?"

I couldn't be everywhere at once. And I couldn't return to the crystal without other vampires to flank me. "Larisa, Clara, and Fang will look after her."

"Fang might want to come with us," Kingsnake said. "Ever since I told him about Beast, he's been fascinated."

Cobra grinned. "The little guy is always looking for action."

"Well, I don't think action is possible with Beast," I said. "The scale alone would make it impossible."

"I think he wants to see for himself, nonetheless," Kingsnake said. "He's always liked a strong woman..."

I felt her long before she stepped into the room. Her anger was like a hungry fire, growing bigger with every log that was added. I sat at the large table with my back to her, my glass of scotch in front of me.

She drew closer, her bare feet changing in sound once they hit the rug. "You would rather drink alone all night than come to me?"

My eyes remained fixed on the glass, the amber contents nearly gone. "I'm still angry."

"So am I," she snapped. "But no amount of anger would ever make me want to be apart from you." Her footsteps headed in the opposite direction. The door closed behind her, and then the castle was silent.

I finished off the rest of the glass before I followed her into our chambers. When I stepped inside, she stood on her side of the bed, dropping the white nightgown and revealing the beautiful skin I'd kissed countless times. Her tits were out, nipples high and proud, and her long hair framed her shoulders in the sexiest way.

My anger vanished at the sight of her.

She pulled back the covers and slipped between the sheets before she blew out the candle on her nightstand. The fire continued in the hearth, but it was slowly dying, plunging the room into darkness.

I undressed then got into bed beside her, my hand immediately gliding over her body because I couldn't resist the softness of her flesh. My lips kissed her shoulder and then her neck as my arm circled her soft belly. I pulled her into me, letting her feel my hard dick right between her cheeks. She was the only woman who could sheathe my anger like the scabbard over my sword.

I'd never craved a woman without craving her flesh, without longing for a taste of her blood. But with Harlow, not only did I not want it, I *despised* it. My fangs were never tempted to protrude, and when her pulse vibrated against my mouth, I felt absolutely nothing.

All because I loved her.

From the moment I'd met her, I didn't crave it. And it made me wonder if I'd always loved her, since that first night we were together.

She wouldn't roll over to face me, giving me the cold shoulder despite the invitation to bed.

I continued to kiss her as I tugged her into my body. Then I hooked my arm underneath her thigh and hoisted her leg up, opening her from the side so I could guide my hips where they needed to be and push my head into the wet flesh waiting for me.

My cock twitched when it felt her wet kiss, and I pushed forward to sink farther inside, gripped by her tightness.

Her breathing instantly changed, and all the anger she felt evaporated like water in a hot pan. Her little body took all of me and she reached behind herself to grab my ass, to tug me closer because she liked the way it hurt.

I propped my knee and thrust inside her, taking her in a position I hadn't before, sheathed in the cream that she made for me. My arm slid underneath her neck and turned her head to face me, so our eyes would lock as our wet bodies moved together.

She cupped the side of my face and kissed me, her fingers sliding into the hair at the back of my head. Our bodies suddenly slowed down, grinding together rather than thrusting, savoring the feeling of our touches and kisses.

I spoke against her mouth, one hand on her perfect tit. "I'm sorry…"

She breathed into my mouth, her hips grinding back against me. "I'm sorry too."

TEN
VINE

Our kingdom might be silent now that the intruders were gone, but the echo of their destruction continued to reverberate against the rock and stone. They'd managed to escape and make it to the surface before we could retaliate.

I made the long journey deep underground, crossing all the bridges to arrive where I desired, the blue shine of the crystal visible from leagues away. The gates opened at my arrival, and I stepped into the domain that was forbidden from everyone else.

I crossed the courtyard with trees made of stone, the light from the crystal so bright it hurt to look directly at it. Even when I looked down, it was uncomfortable, because the gold tile reflected the light the same way a mirror reflected sunlight.

When I entered their fortress, I approached the throne room where the three chairs sat. Last time, it had been only Lord Ashe who entertained me, but now all three Demon Lords were present—fully aware of the travesties I had failed to prevent.

My hands clasped behind my back, and I awaited judgment from the beings that gave me their endless stares. There was a quiet hum in the background, the power of the crystal distinguishable in the silence. It was a tenor, deep like the bottomless chasms, the life of the underworld.

Minutes passed, and nothing was said. Prepared for the onslaught of insults and heated disappointment, I waited for punishment to be announced, but the silence continued, as if it were my responsibility to interrogate myself. "The broken bridge is being repaired as we speak. Construction will continue around the clock until it's fixed."

"And the traitorous snake?" It wasn't Lord Ashe who spoke, but Lord Stone, the Demon Lord to the right. His appearance was much different from the others, with rubbery black skin that was shiny like oil. He had no hair at all, his bald head shiny like the rest of his skin. His eyes were too big for his head. His mouth too big for his face.

"She's been punished." It wasn't she who had received the beating, but one of her hatchlings who were imprisoned in the vault. He was beaten until large tears dripped from her eyes. Only then had I stopped. "I warned her what would happen if she chose wrong again."

"She's served us a long time," Lord Stone said. "Strange for her to have a change of heart so suddenly."

"The vampire can speak to snakes." No words were spoken among them, but I saw the connection between their eyes, the way an entire conversation passed within their minds. Beast had been transfixed by him the moment their eyes locked. "How, I do not know."

Lord Opal held his silence as he stared, not once blinking as he regarded me, his look empty as if he didn't know who I was. Each Demon Lord was drastically different from the others, their secrets still buried deep behind their eyes.

Lord Stone narrowed his big eyes on me. "Perhaps all vampires have this ability...or perhaps it's only their kind. In whichever case, the Teeth failed to inform us that the humans have a powerful ally."

"Rancor said this vampire is acting of his own accord."

"*For now*," Lord Stone said coldly. "Until more of his kind reach these shores. We were supposed to conquer these humans and put them to work just the way we did with their relations on this side of the mountains. A vampire army changes that—drastically."

"Are you suggesting we attack now?" I asked.

Lord Stone leaned forward slightly, his large eyes formidable in his strange face. "I suggest we take these humans while they're ripe for the picking. Defeat them. Enslave them. We scour their lands for what we seek, and as a token of our mercy, leave them to live off the barren land rather than execute them all."

"King Rolfe pleaded for his kingdom and insisted they would never surrender." I despised humans, viewed them on the same level as livestock on a farm. But this one had more…substance.

"Put a sword to his wife's throat, and he'll change his tune. Chop his pretty daughter into little pieces, and he'll bend the knee. He will fall like the others before him—and he won't be the last. Prepare the armies to destroy their kingdoms—and put our new prisoners to work."

ELEVEN
HARLOW

I was dead asleep when I felt it.

The earthquake.

It was gentle, so slight that I wasn't entirely sure if it was real or just a vivid nightmare. But when I opened my eyes and looked around, Aurelias was already sitting upright because he'd heard it too.

When I sat up, he turned and our eyes met.

It was a long stare, an entire conversation passing between us without a spoken word. Terror gripped me by the throat and squeezed. My heart suddenly hurt, like a powerful fist had punched me square in the chest. Fear like I'd never known kicked me right in the stomach because I knew what that vibration meant.

Aurelias moved his hand to mine and squeezed it—like he felt my terror. "It'll be okay."

I continued to breathe hard, looking out the window as if I would see an army rushing us in the distance.

"Baby." He commanded my gaze.

I looked at him.

"I would never let anything happen to you."

"I'm not worried about me," I whispered. "I'm worried about my family...my kingdom...and everyone I love."

When we stepped into the great room, it was clear everyone else had felt it too.

My father was dressed in his heaviest armor, sleek and black, with jagged grooves in places to catch his enemies' swords. Uncle Ian was dressed the same way, both of them prepared to fight on the front lines rather than hide behind their armies.

I was scared for Atticus, but I didn't say it.

My mother wore a hard stare, but I knew her well enough to know she was as scared as I was.

Kingsnake and Cobra were there with their wives. Fang was around Kingsnake's shoulders.

A guard ran into the room with a scroll in hand. "King Rolfe, one of the dragons from the north just landed. The rider has a message."

My father snatched the scroll out of his hand and forced it open. His eyes shifted back and forth as he quickly read through it. "It's Atticus. The army of demons has emerged from the land between us. They're near the outpost, and the demons are twenty leagues south."

"They're dead center between us," Uncle Ian said.

My father let the parchment bounce back into its roll before he handed it to my mother, knowing she would want to read it herself. "General Macabre, prepare our men for war."

General Macabre skipped the polite nod and the bow and immediately dashed off to execute his orders.

This was really happening.

Aurelias placed his hand on my shoulder, aware of every surge of terror that gripped me.

My father looked at his brother. "If we don't ride out to meet them, Atticus and the others will be slaughtered."

Uncle Ian gave a slight nod in agreement. "Then we lead our army into battle—side by side."

I wanted to cry. Burst into tears on the spot. But I had to be strong, be strong the way my father taught me to be.

"We'll have the riders carry their boulders to the battlefield," my father said. "They'll have to carry them over a greater distance, but that plan can't change. Fire is useless against these beings, and we can't let the dragons land

and be swarmed and killed." He turned to my mother, and a long stare ensued, in front of everyone. "I will leave an army behind to protect HeartHolme in case we fall. The gate is strong, and the fortress is unbreachable. You can defeat a bigger army with its fortifications. Emerge victorious—and then flee. Sail across the sea far away from here."

My mother listened to all of this with a straight face, but her labored breaths betrayed her...and the shine in her eyes. After a long pause, she forced a nod.

"Give them hell, baby. And don't surrender." My father turned to Aurelias and the other vampires. "Aurelias, protect my family. And the others, protect my kingdom." He turned away without saying goodbye, not to me, not to his own mother, not even to his wife...because it was too hard to say what he didn't want to admit.

He walked out—and I feared that was the last time I would ever see my father.

That was the moment I burst into tears.

Aurelias immediately cocooned me into a hug, covering me with his arms to shield me from the eyes in the room. Avice cried as well, holding on to Lila. "I'm sorry." As if he didn't know what else to say, he repeated it. "I'm sorry."

I pulled away. "Please go with him."

He looked down at me, his face hard.

"Please protect my father."

"I came here to protect you—"

"*Aurelias.* My father speaks like he knows he's going to die...he's never done that before. I know what we're up against because I've seen it with my own eyes. If my father falls, so does the army...and then HeartHolme. I know you're just one man, and one man can't possibly make a difference, but I know *you* can make a difference."

He stared at me, his eyes shifting back and forth between mine.

"She's right." Kingsnake appeared. "They'll take down the king first to demoralize the army and then destroy them in a quick takedown. If we want to protect the army, we must protect the king."

Cobra appeared too, in silent agreement.

Aurelias stared at his brothers before he looked at me again. Then he gave a nod. "If we don't return, Larisa and Clara will take you back to our lands. They'll make sure you and your people are taken care of." He cupped my face and kissed me before I could say anything else.

I'd gotten what I wanted, but now I was even more terrified...terrified I would lose him too.

He pulled away, his eyes heavy with sadness. "I love you, baby."

"I love you too."

TWELVE
HUNTLEY

I didn't tell Ivory I loved her before I left.

I didn't tell her that my soul would be waiting for hers when her time came.

I didn't thank her for giving me children I adored.

Because she knew.

She already knew all of that, and listening to me say it for the last time wouldn't make our parting any less difficult.

Ian didn't say a word while he walked beside me as we left the castle, walked down the stone streets and to the stables where our horses would be waiting for us. The alarm had been sounded, and the soldiers hastened to prepare to ride out to battle, to take on the demons from the other front in the hope our numbers would defeat theirs.

"Huntley."

I turned at the sound of my name, coming face-to-face with the vampire I'd ordered to stay behind. His two brothers were behind him, all wearing different armor with different snakes to represent their kingdoms.

"We're coming with you."

"Your orders are to protect my family—"

"You aren't my king, so I don't take orders from you. But your daughter is my woman—so I obey hers. She asked me to protect you."

I was touched by my daughter's gesture, but also furious at the same time. "Aurelias, I'm riding to my death. All the men who ride with me...they ride to their deaths too. I should have listened to you and not entered their kingdom...because we know that's the reason they're here. This is my fault—and I deserve what's coming."

Aurelias's eyes dropped for a brief instant.

"You've stayed in this land to protect my daughter. Protect her—*not me*."

Aurelias stared, his dark eyes hard. "The battle is not lost, not if the king still stands. Your people look to you for courage and valor. Give that to them, and you may prevail. You told your wife not to surrender, yet that's exactly what you're doing."

"I have not surrendered—"

"But you've accepted defeat, and that's the same thing."

I stared at him, the shame burning my veins.

"You have my sword, Huntley. And you have my brothers' as well."

I didn't know what to say.

"If we fall, Clara and Larisa will take your people back to our lands. I give you my word they'll be well taken care of." His eyes continued to bore into mine. "But we can do this, Huntley. We've got them flanked on both sides with the soldiers of all the Kingdoms, all of whom respect you. I've seen many kings come and go, and not a single one has your strength and integrity. I will gladly fight for you—and I know your men will too. This may not be the battle we anticipated, but perhaps it's the battle we needed."

I looked into those dark eyes, seeing a man I'd deeply misjudged for a long time. "You're a good man, Aurelias."

His eyes lost their hardness.

"If I don't survive, you have my blessing to marry my daughter."

He inhaled a slow, deep breath, emotion visible across his face.

"If that's what she wants..." I didn't want my daughter to be like Aurelias. I wanted to see her again someday, not forsake her soul, not forsake her ability to have children… to be denied the greatest joy she would ever know. But I recognized love easily because I'd been in love for twenty years without respite, and I could spot it in the dead of night. I knew my daughter loved this man, and I knew he loved her more.

Aurelias clearly didn't know what to say to that because all he did was stare.

"Grab your horses. Prepare to ride."

After another long stare, he nodded and left with his brothers.

I watched them walk away before I turned back to the path.

Then I saw her standing there, tears in her eyes, a grown woman in the eyes of everyone but me. What I saw was a little girl with her hair in a braid, wearing a dress she hated but was forced to wear for the luncheon with the stewards. She was afraid, as if she would be punished when I found out she'd taken the cookies from the jar in the middle of the night. But my resolve for discipline had never been strong with her, so we ate the cookies together in front of the fire and never told her mother.

I almost cried at the memory.

Harlow walked up to me, a scared little girl looking to me to make her feel better, to make all of this go away like I always did. She opened her mouth to speak, but nothing came out. She tried again, but her voice cracked with tears. "You—you can't leave without saying goodbye…"

It took all my strength to hold everything back, to restrain my emotion not just in front of her, but my men. They all had to say goodbye to their families. They all had to endure this horrible burden. "I will never say goodbye to you, sweetheart." My arms circled her and brought her to my chest, my chin resting on her head. My eyes closed once my face was no longer visible to her, and that was when I felt the tears burn behind my eyelids. Battling them was like battling the rain clouds...hopeless.

She cried in my chest, holding on to me like I was a stuffed doll even though I was covered with solid armor. "Come back. I need you to come back."

I steadied my breathing. Forced myself to calm. To treasure this moment with my daughter...because it might be the last one I ever had. "From the moment you were born, I knew you were destined for greatness. You had your mother's strength and sass. You had my tolerance for bullshit. And now you're a grown woman, and I'm so proud of you."

She continued to cry.

"You can do this, sweetheart."

"I don't want you to go."

"But I must." When I finally composed my face, I pulled away to look her in the eye. "It's not only my duty to fight for our people, but it is my honor. There are things worth dying for, and this is one of them. If I don't come back—"

"Stop."

"Know that I gave my life for what I believed in. You. Your mother. Our people. And I would do it again even if I knew how it would end. I know you understand this because the blood of kings runs in your veins. I know you're proud of me, even if it's too difficult to say right now."

Tears spilled down her cheeks, her blue eyes crushed by despair.

"Harlow."

She continued to cry.

"Sweetheart." I squeezed both of her arms. "Come on."

She inhaled several breaths quickly, over and over, forcing herself to slow. She closed her eyes and sucked in a breath before she held it. When she opened her eyes again, they were soaking wet, but the soul-crushing sobs had stopped.

I smiled. "Attagirl."

"Father…" She dropped her chin, new rivers flowing down her cheeks.

"These demons may be more powerful than us, but we have more to fight for. They fight for crystals and immortality—but we fight for love." I cupped her cheek. "And you know how damn much I love you. Nothing will stop me from coming back to my girls. Nothing will stop me from walking you down the aisle on your wedding day. Nothing will stop me from holding your firstborn in my arms and watching your smile light up the darkest night. *Nothing.*"

Her hands grabbed on to mine as the cries started up again. "Nothing…"

"*Nothing*," I repeated.

She nodded. "I love you, Father."

"I love you too, sweetheart." I cupped her cheeks and pressed a kiss to her forehead.

She squeezed my wrists before she let me go, before she stepped back so I could walk into the stables and grab my horse.

But then I saw my wife standing there, dressed in her uniform and armor, regal and strong…with pain behind her eyes.

I'd found the strength to console my daughter, but I didn't have the strength to do the same with my wife. Not when she could see right through me. Not when she knew all my fears because I couldn't hide anything from her. Not a single thought. Not a single emotion. She would never ask me to stay behind while our soldiers fought for us, because she knew I would never agree. If my people prospered, I prospered. If they died…I died with them. We shared a stare of despair and longing, but we didn't exchange a word, didn't exchange a goodbye.

I turned away and stepped into the stables to fetch my horse...knowing that might be the last time I ever saw her.

The entire army left on horseback.

Ian and I rode in the lead, the vampires directly behind us. The dragons had started their attack by grabbing the boulders the soldiers had found, and they carried them to the battlefield twenty leagues in the distance.

It was a long ride, the sound of thousands of hooves beating the cold earth, the cacophony the drumbeat of battle. Riders carried torches to illuminate the way because it was still night. Traveling by horse would normally be dangerous, but I feared what would happen if we didn't ride out to meet the battle.

My son would be killed...along with everyone else.

With my brother beside me and all our soldiers at my flank, we rode out...and then felt the ground rumble once a dragon dropped a boulder from the sky. The cries of battle became audible, and the fiery veins within the demons' flesh became visible. The sky had turned to a lighter shade of blue, so sunrise was on the horizon. Once the sky changed, visibility would be better, and perhaps that would help win the war. We couldn't see in the dark, but I suspected the demons could.

The horrors of the battle became visible, the seven-foot demons dominating our soldiers. Before I was close, I saw one stomp on a soldier until his head popped off his neck in the mud. I saw another get a sword through each of his eyes, but instead of killing him, the demon laughed and pushed him aside to fend for himself.

I felt no fear, but my stomach dropped when I thought of Atticus.

I raised my fist and brought the army to a halt. "Circle them until we meet the Kingdoms on the other side. Form a perimeter and attack on both sides. General, to the left. I'll take the right."

General Macabre nodded then took his half of the army with him.

Ian stared at me, his face hard in light of the slaughter, like he refused to feel anything.

I could make a speech to rally the men, but the longer we waited, the more the Kingdoms suffered. "Kill these motherfuckers." I yanked on the reins of my horse and pulled him away, leading the charge in the other direction.

"We stay together," Ian said as he rode at my side. "We live together, or we die together."

When we circled the demons the other way and met the line of Kingdoms, we realized how poorly we were faring in comparison. While the Kingdoms had more men than we did, the demons were just too strong. There were bodies of my kin on the ground, burn marks all over their flesh…charred just like Ivory's neck.

The memory of my wife's scarred neck sent me into a blind fury. She would carry that for the rest of her life—because I hadn't been there to protect her. Now I was here, protecting her, our children, and our kingdom.

We left our horses behind, and I went first. I released a scream so loud, it momentarily paused the fight of those in my vicinity. Demons and humans all turned to regard me, stepping into the battle with my sword and axe in hand. At that moment, General Macabre sounded the horn on the other side, to let our brethren know we hadn't abandoned them to their fate.

One of the demons released the soldier he had by the neck, his flesh so badly burned the bone was visible, and marched toward me, grinning like this provocation was fun rather than a deadly assault. "The king has arrived at the ball," he said with a grin. "Good thing I'm holding your dance card."

I'd never faced these opponents before, only briefly down in their kingdom, but the snake had ended that attack almost as soon as it'd begun. This was my first time in battle, first time facing an enemy taller than me, but I gripped my weapons like it was no different from the battle of the Three Kings.

The demon gave a curtsy, a ridiculous gesture when a soldier screamed before a sword sank deep into his stomach behind him. "Let's dance."

I spun my sword around my wrist and gripped my axe, ready to chop this fucker into pieces like firewood.

He stared at me, and then an instant later, he rushed me. He sprinted to me and brandished his sword, swinging it to swipe my head clean from my shoulders right at the start, but I ducked his blade and slammed my hand down onto his forearm, making him growl and loosen his grip on the sword.

I struck him again before he could recover, making him drop the sword altogether. I had the upper hand in that moment, so I continued the onslaught as if my life depended on it, striking him in the face then slashing my sword across his other arm, which immediately oozed with blood that looked like liquid fire.

He screamed before he came at me with his bare fists, swinging for my face and then kicking me in the chest.

I fell back but quickly rolled, getting out of the way of the sword he nearly struck me with. My axe hit his chest and embedded in his chest piece, stuck deep inside the metal. I rolled away again before he came down on me, and then my sword met his. He gave a menacing stare before he rained down a flurry of blows on me so quickly, it was hard to keep up.

But I met his sword each time and pushed back with my own fury.

He stepped back, eyebrows hooded in annoyance. "The king knows how to play."

"He knows how to kill too." I launched another attack, and then our swords came together. They danced in the light of the torches, the steel clanging together mixing with the sounds of the dying. The cold ground was slippery with mud because the snow had melted under the heat of their fire, and now the ground was uneven. It was a hindrance to both sides, something I hadn't prepared for, but I remained level and focused all my efforts on winning.

We broke apart again as we circled each other. A soldier fell behind him, and a demon stepped on his chest, forcing him face first in the mud where he flailed about as he drowned in the dirt, the demon on top of him laughing hysterically.

But there was nothing I could do.

Then a dagger flew through the air and impaled the demon right in the eye. His foot left the soldier, and he stumbled back as his hands grasped the hilt sticking out of his head. It was enough time for the soldier to crawl away, gasping for air.

Aurelias came with his sword and finished the job on the demon.

My eyes moved back to the demon before me.

He watched me, a snarl on his face. "You're strong for a human. But not strong enough." He launched at me again, and this time, he gave me more strength than before. His sword came at a slightly higher angle than I was used to, so I had to adapt to that quickly. Otherwise, I would lose my head.

His force pushed me back through the mud, my boots sliding and losing their footing, but my sword always met his. I never failed to block his hits, and that seemed to infuriate him more and, therefore, push him harder.

We kept going, and sweat broke out on my face despite the cold temperatures. We were locked in concentration, each of us trying to break the other's defenses, my axe still lodged in his chest.

I faked for the first time, knowing he would trust it because I'd never done it before, and then I took the opening to strike my sword into his neck. The blade struck his bone but didn't slice through. It was lodged the way the axe was in his chest.

He stumbled slightly but didn't fall, blood oozing down his front. Then he gave me a sick grin as he barreled down on me, holding a sword while I was weaponless.

"Huntley!"

I turned to see Aurelias.

He tossed his sword to me.

I caught it by the hilt and met my enemy's blade just in the nick of time. "This. Ends. Now." With a burst of energy, I gave him a flurry of blows he couldn't match, knocked the sword from his hand—and finished the job.

This time, I got the blade through his neck—and my sword came free.

His body dropped into the mud, my axe sticking out of his chest.

I turned to Aurelias and tossed the sword back. "Thanks."

He was already gone, rushing into battle to take on two demons at once.

I pulled out my axe, picked up my sword, and jumped back into the battle.

Without the vantage point of the castle walls, it felt like chaos. There was no way to know how many men we'd lost, how many of their side had fallen, if there was an end in sight to this massacre.

My armor was stained with dried mud, and everyone else was covered in the dirt. Dragons flew overhead and dropped their boulders on the enemies below. Every time that happened, the earth shook beneath our feet. The boulders would roll with the momentum, and in one instance, I almost got demolished, but I was able to maneuver at the last second.

I kept my eyes on Ian, who was a short distance away, covered in mud, blood, and sweat. In armor identical to mine that our sister had built for us, he fought on, the same crazed look in his eyes. The only ones who seemed unfazed by the arduous battle were Aurelias and his brothers. They were dirty like us, but they did not possess the same kind of exhaustion. They were always flanked around me a short distance away, close enough to intervene if I was ambushed by a group of demons.

Every time I moved forward in the battle, I hoped to see my son's face, holding his mighty sword, striking down his enemies before him. But every soldier was another face I didn't recognize—both dead and alive.

A blue dragon flew just overhead. ***I don't see him.***

My heart grew progressively weaker, because even if we were victors in this battle, I feared Atticus would be dead...his body covered in a puddle of mud. No father should ever live long enough to see their child die, and I wasn't sure if I could carry on if that happened. I could look death in the eye and face it, but not if he was there to take one of my children.

A mighty roar issued through the clearing, and then three demons emerged, their eyes moving to mine and locking in place. Once they found their target, they began to run, splashing through the mud and knocking down people in their way.

Keep looking.

I should help retrieve boulders—

Find my son, Storm. It was the first selfish act I'd committed. Storm could save the lives of my people, but I wanted him to find my son instead. I brandished my sword and prepared for the onslaught of demons coming my way, demons determined to rip my head from my shoulders to demoralize my people. That meant our soldiers were a threat to their victory—and that was a good sign.

But one demon was enough of a challenge, so three would be an impossible feat.

Ian joined me, raising his sword to block the incoming steel just in time. I blocked both swords from my assailants with my axe and sword, but I wouldn't be able to do that for long. I dodged a hit by one then blocked the other, moving with a speed I wasn't aware I was capable of. Instead of thinking about every detail of the battle, I cleared my mind and acted on instinct, moving, blocking, striking, taking on two demons at once with ease. But as the minutes passed, my muscles fatigued, and I lost the speed I needed to keep up the fight.

The demon on the right grinned, like he knew I would fail. "The king isn't as mighty as they say." He pushed forward, forcing me back into a puddle that went to my shins and made it hard to move. He had the upper hand because my feet were rigid, and all I could do was twist and turn my body to meet his blows. If I tried to move, I would probably slip. I knew I couldn't hold this. I knew I would be defeated if I didn't leave that pool of mud or defeat one of them.

But then Aurelias emerged, blocking the sword with his black blade and shoving the demon back. He pushed through the mud and forced the demon back onto dry land, using strength and speed I couldn't match as a human.

The other demon dropped his focus for just a second to watch the vampire pass, and that was enough for me to slice my blade into the flesh of his arm and make his insides ooze out. I struck him again, hitting him hard enough to force him back. That was enough time for me to get out of the pool of mud and find firm ground to dig my boots into the earth.

The demon released a war cry then swooped down toward me, slicing his blade through the air as he barreled down on me, trying to push me back into the mud. I faked to my left and dodged his hit, turning the other way so the mud was no longer at my back. He released another scream as he came for me, furious his plan had been foiled. "You pathetic human." His blade moved quicker than before, so fast I struggled to keep up, barely making my blocks in time. Sweat dripped down my temples and burned my eyes, but I didn't have a single moment to wipe away the beads of salt. "I'll burn you the way I burned your pretty wife."

Our swords came together, and then time stopped. I looked at him across our joined steel, and I felt the air leave my lungs. The battle raged around us, but time had stopped for the two of us. Images of my wife's wet eyes came back to me, the destroyed flesh that would leave her beautiful neck scarred for the rest of her life. It was hard to look at her—and it would always be hard to look at her.

Strength that came out of nowhere burst from my arms, and I shoved him back, a demon a foot taller than me that had the density of the earth. Vitriol wanted to spill from my lips, but I needed to save my energy for the fight, because words wouldn't break through attacks and blocks. Only brute force.

He grinned like he'd gotten the reaction he wanted. "Looks like the little pathetic human is upset—"

I grabbed my axe from my back and used both weapons to bear down on him, to swipe and block simultaneously, to make him sweat from the speed of my ferocity. His grin dropped as I continued my assault, having to focus all his energy on my attack.

He had to move his sword faster to block both of my weapons, on the defensive rather than offensive, and he was the one who was driven back into the throes of battle. Humans and demons around us screamed as they perished from bloody assaults. It seemed to just be the two of us, locked in the only battle that really mattered. I swung my axe for his head to cave in his skull, but he cut it down with his sword—and severed it in two.

Now his grin was back worse than before. He pushed me back with his blade, striking at my armor because the power had shifted, and now he was on the offensive. Invigorated by my broken axe, he pushed me back toward the puddle of mud, moving so fast I could barely keep track of where his blade was. "Should I burn your face so you'll match?"

I released a scream as I fought back, wanting the upper hand but unable to attain it. The battle had raged for hours but it felt like days, and my muscles had fatigued fighting opponents bigger and stronger than me. I tried to push back, but my boots slipped into the mud, and then the watery grave covered my chin.

"Or should I drown you in filth?"

I gritted my teeth and continued my fight, my boots losing their grip on the slippery ground. I pictured my death, the demon shoving my face into the water as he laughed, my body convulsing as my lungs inhaled the dirty water. I wasn't afraid to die, but I didn't want Ivory to live with that image of me.

He blocked my hit then kicked me in the chest.

I fell back, splashing in the shallow pool of dirt.

Fuck.

He moved over me, his hand reaching for my neck.

I tried to roll without turning over, tried to kick. My blade got lost in the mud, and I couldn't find it.

"Come here, Your Majesty."

Just when his hand reached for me, he stilled and then stumbled, his grin gone and his eyes empty. He suddenly dropped to his knees, his hand reaching behind as if to grab something. And then he fell face first on top of me.

I moved out of the way through the mud, my face covered in it, and I saw the demon hit the mud and then sink, only the sword protruding from his back visible. I stared at it for several seconds as I breathed before I looked up to see Aurelias.

But it wasn't Aurelias.

It was Atticus.

Horror was written across his face as he looked at me, like a scared little boy who had just had a nightmare. "Father." He rushed to me, splashing through the mud before got to me and grabbed me by the arm.

Wide-eyed and shocked, all I could do was stare. I was aware of my body leaving the puddle but wasn't sure how it happened. I stood on my feet in the mud and looked at him, possessing Ivory's eyes but my face. I gripped his shoulders before I crushed his body into mine to hug him, to squeeze him tight despite the heavy armor that separated us both.

He breathed hard against me, scarred by what he'd just seen.

I cupped the back of his head and felt my lungs gasp for the same air. The battle continued around us, screams piercing the morning light. Sunrise had arrived, and the gruesomeness of the battle became even more visible.

I pulled away to look at him, but words failed me.

They seemed to fail him too.

We stared at each other.

I gave a nod.

He gave a nod too.

"Let's stay together," I said.

He nodded vigorously. "Yes...let's stay together."

THIRTEEN
HUNTLEY

The battle raged on, but I kept my son close to me, never fully paying attention to my opponent because Atticus was more important. But I never needed to help him. He was more than twenty years younger than me, so his youth gave him a surge of strength that my decades of experience couldn't match.

I'd personally trained my son to fight, had him train with General Henry, put him through a ruthless conditioning program every day since he was twelve years old. It had obviously paid off—because he was a monster. Battle was no place for emotion, but I couldn't deny the surge of pride I felt.

Kingsnake emerged through the fray, just as dirty and bloody as the rest of us. "We're winning."

I sliced through the neck of my opponent and watched him go down. My body was spent, pushing even when I had nothing else to give. A battle against men was already hard enough, but the battle against these powerful beings was excruciating. I turned to Kingsnake, my son in the background taking down his opponent.

"They have the strength, but we have the numbers," Kingsnake continued. "But victory isn't guaranteed, so we need to fight like we're on the verge of loss."

I nodded in understanding.

Atticus decapitated his opponent then stepped back, breathing hard because he was exhausted by the fight. Everyone was exhausted.

"Use your dragons," Kingsnake said. "If they land and fight head on—"

"I won't risk them."

"You could save more lives—"

"This is not their war." I wouldn't let the dragons sacrifice their lives for us, not when they'd won us our previous war, not when they had already done so much.

Kingsnake didn't press his argument.

"Spread the word that the battle is ours. The morale will push them on."

Kingsnake turned to do as I commanded—even though he was a king himself.

I moved to Atticus. "Kingsnake reports that we're winning."

Undeniable relief moved across his face. "Thank the gods..."

"We have to push a little longer. Victory will be ours."

He nodded, too tired to say much else.

I grabbed him by the shoulder. "You're a stronger fighter than I was at your age."

His eyes locked on mine, a subtle hint of emotion there.

"I'm so proud of you." I said it now because I feared I wouldn't be able to say it later, that the demons would claim one of us—or both.

His eyes held mine until he couldn't meet their look anymore. "Let's finish this, Father."

I released his shoulder. "Let's finish this."

Once there were more humans than demons, every fight was unfair. Three to five humans attacked each demon, so their numbers diminished with increased speed. By midday, the last demon had been struck down—and the war was over.

I stood there and surveyed the mass slaughter, the piles of bodies, friend and foe, on the melted snow. It was a cloudless day and the sun was bright, the sky already filled with birds waiting to feast. I'd been the victor in battle before, looked at the sea of dead around me, but it had never hurt as much as this did.

So many of my people had died.

The bodies stretched as far as the eye could see. Heads were missing from bodies. Arms stuck out from piles of mud. The stench from the dead was already rising with the heat. I couldn't remember a time when I'd been this tired, when I was this close to the verge of collapse. I wanted to assume my age was the cause, but in my heart, I knew this battle was different from all the others.

There were tears behind my eyes, but I didn't let them fall.

My men had died—but theirs would return.

Aurelias walked up to me, just as tired as I was. He didn't say anything, as if the look on my face was enough to erase whatever message he had.

"So few are left..."

His eyes softened in sadness, and he looked away. "A king should celebrate his victory."

"*You call this a victory?*" I said coldly. "My men are dead forever, but those motherfuckers come back with a couple of scars." The one who'd scarred my wife would be back, and the only good thing about that was I'd have the pleasure of killing him a second time. "Less than half of our

Kingdoms remain." It was still chaos, people searching for those who were still alive to see if they could be healed before they perished. People needed food and water. I hadn't seen the stewards of the Kingdoms...probably because they were all dead.

"We were victorious because your forces surrounded them on all sides. Many lost their lives, but the other outcome would be extinction. I don't mean to sound insensitive—"

"Then don't speak."

Aurelias held my gaze but said nothing more.

I should thank him for his service, but I was too heartbroken to be grateful for any damn thing.

Aurelias turned away and walked to where his brothers stood together.

I looked at the dead all around me again, the beautiful sunshine a direct contradiction to the darkness across the surface.

Storm flew across the sky then landed beside me, his heavy body making a distinct thud when he landed. **Shall I return to HeartHolme to notify the queen?**

I was so demoralized I hadn't even thought about my wife, whose heart raced, waiting for news of my death or my survival. *Yes.*

Storm remained beside me. ***I'm sorry for your losses.***

I inhaled a deep breath. *I know you are, Storm.* He was the only one who understood my pain. Understood my heart because he knew it so well.

He pushed from the ground then flew into the sky. The flap of his wings died a moment later.

Atticus carefully stepped around all the bodies as he came toward me, kicking aside the demons but avoiding our kin. He reached me, his arm resting on the hilt of his sword. His eyes were tired, and his skin was pale. There hadn't been time for food and water, as most of the carts had been upended or destroyed. "General Henry is confirmed dead."

He would have found me already if he were still alive. I gave a nod in understanding.

"General Macabre as well."

I gave another nod. "They were good men."

His eyes dropped to the ground.

"But good men always die."

He looked around at the battlefield, his innocent eyes forever scarred by the sight. I wanted to protect him from this, to shield my children from the horrors of war, but I didn't have that privilege. I had to watch my son absorb all the pain and the horror of what had just happened.

It broke my heart.

My brother walked up to us, and he went to Atticus first, embracing him in a bear hug like he was his own son. He squeezed him hard then pressed a kiss to his temple. My brother loved my children like his own, and I loved Lila like my own as well. He gripped Atticus by the shoulder. "You fought valiantly today."

Atticus nodded, but his eyes were empty.

My brother looked at me next. His eyes were heartbroken just like mine. We'd survived the night and made it to day, but we'd lost so much. We'd lost the people we'd vowed to protect. We'd lost soldiers and civilians. We'd lost women and children. We'd lost...everything. And the demons had lost nothing.

Ian moved into me, and we embraced, a one-armed hug that was solemn and depressing. He pulled away and looked across the sea of dead. "Storm will notify Ivory of our survival?"

I nodded.

"Good."

We stood there together, absorbing the magnitude of our loss in silence. The only thing I was truly grateful for was the fact that my brother and son stood with me in that moment, that the people I loved most were still with me. But that graveyard was full of brothers and sons...of entire families.

"We should ride back," Ian said. "The demons will return. We need a plan."

"There are more of them?" Atticus asked, snapping out of his reverie.

Ian and I both turned to him, and we realized he didn't know the truth.

I didn't have the heart to tell him.

Ian did the dirty work for me. Told him about the crystal and its ability to reincarnate the demons. We'd killed them, but they would be back.

Atticus said nothing for a while. "Oh fuck." Now his shoulders dropped in hopelessness.

"We need to destroy the crystal or flee." Ian looked at me again. "Those are the two options. Or maybe we should choose both options. Send away our people and leave behind a group to destroy the crystal. If they fail, at least the others will survive."

I didn't have the heart to plan our next move. It was too broken. "Return to HeartHolme with Atticus. I need to stay here."

"Why?" Ian asked.

"Because my people need me right now." They needed me to mourn with them. To carry the dead to the pyres. To help those in need. War was more than the battle—it was the aftermath, and I wouldn't desert them to rush back to my castle to plan the next move. "I'll lead our people to HeartHolme once they're ready."

Atticus stared at me for a moment before he walked into me and embraced me.

I held him, my palm against the back of his head, mourning in silence.

We stood that way for a long time before he pulled away and wordlessly walked away. My brother joined him.

Aurelias returned to me. "Shall I return to HeartHolme?"

"Yes. I'll remain here with my people."

"My brothers have agreed to accompany me to the crystal to destroy it."

My eyes were on the muddy graves when he spoke, so I redirected my gaze to him. "We just need to gather the supplies for the detonators, then we'll go."

"Gather what you need in my absence. When I return, we'll forge our plan."

He was quiet for several seconds. "With all due respect, we may not have that time. The demons could be back in just a few days, and we simply don't have the numbers to defeat them a second time—"

"I'm aware, Aurelias."

"If we destroy the crystal before they leave, they may not attack us again since their deaths will be permanent."

"I need to be here with my people—"

"Then my brothers and I will gather what we need and depart, even if you haven't returned."

My eyes narrowed.

"I respect your decision, but now you need to respect mine."

I wanted to lash out and order him to listen, but then I remembered that he'd had my back in that battle, that he'd risked his life for me and my family, that he only wanted to help. "You'll need more than the three of you to be successful. Whatever lies in wait there will be bigger than the three of you."

"I know," he said. "We'll have to take more men."

"You'll need men like me and Ian."

He regarded me in silence. "I'd rather Harlow lose one of us—not both."

"That crystal isn't your burden, Aurelias. It feels wrong to allow you to risk your lives."

"I didn't ask my brothers. They volunteered. And if these demons aren't defeated, they'll travel to other lands and destroy those too. And who's to say the next one won't be ours? This mission isn't completely altruistic."

"I think it is, but you're trying to mask it in selfishness."

He stared.

I stared back. "I'll return when I can."

"I admire your dedication to your people. My brothers are the same way."

I let the compliment hover in the air between us.

He turned away and prepared to walk off.

I didn't want to say it because it made me uncomfortable, but I forced it out. "And I admire your dedication to my daughter."

FOURTEEN
HARLOW

We were all on edge.

We didn't sleep or eat. We didn't pass the time with conversation. All we did was sit in silence and wait. There was no point in us being in the same room together because we didn't speak to or even look at one another.

My grandmother spent her time looking out the window and to the city of HeartHolme beyond. Mother chose to pace, her arms crossed over her chest, dressed for battle with her sword on her hip.

The air was so heavy, I could barely breathe.

I'd asked Aurelias to protect my father, but now I feared I would lose them both.

My mother suddenly halted in mid-pace, her hand moving to her chest like she might collapse.

"Mother?" I tried to get out of my seat so quickly that I knocked over the chair and tumbled to the floor. I crawled forward and got to my feet, almost tripping again in the process. When I reached her, I grabbed her by the arm.

Her eyes were closed, but tears streaked down her cheeks like rain from a storm.

"Mother…?" I was scared, more scared than I'd ever been.

She opened her eyes and gasped for breath. "Father is okay," she said as more tears fell. "He's okay…"

Grandmother and Aunt Avice came over to us in a rush. "What about Ian?" Grandmother asked.

She nodded. "Storm said he only has a few scratches and a gash on his arm."

Avice clutched her chest and nearly dropped.

"Atticus is okay too," she added.

All of that was good news, but there was still someone left. "Aurelias? His brothers?"

Mother went quiet, like she was speaking to Storm. "He said he's not sure. He's not familiar with them."

I had so much to be grateful for, but I felt like I'd been delivered horrible news. I turned to look at Larisa, Clara, and Fang as they stood near one side of the table. Their eyes were heavy like mine. "Can you ask Storm to go back? We need to know."

"They'll be on their way back by now," Grandmother said. "Everyone is in need of sustenance and rest. If they are alive, they'll be here soon."

My heart had plummeted into my stomach, because that could take at least a day.

"I'm sure they're okay, Harlow," Mother said. "Of all the soldiers on that battlefield, they're the strongest."

I wouldn't be able to live with myself if Aurelias had died because I'd asked him to protect my father. His death would be my fault, and it would eat me alive from the inside out.

"We've emerged victorious, and our loved ones are returning to us," Mother said. "We have much to be grateful for."

"How many men did we lose?" Grandmother asked.

Mother hesitated, communicating with Storm in silence. She closed her eyes as she told us. "Over half."

"Oh no..." I inhaled a slow breath, the loss like a whip across the back.

It was silent, the news devastating.

We'd won the war, but we'd lost our people. Even if the demons were truly vanquished and peacetime had arrived, it would take generations to rebuild our population, generations for families to heal.

I knew my father's heart, and I knew he hurt more than anyone else. He hurt as much as the mother who'd lost her son. The father who'd lost his daughter. The brother who'd lost his twin. He hurt as they all did, just as he would have if he'd lost us.

I knew he was broken. Completely and utterly.

The next day, we heard the horn to sound their arrival. The gates opened to allow the survivors inside Heart-Holme. Riders rode in, all of the soldiers weary on their steeds, their armor dented and covered with mud.

I witnessed the aftermath of war firsthand—and it felt nothing like a victory. Every soldier wore a haze in their eyes, like all they could see were the horrors they'd witnessed. Some were injured, their arms in slings. Some had faces so bloody they could barely see.

I pitied them, but what I cared most about was one face in particular. I stared at the soldiers as they entered the gate and waited for that face to come through. I stood with Larisa, who had Fang around her shoulders, and Clara beside me.

Larisa spoke. "Fang says Kingsnake approaches with both Cobra and Aurelias. They're at the back of the line."

I closed my eyes and felt the painful ache of relief. It'd been the longest day of my life waiting for that news.

More soldiers filed in, and finally, Aurelias and his brothers entered last, just as dirty and banged-up as everyone else.

The relief I felt at the sight of him…was indescribable. I wanted to swallow his body with mine and be connected forever. I wanted to feel him in my arms and never let go. The urge to bring us close together was irresistible.

His eyes locked on mine, and I swore I could feel exactly what he felt.

He dismounted the horse and handed it off to the stable hand before he walked to me.

Fang had already left Larisa's shoulders and slithered rapidly across the ground to snake up Kingsnake's body and wrap around his shoulders, squeezing his neck to hug him.

I rushed into Aurelias and collided with his armor. It was covered in dirt and it transferred to my clothes, but I didn't care. I rose on my tiptoes and kissed him hard on the mouth, not caring that my mother and grandmother were there to witness the inappropriate display of affection.

Aurelias didn't seem to care either, because he cupped my face and kissed me just as hard, his arm circling my waist to bring me in as close as possible. The sound of the soldiers coming home was quiet now that we were locked together, as if we were all alone.

Aurelias was the first one to pull away, his hand still on my cheek.

I stared into his eyes and treasured the sight of his handsome face, the brightness in his dark eyes, the drops of mud on his cheek. "Thank you for protecting him."

"He's a strong fighter. Held his own well." His hand dropped from my cheek.

"Where is he?" I pulled away to look, seeing my mother staring at the open gates, waiting for him to emerge.

Then Uncle Ian and Atticus rode in, war-torn and disheveled, but there was no sign of my father.

"He decided to stay behind and honor the fallen and comfort the families who'd lost loved ones," Aurelias said. "He'll return with them in a few days."

My mother rushed to Atticus and embraced him, squeezing him like he was still a boy.

Uncle Ian moved to Aunt Avice and Lila, hugging them both simultaneously.

I missed my father and was disappointed he hadn't come home, but I was unsurprised by his decision. "I'll see him soon, then." I left Aurelias's embrace and walked over to my brother.

He pulled away from Mother and looked at me, his boyish grin coming through. "Disappointed?"

His question nearly made me sob on the spot. "Atticus..." I moved into his chest and hugged him, gripping him hard, so thankful that my little brother had come home in one piece. "I'm so glad you're okay."

He pulled away. "We almost weren't. We weren't prepared for them to come out of the ground like that."

I couldn't even imagine.

"Thankfully, we had our soldiers in front so we had a line of defense for the civilians...not that it lasted long. We lost a lot of people. A lot."

"I heard."

"Father is... There are no words."

"I know."

He dropped his chin in solemnity. "Uncle Ian told me these things are like cockroaches, come back even after you've cut off their head. When I thought it was over, I could accept the sacrifice of so many good people, but knowing it's not over... It's fucked."

"I know."

"We won't survive another siege."

"Father will figure it out. He always does."

Atticus looked past me, and he seemed to see Aurelias because he looked at me again and said, "Uncle Ian tells me you're in bed with a vampire."

"Uncle Ian would never say anything like that."

"Fine. He mentioned you're in love with one."

"I am." I said it proudly. He'd joined my father in battle to protect him. Accompanied him to the east and kept him alive. He'd sacrificed as much as any one of our soldiers, all because he loved me. "And he's in love with me."

"You know that's weird, right?"

I grinned.

"You could literally have any guy you want, and you go for one with fangs?"

"His fangs aren't exposed, Atticus."

"Whatever. He has 'em."

"If Father is okay with it, then you should be too."

"It's not like my opinion matters to you anyway," he said. "And there's a difference between being okay with something and tolerating it. Father tolerates it."

"You just got back, and you want to argue?"

"Just wanted to say my piece," he said. "Now I'm going to get something to eat because I'm fucking starving."

"How about you shower first?" I suggested. "You smell…" Like a sweaty horse. Like death. Like blood and guts. "*Bad.*"

"Good idea," he said. "I want to take this shit off anyway." He stepped aside and walked away.

Aurelias came back to my side. "I need a shower too." He grabbed the front of my shirt, which was caked in the mud from his armor. "Care to join me?"

"I'd love to."

I joined him in the shower, and the warm drops of water immediately soaked my skin and dripped down. My fingers touched his hard body, feeling muscle everywhere they moved. His fair skin didn't have a bruise or a scratch, so his hard armor had protected him well...or his sword had.

We didn't speak as we washed each other, as we let the soap wash away all the evidence of battle. The mud was out of his hair and off his cheeks. His dark eyes maintained their intensity, like he was still on the battlefield in his mind.

I wanted to enjoy him the way I did every night, but I wasn't the one who'd just watched so many people die. Even though he didn't show it, I knew he carried a burden of horror. It wasn't his people who'd fallen, but they were still the people he fought for. "Are you okay?"

His eyes hardened on mine. "I've fought many battles."

"That wasn't what I asked."

His eyes dropped. "They're all the same. The battles. The dead. The stench."

"You don't have to put on a front with me."

His eyes remained down for a moment before he looked up again. "It's not often that the loser of the battle is actually the winner."

I swallowed.

"They know we lost over half our soldiers. They know they'll destroy us when they return. Your people paid a heavy price for an empty victory."

Now my eyes were down.

"Our only hope is the destruction of that crystal. Perhaps if we destroy it before they attack, they'll think twice about pursuing another war."

"Why?" I asked.

"Because their lives will be on the line as much as ours," he said. "The humans have an afterlife—and I suspect they don't. They fight viciously because they have nothing to lose, but once they do have something to lose, they'll be far more cautious. If there is another battle, it'll be far different from the first."

"We must destroy that crystal."

"My brothers and I need to gather a few things before we leave."

"You're going?" I asked quietly.

He nodded. "We're the only ones strong enough to pursue it."

Just when I'd thought the worst was over, I realized the worst had yet to come.

His fingers cupped my cheek, and his eyes softened, feeling the terror that surged in my heart. "I'm here now."

"But I just got you back..."

"And you'll get me back again, baby." His hand guided my head back so he could kiss me, part my lips with his to slip his tongue into my mouth. The water cascaded around us as our kisses deepened, as we both forgot the conversation we'd just had. His hand gripped my ass, and he tugged me into him, his hard length right against my stomach.

My back hit the wall, and he turned the faucet, cutting off the water that drenched our skin. He guided me out of the shower and to the bed, laying me down right on top before he moved over me. Our bodies wet and soaking the sheets, we came together, and he entered me, sinking inside nice and slow.

My hands scratched his back as I moaned in his face, reacquainted with his body as well as his soul...or what I felt was a soul.

He rocked into me slowly, his eyes on mine, kissing me between his moans, whispering his love to me and only for me.

I woke up to the shift of his body.

My eyes opened to see him leave the bed and grab his clothes from one of the drawers. He was quiet, so quiet it wouldn't have woken me up, but the second his warmth was gone, I felt cold. I looked outside, seeing that it was pitch dark, sometime in the middle of the night.

He pulled his shirt over his head then moved for his trousers.

"What are you doing?" I asked in a raspy voice.

He stilled before he continued to dress. "Go back to sleep, baby."

"I can't sleep without you."

"I'll be back shortly." He pulled on each one of his boots before he stood up again.

"What are you doing?" I repeated.

He straightened then looked at me, and his annoyance was undeniable. "I need to speak to Kingsnake."

"*Now?*" I asked incredulously. "It's the middle of the night."

"And the night isn't our preferred time for sleep," he said. "Go back to bed, baby." He leaned over the bed and came to me, pressing a kiss to my temple. "I'll be back before you wake up." He walked out and quietly shut the door behind him.

I lay there and listened until his footsteps were no longer audible. I was disappointed he'd left, but there was something else that bothered me. Something just didn't feel right. He'd slipped out in the middle of the night before, but he never told me where he was going. I left the sheets and walked to one of the windows, which had a partial view of the main doors that led to the castle.

I stood there and waited, my heart racing more and more, afraid I would see him walk through those doors. Minutes passed and nothing happened, so I assumed he'd gone down the hallway to Kingsnake's bedroom so they could drink and talk about all the horrible things they'd seen in battle.

But then I saw him walk out...and leave the castle.

FIFTEEN
AURELIAS

I walked through the kingdom, torches aglow along the streets and the alleyways. It should be a quiet night, but once the soldiers had returned to HeartHolme after the battle, everyone was stirred up. There were people on the street at this time of night when there normally wouldn't be. Citizens retrieving food and medicine.

It was a long walk to her house in the village, a small but handsome cottage just a few streets from the pub I'd visited when I'd first come here. That was how I'd met her—Annabella. She was interested in me, but I'd told her I was unavailable.

But I'd also told her I was hungry.

Long story short, we developed an arrangement. She allowed me to feed, and I compensated her with vampire silver, something that would fetch her a fortune once the war was over. She was also compensated in other ways, but that was her prerogative.

I arrived at her door and knocked.

It was the middle of the night, so I didn't expect her to be awake, but she opened the door almost immediately, as if expecting me.

She looked me over, and the relief that swept through her was like a heavy wind. "You're alright."

I gave a slight nod. "You're up late."

"I thought you might come by…if you survived."

"Can I come in?"

"Of course."

As I stepped inside, she moved into my body to hug me.

We'd never done this sort of thing before, so it caught me off guard. I allowed it but didn't reciprocate. I gently pried her hands off me then shut the door to her cottage. The famine was so acute that I couldn't feel my hands or my fingers. That battle had been intense, and since I had more strength than several men put together, I'd had to work much harder to compensate for their weakness. All the blood I'd ingested before I left was spent on that battle. I'd continued on nothing, and the only reason I could be with Harlow afterward was because my need for her was the only thing stronger than my hunger. But once she went to sleep, my needs came back to the surface.

Kingsnake and the others had fed the instant they returned, but I didn't have that opportunity.

"I'm so glad you're alright."

I turned around to look at her. She was a young brunette who had two dots scarred along her neck, scars from my fangs that had pierced her flesh over and over. I could feel her need burn inside her, along with all the other emotions I didn't reciprocate. All I wanted to do was feed, grab her lithe body and tear her flesh with my fangs, but I had to be polite about it. "As am I."

Her eyes looked into mine, and the sensations inside her chest deepened. "Why don't you feed from Princess Harlow?"

The question provoked me, made me angry, but I was so hungry, I didn't give in to it. "Because I don't want to."

"She won't let you?"

"*No,*" I said harshly. "I don't want to."

"How can you be with a woman you don't want to feed on—"

"I'm very hungry, Annabella. I served your kingdom in a war that wasn't mine to fight. I prevailed and will continue to fight for your people so the demons don't enslave or drive you to extinction. I'm here to feed. Can we get on with it, or should I leave?" If she really asked me to leave, I wouldn't know what to do. The hunger was driving me insane. I'd never been so weak. When Harlow and I had left the shower, I normally would have carried her, but I was so weak I had been afraid I would drop her along the way.

Offense moved through Annabella, but she tried to hide it from her face. "Sure." She flipped her hair back over her shoulder then tugged her top down, revealing her bare shoulder and the top of one of her breasts.

The sight of her pale flesh made my fangs pop out quicker than daisies in spring.

I moved into her, my arm circling her lower back to support her against me, while my hand slid deep into her hair, pushing it back to enable my fangs to sink deep into her flesh and then latch on.

Once the blood started to pour into my mouth, I instantly felt invigorated. It was so good, the metallic taste, the strength it provided me. With her tight in my arms, I fed, feeling the last few days of exhaustion slowly evaporate.

She was breathing hard against me, those breaths turning into gentle moans. Her hand fisted my hair, and she tilted her head farther, loving the feeling of my bite. She loved it so much that her fingers moved down the front of her trousers and into her panties. She touched herself, blood draining her body and entering mine, her arousal so profound that it was like the sound of drums in my ears, so loud that I couldn't hear anything else.

I fed as she rubbed herself, as she made herself come while I gripped her hard and bit her harder. Her fingers dug into my scalp as her hips started to buck uncontrollably.

I finally felt satiated, finally felt my hands and fingertips again, and I knew if I didn't stop, I would take more than I should. Her pleasure had passed and my stomach was full, so I slowly withdrew my fangs and saw the two little rivers of blood.

Her eyes were heavy with satisfaction and weakness, and she could barely stand since the life-force had been sucked out of her.

My arms circled her waist, and I escorted her to the couch, helping her lie down, the blood staining the cushions. Just as I pulled the blanket over her, I felt it. It was weak at first, like it was far away. But then it became louder and more prominent, like it was beside me.

It was Harlow.

I could recognize her mind in a crowd. Could feel it even from a distance.

And she was...devastated...broken...angry.

It came out of nowhere, was so sudden that I didn't know how it had crept up on me without my realizing it. My mind immediately went to the window, and I stilled when I saw her face.

With tears down her cheeks and eyes so watery they looked like pools, she stared back at me. She conveyed so much with so little that I didn't need to feel her emotions to know exactly the turmoil that flooded her mind. She was hurt by my betrayal, but also so furious she could kill me if she had a sword.

For the first time in my life, I was rooted to the spot, completely paralyzed. All I could do was stand there and feel the damage I'd caused, feel the heartbreak my betrayal had elicited. She'd witnessed everything through that window, and I had been too hungry and overloaded with Annabella's emotions to feel Harlow's.

Fuck.

I moved for the door to go after her.

She took off, disappearing from the window.

I made it out the door and onto the road, seeing her run as fast as she could, desperate to get away from me.

"Harlow."

She ran like her life depended on it, wearing one of my shirts and her lounge trousers, putting on whatever she could find when she'd decided to follow me. She must have kept her distance so I wouldn't feel her mind.

"Harlow." She was fast, but I was faster, especially now that I had fed. I caught up to her and grabbed her by the arm. "Let me explain—"

Bam! She didn't slap me like she had before. No, this was a punch right to my face. A good punch too, just like her father taught her.

I hadn't anticipated it, so it was a shock to my system, a painful one.

She was so angry, she could barely put words together, seething in blind rage. "*Don't you fucking touch me.*"

"Harlow—"

"I swear to the fucking gods, I will kill you."

"Please, just listen to me—"

"No, you listen to me." She shoved me hard in the chest, exerting more force than I expected her to. "You *lied* to me. You told me you fed on animal blood, but every night that you've slipped out of my bed, you've been down here...*with her.*"

"Harlow—"

She ignored me. "I asked you. No, I *begged* you to feed from me, and you're the one who stormed out in a rage. Stormed out like I was the problem, when you were down here *with her*. Is she better than me? Is she prettier than me—"

"Fuck no."

"But you still prefer her to me."

"It's not that I prefer her—"

"Oh, you clearly do."

"Harlow, I can't feed from you."

"Why?" she demanded. "What possible justification would you have to cheat on me with someone else?"

"Whoa. I didn't *cheat* on you."

"According to Larisa, feeding on someone else is like fucking them."

"That's not how it is—"

"*I watched her come for you.*"

"That was her doing. I didn't touch her—"

"But you made her come. You snuck down to her cottage in the middle of the night, bit her while she played with herself, after you told me you were with your brother. Aurelias, you fucking betrayed me."

"Harlow, I can't feed on you!" I yelled. "You expect me to protect you when I'm weak on animal blood? Protect your father in battle when I've had deer blood for lunch? I can't possibly face these enemies if I'm not at my fullest potential."

"I've offered how many times—"

"And how many times have I told you no?" I snapped.

"*Why?*" Her voice rose, our shouts audible to anyone nearby. "Tell me why, for fuck's sake. What possible justification do you have to do what you did? To lie to me? To feed on someone else instead of me?"

I stared at her, breathing so hard my lungs were about to pop.

"Go on, asshole," she snapped. "Say it."

It all flashed before my eyes, my uncontrollable bite, the blood that got everywhere, the moment I realized she didn't have a pulse but I continued to feed anyway. The unstoppable tears. Her dead, open eyes. The look that would haunt me for the rest of my life, the terror that reared its head any time I had a slight moment of happiness.

When Harlow realized I had nothing to say, the moisture in her eyes reappeared. She clearly hoped I'd have a justification for what had just happened, that I would make it all better with a simple explanation, but I didn't have one.

My voice came out weak, broken. "I just can't..." The self-loathing was insufferable. I hadn't thought I could hate myself more than I already did, but I managed to top it. I was too much of a coward to admit what I'd done, to look her in the face and tell her the horrible thing I was guilty of. And then I hurt her, could feel just how deeply I'd wounded her, and I still couldn't bring myself to do it. "I'm sorry—"

"*You're sorry?*" She spoke with derision, but her voice cracked with tears. "You're sorry." She repeated the words like she didn't understand them or was saying them for the very first time. "Fuck you, Aurelias."

I dropped my gaze, unable to look at her.

She turned away and walked off. "Fuck. You."

When I made it to the castle and her chamber doors, my things were already in a pile outside. The armor that hadn't been cleaned, my uniform that I hadn't given to the maids, and the rest of my belongings. It was all in an untidy mess, like she'd flung everything out unceremoniously. The only thing she seemed to care for was my sword, which had been placed against the wall, the golden serpent crest on the scabbard.

I stared at it all before I lifted my eyes and looked at the door.

I could see her in my mind's eye, curled up in bed with the sheets tight around her...sobbing. Her emotions were the most intense they'd ever been, like her life was at risk, when her only wound was a broken heart.

I couldn't stay with one of my brothers. I couldn't be anywhere near her because I couldn't bear to feel her pain. All I wanted to do was rush in there and kiss her tears away, cocoon her body with mine and chase away her misery, but I couldn't because...I was the cause of her misery.

I had been so uncomfortable with my hunger, but now I preferred starvation to this heartbreak. My eyes dropped down to my belongings again, and I gave a sigh before I gathered them, unable to hear her cries because of the thick door but able to feel them as if they were my own.

"Need a hand?" Kingsnake appeared, his eyes hard in distress. His emotions were swirling clouds of despair, like he'd figured out exactly what had happened just by observation. He grabbed one of my bags and the sword.

I picked up the other things, and we turned away from the door to head down the hallway.

"You're welcome to stay with us," Kingsnake said. "Fang said he'll let you have the couch."

I ignored the offer.

Kingsnake let me lead the way.

We left the castle again and stepped into the night air. It was cold, just like home, the way I liked. If I'd had a beating heart, it would beat slowly, so slowly it nearly stopped altogether. I was empty inside, a step worse than depressed. I was outside the castle walls and far enough away that I couldn't feel Harlow's misery, but the memory haunted me.

We arrived at the cottage Lady Rolfe had offered me, and it was still vacant. I stepped inside the dark and cold dwelling and dropped everything on the couch. Kingsnake threw some logs into the fire and set it ablaze before he lit a few candles in the room, trying to make the place feel like home when home wasn't a place...but a woman I'd betrayed.

There was a cabinet stocked with booze, so I hit that hard.

Kingsnake took a seat in one of the armchairs. "We can talk about it...if you want."

I set the glasses on the table and fell into the armchair across from him. My fist curled under my chin, and I stared at the fire.

"You didn't tell her."

My eyes remained on the flames, flames that reminded me of the fire in Harlow's soul. She was hot and wild, burning everything in her path. She wasn't barren and cold...like I was. "I tried to warn her."

"Warn her of what?"

"That heartbreak can ruin your life. She didn't believe me."

Kingsnake stared at me.

"Told me she wasn't afraid of getting hurt. Well, now she knows it fucking sucks." And I was reminded of how much it fucking sucked. I'd known that I would never fall for another woman after Renee, that no amount of time would heal that wound, that no woman would ever be worth a trip down memory lane. But it had happened anyway.

"She wouldn't be heartbroken if you told her the truth."

I ignored him.

"You can still fix this—"

"No."

"*Aurelias.*" He said my name with such frustration, like he wanted to smack me upside the head with a rock. "It has already happened. It's already done. Telling her won't change what's already in the past. They are just words."

"*Just words?*" My eyes shifted to him, incredulous at that insensitive statement. "Trust me, they are more than just words, Kingsnake. You can't tell a story without reliving it, and I'll never tell that fucking story as long as I live. If that means I lose Harlow—so be it."

"How can you say that—"

"Because we're done anyway," I snapped. "After we destroy the crystal, the demons will move on elsewhere, and then we'll return to our lands and resume our lives. We always had an expiration date, and now that date has moved up. The outcome doesn't change, just the timetable."

Kingsnake dropped his chin, not touching the drink in front of him.

I didn't touch mine either.

"Wouldn't you want to end on good terms rather than bad?"

"It'll make it easier for her." It would be easier for her to let me go when she hated me, when she never wanted to see me again anyway. She would move on with the next guy and fuck me out of her system. The bitterness in her heart would erase me. "A lot easier to get over someone when you hate them."

He gave a slight shake of his head. "If you love her, you should tell her the truth."

"The truth doesn't change what I did."

"It changes the context—*and that changes everything.*"

I shifted my gaze back to the fire.

"Aurelias—"

"You've voiced your opinion. It's done."

He gave a heavy sigh.

"And if you go behind my back and tell her—we're finished."

He gave another shake of his head. "Perhaps it would be easier for you if someone else told her—"

"*No*," I snapped. "This is my business to share with whom I will. Cross that line, and you can never uncross it."

SIXTEEN
HARLOW

I stayed in my room through the night and the next day.

Didn't leave the bed but once.

The sheets smelled like Aurelias, so I asked the maids to change everything so I could smell sterile soap instead. I watched the colors of the sky change as the position of the sun moved. Aurelias never came to speak to me, and I suspected he wouldn't. We could have another argument, but it would be identical to the one we'd already had...as well as the outcome.

I couldn't get the image out of my head, the way he squeezed her to him, his hand deep in her hair. It was more than just a feed, but a sexual encounter, her fingers down her trousers to get off on the pleasure he gave her.

It scarred my eyes...and my heart.

Anytime I thought about it, additional tears came to my eyes.

A knock sounded on the door.

I sat up right away, in the same clothes I'd worn the night before, my hair a mess because I hadn't brushed it. I feared it was him—the last person I wanted to speak to. Unsure what to do, I stayed quiet.

"Harlow?" It was my mother, the concern in her voice breaking through the door and reaching my ears. "Honey, are you alright? You haven't come out for breakfast, lunch, or dinner. I need to tell you something."

I quickly wiped away my tears with my fingertips, even though it would be impossible to hide my heartbreak from my mother. She would see right through it. She probably already suspected it if she was at my door. "Come in."

She opened the door and looked at me, and it only took a few seconds for her eyes to match mine. "Honey..." She came to the bed to hold me, and that gesture made the tears break free. She was dressed in her armor, but she sat on my bed and pulled me to her.

Like a child, I moved into my mother's lap and clung to her. The tears poured down my cheeks.

She didn't interrogate me. She pressed a kiss to my forehead and stroked my hair, letting me release everything I needed for as long as I needed. She rubbed my back and stared down at me, waiting for me to return to a sense of calm.

"Aurelias left with his brothers yesterday to search for supplies for the detonators," she said. "I didn't think much of it at the time."

I sat up, no longer leaning on her for support.

"You don't have to tell me what happened, honey. But I'm here."

I always told my mother everything, so now, I told her the truth, the whole tale.

She continued to stroke my hair and said nothing. Didn't get angry. Didn't cast her judgment.

"I threw him out, never want to speak to him again."

"I'm sorry..."

Now my eyes were dry, so dry they were red and irritated. I expected her to say more, but she kept her opinions to herself.

"Did he explain himself?"

"He said he wouldn't feed from me...but wouldn't tell me why."

"I think it would be disrespectful to your father if he did. I think it would be disrespectful to all of us."

"He would have told me if that were the reason," I said. "And I thought he wasn't allowed to feed on our people."

"Your father granted them permission—but only from volunteers."

I felt blindsided. "He never told me that." Which meant Aurelias had been doing this a long time, even back in Delacroix. He'd probably never fed on animal blood once. There had been other beautiful women he'd spent his nights with.

"I'm sorry."

"He's been lying to me since the beginning…"

She continued to rub my back.

"I'm so stupid."

"You aren't stupid, honey."

"Well, I feel really fucking stupid right now."

"That man has risked his life to protect you multiple times. He's risked his life to protect your father. Even now that the relationship is over, he's still here, trying to find what they need to destroy the crystal. His deception is a direct contradiction to everything he does for you."

That was why I hadn't suspected his betrayal.

"It was perfectly reasonable for you to assume his love was real, that his character was as true as yours. You aren't stupid, Harlow."

I'd grown tired of discussing him, especially now that I wanted to start crying again. My mother made me feel better momentarily, but she couldn't erase a pain as profound as this. "You said you had something to tell me..."

Her fingers glided through my hair. "I'll be joining your father today. I think he could use some support right now."

I nodded in agreement.

"Until the vampires have what we need for the detonators, there's nothing we can do right now. The demons won't be able to attack again for several days. The kingdom will be safe in my absence."

"Yeah..."

"Would you like to come with me?"

And face Father, the man who could see right through me like a blade that pierced me from front to back. No thanks. "I'm okay." I forced a smile and gripped her hand. "I think it'd mean a lot to him if you joined him."

She kissed me on the temple. "I'm sorry you're hurting right now, honey. But it'll get better. I promise you."

My mother left.

If our circumstances had been different, I knew she would have stayed, but after losing half of our people, I knew my heartbreak wasn't the priority.

I finally left my bedroom to enter the great room because I was starving, but of course, I picked the worst possible time because Aurelias and his brothers were already there, sitting at the table sharing a bottle of booze.

Aurelias faced me, so our eyes met instantly. His stare remained, guarded and intense, but I looked away, feeling his heat on my cheeks afterward. I felt awkward turning around and leaving when this was my castle, so I crossed my arms over my chest and stood there.

Kingsnake and Cobra didn't say a word as they left. Cobra grabbed the bottle from the middle of the table and took it for himself, leaving the partially full glasses behind.

Aurelias's arms rested on the table, and he pulled them back toward his body and crossed his arms over his chest. He slouched in the chair, like he didn't care about me or the conversation about to be had.

It was interesting because I was the one who'd been betrayed. "You aren't obligated to stay. We aren't together anymore, so there's no reason for you and your family to further risk your lives for us."

His eyes burned into mine, and slowly, the anger tinted the edges. He got to his feet and came around the table, his full height like a mountain over a valley. "Together or not, it doesn't change anything. I love you." His words were beautiful, but he spoke them with such anger. "I'm not leaving you until I know this is finished. I know you hate me for what I did, but when I told you I loved you, I meant it. I fucking meant it."

"I could tell you meant it when you lied to me and snuck off with that woman." I didn't know what possessed me to say that, to fire up an argument that would go nowhere, but I was hurt that he could say such beautiful things to me but then torch what we had.

His expression remained as hard as ever, and he didn't respond.

"How is this so easy for you?" I'd cried in my room for two days, and he'd left with his brothers to handle business as usual. He didn't look heartbroken or remotely wounded.

"Who said it was?"

"You don't even look sad. You look pissed off—"

"If you could feel my emotions the way I can feel yours, you would know the extent of my despair. And you would know the extent of my self-loathing, because any time I'm in your presence, I have to *feel* just how much I hurt you…and that's unbearable."

I looked away, this conversation somehow making me feel worse. "If you change your mind, you're free to go—"

"I'm not free to go until you're free of those demons."

I continued to avoid his gaze because his hard stare was too much to bear. "Then hopefully this ends soon, so we can both move on with our lives." I expected him to apologize again, to beg for my forgiveness, to fight for me like he couldn't live without me. But he had this calm resignation to his presence, as if he'd already made peace with our separation. That seemed to hurt more than the actual betrayal. I realized then that I loved him more than he'd ever loved me...had since the beginning...and always would.

SEVENTEEN
HUNTLEY

I worked from sunrise to sunset alongside my people, pulling the dead from the shallow graves in the mud and carrying them to their final resting place on pyres. One by one, they were lit—and together we watched them burn. Sobs filled the night, cries of anguish that would fill my dreams for as long as I lived.

We'd burned the demons in Delacroix, but now, we left them to rot in the mud.

I hadn't bathed since before the battle. I ate what everyone else ate, fruit and stale bread, whatever had survived the carts. I was malnourished and tired, but I didn't dare complain. It was a momentary discomfort, while the death of my people was permanent.

I'd just placed a boy no older than twelve on the pyre, a boy who had barely had the chance to reach puberty before he was killed by those monsters. It was hard to look at him, but to avoid his face felt like a dishonor. I grabbed a rag and wiped his face clean, removing the mud so his parents, if they were still alive, would be able to recognize him. It nearly brought me to tears, but I swallowed back the pain in my throat and carried on.

Then a mighty roar pierced the sky.

"Rooaaaaarrrr!"

I looked up to see Storm's brilliant scales and majestic body, a powerful beast that had become more than a companion, but a friend. He landed on the dry ground and folded his wings, and that was when I noticed the rider.

In her uniform and armor, her hair pinned back, sat my wife.

A tightness flushed through my chest at the sight of her. The ache started off dull then intensified into a crescendo. I suppressed as much of the pain as I could, but the sight of her face made the fight impossible to win.

She reached the ground then walked toward me, her cape billowing in the breeze, her sword at her hip. Her stare was hard and focused, and there was no relief at the sight of my well-being. She knew my sorrow because she felt it too.

I turned to her, walking across the dried mud to meet her.

When she was close, her eyes softened at the sight of me.

I knew my face was red from the sun exposure and my hair was filthy with mud. I knew my eyes were empty because I was hungry and tired. I didn't possess the regalness of a king in that moment. Battle had aged my appearance and claimed my strength.

She cupped my face as she looked up at me, her eyes full of the same sorrow that burned in my heart. No words were forthcoming because there was no consolation that would soften this blow.

But just having her there was enough.

My hands gripped her wrists, and I rested my forehead against hers as I closed my eyes. The pain was all-consuming, unbearable. The battle of the three kings had been horrible, but it didn't hurt the same way this one did. We hadn't lost nearly as many people. Our losses were negligible compared to this. Even if we defeated these demons…would there be anything left?

"They will pay."

My eyes opened to look at her.

"They took what matters most—our people. But now we'll take what matters most to them—their immortality. We'll destroy that crystal. Shatter it into shards. And then we'll kill them all."

My tent was modest. Just a cot on the ground with a couple apples and dried nuts. But I didn't care about comfort right now, because the softest bed and the silkiest sheets wouldn't subdue this pain.

Ivory didn't care about the modest accommodations. She'd never been one to complain.

A fire burned outside the tent, casting light through the thin material. To anyone who passed by, our silhouettes would be visible, but privacy wasn't my concern right now. I sat there with my arm propped on my knee, looking through the slightly open flap into the darkness outside. It was cold, but the cold never bothered me.

It didn't seem to bother Ivory either, probably because her depression masked her nerves.

"It'll take another day to pull the fallen out of the mud and commit them to the flames..." We wouldn't leave until everyone had been burned. We would never leave our own behind.

"Aurelias and his brothers have begun harvesting the items needed for the detonators."

I couldn't think of our future plans. I was trapped in the past, trapped in the brutal memories of war. It was easier for Aurelias to bounce back because we weren't his people. He wasn't responsible for any of them...but I was. "Good."

"By the time we return, they may be ready to proceed."

Death was heavy, and it made me apathetic. The battle had been won, but the war still stood in the balance. But I couldn't get myself to care, even though I still had the other half of my people to protect.

"Huntley."

My eyes had been focused on the flap opening, not on her. But I obeyed and gave her my full attention.

"I know this is something you don't want to discuss. In another instance, I would keep it from you. But—"

"What is it?"

She gave a quiet sigh. "Aurelias and Harlow have parted ways."

It took me a second to process that statement because Aurelias was only here because of her. "How is that possible?" It had taken me a while to accept him, but I knew his dedication to her was real. He wouldn't have risked his life so many times if he weren't willing to die for her.

She hesitated before she answered. "Harlow caught him feeding on another woman."

I stared at her blankly. "And?"

"I guess it was a sensual encounter."

I still didn't understand the problem. "He's a vampire. This shouldn't be a surprise to her."

"Well, he lied to her and said he was feeding on animal blood."

"Why would he lie?"

"Because she'd offered herself many times, but he always said no."

Now I was distressed. The idea of his fangs piercing her flesh and taking what didn't belong to him made me deeply uncomfortable.

"And she's hurt that he would feed from someone else."

"I asked him not to." *Ask* was putting it nicely.

"I told her that. It's not a good enough reason to justify his betrayal."

I looked away, caught up in the unpleasant situation I'd tried so hard to avoid. But I hadn't been able to avoid it from the moment Aurelias had arrived. "At least Aurelias is willing to gather the detonators for us to use before he leaves."

"I didn't get that impression."

My eyes shifted back to her.

"I think he intends to see it through, regardless."

"Why?"

"I never voice my opinions to Harlow, so she can make her own decisions without interference. But I don't think Aurelias would have made this many sacrifices for her just to walk away in the end. I understand why she's hurt by his actions, but I think his needing to feed has nothing to do with his love for her."

I gave a slight nod in agreement.

"We know his character. He's noble, honest, committed... He wouldn't leave her unprotected. He wouldn't work this hard for our people just to abandon us at the finish line."

Once the dead had been burned and the rites of passage had been read, the survivors began their journey to HeartHolme on foot and horseback. Ivory and I rode Storm back to HeartHolme, reaching the stone city in just a few hours.

Word of my return had spread fast because Harlow was there to meet me when I landed. She ran to me as fast as she could, her brown hair flying behind her, and she landed against my chest with a hard thud.

"Father." She gripped me tightly, her face in my chest.

I hugged her as my chin rested on her head, remembering our final conversation and how much those words had haunted me after I said them. I held her longer than I normally would, grateful that I had made it back when others hadn't... And then I felt like shit for thinking it. "Sweetheart." I kissed her temple then let her go.

"I'm so glad you're back."

My arm moved around her shoulder, and I walked with her through the gates and to the castle.

"I'm sorry for everything you had to go through."

It was hard to be upset when I was reunited with my daughter, with my firstborn, the little girl who'd made me a father for the first time. Pride flooded through me because I had two exceptional children, all thanks to the woman who'd survived childbirth and gave them to me.

We walked to the castle and up the stairs to the great room. My mother was there, and I embraced her as she squeezed me the same way I had Harlow. Then I turned to see Aurelias, standing in his uniform and armor, his heavy sword across his back, ready for war as if it was on our doorstep.

The energy in the room immediately changed.

Even if I didn't know about Harlow and Aurelias, I would have realized it in that moment. I noticed his eyes were on Harlow, while her eyes were anywhere but on his.

Aurelias shifted his back to me. "We were able to find the components we need for the detonators. Because of the size of the crystal, we'll need as many as we can make. At least fifty. We should be done tomorrow, so we can head out soon afterward."

I gave a nod.

He gave a slight nod to me and walked away, leaving the great room and taking the stairs as if he intended to leave the castle altogether.

Harlow's energy was different now. Her arms were crossed over her chest, and she looked forlorn when she'd just been ecstatic a few seconds ago.

My mother looked at me, and a quick exchange took place between us before she walked off to her chambers down the hallway.

"Take a seat, sweetheart." I pulled out the chair for Harlow then moved to the head of the table, my heart racing in discomfort. Just when I thought I'd grown as a father and accepted my daughter was an adult woman with adult relationships…I regressed. It made me so uncomfortable, I almost chickened out. "Your mother told me what happened between you and Aurelias."

Now she was uncomfortable, judging from the way she abruptly looked away. "I don't want to talk about it."

"Neither do I."

She turned her head to look at me.

"But we're going to."

Her eyes shifted back and forth between mine.

"Aurelias and I had a conversation, and I made my wishes for you very clear. I asked him to never turn you into one of them—and I asked him to never bite you. He made it sound like he didn't have those desires anyway, but nonetheless, that was my request."

She looked away again, her eyes on the table.

"I realize now that it wasn't my place to make one of those requests. If being one of them is something you want...that should be your decision." The pain was unbearable, but seeing them together and the commitment Aurelias exhibited made me realize this wasn't a short-term relationship—despite what they'd said about it. The only way they could be together was if Harlow turned, and if he was the love of her life...then I would understand. If that had been the only way I could be with Ivory, I would have made the same decision.

"I don't want to be one of them."

"But if you change your mind—"

"We spoke about it," she said, lifting her head. "It's not something I ever want."

I tried so hard to hide the relief on my face, but I knew it came through. And the sigh I released was obvious too.

"I want children. I want to join you in the afterlife. There's no man I'd ever love enough to make that sacrifice."

I was quiet for a while, so relieved that I needed that time to let my muscles relax. I'd dreaded the moment she would come to me and tell me we would only know each other on this mortal plane...and never beyond that. "This is your relationship so it's not my place to influence you, but I think Aurelias is confined to the needs of his race... and had no other option. If he can't feed from you, he needed to find a substitute—"

"He lied to me." She turned to me. "How can you be okay with that?"

"I just think you shouldn't focus on this transgression in light of the sacrifices he's made for you. Nobody remembers when you do something right, but they never forget when you do something wrong."

She shook her head, clearly pissed off by that. "Wow…"

"Harlow—"

"You're the last person I'd expect to say that."

"I know he loves you. Really loves you. Would do anything for you."

"He could have fed from me—"

"That wasn't an option—"

"Yes, it was. It was always an option. But he won't do it, and he refuses to tell me why."

"It's because I asked—"

"*No, it's not,*" she snapped. "Otherwise, he would have just said that—but he didn't. He's hiding the truth from me, and whatever that truth is, it's worth losing me over. So, he obviously doesn't love me as much as you think."

I was hungry for a real meal, desperate for a hot shower, but all those desires disappeared in light of my daughter's pain. "I don't want you to lose the best thing that ever happened to you over this—"

"Father." Her eyes started to water as she stared out the window, like I'd just poked an unhealed wound. "There's no future for us. There never was. Whether it ends now or ends next week, it still ends. I'm not willing to give up my soul for him, and he's not willing to give up his immortality for me. It's over."

My body stilled, all my muscles suddenly tight. "What do you mean by that?"

"By what?" She swallowed and blinked, and then her eyes were dry once more.

"He's not willing to give up his immortality."

"He said it's possible to reverse it. To restore his soul and make him human once again, to live one life as a mortal. But he's not willing to make that sacrifice, and he wouldn't let me make a sacrifice he's not willing to make himself. Not that I would anyway."

I stared at the side of her face, this news a blunt trauma to my bare chest. Anger simmered inside me, quiet at first but then a boil a moment later. My fingers automatically tightened into fists, but I forced them to relax. Otherwise, I might strike the table. "How long have you known this?"

"Since we arrived in HeartHolme."

In just a split second, my entire opinion of Aurelias had changed. I'd seen a man who would make any sacrifice for my daughter, would die for her, would protect me because she asked, would fight in a war that wasn't his to fight. But now, I realized that wasn't true...because he wouldn't make *any* sacrifice.

There was one he refused to make.

He could have my daughter for the rest of his life—but he chose not to.

EIGHTEEN
AURELIAS

I sat by the fire in the cottage while my brothers stood at the dining table, mixing the contents of our supplies to create the detonators. This was Viper's domain, but we'd have to make do without him.

The women were at the bar having a drink, probably talking about their husbands, and I sat across from Fang as we played a game of cards. He held his hand in his coiled tail, his luminous eyes focused on the cards like they were prey. Then he placed his set on the table, showing a winning hand.

I gave him a cold stare. "How do you do that?"

I'll never tell.

"A snake can't be this good at cards."

And a man can't be this ssstupid at cards... but here we are.

My eyes narrowed in anger.

Fang grabbed all the cards and shuffled them so we could play again. **Harlow is a good player.**

"Has ever she won?"

No.

"Then how is she good?"

Ssshe'sss sssmart. Hasss potential. A lot more potential than the rest of you.

"Kingsnake." I turned to my brother, whose head was down as he focused on his work. "Has Fang always been this much of an asshole?"

"Yep," he said, not taking his eyes off what he was doing. "Since the day I met him."

Fang finished shuffling the cards then started to disperse them.

"Maybe you should play a more worthy opponent. Win some money out of it."

There'sss no sssuch thing as a worthy opponent for me.

"Not at all arrogant."

A knock sounded on the door.

My heart gave a jump because I hoped it was Harlow, but I would have felt her mind long before she got here, so I knew it was someone else.

Cobra was closest to the door, so he opened it. "Yes?" He was used to being the king of his fortress, barking out orders like everyone was his servant.

"King Rolfe requests Aurelias join him in his study." It was one of the guards from the castle, the kind that were positioned at the doors and windows at all times in case someone ever tried to storm it.

"Looks like we'll have to finish this later." I got to my feet.

We already know how that will end.

"Asshole," I said under my breath as I walked out.

I walked ahead and ignored the guard who remained behind me. He seemed to keep his distance on purpose, as if he wanted to avoid my company because I was a vampire with razor-sharp teeth.

I entered the castle then found his study on the third floor, a floor higher than the great room and Harlow's bedchambers. I'd never stepped foot on this floor at all, let alone been inside his study, which was decorated in dark mahogany with maroon rugs and curtains. The fire in the stone hearth was lit, and he sat behind his desk, arms on the armrests, and his stare was hostile. Once I entered the room, I felt it...his anger.

I slowed my step as I approached the armchair that faced him. Perhaps his anger had nothing to do with me. Perhaps he and his wife had had an argument about something. But more than likely, Harlow had told him what I'd done when he returned to HeartHolme, and now he wanted to scream at me for hurting his daughter.

I dropped into the chair, rested my ankle on the opposite knee, and waited for his wrath.

He was silent.

I stared.

We were back in time, to when he kept me locked up in the cell in the dungeon and he refused to speak first... because I was beneath him.

A solid minute passed.

I abandoned my pride and went first. "I can't feed on Harlow, so I had no other choice. I didn't tell her because I knew she wouldn't understand." I spared him the details of when she'd begged me, when she'd exposed her neck to me and tempted my resolve. It would infuriate him to know that his daughter stupidly tried to lure a vampire into feeding. "But I couldn't fight those demons and win if I was in a weakened state. I'm sorry that I hurt her, but there was no other option."

He stared me down and didn't blink.

"Whether we're together or not, I love her, and I'll fight for her until the job is done."

Huntley was still as angry as when I'd walked in the door.

There was nothing else for me to say. "What do you want from me, Huntley?"

He fired off immediately. "I want you to take back what you said."

My eyebrows arched up my face.

"You don't love my daughter."

It was like a punch to the face, the kind that broke your jaw. "Excuse me?"

"You heard what I said, Aurelias," he said coldly.

"I fed from the woman," I snapped. "I didn't fuck her—"

"That's not what I speak of."

I sank back into the chair, having no idea what he referred to.

His eyes flashed in anger, like he wanted to draw his sword and stab it through my stomach. "You could be with my daughter forever, but you've chosen to return to your lands and continue your life of drinking and fucking." He didn't raise his voice, but the anger in his tone was as sharp as my dagger. "When I was a young man, there was a different woman in my bed most nights of the week. I fucked whores and women who fucked me for free. I never grew tired of it, would have continued to do that even now. But then I met Ivory... and that shit stopped dead in its tracks. It stopped because I met the one woman I couldn't live without. From that moment, there was no sacrifice I wouldn't make for her. *None.*"

I wore a steely gaze to buffer his anger.

"You could have my daughter, but she's not worth it to you."

"It's not that she's not worth it—"

"You would rather live forever fucking other women than live one life with her. *Period.*"

"Huntley, it's more complicated than that—"

"It's not complicated. If it were Ivory, I know what my choice would be."

"With all due respect, you've never been offered immortality—"

"You could make me a vampire right now," he snapped. "I would be stronger, and I would live forever. But that doesn't tempt me whatsoever. I will die and be buried beside my parents in the cemetery in Delacroix, and then one day, Ivory will join me. We will be together in the afterlife, our souls bound as one, for eternity."

My eyes shifted away.

"Look at me."

My eyes came back to his with my own anger. "When I told Harlow this, she completely understood. You're getting angry about something that is frankly none of your business—"

"None of my business?" he asked coldly. "My daughter's heartbreak will always be my business."

Huntley and I had forged a relationship of friendship and camaraderie, and now, it was long gone. We were enemies once again, an invisible line between us. "As you know, we are no longer together. So this conversation is moot." She'd dumped me, and in the days that had passed, she seemed to hate me more. I'd lost hope that there would be a reconciliation. Her pain was still hot as a bonfire, so it was physically painful for me to be around her.

"I want you to leave, Aurelias."

I heard the threat in his voice.

"I appreciate what you've done for us." He had to force it out, force himself to be diplomatic when he didn't want to be. "But your time here has come to an end. You're no longer welcome here."

In a daze, I sat there, hurt by the request on so many different levels. "The crystal—"

"We'll destroy it with the detonators."

"You can't speak to Beast—"

"We'll figure it out."

"If they attack again—"

"Then your presence will make no damn difference." He slammed his fist on the desk as he rose to his feet. "We may not be vampires, but we are not weak. We defeated those demons, not once, but twice. Don't take pity on us because we don't need it. Now grab your things and leave."

I remained in the chair.

"Leave."

I slowly rose to my feet. "I've lived over fifteen hundred years."

He gave a quiet sigh, like he didn't want to hear my tale but didn't interrupt me.

"I've lived fifteen hundred years as one of the strongest vampires in nature, a creature at the top of the food chain, with abilities that make me nearly invulnerable. But it wasn't always this way. Once upon a time, I was human. My father and my brothers and I left our farmhouse to transport our harvest to sell at the market. While we were away, raiders came to our farm and raped my mother...and burned her alive." This story might be ancient history, but it still hurt to tell it, to know that my mother had died a gruesome death when she was the most loving person I'd ever known.

Huntley's anger dampened...like my words were a bucket of cold water.

"We were too weak to defeat the raiders, so we turned, all of us. I never want to be weak like that again, to fail a person I loved because I was physically inept. That's why I can't be human, not because I don't love Harlow, but because once I'm human...I'll be unworthy of her." I swallowed, picturing myself as a weak man who couldn't help my mother. "I wish...more than anything...that Harlow were already a vampire. But she's not..."

Huntley was quiet, staring at me with the desk between us. "Tell me why you won't turn her."

My eyes had drifted elsewhere as I'd told the story about my mother. Now they'd found his again. "You don't want that for her—"

"I still want to know why."

I remained silent.

"Aurelias."

"I—I can't."

Huntley stared at me before he came around the desk. He stood directly before me, and instead of wearing a heavy scowl, he regarded me with gentleness. "It's because of your fiancée..."

Alarm shot through me. He'd figured out my secret...and he couldn't even read minds.

"I'm sorry."

My eyes avoided his, the shame so heavy it made me sink into the stone floor. My breathing had picked up, and flashbacks of that horrible night came back to me, the blood on her white dress. "I—I would never..." I shook my head because I couldn't get the words out. "Harlow..."

His hand moved to my shoulder, and he squeezed me, squeezed me the way he did with his own son. "You need to tell her, Aurelias."

I avoided his gaze. "I've never told anyone..." My brothers knew because they were there. We never spoke about it because any time they tried, I shut down.

"She needs to understand."

I shook my head, like a boy disobeying his father.

"This isn't how you want to leave things."

I missed her so damn much. She took one look at my stone face and assumed I felt nothing...when I felt far more anguish than she did. Not only did I feel my own, but I felt hers too. "I can't do it." My voice came out as a whisper, not strong enough to remain steady. "Keep this to yourself." My eyes lifted to meet his, hoping his integrity was as strong as I knew it was.

His hand was still on my shoulder, his look and touch giving me more affection than my own father ever had. "I would never betray your confidence, Aurelias. And besides, she needs to hear this from you—not me."

I was alone in my cottage, drinking in front of the fire with the cards left on the table, when the guard came to the door. "King Rolfe requires your presence in the castle." It was late into the night, a couple hours after dinnertime. I hadn't fed since Harlow had caught me, and the hunger had started to tug on my limbs. But I hadn't sought out Annabella because the guilt was too strong.

"I'm coming." I set down the bottle and walked out, making the long walk to the castle. It was a cloudless night, the stars bright up above, the air frigid without the cloud bank to trap the heat to the surface of the earth.

I entered the castle and the great room, finding Huntley and Ivory there. Huntley wasn't dressed in his uniform, just his trousers and a shirt, as if he'd been retired in his bedchambers. The news must not be urgent. Otherwise, he would be dressed for war. I approached the table, and Huntley held up a scroll.

"A fleet of ships approaches the coast. They would have already landed by the time I received this message."

My heart dropped into my stomach. "My father..."

"That's my guess as well. And it's also my hope—because we can't afford another war."

In all the chaos, I'd forgotten about my initial request for aid. Their support would have been helpful days ago when the demons attacked us, but if we were attacked again, we would fall without help. "I'll fly out to meet him."

Huntley tossed the scroll on the table. "And I'll join you."

I rode Pyre, and Huntley took Storm. We left HeartHolme and flew through the darkness because the dragons could see in the dark even if Huntley couldn't. After a few hours, we saw the bonfires across the ground, the campsite for my father and his soldiers.

The dragons landed, and we walked to the camp, tents erected because the vampires didn't want to spend another moment on their galleons. They'd probably taken their slaves off the ships and kept them close so they could feed.

It was exactly what I had done when I'd traveled here, had a ship full of women who would receive my bite whether they wanted it or not. A flush of guilt moved through me at the memory.

We walked into the dark camp, and it didn't take me long to locate my father's tent. It was a tent large enough to accompany ten people, with guards stationed at every corner and the opening flaps. There were also flags posted outside, showing the Golden Serpent.

When I approached the tent, the guard recognized me instantly. "King Serpentine, Prince Aurelias has arrived."

It took a few seconds for him to emerge through the closed flaps, dressed in his black armor identical to mine, the golden serpent across his chest, brilliant in comparison to the dark colors. His eyes were only for me, not for Huntley who stood beside me. My father's eyes were as formidable as I remembered, dark like mine and irritable. Of all my brothers, I looked the most like him. Another reason he preferred me to the others. His emotions matched his stare, endless in their depth with a note of desperation.

"Son." He didn't embrace me with a bear hug the way Huntley did with his children. Instead, he came close and pressed his hand against my shoulder. Affection burned in his eyes, and then there was an emotional pull inside his chest. "I've been worried."

Then what took you so long? "Thank you for answering my call for aid."

He gave a slight nod then shifted his gaze to Huntley.

I knew my father had a lot more to say, but with a human in our presence, he held his tongue. "This is King Rolfe, King of HeartHolme and the Kingdoms." I gestured to Huntley beside me. "We've been fighting this war together."

My father stared at him, the same height as Huntley and just as burly.

"King Rolfe, this is my father King Serpentine, King of Vampires and King of Kingdoms."

Huntley extended his hand.

My father hesitated before he took it, his prejudice difficult to overcome. Like there was a bad stench in the air, my father's nose hiked up in a subtle look of disgust. I'd been hateful toward humans my whole life, but my father's discrimination was far worse.

"Thank you for coming to our aid," Huntley said. "We have much to discuss."

All my father could muster was a nod before he looked at me again. "We need to speak." He gave a quick glance in Huntley's direction. "In private."

I nodded before I turned to Huntley. "I'll escort my father and our people to HeartHolme in the morning. Don't make accommodations for us within the city. Our tents and supplies will be plenty." And I wanted them nowhere near the people of HeartHolme.

Huntley's eyes shifted back and forth between mine, his mind shrewd. "Then we'll speak in the morning."

My father returned to his tent.

"Let me walk you." I walked with Huntley beside me, moving through the camp. We hadn't attracted as much attention on the way there, but on the way back, we had a lot more stares. They could probably smell Huntley's blood, which had a distinct composition. Harlow's was the same, but I was so numb I didn't notice it most of the time.

When we approached the dragons, Huntley stopped.

I could feel his displeasure, feel his discomfort.

"Can I trust you, Aurelias?"

I met his stare.

"I can't read minds, but I know your father despises me."

"He's not a fan of humans."

"Then why travel all this way to fight for them?"

There was only one reason strong enough. "Me."

He continued his hard stare. "An army of vampires has just arrived in my lands when they know we're weak and wounded. It wouldn't be difficult for them to overrun HeartHolme and take it for themselves." His gaze penetrated mine, searching for the reassurance he needed. "Can I trust you?"

"I would never let that happen, Huntley."

He stared at me for a moment longer before he gave a nod and walked to his dragon. He climbed on top and secured his body to the saddle then jumped to the skies, Pyre following him. When the sound of their powerful wings disappeared, I knew he was gone.

I returned to my father's tent and walked inside.

There was a king-size bed with a naked brunette in it, the sheets covering her tits. Her neck had two bloody marks, and there were a few drops on the pillow. She was passed out, like my father had taken a little too much.

My father sat at a table, bottles of booze and glasses on the surface. He stared at me and silently commanded me to sit.

I sat across from him, my own flesh and blood, and somehow felt as if I'd stepped into enemy territory.

His dark eyes stared hard into my face with a hint of disappointment. "I've sailed across the sea with half our army…because you're obsessed with a woman. And not just any woman, but a human woman who smells as bad as that man who calls himself a king."

His words immediately incited anger from me, and for a moment, I forgot that my emotions were discernible. It'd been a long time since I'd been in the company of my own people. "The woman I love is his daughter—and he's a great king."

His disappointment simmered. "What happened to my son?"

"Humans are more capable than you realize."

"Are they now?" he asked coldly. "Because I could have ripped his head from his shoulders. You think that pathetic armor would have stopped me?"

It physically hurt me to hear him insult Huntley. I hadn't realized the depth of my affection until that moment, when I felt possessed to defend him...a human. "If you aren't here to help, then you should leave."

"I'm here to get my son back."

"Then the sooner we finish this war, the sooner we can return."

"I do this for him, then what does he do for me?"

"You aren't doing this for him," I snapped. "You're doing this for me."

"You win his war then get to take his daughter home?" he asked incredulously. "That's romantic..."

I didn't tell him I would leave Harlow behind, not when that would only make him angry.

"There are so many women to choose from, Aurelias," he said. "Human women...since you seem to be into that."

My anger reared its ugly head, but I battled it back. I'd only loved two women my entire life—and neither were vampires. My life would be so much easier if they were.

"Human women are only good for two things—feeding and fucking. If you want to devote your life to someone, there are plenty of vampire women that will have you, Prince of the Originals, my successor."

"You can't choose who you love, Father." I never would have chosen this. My love for Harlow had complicated my life. Now I was broken because I'd lost her. She was stubborn and proud like her father, so I knew she wouldn't take me back after what I'd done...not without the explanation to justify it. "We'll travel to HeartHolme in the morning and camp outside the castle walls. The plan is to return to the east to destroy the demons' source of immortality. That may provoke an attack, or it may not. Then we leave and return home."

"A king coming to their aid should be treated with greater respect than that. I deserve the biggest bedchamber in their fortress."

"No."

His eyebrows rose.

"No vampire will enter HeartHolme—including you."

"You don't trust me, son?"

I told the truth. "No."

His stare hardened. "It sounds like you don't really need us..."

"We already had a battle a few days ago. They lost half their people in the attack. They won't survive another, not with their numbers."

My father crossed his arms over his chest, his head cocked slightly. "How sad..."

I ignored the comment. "I'll need to take some of our kind to the crystal. The demons are strong, a challenge even for me. The humans won't survive the journey."

"How many?"

"At least fifty."

He continued to look disappointed by the whole thing.

"You didn't have to come."

"And leave you here to die?" he asked coldly. "My firstborn? My successor? My only son who knows what it really means to rule with an iron fist?"

His only son who hated humans as much as he did…that was what he meant to say. "How are things at home now that the Ethereal have been defeated?" I tried to change the subject, to reclaim a glimmer of what our relationship had been previously.

"Defeated?" He grabbed a bottle from the table and poured himself a glass. "Welcomed with open arms sounds more like it."

"Kingsnake and Cobra mentioned what happened."

"They didn't deserve to be pardoned, but your brothers were willing to fight me for it." He took a drink. "I had no other choice. And then Cobra wedded one of them…"

I had been cold to her the moment I'd known her true origins, but I knew I needed to be better after everything Cobra had done for me.

"Did they say how the Ethereal were feeding their immortality?" His tone was low and sharp, packed with unspent rage.

I shook my head, afraid of the answer.

"Human souls. Every person who's passed since the Ethereal's rise to power has been spent feeding their immortality." He watched my face, waiting for my reaction.

It took me a moment to absorb that information and the painful consequences. That meant when Mother died... she never passed on. And that meant when Renee... I couldn't finish the thought. It was too horrible. So horrible, I nearly fell out of the chair.

My father felt everything I'd just felt and gave a nod. "And your brothers defend it. Insist we need to move on. If they weren't my sons, I would have killed every single one of them and anyone who supports the Ethereal."

I was beside myself with loss. Didn't have a word to say.

"They're cowards for not telling you."

I swallowed and looked at the bottle between us. Then I reached for it and drew it close, drinking straight from the top instead of pouring a glass. I hadn't felt misery like this since Renee had died. It nearly brought me to tears.

My father's voice softened. "I'm sorry, son. I should have told you at a better time."

I stared at the table between us.

"Son."

I finally lifted my chin to look at him.

"There's nothing you could have done. Nothing anyone could have done. Whether we accept their kind or not... what's done is done."

I stared at his face but couldn't truly grasp his words.

"It's not your fault."

"It is my fault. It's completely and utterly my fault." She was dead because of me. She didn't have a soul...because of me.

"I remember Renee," he said gently. "She wouldn't want you to feel this way—"

"Stop." I didn't want to talk about her. I never wanted to talk about her. Not now. Not ever.

My father leaned back in his chair and turned quiet.

I took another drink from the bottle then cradled it close. "I'll see you in the morning." I left the table, taking the bottle with me.

"Aurelias."

I walked out of the tent and didn't stop.

I was awake all night.

I didn't make myself comfortable in a tent. I leaned against a tree and drank alone, looking at the stars and watching them change position as the night passed. The sky changed colors as we left the darkest part of the night and approached the morning. Dark blue was replaced by pink, purple, and orange.

The camp started to pack up and prepare to depart. My kin readied their horses and the carts. When I looked out to the sea, I saw the fleet of ships, at least a hundred floating away from the shore.

It took a few hours to prepare for departure. My father brought my horse for me, a black mare that had a bad temper but wouldn't dare disobey me. When I saw her, she immediately dipped her head so my hand could embrace her cheek. "Nice to see you too, girl." I patted her flank before I climbed into her saddle.

My father approached on his dark horse, a king in his heavy armor, his eyes guarded like the memory of our conversation was still fresh in his mind. But he didn't speak it out loud, didn't ask questions I didn't want to answer. "Lead the way, son."

We left the shore and rode to HeartHolme, the journey taking the full day on horseback. By the time we arrived, it was sunset, the torches of the city had already been lit to illuminate the oncoming night. The gates were open, as if the survivors of the battle had just entered Heart-

Holme that afternoon. They remained open as we approached, but no vampire would be allowed entry under my watch.

My father and I brought our horses to a walk near the gates.

"Looks like they're inviting us inside." He stared at me, the reins tight in his hand.

"We make camp outside the walls," I said. "No discussion."

My father wore a hard stare, like he wanted to argue but didn't want to waste the energy.

"We'll speak with King Rolfe in the castle, but you're to return here once those conversations have concluded."

"I've brought my own whores, Aurelias."

"I don't care," I said coldly. "I'd appreciate it if you could show more respect toward King Rolfe. It was obvious you despised him."

"I don't play games," he said. "You know that."

"It's called manners, Father."

"I'm the one coming to his rescue," he snapped. "So I won't bow to him."

I let the conversation die, knowing I would get nowhere with my father. He was set in his ways, set in his stubbornness. It made me realize how intolerable I used to be, why Kingsnake had punched me in the face when I called Larisa a bitch. I was a much different person now, and I hadn't realized how much I'd changed until I was faced with my past. "Let's go."

We entered the gate together then took the long walk to the castle. My father looked around as we passed through the city, down the alleyways between homes, at the humans as they passed on the cobblestone streets. He seemed unimpressed.

We made it to the castle and up the stairs to the great room, where Huntley waited for us. He didn't wear his armor, just his king's uniform. Now that he knew my father was more foe than friend, he wasn't nearly as kind as he'd been previously. In fact, the only greeting my father received was a stare.

When we stepped into the room, the tension was paramount, so thick it was like smoke in my lungs. My father and Huntley stared each other down as Kingsnake and Cobra stared at my father and waited for his gaze to meet theirs.

Harlow was there, and of course, my eyes went straight to hers.

They locked, and that connection provoked a surge of emotion inside me. After my conversation with Huntley and the news my father had shared with me, I wanted to head straight into her arms and get lost in her touch.

But she looked away, and then a second later, the anguish came through. Her turmoil was so raw, like my betrayal had just happened a few minutes ago rather than days. It physically hurt her to be near me, to look at me and remember what I'd done. Her pain was far greater than her longing…and she didn't long for me at all.

My eyes left her face and didn't return.

Kingsnake approached my father. "You came." Unlike with us, there was no affection exchanged.

"I was left with no choice," Father said. "Since three of my four sons are here…while the last is now in charge of our kingdom." He stared at Kingsnake coldly, as if it had somehow been his fault when I refused to return.

Cobra patted Father on the arm. "Come on, lighten up. They have great pot roast down at the pub."

Father stared at him like he had no idea who he was.

Larisa and Clara stayed back, like they knew their approach would be unwelcome.

Fang was around Larisa's shoulders. **Sssnake killer…** He released an audible hiss.

Father shifted his gaze to Fang. "Keep your pet away from me, or I'll cut his fangs out."

"Don't talk to him like that." It wasn't Kingsnake who said that, or even Larisa.

It was Harlow.

My father slowly turned to look at her last. He seemed to figure out who she was, probably because she was young and gorgeous. His gaze shifted to me, as if he expected an introduction or explanation.

I likesss her. A lot.

I instinctively moved toward Harlow, putting myself between my father and her, not that I feared my father would hurt her. It was just instinct. "Father, this is Harlow." I gave no other introduction because she didn't need one. I'd already told my father I loved her. Nothing else needed to be said.

Father pivoted his body toward her and regarded her with a stare.

She stared back but said nothing.

"I've never met a human who likes snakes."

"If all snakes were like Fang, I'm sure all humans would like them," she said.

Ssshe lovesss me.

My father turned back to the table. "Let's talk logistics." He pulled out one of the chairs and took a seat. "My people want to be here as briefly as possible...especially when they are living in tents." His venomous stare was reserved for me.

We approached the table, and just when I thought Harlow would take the seat beside me, she moved to the other side, taking the seat next to Larisa, where Fang slithered around her chair and then into her lap.

She smiled and started to scratch his head with her long nails, nails that used to scratch my back every night.

Everyone else took a seat, Huntley and Ivory across from my father and me.

My father glanced at me and then Harlow, probably suspecting trouble since she'd chosen a snake over me.

Kingsnake spoke first. "We've made fifty explosives to take with us to the crystal in the east. We were unable to find the components to make more, but fifty should be enough, assuming only half of them work."

"Why would only half of them work?" I asked.

"Because I'm not an expert like Viper is," Kingsnake snapped. "We take fifty vampires with us, destroy the crystal, and then return. With the destruction of the crystal, there's a chance that the demons will flee elsewhere in a desperate attempt to find another crystal to fuel their immortality. Because, if they fight us without it, they're gone for good. Or they'll realize they've decimated the human population to less than fifty percent of what it once was...and take their chances. There could be crystals under this earth, so they come here, conquer us, and then take everything that's underneath."

"What are their numbers?" Father asked.

"At least thirty thousand," Kingsnake answered. "Based on the last battle."

"And how many men do we have?" Father asked.

"We lost half our army and our civilians in the last battle," Huntley said. "So we're down to about forty thousand people. Half of that is military, the other half is civilians, women, and children. We're outnumbered nearly two-to-one."

"More like fifteen to one," Kingsnake said. "Based on strength..."

Huntley stared at him, probably offended, but he didn't say anything.

"The vampire army evens the score," Kingsnake said. "Dramatically."

"If they do come, we'll win," I said. "And with that crystal destroyed, we'll never see them again."

"What does that mean?" Father turned to me. "See them again?"

"Their powerful crystals bring them back to life," I said. "Every time they die, they return with new scars. So not only are they immortal...but also invincible."

My father stared for a long while, trying to absorb that information. "How?"

"I have no idea how it works." The demons were the only ones who could explain it, but they would never share that information.

"We also have the Exiles of Palladium," Ian said. "There are about five thousand of them. They'll fight with us."

"Five thousand humans?" my father asked. "Won't make any difference."

"Don't count your wins until you've won," I said coldly. "That's what you taught us."

My father stared but kept his words to himself.

"I will accompany you to the crystal," Huntley said. "It seems wrong to have only vampires in this fight. It would be wrong to allow you to risk your lives if I'm not willing to do the same."

My father turned to regard him, and a long stare ensued.

"You belong with your people," I said. "We'll handle the crystal."

His eyes were glued to mine. "*I insist.*"

"We also have the Teeth," Ian said, cutting through the tension. "But by the time they arrive, the war will probably be long over."

"When should we leave?" Kingsnake asked. "We don't have time to waste."

"Tonight," Huntley said. "We leave by dragon this evening and travel across the east in the cover of darkness. We'll be able to reach the secret tunnel without their realizing we're even there."

Kingsnake nodded in agreement. "Any objections?"

The room was silent.

"Then prepare for departure." Huntley was the first to rise to his feet. Everyone else followed suit.

Kingsnake went to Larisa to speak to her quietly, and my father rose from his seat to depart the room and return to his campsite outdoors. Fang slithered off Harlow's chair and moved around Kingsnake's shoulders. Ivory and Ian walked away, deep in thought. One by one, everyone left.

Except for Huntley and me.

I remained at the table because, unlike everyone else, I had nowhere to go. Harlow had been my home, but now she treated me like a stranger. All I had was my cold bed in an empty cottage...bottles of booze waiting for me.

Huntley returned to his seat, the one across from me. "You and your father don't seem very close."

I slouched in the chair. "It's a challenge..."

"Challenging how?"

I looked out the window behind him, seeing torches in the distance. "I'm not the same man I was when I left." My father tolerated my brothers, but he'd never had to tolerate me. Now, that was over. "He's not happy about that."

"How have you changed?"

I turned my gaze back to him and decided to be honest. "My brothers have always had a more conservative stance on human relationships—treating them like equals rather than inferiors. My father and I, on the other hand, have seen the human race as nothing more than livestock."

He listened without judgment.

"Obviously, I feel very differently about that now." It wasn't just Harlow who'd softened my heart, but the man across from me, a man I was forced to admire because of his selflessness and his bravery. "I was the favorite son, but now he feels nothing but disappointment for me. Never thought I'd live to see the day." I released a painful laugh, a sarcastic one. "I lost my relationship with my father for a woman who doesn't even want me anymore."

Huntley's eyes glanced down momentarily.

"You can't come with us, Huntley."

"I don't need your concern—"

"You need to stay here to keep my father in check."

He stilled at my statement.

"I told my father they're not allowed to enter Heart-Holme for any reason. He should obey that request, but just in case he doesn't...you need to be here. If he knows you aren't here, it might make him do something he wouldn't do otherwise."

He continued to stare, his thoughts swarming with so many different emotions that none were distinct. "I don't understand your family politics. A father should unite his family, but ever since he has stepped into our lives, I've seen him divide all of you. You all behave differently around him...almost as if you're afraid."

We were afraid.

"I would never want my children to feel that way about me."

"Because you're a good father, Huntley. My father is...complicated."

"Why is he so complicated?" he asked.

"Well, he wasn't this way when my mother was alive. He was a good man then. Taught us how to hunt, how to provide, spent time with us because he wanted to, not because he had to. I guess we continue to tolerate his extremism because we remember the way he used to be."

"Why did you hate humans as much as he did while your brothers didn't?"

Another complicated question. "I guess I hated humans for what they'd done to my mother. My brothers were wise enough to understand that just because a few men were evil didn't mean everyone was evil, but I disagreed.

I held on to the grudge, held on to that pain—and so did my father."

"Does Harlow know what happened to her?"

I shook my head.

"Why haven't you told her?"

I stared at my hands on the table. "For the longest time, I tried to hold back as much as possible because I knew where our relationship was headed—and I didn't want it to happen. But in the end, it didn't matter, because I fell hopelessly in love with her anyway." I didn't meet his gaze as I said that so I could avoid the discomfort in his eyes.

Huntley said nothing, just as I expected him to.

I continued to stare at the table.

"I'm sorry...that your father treats you this way."

I lifted my gaze.

"I love my children differently, but I love them the same."

I knew how much he loved his wife and children because I felt it whenever they were in the same room together. "I feel your love whenever you're around your family, and my father has never felt that for me, for any of us. At least, not since we've been vampires."

Huntley stared at me, softness in his eyes, sadness in his heart. "If I lost my wife..." He paused for a long time, like saying the words was enough to make him inconsolable. "I would never be the same. But if anything, my love for my children would deepen because they'd be all I had left." He swallowed. "You're a good man, Aurelias. So are your brothers. You all deserve that kind of love."

I couldn't hold his gaze any longer and dropped it, looking at the table again, his stare suddenly too much for me. I'd never realized my father's love was conditional until now. I'd never realized I was only the favorite because I had the same poison in my heart. Now that love had replaced my bitterness…I'd lost my place.

NINETEEN
HARLOW

Our relationship had come to an abrupt halt, but he continued to be a part of our lives like he'd always been there. He continued to fight alongside us like he cared for us as much as we cared for ourselves. I was in my room, trapped in my misery, but he carried on like nothing had changed.

I would give anything to feel him the way he felt me.

To know I wasn't alone.

He never came to my bedchambers. Never tried to speak to me. The most he ever did was stare at me. Now that he was about to leave to destroy the crystal, our relationship would be over soon anyway, but it was all I could think about.

They were going to depart in an hour, so I walked down to his cottage, my beating heart in my throat. I tried to swallow it back, but it was lodged in the space. A rush of nerves flooded me, and I hated the fact that he felt all of that.

The door opened when I hadn't even knocked, and he stood there, staring at me in the heavy armor that would keep him alive on this dangerous journey. His dark eyes had storm clouds, and his breathing was immediately different, like his dead heart had jumped into his throat as well.

I stared.

He stared back.

I'd had the courage to come all the way down there, but I didn't have the courage to speak. My eyes dropped to the floor, and I let myself inside the small cottage, the fire almost out in the fireplace, frost pressed up against the windows.

He shut the door behind me then faced me again.

Now that I was the recipient of his stare, I froze in place. I had so much to say, but not a single word would form on my tongue. I was still wounded by his betrayal, but no amount of anguish would make me stop loving him. "I'm scared..." That was the best I could articulate, sounding like a child.

He stepped closer to me, eyes locked on mine with desperation. "I've been there before. I'll be alright."

"They'll know you're coming—"

"But they won't know I'll be accompanied by an army of vampires and explosives."

"You don't have to do this." He was doing it for me, even though I'd ended things.

His eyes hadn't shifted. Hadn't blinked. "Yes, I do."

When his stare was too much, I shifted my gaze elsewhere. "Aurelias—"

He moved into me, his hand cupping my face as his lips landed on mine, backing me up into the wall in a fluid motion.

I was instantly swept up in his embrace, and my lips moved with his on instinct. His affection was warm coffee on a winter morning, cold sheets on a summer day, rain to the rose garden outside the castle walls. The heat thawed my angry heart, and I pooled into a puddle on the floor at his feet.

But then reality came back to me, and I spoke against his lips. "Tell me why." I pulled away to look at his face, to see his reaction because his expression was the only tell he had.

He stilled at the question.

"Tell. Me. Why." My eyes shifted back and forth between his, knowing there was a secret guarded behind that strong gaze. He'd locked me out in the cold and barred the door. His heart had been blocked, and there was no way inside.

His eyes remained hard and impenetrable. His breathing had picked up slightly, and not because of the kissing. Conflict was written across his gaze, the internal debate exploding inside him. But he dropped his head and remained silent.

"Why won't you tell me?"

His eyes remained on the floor.

"You would rather lose me than tell me the truth."

He wouldn't look at me.

"Aurelias."

He inhaled a deep breath before he forced himself to look at me. "I can't..."

"You can't explain to me why you would rather feed from someone else? Why you preferred another woman instead of me? Why you would share something so intimate with someone who means nothing to you instead of the woman you're risking your life and afterlife for?"

His eyes shifted away. "I just can't."

It hurt all over again. "This is how you want things to end?" I did my best to battle my tears, to suppress the heat that burned behind my eyes, but his refusal was like a knife in my heart. He either didn't trust me or didn't think I was worthy of his secrets.

"I never want this to end, Harlow. The last few days have been some of the worst of my life, and all I've wanted to do is run straight to you." His eyes found mine again, steady once more. "My father is an asshole, and I found out that my mother's soul is gone forever…"

"What do you mean, gone forever?"

He paused before he continued. "It's a long story. But our enemy back at home was fueling their immortality with the souls of innocents. They call us monsters because we feed on blood, but the only soul we destroy is our own."

"I'm sorry…" I didn't understand the weight of his words, but his sadness was like ice in my heart. "And I'm sorry about your father too."

His eyes were elsewhere now, staring past me out the window. "My father is an asshole because my mother was raped and murdered. I understand that's something you just don't get over. And knowing her soul is long gone and there's no afterlife for her has fueled even more rage. I understand it…but I can barely tolerate it."

My heart sank when he confided that horrible news to me, especially when he breezed over it so casually. "I—I didn't know that."

"It's hard for me to talk about."

"I'm sorry." My words felt empty because they would never compensate for the weight of his pain. They were just air and nothingness, and his grief was as real as a solid piece of stone.

"I know you are." His eyes found mine again.

"I don't understand why you can confide this to me...but not what I need to know."

His eyes were gone again. Shifted somewhere else instantly. "Because it's infinitely more painful than what I've just told you."

How could anything be more painful than that?

When I didn't say anything, he spoke. "I need to leave."

My heart gave a lurch, afraid this would be the last time I saw him. "Aurelias, I hate this."

"Not more than I do."

"What you did is unforgivable...but I want to forgive you."

His eyes hardened on my face, growing intense like he might grab me and kiss me again.

"Give me a reason to forgive you."

His eyes grew guarded.

"Give me a reason," I whispered. "Please..."

His eyes dropped.

"Tell me why."

His eyes never rose to meet mine again. He stepped around me and grabbed his sword where it leaned against the wall. He hooked it into the scabbard across his back then moved to the door.

I turned and watched him go, his back to me now.

Without looking at me, he spoke. "I'm sorry, baby." Then he walked out and left the door wide open.

TWENTY
AURELIAS

I met my brothers in the clearing where the dragons waited for us. It was dark now, the torches our only source of light. Fifty vampires were there too, all Originals, all with the same ability I possessed.

And Huntley was there, ready to see us off. "My brother is going to accompany you so he can communicate with the dragons. With this many dragons leaving our kingdom, it's imperative we keep them safe."

"I understand."

"Got the detonators?"

"Yes." Kingsnake held up the sack over his shoulder.

Huntley looked at me again. "This is where I tell you how much I appreciate your sacrifice...but there are no words of gratitude I could ever express that would equal your actions."

"I'm not doing it for gratitude, so you can save your breath."

For the first time ever, Huntley cracked a smile like he might laugh. But then it disappeared as quickly as it arrived. "We were both down there. We both know what awaits you. You may be a vampire, but there are things out there we don't understand. Be careful, not arrogant."

I nodded in understanding.

"I wish I could fight by your side, but you're right, my place is here with my people."

I nodded in agreement.

"Please come back—all of you." He looked at my brothers and grabbed each one by the shoulder before he walked off and joined his wife. Harlow didn't come down to see me off. She'd remained in the cottage after I left, her mind burning in pain until we were so far apart I couldn't feel it anymore.

"Let's go." I approached Storm and climbed up.

Cobra remained on the ground, looking up at me with his hands on his hips. "I'm just supposed to climb up?"

"Use the ropes from the saddle."

He grabbed on to the rope and slowly hoisted himself up, finally getting into the saddle. "You want me to spoon you, or you want to spoon me?"

"You're behind."

"Hope you don't mind my hard dick in your back…"

"Why is your dick hard?"

He moved behind me, chest pressed to my back. "Have you seen my wife? It's always hard."

We flew across the mountains in the dead of night, so there was nothing to do but look at the stars. I hadn't slept in nearly two days and I was tired, but the impending mission was enough to keep my mind wide awake.

"Things still aren't good with you and Harlow?" Cobra asked from behind.

It took me a while to answer. "No." Cobra and I were never the kind of brothers to have the heart-to-heart conversations. Kingsnake was the only one I had somewhat serious conversations with.

"Shame. She's got a great ass."

"You want me to throw you the fuck off right now?"

"What?" He shrugged. "Clara has a great ass. It wouldn't bother me if you said it."

"I've never looked at your wife's ass."

"Well, maybe you should."

"We're about to enter the domain of the demons, and you're acting like it's all a joke…"

"Life is a joke, man. Lighten up." He clapped me on the shoulder.

"I'm serious, Cobra."

"I'm sorry, are there demons here right now?" he asked incredulously, looking around left and right. "We'll be fine. I've kicked demon ass twice now. And if we are gonna die, I'd rather die with a laugh than a cry."

We spent the rest of the journey in silence, the air slowly growing warmer as we headed farther east. By starlight, we were able to see that the mountains had been replaced by desert, and we traveled across the open world in the hope no one below saw our progression. Maybe one or two dragons wouldn't be enough to be spotted—but twenty-six dragons was a different story.

We arrived at the mountains where the Exiles of Palladium were located and began our descent, Ian in the lead like he knew exactly where to go. He landed in the brush moments later, and then he dismounted.

The rest of us left the dragons and joined Ian, the sky changing from shades of black and blue to the light colors of dawn. He hiked into the mountains, taking a path through the trees and toward higher ground. We all followed in a line, hiking upward without asking any questions.

After twenty minutes, we were at a much higher elevation, and the torches became visible. I assumed we'd arrived at the territory of the Exiles, the people who knew exactly where the hidden passage was.

Finally, soldiers came to greet us, and they seemed to recognize Ian. They spoke briefly, and then they escorted us in a different direction entirely, through a cave and into a mountain. It was dark inside, so the guards lit flames to guide our way.

Ian came to a stop when the walls started to narrow. "This is where I leave you. The Exiles say this passage will take you into the demon domain. I need to remain with the dragons while you're away."

I looked into the narrow tunnel, dark with cobwebs in the corners. This was the passage that Beast had told us to take, where she would check for our appearance on a daily basis. "We can take it from here."

"Good luck." Ian gave us a nod before he walked away.

When he was gone, it was just us, vampires in a land very different from our own, fighting for a cause that didn't benefit us whatsoever.

Cobra came to my side. "This should be fun."

Kingsnake came next. "Never thought I'd say this, but I wish Viper were here. Detonators in dark places are his forte."

"So, there's a giant snake that lives down here." Cobra looked up to the ceiling, a large spider web visible. "You don't think giant spiders do too...right?"

Kingsnake took the first step forward. "We're about to find out."

We made the long journey downward, moving closer toward the center of the earth, the air growing progressively staler as we traveled. We could see in the dark, so we didn't need to light torches to guide our way. The path seemed to go on forever, and with every passing hour, we grew more demoralized.

Then the path ended, opening into a giant chasm that was dimly lit by the various crystals that were embedded in different surfaces. It was a different kind of quiet, different from falling snow on a winter night, different from a quiet bedchamber at midnight. In a place like this, every sound echoed, and the fact that there was no sound at all...meant there was nothing at all.

"Now what?" Cobra asked.

"We wait for Beast," I said. "She said she would check the passage once a day for our presence."

"Then we should rest," Kingsnake said. "Put a few vampires on guard while the rest of us sleep."

I was dead tired, so that sounded like a great plan. A few vampires volunteered, while the rest of us tried to find flat surfaces so we wouldn't roll off over the edge. I unrolled my cot against the wall and got inside, so tired I fell asleep the second my head hit the small pillow. It'd been several nights of no sleep, and I didn't realize how much I needed rest until I finally got to have it.

I woke up to someone shaking me. "She's here." It was Cobra's voice.

My eyes snapped open, and I immediately sat up. "How long's it been?"

"About ten hours."

I blinked several times, my mind feeling sharp instead of dull. I got out of the cot and packed my things, but then realized it made no sense to take my pack any farther than this. I couldn't take unnecessary weight into battle. I left it where it lay and approached the entrance to the chasm.

Beast dipped her head to come close to me, her bright yellow eyes burning into mine with interest. Her head was as big as the chasm opening, her sharp fangs the size of boulders. **You've returned.**

So have you.

Do you have a plan?

Yes.

What isss it?

We've made explosives to destroy the crystal.

Explosssivesss?

It was hard to describe, especially to a snake. *It's basically a concentrated ball of energy, and once it hits something hard, all that energy releases at once. It's like an earthquake.*

Fassscinating.

What information can you share with us?

They sssussspect you're coming. Vine is very angry that you made a fool of him.

He didn't leave me any choice.

The Demon Lordsss are prepared.

What are their abilities?

Magic.

Such as?

I've never witnesssed their powersss, but I know they can wield the elementsss…like fire and ice.

I hoped fifty vampires would be enough.

If you fail, it'll be the death of my hatchlingsss. She brought her face closer. **You. Can't. Fail.**

I know.

She pulled her face away. ***The only way to reach the cryssstal is to climb the fortresss. It'll be quicker if I take you to it. The othersss will need to fight the Demon Lords to give you the chance. Once that cryssstal isss gone...ssso are their powersss. The quicker you accomplisssh thisss, the quicker the fight will turn in your favor.***

I understand.

And Vine will be there...and he'sss angry.

What are his abilities?

He'sss their chosen sssuccesssor. He'sss ssstronger than the other demonsss, blesssed with unparalleled ssspeed and ssstrength. Once the cryssstal isss desssstroyed, he'll have the abilitiesss of a normal man, but I sssusssspect he would ssstill be a worthy foe.

I turned to look at Kingsnake and Cobra. "Did you hear all that?"

They both nodded.

I'll take you all to the fortresss. The sssecond we arrive, they'll know.

Will you help us?

I fight for the livesss of my hatchlingsss. They will receive the bite of my fangsss and the sssting of my venom. Once the attack beginsss, the demonsss will come to their aid. I'll fight them off.

I looked at my brothers. "Ready for this?"

Kingsnake had a hint of hesitation in his eyes, but he didn't give voice to it. "Yes."

Cobra didn't have any more jokes up his sleeve. "Let's kill these motherfuckers and destroy that crystal so we can get back to our wives."

Beast dipped her head so we could walk onto her body and down her neck.

"Let's go." I took the lead, stepping onto her hard scales and waiting for everyone else to walk on.

My brothers came next, followed by everyone else, taking a spot on the beast's neck or farther down her body. None of them was hesitant, not when snakes were such an integral part of who we were.

Let'sss kill them all.

Beast slithered through the different chasms, knowing her way underground even though everything looked the same to me. There were small clusters of different-colored crystals stuck into the walls and ceiling, and they must have been what Beast used as markers for guidance.

Twenty minutes later, we returned to the place where she'd taken us before, giving us a view of the fortress behind the tall iron gates. In silence, she studied the area, seeing the bright-blue crystal that shone right above the fortress, the tip poking through the hole in the ceiling. It was quiet. There were only two guards posted, both on the other side of the gate, like even they weren't allowed entry.

Beast moved, gripping the chasm walls and sneaking around the sides, staying out of sight as she approached the fortress from an invisible angle. She was quiet, her scales sliding over the rocky terrain without making a sound. Rocks didn't come loose and tumble down. She was a professional at stealth.

Get thossse explosssivesss ready.

I readied my bag. *I've got them.*

She exposed herself for the first time, climbing up the chasm and then the walls of the fortress, reaching the top in a few seconds.

I quickly jumped off, my eyes squinting from the intense light of the crystal.

Good luck. She slithered away, back down to the ground so the rest of the vampires could jump off. Just as she'd said, the second we arrived, they were aware, because a loud horn sounded from nowhere, deep in tone, reverberating off all the walls of the chasm.

The guards quickly unlocked the gates even though they were outnumbered, being cut down by the vampires and their black blades.

I pulled out the explosives one by one and stuck them to the crystal, using the sticky solution one of Huntley's men had made for me. I had to hold each explosive for several seconds to make sure it was truly attached before I moved to the next one. I was unable to watch the battle below, unable to check on my brothers because I had a job to do and I couldn't deviate from it.

One by one, I attached the explosives to the crystal, moving higher up, as high as I could go to cover it all.

Then an earthquake erupted, and I tripped forward, catching myself with my hands but hurting my wrist to break the fall. The vibrations continued, so intense that my body bobbed up and down uncontrollably with the movement.

Then it stopped—and a high-pitched scream came from every direction.

"What the fuck?" I pushed myself to my feet and looked toward the gate. As far as I could see, a line of demons was rushing to the fortress to kill us all. There had to be hundreds, all traveling over the same bridges to reach us.

I looked back at the crystal, knowing I needed to get these explosives higher if I was going to destroy it completely. *Beast, I need your help.*

I'm busssy. She issued an angry hiss and then slammed her body into the bridge that connected to the fortress, breaking it clean in two to stop the demons from crossing.

I need to get these explosives higher— Something hard collided with my back, and I hit the ground, the wind knocked out of me. It all happened so quickly, I could only operate on instinct, rolling out of the way even though my body screamed in pain. It was a good thing I did—because a golden blade slammed down beside me.

Vine looked down at me, dressed in full armor, unlike the other demons, wearing the most savage expression I'd ever seen. His face was tinted red like a ripe tomato, and tremors rocked through his body because his rage couldn't be contained. "Foolish. Fucking foolish." He came down on me again.

I rolled out of the way over and over, dodging his blade on the ground without having the opportunity to rise to my feet. All I did was evade, my wrist aching along with the rest of my body. I finally had the chance to kick him in the shin and interrupt him momentarily to get to my feet.

But his blade sliced across my chest, cutting right through the golden serpent. Now I had a crack where his sword had been, his golden blade having the ability to slice right through my armor.

I dodged another swipe of his sword as I pulled out my blade.

"Your armor will fail you." He launched at me, releasing a flurry of hits I could barely keep up with. One after another, all with the same strength and intensity, all the while he looked at me like he couldn't wait to stab that sword through my throat. I knew that was how he wanted to kill me, to silence my voice so I would never speak again as I lay there dying. But anticipating his attacks wasn't enough for me to win—not when he was this fast.

He released a scream then kicked me in the chest, making me fly back across the ground to the edge. He moved quickly to finish the job, to shove me hard with his shoulder and make me catapult off into the ground below.

I ducked at the last minute and shoved myself toward him, making him trip over me and roll toward the edge.

I kicked him as hard as I could, threw my entire body into it, knowing I had to kill him before he killed me. Harlow's face came into my mind, and I knew if I died, she would die next. A surge of strength flooded through me, and I overpowered him, making him fly several floors down to the gold-plated floor below.

His body hit the floor with a loud thud, and then he lay still.

I stared at him for a moment to make sure he was dead before I faced the crystal once more, out of breath, my wrist throbbing.

The screams erupted again, and then I felt the heat from the flames. I looked down, seeing massive fireballs unleash and fly across the floor and to the chasm below. Then I saw a vampire get struck by a lightning shard, hit so hard he was flung over the edge. Bumps formed on my arms as my stomach dropped. *Beast, help me.*

Hold on.

I ran to the remaining explosives and pulled them out of the bag.

"Did you really think it would be that easy?"

I turned and saw the fist as it flew at my face.

The hit was so hard, I crashed down to the ground, and the world went black. But then I jerked awake again when I felt it, the blade piercing straight through my armor, my dead heart, and impaling the stone below me.

I screamed in pain, the golden element making me burn from the inside out.

Vine stood over me, an angry gloat on his face.

I tried to move, but I was stuck in place, the blade too strong for me to pry free. I couldn't reach the hilt, so I grabbed it by the blade and tried to pull it out, cutting my hands through my gloves in the process.

Vine watched, fascinated. "Foolish." He came around, taking his time, his boots heavy against the stone.

I saw what he intended to do, to stomp his foot hard on my face over and over until my skull shattered and it was just a pile of blood, guts, and brains left over. *Beast, he's going to kill me.*

Vine stood over me, looked up at the explosives glued to the crystals, and then looked down at me again. Screams sounded from below, vampires being outmatched by the Demon Lords below. My brothers could be some of them. My job was to destroy the crystal, but I'd failed.

I'd failed Harlow.

He raised his boot over my face and prepared to stomp. "What a handsome face to waste."

I grabbed his boot and tried to tip him over, but he stomped down on my hand and made my wrist ache even more. He kicked me in the side of the head, and both my nose and mouth started to bleed. I couldn't outmatch him, not when I was pinned in place, bleeding out everywhere.

"*Hisssssssssss.*" Beast's massive jaws snatched Vine off me, and she crunched her teeth together, breaking his spine and all of his bones. Instead of swallowing him, she flung him out of her mouth and into the abyss. ***I can't help you and your kin at the sssame time. You mussst choossse.***

"I need to reach higher to destroy the crystal." I tried to pry the sword free, but it just made my hands bleed more. The crystal was more important than any life below, because as long as that crystal persevered, the battle would rage on.

Beast grabbed the sword with her teeth and pried it free. ***Hurry. We only have sssecondsss before he'sss back.***

I forced myself up, my hands slippery with blood, and grabbed the sack of explosives before I climbed onto her head, dripping blood all over her brilliant scales. I swayed and nearly toppled over.

Can you do thisss?

"Yes."

She raised her head so I could reach. ***Hurry.***

One by one, I stuck them to the sides of the crystal, moving up toward the base so it would destroy the entire thing once the explosion happened.

Hold on.

I dropped to my knee as Beast jerked to the right.

"*Hiiisssssssss.*"

I knew Vine had returned, aiming his blade at Beast.

I kept going, sticking the explosives, quickly running out.

Then an explosion happened below, down where the fighting was.

He'sss pulling them off.

I gritted my teeth and kept going. "Fucker…"

More explosions sounded, Vine removing the ones I'd put at the bottom and throwing them at my own kind.

"Done."

Beast immediately pulled away and moved toward Vine.

I jumped off her and landed hard on my side, my entire body crying out, more blood being squeezed from my muscles.

She struck at Vine, but he cut her across the nose with his gold blade.

"You betray me, bitch?"

"*Hiiiiisssssssss.*" She struck him again, biting his torso clean in two before flinging his body over the edge. ***Is it ready?***

"Yes." I climbed back up her body. "Move away."

She pulled away from the fortress, and that was when I had a clear view of the chaos. The Demon Lords had unleashed fire and ice on the vampires, burning them alive or freezing them in place. Demons launched themselves across the bridge to get into the fight.

I quickly scanned for my brothers, but I didn't see either.

Dessstroy it.

I grabbed the last explosive I'd kept just for this and threw it at the crystal. At the moment of collision, the explosive detonated, causing all the others to do the same. A fiery storm of flames and clouds appeared—and then the crystal shattered. Shards poured down everywhere like sharp drops of blue rain. It flowed through the roof, ejected in all directions.

The battle came to a halt as everyone stared, some in relief, and some in terror.

The high-pitched scream returned, a cacophony of several voices at once.

"Get us out of here."

My hatchlingsss. If I don't get to them first, they'll kill them all. She traveled back to the battle and lowered her head so others could climb on.

"Move out!" I ran into the fray and ordered everyone to leave. Now that the crystal had been destroyed, the demons were just standing there and looking up, as if it would reform by sheer will alone. Instead of taking the opportunity to strike them down, I chose to grab every vampire I could. "Run to the snake." I pulled one of my kin from the ground and got him upright. "Go." I kept going, looking for my brothers. "Kingsnake. Cobra."

The demons across the bridge screamed in rage, and then more of them started to come, barreling down on us with a vengeance.

We need to flee.

Not without my brothers. "Kingsnake! Cobra!"

"Here!" Kingsnake shouted from the rubble of the fortress, which seemed to have rained down on them both.

I rushed over, aware of the wave of demons on their way to us. "Move."

Kingsnake's armor was barely put together anymore. It was covered in soot from the flames. One arm was completely bare, bloody. "Cobra..." He grabbed our brother by the arm, but he was limp.

"No..."

"He's still breathing," Kingsnake said. "I'm struggling to breathe myself."

"Get him up and go to Beast."

Kingsnake's eyes were heavy.

"I'll stop the demons from getting to you. I need you to carry him."

Kingsnake continued to wobble in place.

"Larisa." I grabbed his shoulder and shook him. "Think of Larisa."

He blinked several times before he clenched his teeth and rose to his feet.

"There you go." I turned away and pulled my sword free. I felt just as shitty as Kingsnake did, in no shape to fight the horde of demons that were hell-bent on killing me after I'd destroyed their immortality. But I gritted my teeth and faced them, giving my brothers a chance to escape.

They came down on me, and with strength I didn't know I had anymore, I met their blades with mine, taking on five at once, slicing through their flesh and knocking them aside. They were much easier foes than Vine had been, so it was a less-strenuous match.

ature *I have them. Run.*

Across the crowd, I saw him.

Vine.

He must have returned before I'd destroyed the crystal. My death was promised in his eyes, his golden sword held at the ready, prepared to part the crowd and take my life.

I knew I stood no chance, not in my weakened state, not when I'd lost so much blood. I cut down the demon nearest to me and sprinted as hard as I could, launching off the edge of the platform and into the abyss.

Beast broke my fall with her head, catching me before I disappeared into the darkness. Then she dove, the sounds of the battle growing distant and then silent the farther we traveled. I didn't have time to check on my brothers, not when we were dropping so fast, not when I felt so weak.

Beast traveled down most of the time, but then moved upward, rising to a platform that contained a large cage covered with golden bars. She slithered up, making her body flat so we could step off.

I went straight to Kingsnake and helped him get Cobra onto the floor.

Cobra was conscious this time, so that was a good sign. "I got stabbed...a lot."

I looked him over, seeing all the places where his armor had been impaled. It had been weakened by flames first, making it easier for the blades to puncture the protection.

"Fuck, Clara is gonna be pissed."

I need your help.

I looked up to see Beast staring at me. *We're all injured—*

I don't take you to the sssurface until my hatchlingsss are free. Her eyes turned venomous. *Vine will be here sssoon to make good on hisss promissse. Thisss mussst happen now.*

I looked at the golden bars of the cage, a cage that was three stories tall. I rose to my feet and approached, seeing snakes that were still enormous, but much smaller than her, curled up in the corner, all piled together. One of them had bloody gashes all over their body.

Sssave my hatchlingsss.

I tested the bars, trying to shake them, but they seemed to be anchored in place. The rest of it was solid rocks and earth. "I wish I had more explosives..." I turned to her. "Have you tried to break through these?"

They're sssolid gold.

"Aurelias."

I turned back to my brothers, seeing that Cobra was the one trying to speak to me.

"I've got you." He slowly moved his hand into his pocket and pulled out an explosive.

"Are you insane?" Kingsnake asked. "You've just been carrying that around like an idiot—"

"That guy on the roof threw it. It didn't go off...so it must be faulty." He lay still again, as if that information had taken all his effort to relay.

I took it from him and walked away before I opened it. I checked the contents and tightened the vials, rebuilding the explosive from scratch in the hope it was just improperly pieced together.

Beast watched me with hard eyes.

"Let's try this again." I carried it to the gold pillars in the center, placing the explosive on the left side of the pillar in the hope it would destroy the one to the right of it as well. "I'm not sure if this will work with solid gold, but we'll see."

The snakes all poked their heads up to watch, but they stayed back in their corner.

Hide.

The snakes buried their heads underneath their bodies.

We backed away, and I picked up a rock and chucked it at the explosive.

Fire immediately erupted, a powerful detonation that shook the world around us. Once the flames had dissipated, I assessed the damage. None of the pillars had shattered—but they'd bent. The ones in the middle had both bent outward, increasing the space in between. "They should be able to fit."

Come.

One by one, the snakes slithered through, going straight to their mother. She dipped her head to kiss each one with her tongue and closed her eyes as she held them close to her face. A tear emerged, streaking down her scales.

I didn't want to interrupt their moment, but we still had to get the fuck out of there. *Beast, we need to go.*

She pulled away from her hatchlings. **Come**. She then angled back toward us and allowed us to walk across her head and down her neck, to get situated on her scales before she pulled away from the platform.

A scream pierced the darkness, making the rocks vibrate.

We mussst hurry.

She traveled down then up again, seeming to take a different path from the one we'd taken there. Instead of going straight to the surface, she slithered down a series of paths, and the farther she moved, the quieter it became.

It was the first time I'd felt relief.

She made her way back to the passage that we'd taken here and allowed us to climb off in the rocky opening. Her hatchlings had followed her.

Kingsnake had Cobra's arm over his shoulder as he escorted him forward.

We'd returned with only a handful of vampires. Most of them had died in the battle. Guilt crushed my lungs, knowing it had happened because of me. *Thank you for everything, Beast. Where will you go now?*

Away from here. Sssomewhere my babiesss will be sssafe.

To the northwest, there's land given solely to the dragons. I'm sure King Rolfe would let you live there if you wanted.

Dragonsss?

They're like you—but with wings.

Fassscinating.

Meet us on the other side of the mountains to the north. There's a kingdom there called HeartHolme. I'll have your answer then.

I'll sssee you then, sssnake friend. She turned away and dove deep into the chasm.

I caught up to Kingsnake and Cobra, pulling Cobra's other arm over my shoulders and helping him through the long tunnel.

"I can't believe we're still alive," Cobra said.

"It'd be stupid to croak at the end, so don't even think about it," Kingsnake said.

"Can you imagine how angry Clara would be?" Cobra said. "She would bring me back to life just to kill me."

When we left the tunnel, the Exiles were there to intercept us. We were escorted into their humble fortress under the mountain, given cots to lie on. We'd been bleeding a long time, and those wounds closed naturally, so there wasn't much medical attention they could provide.

What we needed was blood.

When Cobra's armor was removed, the extent of the damage was visible. He had scars from all the places he'd been stabbed. His previously flawless skin was now tarnished by the battle.

Kingsnake was scarred too, but knowing him, he was just happy to be alive.

Every time I moved or breathed too hard, the wound made me wince in pain, but if I'd survived this long, I would probably pull through. The others were in similar shape...and most of them didn't make it at all.

Now I knew how Huntley had felt after the battle that had claimed so many of his people.

Ian walked in sometime later and took one look at all of us before his face paled. "There are so few of you..."

I sat up in the cot, exhausted. "Yeah."

"What happened?" Ian came to my bedside and pulled up a chair.

I told him the whole tale. "They were pissed."

"You think they'll come for us?"

"I think there's a pretty good chance they will. We need to get back and warn Huntley."

Ian gave a nod before he looked at Cobra. "You look like you're in no condition to travel."

"We need blood, and there's none of that here." The Exiles were suspicious of us, keeping their distance like we might bite their arms off. "We need to head back. If we haven't died yet, then that means we should pull through."

"Are you sure?" Ian asked.

I nodded. "Huntley needs to know what's coming."

TWENTY-ONE
HARLOW

I couldn't sleep.

It'd been three days, and I'd slept on and off only briefly. Every couple of hours, I left my chambers to ask my father if he'd received any news—and the answer was always the same. I hated the way my final conversation with Aurelias had ended. It'd been on my mind every moment he'd been gone. I was hurt he wouldn't repair the damage he'd caused, but I loved him so much that my heart was still tied with his irrevocably.

I left my bedchambers and entered the great room, expecting no one to be there so I could look out the large windows to the city and field beyond, to check for the scales of dragons in the torchlight.

But they weren't there.

"Sweetheart."

I turned behind me to see my father sitting at the table, wearing his lounge trousers without a shirt. A nasty scar was on his shoulder from where he'd been stabbed. Other marks of battle were on his tanned skin, old scratches and cuts. He was a burly man with lots of muscle on muscle, a bear without fur. I approached the table. "I'm so tired, but I can't sleep."

"Neither can I."

I took the seat across from him, seeing the bottle of scotch and his glass. I would normally reprimand him for his drinking, but tonight, I didn't care. In fact, I grabbed the bottle and took a drink myself.

My father didn't pass judgment.

"They should have been back by now."

"It's unrealistic to have any expectations."

"But you've been there."

"I don't know what the circumstances are. Because this time, the demons probably knew they were coming. They may have had to sneak to the crystal, find another way of getting the job done. I'm worried…which is why I drink and not sleep, but that doesn't mean they're unwell."

"We don't have any dogs in the fight, so why are you up all night?" Uncle Ian hadn't traveled with them underground. He was safe with the dragons, waiting for the vampires to return. If things went south, all he had to do was fly away.

"I do have a dog in the fight." He crossed his arms over his chest as he slouched in the chair. "A couple…"

My father had despised Aurelias at their first interaction. That hatred lasted a long time. But now, it was different. Their journeys and battles had changed their relationship. "You've grown close."

He was quiet for a while. "He's a good man."

I said nothing.

"Reminds me of myself."

I was hurt by Aurelias's betrayal, also hurt that my father seemed to tolerate that betrayal, but I kept that to myself. Because if you looked past that, Aurelias really was a remarkable person. One day, he would find a vampire woman who could give him what he wanted, and he would marry her…and she would be the luckiest woman alive…or unalive. By the time that happened, I'd probably have been dead for several hundred years, my descendants ruling the Kingdoms while my body rotted in a grave. The pain made me swallow, because I knew I would never love another man the way I loved him. I would meet someone new someday, but he would never compare to the man I'd already loved and lost.

"You alright, sweetheart?"

My eyes lifted to his again. "Yes…just worried."

"I've seen Aurelias and his brothers in battle, and they're definitely superior to the demons we've fought. I have faith they'll return. But until they do, all I can do is sit and drink."

I gave a nod. "It's only been a few months, but I can't remember how life used to be. It's hard to believe it used to be normal, peaceful. I would read books after dinner... and now I can't focus beyond more than a few sentences. War is always right on our doorstep, and people are always dying."

My father released a heavy breath. "This is a life I never wanted you and your brother to know."

"And if we survive it, I'll never forget it."

"If Aurelias does return and the demons attack us once more, we should win with the vampire army."

"But they have to destroy the crystal—and return."

"Aurelias knows the consequences if he fails." He looked at me, the subject of Aurelias's motivation unspoken. "He knows he can't."

He would put his life on the line for me several times, but not tell me his secret. There were times when I was moved by his protection and bravery...and then burned by his abandonment.

A guard entered the room. "Your Highness, the dragons have been sighted to the east."

My heart lurched as I got to my feet, knocking over the chair in my haste. "How many?"

"It seems they are all accounted for."

I turned to my father. "They're back."

He took his time getting to his feet, not jumping in excitement the way I did. "The dragons are back. Doesn't mean their riders are."

It was dark and cold, the wind harsh as it swept over the flat land. There was a line of torches in a circle for the dragons to land and for us to see. My father put on a coat and came out with my mother. A guard had been sent to King Serpentine's tent to inform him of the dragon's return, and when he arrived, he was in his full armor, like he was about to enter battle rather than reunite with his sons.

Twenty minutes passed before the first dragon landed, Nightshade. Uncle Ian was the rider, and he immediately unfastened his legs before he dropped down. He moved to my father, who had walked to him the second he landed. They shared a quick one-armed hug before they looked at each other.

Uncle Ian spoke without being questioned. "The crystal is destroyed."

My father's gaze had been hard and serious, but slowly, a smile moved on to his lips. It even reached his eyes. "I knew they would succeed."

"Most of the vampires are gone," Uncle Ian said. "Only a handful remain…and most of them are injured."

My father's smile disappeared.

My heart dropped like a stone. "Aurelias?" I moved forward, needing to know he was still alive. "Tell me he's made it, Uncle."

Uncle Ian's eyes shifted to me. "Yes."

My hands came together against my chest in relief.

"But he's injured. So are his brothers. They'll survive, but they aren't in the best shape."

Dragons started to drop behind him, one by one, some with riders and some without.

Uncle Ian continued to stare at my father. "Aurelias says there will be repercussions."

"They'll come for us."

He nodded. "They'd rather risk permanent death than let us live."

My father took this news with a straight face. "Then we prepare for war."

I turned to the other dragons, searching for Aurelias on one of them. Finally, Storm landed, and that was when I saw him, Cobra sitting in front of him and tied to the saddle. Clara and Larisa rushed forward to help Aurelias get him down to the ground.

"Baby, I'm okay." Cobra winced as he straightened and stood on his own.

"You are not okay." Clara threw his arm over her shoulder to support him. "You look dead."

"Well, I am dead…"

"You need to feed. Come on." She continued to help him walk away.

Larisa disappeared with Fang to find Kingsnake on another dragon.

Aurelias hopped down next, looking as pale as his brother, but his eyes still shone when he looked at me. His face was bloodied and bruised, and there was a huge gash in his armor. It barely looked intact.

I moved into him and hugged him tightly.

He squeezed me hard, his chin resting on my head, his hold not as strong as it normally was.

"Are you okay?" I whispered.

"I'm okay." He pressed a kiss to my forehead as he gripped the back of my neck.

"Let me help you." I put his arm over my shoulder so I could support him the way Clara had supported Cobra, but just his arm alone was too heavy for me.

"It's okay, sweetheart." My father walked over, his eyes on Aurelias, full of admiration and pride. "I got him." He threw Aurelias's arm over his shoulder and walked him across the field back toward the castle.

I watched them stop at King Serpentine, who shared a couple words with his son. His face was as hard as it'd been when he'd walked down there, like something displeased him, perhaps the fact that most of the vampires had died in the attack. Then my father and Aurelias kept going, heading back toward the castle where they could rest. People helped the other vampires and escorted them back to their tents.

I followed my father and Aurelias, but instead of walking into the castle, they moved to the line of tents where the vampires were camped. My father escorted him to one tent then let him stand on his own. There was a bonfire there, illuminating the space and the other tents in the distance.

Aurelias turned to look at me, knowing I'd been there the entire time.

My father glanced back and forth between us before he silently excused himself from the campsite.

Aurelias unsnapped his chest plate and let it fall to the dirt because it was useless now. His eyes were tired, more tired than I'd ever seen them. But he straightened and held himself upright as he looked at me. "Return to the castle. It's not safe for you here."

"But I'm with you."

His eyes turned guarded before he looked away. "Go to the castle."

"You just got back, and you want me to leave—"

"*I need to feed.*" He didn't look at me as he said it. "It's the only way I'll heal."

My heart fell like a stone once again, dropping into a pit.

"I'll die if I don't." He slowly turned his head to look at me. "So, leave...please."

The memory of his body pressed up against hers, his lips against her flesh, her hand in the front of her trousers... was enough to make me hurt all over again.

He closed his eyes like he felt it.

"Feed from me."

His eyes remained closed. "No."

"Aurelias—"

"*I don't have the energy for this.*" His eyes opened, and he looked at me, his gaze furious. "I told you I won't change my mind."

"I want to make you strong—"

"Harlow—"

"Why not?"

His restraint snapped, and he unleashed a howl that echoed throughout the entire campsite. "Because I'll kill you." He slammed both of his fists against his chest to release his anger.

I stilled at his ferocity, seeing a new side to him I'd never witnessed.

"I'll drain the blood out of you...and I'll fucking kill you." He seethed, breathing hard as the fire of rage continued to burn inside him. "That's why, Harlow. Now get the fuck out of here."

"You didn't kill that woman—"

"*Please.*" He closed his eyes again, restraining his fury.

"Aurelias—"

He opened his eyes and walked toward me, staring me down with threat in his eyes. "I didn't kill her because I didn't love her. But I will kill you because I won't be able to stop. My fangs will hook into your flesh and never leave. I will feel your pulse grow quicker and quicker and then fainter and fainter until it's gone...and I still won't stop. Now, for fuck's sake, leave." He raised his voice and screamed at me. "*Leave!*"

I couldn't stand the redness in his face, the pop of his veins at his temples, the strain of the cords in his neck. He screamed at me, and that made me want to run. I turned away because I couldn't stand this version of him, the man who had succumbed to a forest fire of fury.

I rushed out of the campsite and through the open gate, getting back to the castle quickly because I ran the entire way. Luck was in my favor because I didn't pass my family or anyone else as I fled. I made it into my bedchambers and locked the door, shutting out the outside world so I could be alone. My happiness at his return had been destroyed by his brutality. All I wanted to do was make him strong, to share that connection that Larisa affectionately described, to have that intimacy he shared with a stranger—but he denied me.

I hadn't slept in three days, but now, I cried myself to sleep...and stayed asleep.

When I woke up, the sun was low in the sky, like I slept the rest of the night and through the following day. I sat up in bed, and the last conversation I had with Aurelias came rushing back. Every time I thought there was hope we would be able to work through our problems...that hope was shattered like broken glass.

I showered and got ready for the day, tired of lying in bed like I'd done lately. All I'd done for the past week was mope around in sadness, skipping meals because I had no appetite. But another battle was coming—and this time, it would come to HeartHolme.

I moved to the great room, where my father stood with Uncle Ian and Atticus, looking at a map of HeartHolme and the outside lands. None of the vampires were there, and I was surprised that Aurelias wasn't standing beside my father since they'd become so close.

My father stopped in mid-sentence to look at me. "Hey, sweetheart."

I approached the table, looking at the pawns they'd used to map out the upcoming battle. "Is there any way I can help?"

My father stared at me for a moment. "You can stay within the castle walls and help the injured at the infirmary."

I hadn't expected him to let me do anything at all, so that was a nice offer.

"We've lost so many people that we need to step up to roles we haven't done before," Father said. "Ask the healers to show you how you can help. Thank you for offering."

"Thanks for letting me help."

My father turned his head and looked past Uncle Ian.

I felt him before I saw him, felt his stare on the side of my face. I turned to walk away, careful not to make direct eye contact with him. His dark figure was a blur as I turned and headed toward the hallway so I could leave the castle and report to the infirmary.

But he followed me.

"Harlow."

I stilled at the gentle sound of his voice. It took a heavy dose of strength to relax my face and not look so angry, to push the memory of last night out of my mind. I turned around to face him, seeing that his skin was a healthy color and that fatigue was gone from his eyes. He looked invigorated, and he stood tall with his shoulders back, his injuries resolved.

"I'd like to speak with you."

"I'm on my way to the infirmary. Need to learn what I can from the healers before the battle begins." I thought that was more important than another pointless conversation that never went anywhere. Aurelias and I were at a stalemate, and since he was leaving soon anyway, salvaging this relationship was pointless.

"Please." He was gentle, far gentler than he'd been last night.

"You can talk on the way." I turned away and took the stairs to the bottom of the castle then walked out the double doors. When I made it outside, it was sunset, the sky a beautiful canvas of different colors.

Aurelias walked beside me but didn't say anything.

I didn't speak because I had nothing to say to him. Kept my gaze forward and continued to walk.

When we passed his cottage, his hand moved to my arm. "Please." He didn't grab me, just lightly pressed his fingers into the fabric of my long sleeve, handling me with delicacy because he'd shattered me one too many times.

"Aurelias, I'm tired of having the same conversation over and over—"

"I know."

"I love you so much…" I shook my head, my tears hot behind my eyes. "But I can't keep doing this."

Now his hand gripped me by the waist, and he brought me close. "Please."

When I looked into those dark eyes, I couldn't resist that intensity, the way he looked at me like I was the only woman in his heart. He could hurt me one moment…but make me so weak the next.

He gently guided me inside, shutting the door behind us and bringing us into the darkness of the cold cottage. He went for the logs and started a fire, bringing the room to life with heat and light. Then he came back to me, his hard eyes looking into mine for several long seconds. A sigh escaped his lips, and he dropped his gaze momentarily, like his words were heavy. "I'm only going to talk about this once. Then I never want to speak of it again."

My arms were crossed over my chest because of the chill, but the bumps that formed on my skin had nothing to do with the temperature. I knew this conversation would be different, that we were on the precipice of something new.

His eyes dropped to the floor because he couldn't look at me as he spoke. "There was someone else…a long time ago."

I remembered the first time it had come up. She was barely mentioned, and he offered no detail. I just remember being so jealous, jealous of someone who wasn't even in his life anymore.

"Her name...was Renee." His voice quavered as he said her name, like it brought him immense pain just to put those syllables together. "I loved her very much...and asked her to marry me."

It hurt to hear this. Hurt to know there had been someone else who'd loved him as much as I did. We'd agreed this relationship would end, but I'd claimed him as mine for forever, even during times I didn't know him. But that flush of emotion passed...and I hurt for him.

He paused for a long time, like he might not go on. "She was human...so I planned to turn her." Now he swallowed, the features of his face tightening like he had willed himself to finish the sentence. "But the taste of her blood... I couldn't stop...and I didn't stop." His breath quickened, and then a sheen formed over his eyes.

My world crashed down as I saw Aurelias crumple before me.

"I—I killed her." The tears broke free, pooling in his eyes and streaking down his face. "I fucking killed her."

I didn't feel the tears before they formed. I only realized they were falling when my cheeks became soaked.

"I'd never struggled to stop myself before. But because I loved her...her blood was different." He inhaled a deep breath and closed his eyes, forcing the emotion back deep inside the vault from which it came. When he spoke again, his voice was stronger. "That's why I can't feed from you, Harlow...because I'll kill you." He finally had the strength to raise his chin and look at me, to see tears for him on my face. "That's why I can't turn you... because I'll kill you. I loved her with my whole heart. Could have spent eternity with her in bliss. But somehow..." His eyes flicked away for a moment. "And I feel like shit for even saying this..." He took a breath. "Somehow...I think I love you more."

I moved into him and cupped his cheeks, bringing our faces close together. "Aurelias..."

He rested his forehead against mine. "I should have told you."

"It's okay." My arms hooked around his neck as his arms circled my waist. "I'm so sorry that happened to you."

His eyes remained down. "I know you are, baby." His arms tightened around me and pulled me close, and he moved his chin to the top of my head. "I'm sorry that I hurt you."

"It's forgotten." The context of the situation had changed, and now it didn't feel like a betrayal but a necessity. It felt good to have him in my arms again, to smell him, to know that he was mine.

He pulled away and looked into my face, his old tears still visible on his cheeks.

"I'm sorry that I didn't let it go."

He shook his head. "You had every right to be upset. It was my fault for being a coward."

"You are not a coward, Aurelias." I looked into his eyes, seeing a man I admired as much as my father. "You're the most courageous man I've ever met." No other man would do as much for me as he had. He pledged his life to me, and he couldn't even marry me. He did all this so someone else would have me someday in the future.

"I'm required elsewhere, but all I want to do is make love to you."

After this long separation, it was all I wanted too. "We have all night..."

His eyes bored into mine, like he was tempted to sweep me off my feet and carry me to the bed. "All night it is."

TWENTY-TWO
AURELIAS

I stepped into my father's tent, seeing my brothers there, all healed from the feeding.

I could tell my father was in a sour mood—and not just because I could feel his emotions.

He sat behind the desk and stared at me, accusation in his eyes. "I lost nearly all the vampires I gave you."

"I know."

"Good vampires. Vampires who deserved eternity. But they're dead—forever—because of you."

My brothers all looked at me but said nothing.

"I feel like shit about that."

"Do you?" my father asked incredulously. "We sailed all the way here to fight a battle that doesn't belong to us...all for pussy." He crossed his arms over his chest. "When there's perfectly good pussy back at home—"

"Do not refer to her like that again." My insides tightened in discomfort because it made me sick. I loved to fuck her brains out and she was a hot piece of ass, but only I could think those things. No one else.

"Our people are dead, and you choose to defend her?" He cocked an eyebrow.

"I made the decision to fight, so insult me, not her."

Father stared me down. The tension in the room rose like smoke to the ceiling. "Leave us."

My brothers stood up from their chairs and walked out, leaving us alone.

When they were gone, my father continued his assault. "Will this woman be returning with us?"

I didn't want to answer.

"Will she be your wife?"

"She would be my wife…if things were different."

Anger seethed under his skin. "If what were different?"

"She's human." I wouldn't go into the details that he already knew. "We know what happened last time I loved a human."

"So you're willing to risk all of us for a woman you won't marry?"

"Not *won't*. Can't."

"This is stupid—"

"*Then leave*," I snapped. "You're under no obligation."

"If I pull out the army, all of these people will die, including you."

"Then so be it," I said simply. "She dies, I die."

He continued to stare at me with a note of bewilderment. "I won't abandon you, Aurelias. Or my other sons. But I want something in return. I'll be putting my life on the line to fight these demons. If this woman won't be your wife, then I need to be compensated."

"What do you want?"

My father stared for a long time.

"Name your price."

"I'll let you know when I have it." That was all he said, staring me down like I was an enemy rather than his own flesh and blood. "Be ready."

We prepared the field for battle, knowing the demons would arrive without warning. That meant soldiers would be on rotation as they stood on the line, torches lit up across the field so they could see even if it was dark. The dragons were ready with their boulders. And the vampires didn't need time to prepare since they were physically superior to their human counterparts.

I walked up to Huntley, who stood on the line in his full armor, which had been replaced since his last set had been damaged by Vine's golden sword. Instead of sitting in the warmth of his study or lounging in the great room, he was on the walls with his people, ready for the imminent war.

He turned to me, and there was an undertone of respect and affection to his gaze. It was the way he looked at Harlow and Atticus, a flood of warmth inside his chest. "I have something for you." He turned away and called out to someone. "Elora!"

A woman came from around the corner of the gate. "What?"

"Bring the armor."

She turned and walked off, and then returned a moment later with a brand-new set of armor, which was identical to what Huntley wore—except for the golden serpent on the front. "We've outfitted your brothers, too, since their armor was badly damaged in the east. We would be honored if you wore it."

When I looked at it more closely, I saw the dragon in the background, the symbol of their kingdom. Wordlessly, I took the chest piece from her and fastened it to my body, and it was a perfect fit. "I don't know what to say." It was an expensive gift, something only the king wore.

Huntley patted me on the shoulder. "Don't say anything —just put it on."

Before I walked to the front door, I felt her mind.

I felt her desperation, the arousal that ached between her legs. It was a distinct sensation, heat from the summer sun right on the back of my neck. I stayed in front of the door and absorbed it, so struck by her desire that I was immobile. She wanted me before I even came into the room, so anxious she'd gotten started without me.

My dick was hard when I walked in the door. Naked on the bed with the thin sheets barely concealing her body, she lay there, her hand still between her legs.

I dropped the pieces of armor as quickly as possible and stripped down to my bare skin before I approached the edge of the bed. I grabbed her by the ankle and dragged her to me, bringing her ass slightly over the edge.

"I'm sorry..."

I folded her at the edge and pinned one of her feet against my chest before I sank inside her, smeared with the wetness that had started without me. It felt so good that it felt like the first time, like I'd never been with her before. "Baby, I'm here now." My hand dug into her hair and fisted it while she held on to my shoulders and arms.

I thrust into her hard and fast, doing the opposite of making love to her, but it'd been so long since I'd had her that I couldn't slow down. I just wanted to thrust over and over, make her little body shake underneath me, listen to her moan as I pushed her to the edge of her climax. She'd already hovered there before I'd walked in the door, so she was ready to come once I was inside her —and she did.

"Aurelias..." Her head rolled back, and the sexy tears streaked down.

I tightened my grip on her hair and forced her stare back on me, watching the tears fall from her eyes to her ears. I fucked her like I'd paid for her for the night, except my heart was full of love instead of lust. She didn't seem to mind, the dry spell torture for her too. With a heavy moan, I filled her, gave her a week's worth of a load in a single release.

Her hand cupped my face, and her thumb brushed my bottom lip as she stared at me. "Now you can make love to me..."

My arms were locked behind her knees as I kept her folded underneath me, her little body so bendable. Hours had passed, and we had been locked together all that time, kissing, touching, moving our bodies together because they were still soaking wet. It was the first time

I'd really made love to her because now she knew who I really was.

When I told her the truth, I'd expected her to be appalled...and afraid. But neither of those emotions burned in her body. In some complex way, she seemed to love me more. There were no sour eyes of judgment.

I wish I'd told her sooner.

"I don't think I can come again." Her tightness had been taking me all night, and once the morning came, she would be too sore to have me again.

"Come on, baby." I tilted my pelvis to grind against her, to give her my kiss and my tongue. The sheets were wet and sticky from our sweat and the wetness that dripped down her slit to the bed below. I ground into her harder, pushing her clit with enough force to make her inch toward the edge.

She began to moan into my mouth, starting off small then slowly growing louder, more demanding. Her fingers dug into my sweaty hair as her hips moved back against mine, fighting for that friction that made her tighten around me.

"Almost there..." I could feel her grip me like a firm fist. I could feel the tremble of her lips as she started to pant. My dick hardened inside her because now I wanted to come. My ego burst with my accomplishment, and now I was right at the edge of release.

Her beautiful moans sounded in the stone cottage, masking the sound of the dying flames in the hearth. She grabbed on to me as she writhed, as her nails scratched down my chest. Her hips gave uncontrollable thrusts as she finished, her eyes wet again.

I let myself go, filling her so many times I'd lost count through the hours. It was our longest session, the best make-up sex I'd ever had. I'd been on top of her the entire time because I missed being between those soft thighs with her little body below me. But now the fatigue crept into my veins.

I rolled off her, my head hitting the pillow for the first time that night.

She immediately moved into my body and ignored the sweat that coated us both. She pressed a kiss to my shoulder and closed her eyes, drifting off to sleep almost immediately. Her breathing changed right away.

I stared at the moving shadows on the ceiling and felt my eyes grow heavy. The world was so quiet, just the flames in the hearth. It was easy to forget everything that had happened, everything that was bound to happen, and just drift off in peace.

But then the horn sounded...and that peace was gone forever.

TWENTY-THREE
HUNTLEY

It was an hour before sunrise.

The horn sounded from the scouts in the distance, so the guards sounded our horn as well, alerting everyone in HeartHolme that battle had arrived on our doorstep. I wasn't sleeping in my bedchambers, staying in the barracks with the other soldiers, taking naps here and there. I knew there would be limited warning for the attack, and it wasn't right to expect my men to be on guard all day and night if I weren't willing to do the same.

But now, it had arrived.

There was a jolt of excitement in my heart, not because I enjoyed the rush of battle, but because it was almost over.

This nightmare was almost over.

We could get our lives back. Rebuild our world. Mourn the dead. My children could have the peaceful lives I wanted for them. My wife and I could have our quiet evenings again, our adventures on Pyre when we ventured into the countryside where no one would ever find us.

My brother joined me on the wall. "Are they in sight?"

"No. But they'll be here soon."

He was in identical armor, his heavy sword across his back, and he looked out at the torches. "They're stupid for coming here."

I looked down at the vampire encampment. Once the horn had sounded, they'd immediately readied themselves for battle, leaving their tents in their blades and armor. Different vampires wore different colors, just like Aurelias's brothers. King Serpentine was the most distinguished, his armor different from all the rest. Like me, he would fight alongside his people, and while I didn't like him personally, I respected his leadership.

"They won't stand a chance against the vampires."

Without them to fight with us, we would have been demolished. The only reason the Kingdoms would survive was because Aurelias loved my daughter. I would always fight for my people, but I knew in my heart we would have fallen to the demons without Aurelias. If he hadn't taken Harlow, someone else would have—and we'd all be dead right now.

Aurelias appeared beside me, dressed in the armor we had gifted him, giving him the symbol of his people along with ours. He looked out into the darkness, seeing much farther than we could. "Let's finish this."

Atticus walked down the ramparts and came to my side, a grown man like all the others, but somehow still a boy in my eyes. He was as muscular as I was, inherited my hard jaw and cold stare, but I could still see him smile as I threw him in the air and caught him again. He looked serious now, responding to the call of battle.

I grabbed him by the shoulder. "We'll win this battle, but fight like you might lose."

He nodded.

I wanted to keep him safe with Ivory and Harlow, to shield him from the horrors of war, but why should I ask my people to risk their sons in battle but not my own? As much as it pained me to risk my only boy, he needed to understand that life was about serving others, not being served.

Storm's voice came into my head. *We're ready.*

"The dragons have the boulders ready," I said. "Let's head onto the field." I turned to Ian. "Lead the archers."

"General Atticus will protect the wall while we join ranks," Ian said.

My son was now the only general after both Henry and Macabre had passed. It had slipped my mind. "Let's go."

We moved down to the main gate, which was still open to allow soldiers to pass onto the open field. That was where we met Kingsnake and Cobra, both wearing the same armor we'd gifted to Aurelias.

"I'm ready to go home," Cobra said.

"Me too," Kingsnake said. "Who knows what shit Viper has gotten into…"

Aurelias smirked. "Maybe he'll loosen up for once."

"Or his ass has gotten tighter." Cobra walked alongside his brothers out onto the field, to fight another battle that didn't affect them whatsoever. But they came for Aurelias, who stayed for my daughter.

A pain dropped in my heart when I knew how this would end, that Aurelias would return home and leave my daughter with a broken heart.

He must have felt it because he turned back to look at me.

I avoided his stare and moved forward, knowing I had more important things to worry about right now.

We reached the front of the line, where King Serpentine stood in black armor with the golden serpent on his chest. He took one look at his sons, and the disdain was heavy on his face, repulsed that they were outfitted in armor built by humans. If I hadn't needed him to keep my people alive, I'd have a couple things to say.

Aurelias stood beside his father and didn't speak, his sword over his back as he tightened his gloves.

We stood there for a while, just waiting, and then the sound of their heavy footfalls became audible. Their masses were visible minutes later, a long line of demons that ran straight toward us.

Begin.

Storm took the lead and flew forward, a massive boulder clutched in his talons. He swooped over them and dropped the rock directly on the line, smashing them under the weight. The other dragons came, all following his lead, dropping massive rocks that made the earth shake.

They continued to run, their ranks breaking as they dodged the boulders that fell from the sky. Now when they perished, they were truly gone, no longer immortal. We would never see them again.

They came closer, their war cries louder, the vibrations from their boots loud.

I readied my sword.

Everyone else did the same, bringing their weapons forward to meet the onslaught.

My heart had slowed way down, bringing myself to an eerie calm. Demons a foot taller than me were running me down to cut my head from my shoulders, but I wasn't afraid. I knew this would be over, whether I survived or not. My family would be safe. My wife would be a widow and my children would be without a father, but that would be the worst outcome.

I could accept that.

I was the first to step forward, brandishing my sword to strike down the first demon who came my way. When I was close enough, I realized the difference. They hadn't worn armor before, but now they did—and it was made of solid gold.

This battle might not be as easily won as I hoped.

The lines crashed together, and the battle ensued. A demon swung his heavy blade right for my head, and I ducked, striking my blade against his gold armor and immediately bouncing off.

"Go for the neck!" Aurelias shouted from feet away.

His neck wasn't easily accessible, not when he was a foot taller than me, so I blocked his hits and stayed alive but caused no injury in return. They were more formidable than before because now they had more to lose. The demon moved with powerful speed, crashing down on me and forcing me to dodge rather than fight. When I was knocked on my back, I swiped my sword at his ankle, and that luckily brought him to one knee. It only lasted for a second, but it was enough time for me to jump up and slice my blade across his neck. It only went halfway through, but the damage was done. The blood poured from the wound once I tugged my sword free. He collapsed and bled into the dirt.

But that was only one...and I had hundreds to go.

The dragons continued to drop their boulders and decimate dozens of demons at once, but with their golden armor, they were a much harder foe than I'd anticipated. If they'd worn this armor at the last battle, we probably would have lost.

We were slowly being driven back, pushed against our own gate because their assault was so intense. But the closer we came, the easier it was for the archers to help us. The arrows rained down on our opponents, piercing them in the neck. It took at least twelve arrows in the neck to bring them down, so it was still a challenge to fell them. But our men were starting to get crushed against the wall because we were being driven back so much.

"Forward!" I tried to push the demons back to avoid the screams that came from behind me, but their armor was nearly impenetrable. When I looked at the vampires, they were having an easier time taking them down, but it still wasn't an easy victory.

"*Roooaaaaarrrr!*"

I looked to the sky, seeing Storm's silhouette appear in the light of dawn, and then a line of fire torched the demons in the front. He flew across their entire defense, unleashing a powerful stream of fire that nearly burned me, just from being so close. *They're invulnerable to fire, Storm.*

But gold is not.

I looked at the demon in front of me. The armor had lost its structure and was slowly melting off his skin... becoming liquid.

You're brilliant, Storm.

Your wife is the brilliant one.

The rest of the dragons came, continuing to burn the demons and melt off their armor until it dropped to the soil. With a smirk on my face, I pushed forward, unleashing a fury of blows that felled my opponent in just a few seconds.

The demons behind him no longer looked jubilant. In fact, they looked scared.

Fucking scared.

"Forward!" I raised my sword in the air and commanded my men to rush ahead. We swarmed them, moving away from the gate as the dragons dropped additional boulders, their armor worthless. The demons were hard opponents even without the armor, but once they lost their defense, their hits and blocks became careless. The arrows fired down and took them out in quick succession. Soon, we were too far away from the wall for our arrows to reach, and we pushed back the remaining demons.

The ones in the rear tried to flee.

"Let none escape!" No demon would live while I remained king. They wouldn't crawl back to their cave and regroup. They would all die—and we would have peace. "Get them all!"

I chased down the final group of demons and brought them down with the men who followed me. Not a single one escaped. Not a single demon would leave after decimating my people, after burning my wife, after destroying the peaceful world I'd forged. Blood had splattered all over me, and my armor was nicked from all the hits I'd taken.

I was tired...but fuck, it was over.

I dropped to my knees and looked out to the world beyond, the water crystals in the soil that reflected the sunshine. The dead trees with the sharp branches. The snowy mountains far in the distance. It was the first real breath I'd taken in a long time...but there was still the weight of grief.

More men had died in this battle. And many more had already been slain. Our world had just become much smaller. There were now twice as many women as men because so many had died. While I would rejoice in victory, it still felt like a loss.

A hand landed on my shoulder.

Without looking, I knew who it was.

"I know." My brother's voice was gentle. "I know…"

I continued to stare ahead, my sword impaled in the dirt in front of me. "How many did we lose?"

"Maybe a quarter…"

I released a painful sigh.

"But it's over."

"I'm not sure how to rebuild after this."

"Just be grateful there is a world to rebuild." He pulled his hand away from my shoulder and extended it to me so he could pull me up.

I hesitated before I took it, wanting to stay on my knees forever and avoid the aftermath of war. But I took it and let him hoist me up. I grabbed my sword, and we turned back to the castle together, our swords still in our grip.

When we approached, medics were in the field getting the injured on stretchers. Harlow was one of them, bandaging up the wound of a fallen soldier. I let her do her duty and approached the gate. Aurelias and his brothers had survived. So had his father, who stood off to the side as he spoke to his general.

Atticus came up to me, not a scratch on him. "You alright?"

It was a complicated question to answer. "Yes...physically."

"At least it's over now. There's no one else coming."

I nodded as I gave him a one-armed hug. "I hope this is the only war you'll ever know. And your children will never know one at all." I released him then walked to my wife, who'd been anxious to greet me ever since she'd seen me walk through the gate. Her eyes shone with emotion, not just because I'd come back to her, but because the war had finally come to an end.

I enveloped her in my arms, and she collapsed against me, like she'd lost the will to be strong, finally allowed her body to be defeated by the grief and the anguish.

I held her against me, my chin on her head, and stood there for a long time, not in any hurry to be anywhere else. My family was safe. Our kingdom was victorious. Now it was time to heal. "You saved us...with the gold."

She didn't acknowledge the compliment, and she would never acknowledge it. She pulled away and looked at me, her hands cupping my cheeks and wiping away the spots of blood. "What can I do for you?"

"All I want is a hot shower...and some pot roast."

Despite the sadness in her eyes, her lips tugged up in a smile. "Come on, let's go."

TWENTY-FOUR
AURELIAS

Harlow was on the battlefield, helping a soldier clean his wound with antiseptic before she wrapped the gauze tight around his arm. He gave a grimace in pain at the pressure before he wiggled his fingers to make sure he could still move.

I stood behind her and waited for an opportunity to speak with her, not wanting to interrupt her work. She didn't discriminate with her patients, helping vampires too. Soldiers worked to place the dead onto the pyre to burn, while everyone else tried to save as many people as they could. The demons were left where they fell, a problem for a different day.

When she stood up and turned, she noticed me, and the flush of emotion that flooded her was intoxicating. She moved to me, a bag of supplies over her shoulder, her hands dirty from the patients she'd touched. That was probably why she didn't cup my cheeks like she normally would. "I'm glad you're okay."

I dipped my head and kissed her. "Need any help?"

"No," she said. "You already did your part."

I wanted to shower with her then sleep side by side in our bed. I didn't want to say a word, just be together. I probably should feed, but I didn't even want to do that. All I wanted was her...especially now that our time together would soon be over. But I knew she would never abandon her duty—and I would never ask her to.

"Your brothers are okay?"

"They're fine," I said. "My father too. We lost very few vampires."

"I noticed. That's good to hear."

"You lost a lot more of your own."

"But that was expected."

"After I speak with my father, I'm going to shower and rest. Wake me up when you get back." I was dead tired, but I would never be too tired to hold her and kiss her, to treasure her beside me.

"I will."

I leaned down and kissed her again. "I love you."

"I love you too." She said it against my lips, her eyes on mine.

I wouldn't have very many opportunities to tell her that anymore. I didn't think about the end of our relationship much in the throes of the battles and conflicts, but now that we were on the other side of them, that was all that was left. I'd done my job and protected her...and now it was time to go.

I walked away and found my father minutes later. His guard stepped in my way and wouldn't allow me to enter —and I knew that was because my father was preoccupied with his favorite whore. Not that he was fucking her...but feeding from her.

I should do the same, but I tried to fight it.

The guard eventually allowed me to pass, and I stepped inside his tent, the naked woman passed out on the bed with drops of blood on the pillow.

Father had already taken off his armor and wore only his trousers, not bothered by the cold. There were a few bruises on his arms from the hits he'd taken, but other than that, he looked perfectly fine. He opened a bottle on his desk and poured a glass to wash down the remaining blood in his mouth. He glanced at the woman before he looked at me again. "Would you like some?"

I didn't look at the woman. "I'm okay."

"I can tell you haven't fed."

"I'll do that later."

He poured another glass and slid it across the desk toward me. "You got your victory."

"We lost good men." I grabbed the glass and took a drink.

"And a few good vampires." He sat behind his desk. He was several decades older than me, but the snake venom had smoothed out his skin and made him youthful, looking more like an older brother than a father. Getting the attention of prey was as easy for him as it was for me. His older age actually made him more appealing in some ways.

"Yes."

He stared at me. "Now what?"

I stared at the glass in my head, dreading the answer. "Nothing."

"We just leave?"

I nodded. "You can leave as soon as you want."

"And you?"

"I'll leave…eventually." I didn't have a particular time or date. "I guess whenever Kingsnake and Cobra leave."

He poured himself another glass. "Their dragons are exquisite."

"They are."

"And they have many of them."

I continued to stare at the glass.

"Very impressive."

"If the demons weren't invulnerable to fire, this battle would have been over before it started."

Father stared at me, his eyes hard and intense. "Indeed."

I finished off the rest of the contents and set the glass on the table.

"With the power of the dragons and the power of the crystal, King Rolfe would be the mightiest king that ever lived."

My eyes lifted to look at him. "Even if there was a crystal beneath this soil, he would never use it."

"Men are easily tempted by power."

"Not him," I said proudly. "He's happy with what he has."

My father stared at me, his body an empty vessel. There was no emotion to him, just darkness. It was like he purposely restrained his true emotions so I couldn't feel them, but I couldn't imagine why.

"Thank you for coming," I said. "I really appreciate it... more than words can say."

His stare didn't change.

Our closeness and camaraderie were long gone. He looked at me exactly the way he regarded Kingsnake.

"Rest and recover. We'll talk about our departure in a couple days." I stood and placed the empty glass on the corner of the desk. "And thanks for the drink."

I was dead asleep when I felt her on top of me. Her soft thighs straddled my hips, and she planted her hands against my chest.

I opened my eyes to see her above me, her hair damp because she'd just gotten out of the shower, buck naked with her tits right above me. My hands moved for her hips, and I rolled her over, moving on top of her so I could smother her in kisses, still half asleep but instantly aroused by her smell and the soft touch of her flesh. I kissed her tits and moved down her stomach, traveling lower until I found the lips I wanted to kiss.

I knew she would be sore after our long rendezvous in the middle of the night, so I kissed her instead, tasted her sweetness as I made her pant in pleasure. When she was finished, her little mouth would be around my dick, sucking me hard with those plump lips.

Her fingers dug into my hair as she rocked her hips into me, immediately loving my kiss, her nipples pointed high to the ceiling.

I was tired and sore, not fully awake even as I sucked her nub into my mouth, but I'd rather be delirious and awake with her than lose these moments we had together, because soon, we wouldn't have them anymore…

I was asleep with her in my arms when someone pounded on the door.

"Aurelias!"

The pounding happened again, so loud it shook the entire cottage.

I jerked awake, and she did the same, giving a gasp in fright. The curtains were drawn over the windows, but the sunlight poked through, like it was sometime in the middle of the day.

"Aurelias, open the fucking door!" It was Cobra, trying to turn the locked doorknob.

"Shit, I'm coming." I got out of bed and moved for my clothes.

This time, he threw his body against it, nearly breaking it off the hinges.

I ditched the clothes altogether and opened the door. "*What?*"

Cobra toppled over the threshold and nearly fell to the floor.

I slammed the door. "*What the fuck is so important?*"

Harlow was still in the bed, the covers pulled over her body to hide her nakedness.

I knew whatever it was, it was serious because Cobra didn't make a single joke about my hard dick hanging out. "Father…" He took a second to catch his breath. "He's—he's taken over HeartHolme."

"What?" I exclaimed.

Harlow's response was the same. "What?"

"Kingsnake tried to stop him, but Father locked him up under the castle. Larisa, Clara, and Fang too. I got away…"

I blinked several times because I couldn't process anything he'd just said, either because I was exhausted or shocked. "I—I don't understand."

"He's gonna kill Huntley if he doesn't yield."

Harlow was out of bed, dropping the sheets in front of Cobra because she didn't give a fuck about her vanity right now.

"How the fuck did this happen?" I snapped.

"The soldiers were exhausted, so they slept…there were no guards on post because there was no more threat… everyone else went to bed…so he marched into Heart-Holme with the vampires and took out all the guards and imprisoned anyone who resisted them."

I couldn't believe it. Was it all just a dream?

"We've got to do something fast," Cobra said. "Because they're hot on my tail, and they're going to grab us both in about forty-five seconds."

"My ass, they are." Harlow was dressed in her uniform with her sword at her hip. "Come on, Aurelias."

I pulled on the uniform and armor I'd dropped on the floor, dressing quickly and hooking my sword into place.

Cobra manned the door, checking the peephole to look for the soldiers. "They're coming." He stepped back and withdrew his sword.

I did the same. "Harlow, stay out of the way."

"Don't fucking tell me to stay out of the way!" she hissed.

The door flew open, and twelve vampires came in. Clive was in the lead, my father's general. "Aurelias, we don't want to hurt you. So let's just skip the theatrics—"

"I strike to kill, Clive. I will kill every one of you if you stand in my way. So I suggest you move and let us pass."

Clive gave me a frustrated stare.

"Move."

"I can't do that."

"*He's insane.*"

"He has his reasons, and they are good reasons."

"I ask him to fight for the woman I love, and all he sees is an opportunity?" I asked incredulously. "This is ludicrous."

Clive kept his hand on the hilt of his sword. "You can't stop this. So just surrender—"

I struck with my blade. "I warned you."

His blade met mine, and Cobra and I were quickly in battle with twelve-on-two. I sliced Clive down the arm then kicked him so hard his back hit the stone fireplace. He went limp, unconscious but not dead. Cobra defeated one of the other guards, and Harlow grabbed one of the logs from the fireplace and knocked out the one closest to her.

The others stopped and took a step back.

"Let us pass," I ordered. "Or we'll kill all of you and *then* pass."

They exchanged a quick look before they sheathed their swords and stepped out of the way.

"Good call." Cobra went first.

Harlow and I went next and ran to the castle. We could see the difference already along the way, vampire guards posted in different districts, and when we got to the castle, there were no humans, just vampires.

I kept Harlow behind me as Cobra and I struck the vampire guards down before we entered the castle.

"The throne room." Cobra led the way, taking me up the stairs and to the right, killing our own kind along the way until we reached the throne room, a room I'd never seen because Huntley seemed to never step foot in the place.

It was a horrific sight. Huntley was bound by his ankles and his wrists, on his knees on the floor while my father held a blade to his neck. I saw two red marks on his neck and a streak of blood, like someone had already fed on him. Behind my father stood one of his commanders, Ravine, blood in the corner of her mouth.

Ivory wasn't in the room, so she must have been ordered away.

"Let him go!" Harlow sprinted into the room with her sword in hand, ready to take on my father—which would end in disaster.

Huntley's face contorted in terror as he saw her rush to him. "No!" His scream was nothing compared to the agony inside his chest, the indescribable terror a father felt in fear for his daughter.

My father felt Harlow's murderous intention and turned the sword on her instead. It happened so fast, my father feeling no empathy for her whatsoever, ready to strike her down. Huntley tried to rise, but all he did was tip over and scream.

I got there in time, blocking my father's sword with mine and shoving her back so hard she rolled across the rug.

My father stared at me.

I stared back.

He was the first one to pull away, but he didn't turn his back to me.

Huntley looked at Harlow and mouthed to her, "Run."

She remained on the rug, angry tears in her eyes.

I lowered my sword but kept it in my hand. "*What. The. Fuck. Are. You. Doing?*" I said every word slower than I normally would, pissed off and overwhelmed by his betrayal. My father had questionable moral fiber, but I'd never expected him to be this traitorous. "I asked you to save them—"

"And I did. I have no intention of hurting or killing these people."

"Then cut the king's bindings and let him stand."

Father glanced at Huntley on the floor, who was bruised and bloody from the battle he'd lost with my kind. "He's no longer King of HeartHolme or King of Kingdoms." He pressed his hand to his chest. "I am."

"You're fucked in the head, you know that?"

My father grinned like that was a compliment. "I saved them from annihilation. Now it's time to pay the price. These are my lands now—and so are the dragons."

"The dragons belong to no one," Harlow snapped. "They will turn on you the second you try—"

"*Harlow.*" Huntley tried to silence her with his suppressed growl.

"If they don't cooperate." Father pressed the blade to Huntley's neck again, close enough to make him bleed.

Harlow started to cry again. "Please stop."

"Sweetheart, I'm okay," Huntley said calmly, caring more about being there for her than his own demise.

"Then I'll slay their beloved hero," Father said, the tip of his blade remaining against Huntley's skin. "We'll dig to find those crystals. Not only will we be immortal—*but invincible.*"

I had to make this stop. "Father, you're King of Kingdoms in our lands. How much more power do you need?"

"All of it," he said simply. "All the power."

"Mother would be disgusted with you." I was disgusted with myself for siding with him for all these years. For treating humans so unkindly when they were far better than we were.

"We'll never know," he said without emotion. "Because her soul has been used like logs in a hearth."

"And this makes you feel better?" I asked in disbelief. "I fought for the woman I love, and you dismantle everything I did—"

"You said you wouldn't marry her."

"*What does that have to do with anything?*"

"Because she's not family. And family is the only code I honor."

"Then I'll marry her," I snapped. "I'll fucking marry her right now. Stop this bullshit."

He didn't take the sword away from Huntley's throat. "Too late, son."

"You're so full of it. Even if I made her a vampire and married her, you'd still pull this stunt—"

"You're probably right." He looked down at Huntley, a slight smirk on his lips. "Aurelias, we've always been better than the scum we call humans. They're good for very few things—feeding and fucking. Unlike your brothers, we've always been in agreement about this. Don't let one good lay change your perception."

Anger slithered down my spine.

Father looked at me, like he could feel my rage and was amused by it.

"Aurelias." Huntley spoke with a calm voice. "Get Harlow out of here."

"I think that's wise," Father said. "No daughter should have to watch her father be executed."

Harlow choked back a sob.

"Father." I raised my hand slightly. "Take the blade off his neck and step back."

Father dug the blade in deeper, made the line of blood thicker.

"Stop," Harlow begged. "Please stop."

I stepped forward. "Stop. For me. Please."

Father relaxed the pressure. "I came all the way here for you, Aurelias. And you would ask more of me?" Both of his eyes rose at my request, like I was in the wrong here.

"How can you rule two continents at once?"

"*With dragons*," Father said, his answer already prepared. "With my oldest son, Prince of Kingdoms, ruling in my absence. We would do this together, Aurelias. We would rule two worlds...and then three...and then four."

"I don't share your ambitions, Father. There's only so much fucking and so much feeding we can do."

He grinned. "Well, we have all of eternity to try."

I kept my hand up. "I'm begging you, Father. I'll get on my knees right now and do whatever the fuck you want... just let him go."

His eyes narrowed in offense. "What is your fascination with this man? I'm the strongest vampire who's ever lived, and yet, you care about this man on his knees with his face to the floor."

"Is that what this is about?" I asked quietly. "You're jealous?"

"I'm jealous of no human."

"But you're jealous of my respect for him, respect that he's earned. I'm sorry if my admiration for his integrity and his courage threatens you. Perhaps if you had more kindness and empathy, I would feel the same way toward you." The last thing I should do was piss off my father, but the words tumbled out. "Now take your fucking sword off his neck and let him go."

"You want me to take the sword away?" He turned to Huntley, moving around until he was in position to swipe his head clean from his shoulders. "Huntley, give me your word that you revoke your title as king and grant it to me. That you'll live your life as a mere citizen to obey my command. That you'll never try to reclaim the title with force or secrecy. Give me your word—and I'll let you go."

Huntley's answer was immediate. "*No*."

I'd expected no other answer.

Father looked at me. "He had his chance."

"No!" Harlow pushed to her feet. "Stop!"

Father lifted his sword to slice it through Huntley's neck.

All Huntley cared about was his daughter. "Sweetheart, it's okay."

My father slammed the sword down.

I only had a second to react. My sword wouldn't stop his at this angle. I did the only thing that made sense—and I jumped on top of Huntley.

The sword stuck my back instantly, the weapon being wielded with so much momentum that I crashed into Huntley. The armor he'd gifted me was as strong as he claimed—because the blade didn't pass through. The hit was hard enough to knock the air out of my lungs and leave a bruise that would last weeks, but it didn't kill me. I got to my feet and pushed my father back, raising my sword to block the sword that was coming.

Ravine joined the fight, coming at me alongside my father.

"Cobra!"

"I got them!" He ran forward to Huntley and cut his bindings. Harlow was there too, sobbing on top of her father.

I battled them both, having a surge of strength I'd never had before, rage coupled with sheer insanity. Even my father was surprised, his eyes widening at the flurry of hits I rained down on them both.

Sssnake killer. Fang sprang into action and jumped on Ravine, wrapping his body around her neck and squeezing her so hard, he snapped her spine. She crumpled to the floor. Kingsnake and the others rushed into the room, fighting the vampires who were the most loyal to my father.

I wanted to check on Harlow, but to counter my father's lethal attacks, I needed to give him my full focus. Our blades moved faster than they could be watched, and I had to rely on his emotions to anticipate attacks and make my own. Normally, he would mask his thoughts and feelings, but the battle was so heated, he didn't have the energy for it. I didn't mask mine either because I couldn't.

He caught me off guard by punching me hard in the face.

I stumbled back, and he pushed his advantage, his blade striking me down. "How dare you raise your sword to me."

I blocked his sword with mine and pushed, pushed against his weight as our eyes remained locked together. "Stop this. Please."

He pulled away then struck at me again. All of his blows were to wound, not to kill.

"I don't want to kill you."

"Then surrender." He didn't stop. In fact, it spurred him on, giving him more energy.

Sssnake killer. Fang slithered forward to slide up his body.

Fang, no. I knew my father wouldn't hesitate to kill him. *Help the others.*

"*Hiiisssssss.*" Fang did as I asked and moved away.

"Are you going to kill me?" my father mocked.

Our battle stopped momentarily, and we circled each other.

"You aren't leaving me a choice."

"I brought our armies to these shores, and this is how you repay me?"

"Stop this madness, and we can forget it ever happened," I said. "We can go back home and live our lives. These are good people."

"No such thing, Aurelias."

"I've only loved three women my whole life—and they were all human."

He stilled, knowing my mother was the third one.

"Stop. Don't make me do this—"

He rushed me, his blows cranked to a new level, flying through the air and aimed at my neck. He'd aimed to wound before, but now, he aimed to kill. I was the only thing that stood in the way of his domination, and if he didn't remove me from the situation, he wouldn't get what he wanted. He made his decision.

So I made mine.

I faked to my right, slammed my sword down on his to make the opening, and then my blade went straight through his neck.

I turned away before I saw anything.

But I heard it. I heard his head hit the floor. Then the rest of his body, the sound of his armor striking the hardwood floor. Fighting still carried on in different parts of the room, but I couldn't see it. My sight was blurry...blurry with tears.

I fell to my knees, overcome with the weight of my decision, what lay behind me.

I'd killed Renee...and now I'd killed my own father.

Someone moved in front of me, but I couldn't make out their face. I couldn't even see the floor. The room went silent. A powerful hand moved to my shoulder, and then slowly, my gaze sharpened.

It was Huntley.

His eyes ached with pain as he looked at me, as if he could somehow have empathy after my father had tried to take his kingdom and his head. "I'm sorry." His other hand went to my other shoulder to support me because I started to tip over. "I'm sorry, son." He moved into me and hugged me, hugged me hard like he did with his own son, a bear hug that squeezed and squeezed.

I continued to stare at the floor, the tears so heavy they streaked down my cheeks. I was numb but simultaneously overcome with grief. Despite the fact that it had just happened, my mind already tried to pretend that I hadn't been the one to do it. That someone else had killed him and I didn't get there in time. My father was the only parent I'd had left...and now I had no parents.

Huntley pulled away and looked at me, like he wanted to say something but he had no words. Kingsnake and Cobra approached, and that was when he took his leave to give us space.

I remained on my knees, my bloody sword on the floor beside me.

My brothers each took a knee to be eye level with me.

I didn't meet their gazes, too ashamed of what I'd done. "I—I didn't know what else to do..."

Neither of them spoke.

I clenched my eyes shut for several seconds to stop the tears. When I looked at the floor again, they were dry... but the heat was still in my throat. "I'm sorry."

Kingsnake's voice was gentle. "It's okay, Aurelias."

"It's not okay."

Fang slithered to us, snaking up my body and wrapping around my shoulders as a sign of comfort. ***He wasss a sssnake killer.***

"Fang, not now," Kingsnake said without looking at him. "After we absorbed the Ethereal and defeated the werewolves, Father took over all the Kingdoms and proclaimed himself the king of all Kingdoms, which we thought was unnecessary. If we hadn't challenged him against the Ethereal—innocent people who weren't even aware of their crimes—he would have slaughtered them all. Perhaps he'd been a vampire so long that he'd forgotten his humanity altogether."

"He needed to be stopped," Cobra said. "This probably would have happened anyway."

"Some people change—like you," Kingsnake said. "But some people don't."

My eyes remained on the floor.

Kingsnake moved his hand to my shoulder. "Brother."

My eyes lifted automatically.

"You made the right decision." Kingsnake said it with the confidence of a king. "Instead of coming to his son's aid, he came to this land with an agenda. He's always been an opportunist. He should have respected your love for Harlow, regardless if that love would last forever."

"But—but now we have no father…"

Kingsnake exchanged a look with Cobra.

Cobra clapped me on the other shoulder. "But we have one another."

TWENTY-FIVE
AURELIAS

A lot happened in that moment.

Harlow and Ivory were so relieved that Huntley was unharmed that they spent several long moments together rejoicing as a family. The soldiers took my father's body from the room to either burn him or bury him, but it was probably just to spare me the pain of what I'd done.

Harlow broke away from her family then looked at me.

I felt the dramatic shift, the relief transform into a fiery cataclysm of pain. As she came close, the sheen over her eyes was visible, accompanied by the agony in her heart. I knew the misery she harbored was for me, for the horrible thing I'd done and could never take back...the horrible thing I'd done for her.

She moved into my arms and hugged me tight, squeezing me with the same strength as her father did.

My chin rested on her head, and I closed my eyes. The comfort she gave was instant, a warmth that soothed all the aches in my heart. It was like a thick blanket on a cold night. Or sunshine on a flower petal in winter. It was the comfort no one else could give, only her.

"I'm so sorry." She said it quietly against my chest, so quietly that only I could hear it.

I pressed a kiss to her forehead. "I should be the one to apologize..."

She pulled away to look me in the face, her eyes still wet. She gave a subtle shake of her head. "No."

My hand slid into her hair, and I cupped her face, seeing a woman so beautiful that it hurt my eyes. With blue eyes the same color as that crystal I'd destroyed, she was stunning. I wished I could look at her every day. I wished I could see her in the armor of our people, hundreds of years into the future, perfectly preserved like this.

But I couldn't...and that made everything hurt again.

I would return home, a home that would be forever different without my father, and sulk alone. "Is your mother okay?"

"Yes. They'd locked all of them up in the dungeon."

"How did they get out?"

"Fang pulled it off somehow."

"No surprise there." My father had always underestimated him. Despite the fact that snakes had given us these powers, he didn't treat them very kindly. Treated them the way he treated everyone else, like they were there to serve him.

Kingsnake walked up to me. "Sorry to interrupt, but I need to speak to you."

Harlow rose on her tiptoes to kiss me before she walked away.

I watched her go before I looked at my brother.

"This will sound insensitive, but due to the complexity of our situation, it's a conversation that needs to be had. You're father's successor, and now that he's gone, you're King of Kingdoms. Do you accept?"

I held my silence.

"Because orders need to be given now."

"Why would they follow me when I just murdered their king?"

"Because they know he's been unhinged for a long time."

They should turn on me for what I'd done, but not a single vampire moved against me.

Kingsnake continued to watch me. "Our purpose here is finished. The demons have been defeated. They're safe from Father's wrath. There's nothing left to do but return home, and I know we're all eager to get back."

The dreaded moment had come. It had felt so far away for so long. "Have them bury Father in the cemetery. In two days, we'll depart for the ships."

Kingsnake watched me, understanding that I had just accepted the new position. "And what will you do with the kingdoms?"

"I haven't given it any thought," I said coldly. "Because I just killed my father twenty minutes ago."

Kingsnake backed off. "We'll leave in two days."

It was hard to make love.

There were a lot of reasons for it. One, my heart was heavy with grief. It was saddled with guilt too. And two, I was fucking depressed. Depressed that I would leave her behind in two days and never see her again. I'd done all of this for her...just to leave.

She couldn't feel my emotions the way I felt hers, but I suspected she knew exactly what I was experiencing. She was in my arms in bed, her hand stroking my chest as she rested her head on my shoulder. We hadn't said much since we'd returned to the cottage, and all of our stares were heavy with words that we chose not to share. The worst was now in the past, but it felt like it was in the future.

"Aurelias." She propped her head up, her long hair falling behind her like a curtain.

"Yes, baby." My fingers automatically moved toward it, touching the silky strands.

A tightness formed in her chest, a painful lump in her throat. "I—I know we already talked about this, but..." Her eyes dropped to my chest as she lost the words. "Are you sure you can't stay?" She swallowed, keeping her eyes down to protect herself from the disappointment.

My fingers froze in her hair, unable to bring myself to answer the question.

Silence passed, and she didn't look at me.

I finally found the courage to speak. "I'm sorry, baby."

A wave of hurt moved through her, but her expression didn't change.

"If I were willing to be a vampire, would you be willing to live here?"

Just when I thought I couldn't hurt more, my pain reached new depths. "I don't want that for you."

Her eyes lifted to mine. "It's my choice—"

"No."

"My father told me he would understand..."

"He did?" I asked quietly.

She nodded.

This pain would never end. "If I won't be mortal for you, then you shouldn't be immortal for me."

"They're incomparable. It's one life for an eternal life—"

"Baby." My hand cupped her cheek. "My answer won't change."

Once she realized the future was set and she couldn't alter it, her eyes started to moisten. "Why?"

Now I was the one to avoid her gaze.

"I'm willing to do it for you so we can be together, but your answer is still no. Is it just an excuse? Is it because you don't want to settle down—"

"No." I looked at her again.

"Then why won't you change for me?" Her tears started to get heavier.

This was fucking unbearable. "Because I have three brothers, Harlow. I'll die in eighty years, and they'll carry on without me. Because I've already lived fifteen hundred years, and it passed in the blink of an eye. It's just not enough time..."

"Enough time for what?" she asked, the tears spilling over. "To screw women that you'll never love as much as me?"

"Harlow..."

She left the bed.

"Baby."

She grabbed her clothes off the floor and prepared to storm off.

I got out of bed. "When we spoke about this before, you understood—"

"Things are different now." She pulled on her bra and then her top, moving as quickly as she could, as if she couldn't get away from me fast enough.

"How are they different?"

She shoved her legs through the pant legs of her trousers and tugged them to her waist. "You killed your father to protect mine. How can you do that and then sail away, never to return?" Tears spilled down her cheeks. "How can you risk *everything* for me? And then leave?"

"My affection for your father is independent of my love for you."

She looked away and started to march out.

I put my hand on the door so she couldn't escape. "Harlow."

She tried to tug it open against my weight.

"I leave in a day, and I don't want to spend our time left fighting—"

"You don't have to leave at all." She rounded on me, pained and furious. "Why am I not worth it? If you'd died in battle, you would have lost your life and your soul. But this is too much to ask…"

I took a deep breath. "I wouldn't be the same, Harlow."

Her eyes narrowed.

"I wouldn't be as strong as I am now. I wouldn't be able to protect you the way I have. I wouldn't have been able to save your father's life because I would have been too weak to do so. I wouldn't be the same."

"My father is a human, and he fought those demons alongside you just fine."

"It was a million times harder for him than it was for me—"

"Then get better. Get stronger. Fight harder." Now she yelled. "You've fought for me this whole time, so fight for me now!"

"You don't understand—"

She marched out of the cottage.

I was still buck naked, so I couldn't follow her.

But I probably shouldn't go after her anyway.

I had no idea where Harlow went.

She wasn't in her bedchambers in the castle or the great room. I asked my brothers if they'd seen her, and they hadn't. She wasn't at the front of the castle either, nor with the dragons in the field.

This time, she didn't want me to find her.

I sat in the great room and assumed she would return to her bedchambers at dark because she'd rather sleep alone than sleep with me. There was a bottle of scotch already sitting there, so I helped myself, knowing the last time I had been this low was when Renee died. Or I'd killed her…was what I should say.

Footsteps sounded, but they were too heavy to belong to Harlow. A moment later, Huntley emerged, dressed casually in brown trousers and a black shirt. The bruises were still visible on his face from where my father had tortured him, but the light in his eyes showed nothing but peace.

He took a quick look at me and recognized my sorrow. He pulled out the chair across from me and helped himself to a glass. He took a drink then licked his lips before he relaxed in the chair, looking at me and giving me the opportunity to choose the conversation.

I refilled my glass.

Huntley asked a question he'd never asked before. "How are you?"

I cut myself off and crossed my arms. "Shitty."

He gave a subtle nod. "Anything I can do?"

I shook my head. My father had been buried in their cemetery, and Huntley had given no objection to it. Allowed me to engrave his tombstone with honor rather than corruption. He held no animosity—even though my father would have killed him and taken his kingdom if I hadn't been there.

"Things aren't good with Harlow?"

I stared at him.

"I assumed you would be with her right now since you're leaving soon."

"I think that's over..." I didn't see a scenario where we made up before I left. She'd stormed out, and based on the fact that she'd disappeared, she didn't want to make up. It would probably be easier for her if I left on these terms.

"You haven't changed your mind, then?"

I almost looked away before I shook my head. "She said you would accept her choice to become a vampire. Is that true?"

It was a simple question, but he took a long time to answer it. "Yes."

"You asked me to never turn her."

"And that was wrong of me. If Ivory's father had cared enough to have forbidden her from being with me, that wouldn't have changed a damn thing. I see the love you have for each other, and I know it's real. I would never intervene...even if that meant I would lose her."

If Harlow turned, that would fix everything. But I still couldn't do it. "She offered to be a vampire so we could be together."

Huntley's expression didn't change, but his entire being gave a jolt in pain.

"I told her no."

He did his best to keep the same expression, but it was a losing battle. Relief moved across his face. "Why?"

"Her soul is too pure. I would never allow her to forsake it. I would never allow her to give up everything that matters to her just so she could be with me, not if I'm unwilling to do the same for her. It would be wrong."

Huntley gave a slight nod. "I appreciate your integrity."

"But now, she won't speak with me, and I can't find her. Do you know where she is?"

There was a pause. "I think so. But I can't tell you, Aurelias."

Disappointment moved through me, but I hid it. "I understand."

"It's not my place to say anything, but I'm going to say it anyway." He looked me hard in the face. "Beautiful women are a dime a dozen, but a beautiful woman with a beautiful soul...that's a needle in a haystack. To find someone you love...*truly* love...is almost impossible. If I had the choice, I would choose one life with Ivory rather than eternity with someone lesser."

I stared at his face.

"Harlow will get over it eventually. She'll marry. Have children. I know time works differently for you, so it may take ten years before you realize what you lost, but by then, it'll be too late. You may live forever, but that means your regrets last forever too. Something to think about..."

I didn't want to picture her marrying somebody else. I didn't want to picture her with a swollen belly as she expected her first child. I didn't want to picture the man who had replaced me.

"Regardless of what happens between you, I want you to know that I've come to care for you deeply." Huntley said all of that without discomfort, showed more affection for me than my father ever had. "Not just because of what you've done for us, but because of your noble character and stout heart. If you married my daughter, I wouldn't love you like a son-in-law, but my own flesh and blood. It would be an honor. But if you don't marry my daughter... I'll still always see you as a son or a nephew. If you're ever in need of aid, you know HeartHolme will answer that call."

TWENTY-SIX
HARLOW

My parents had an old cottage in the village, a place they'd used when they'd first gotten together. They never stayed in it anymore because they occupied the castle when they visited, so it was mine to use whenever I wished.

That was where I stayed, knowing Aurelias would never find me. Even if he asked my father, he wouldn't get the answer he wanted. No matter how much my father cared for Aurelias, he would always be loyal to me first.

I sat in front of the fire with a broken heart, knowing I was wasting what precious little time we had left by avoiding him. But knowing he was leaving the next day made it impossible not to think about it, to put that out of my mind and live in the moment with him. Our endless nights together were long gone.

It was over.

I didn't want it to be over.

I knew I was young and would find someone else in the years to come, but I also knew that he wouldn't be Aurelias. That no matter how old I was, I would think about the vampire across the sea...the man who would always have a piece of my heart.

I didn't want that to happen.

I didn't want to settle for someone else.

I left the cottage and headed for the castle.

Kingsnake opened the door, Fang wrapped around his shoulders. He was clearly surprised. "Harlow?" His eyes shifted behind me, expecting to see Aurelias there, but it was just me. He turned to Fang on his shoulder. "Not now."

"Excuse me?"

"Sorry, Fang wanted to know if you were here to play with him."

"Oh." I smiled at him. "Maybe later."

"Everything alright?" Kingsnake asked.

"Actually...can I talk to you for a second?"

"Um, sure." He opened the door wider and allowed me inside his chambers. He was dressed casually, and when I walked farther inside, I saw Larisa was dressed similarly, wearing a long-sleeved dress.

The fire roared in the fireplace, and the curtains were drawn closed, even though it was a beautiful day. I watched Fang leave Kingsnake's shoulders and take a spot on the couch. His tail patted the empty seat beside him.

"Everything alright?" Larisa asked, joining us in the entryway.

"I'm not sure." Kingsnake crossed his arms over his chest as he looked at me. "What is it, Harlow?"

I'd made my decision, and there was no turning back. "I want you to make me into a vampire." It wasn't my first choice for how to be with Aurelias. I'd rather live one human life with him than forever, childless with my family deceased. But if this was the only way...then so be it.

Kingsnake stared at me blankly for several seconds.

Larisa did the same thing.

Even Fang seemed to tense.

"I've thought about it...and this is what I want." I continued to look at Kingsnake.

Kingsnake exchanged a look with Larisa. "But this isn't what Aurelias wants. Otherwise, you wouldn't need to ask me."

"I asked him to be human for me, but he won't. This is the only way."

His eyes softened. "Harlow—"

"Please."

Kingsnake looked at Larisa again.

"I know he won't turn me because of what happened with Renee. He's afraid of...you know. But if you do it—"

"I would never turn another man's woman," he said. "That's not acceptable conduct."

"But this is a different circumstance."

"*Harlow*." His eyes narrowed. "I would be sick to my stomach if Aurelias turned my wife. I would never turn his—not without his consent." His eyes softened again. "I'm sorry. You can ask Cobra if you want, but he'll tell you the same thing. This is something you and Aurelias need to agree on together."

Larisa moved her hand to my arm. "But I agree with Aurelias. It's not fair for you to make the sacrifice if he's not willing to do the same for you. I know you love him, but you deserve more than that."

"You became a vampire for Kingsnake..."

"But he would have become human for me if I'd asked. We ultimately determined this was best for us as a couple."

My eyes dropped to the floor, the sadness gripping me by the throat. "I don't think I'll ever get over him."

Larisa moved into me and hugged me.

"He did all of this for me...just to let me go?"

"I'm sorry." She rubbed my back.

I started to cry, my chin on her shoulder.

Kingsnake drew near, placing his hand on my shoulder. "I'm sorry. Fang is too."

The vampires had packed up their belongings and were prepared to return to the coast where their ships were waiting. They would sail back to their lands far away across the sea, to a place I wouldn't be able to find again even if I wanted to.

A part of me didn't want to say goodbye to Aurelias. Just hide in the cottage until it was too late. To see him ride away for the last time and leave me here alone, a place that would never feel the same after he'd left his mark everywhere.

But I knew how much it would hurt Aurelias to let that be our last conversation, when I stormed out with tears streaming down my face and he was too naked to follow me. And the last thing I ever wanted to do was hurt him.

So, I dressed and left the cottage, running straight into my father.

He was dressed in his uniform but without his armor and sword. He looked me over, seeing me in a long-sleeved dress and boots. My hair was done, and my face was made-up. If this was the last time Aurelias ever saw me, I wanted his memory of me to be the prettiest I'd ever been.

My father gave me a quick once-over. "I'm glad you changed your mind."

We walked together through the city and down the path to the gate. The vampires were ready to go, their steeds saddled for the ride, already lined up in their ranks. My mother and brother were there to say their goodbyes. Kingsnake and Cobra stood with Fang and their wives.

And Aurelias was in the center, wearing the armor my father had gifted him, his family crest combined with ours. He was handsome in the morning light, but his eyes were black and broken. He hadn't noticed me just yet, but when I drew close enough for him to feel me, his eyes shifted to mine.

Our eyes locked, and every moment we'd shared passed between us.

It was the most painful sensation I'd ever endured.

I stopped several feet away from him, because now that I was there, I realized just how brutal this would be. We stared at each other, neither one of us making the first move, neither one of us wanting to say goodbye.

When nothing happened, Kingsnake approached me. "Take care, Harlow." He gave me a one-armed hug.

"Thank you for everything."

"You can call upon your vampire friends for anything." He gave a nod before he stepped away.

Cobra came next. "I know this sucks..."

A painful smile came through at his candor.

"And I'm sorry that it does."

"I know."

He gave me a brief hug then stepped away.

Larisa and Clara hugged me as well. Fang was on Larisa's shoulders, so he leaned in and gave me a little kiss with his tongue. "He says you're a great card player," Larisa said. "And he'll never forget you."

That almost brought me to tears. "I'll never forget you either, honey."

They stepped aside.

That was when I saw my father embrace Aurelias, hugging him the same way he hugged Atticus, squeezing him hard like he didn't want to let go. His palm supported the back of Aurelias's neck. He pulled away and looked at Aurelias. They exchanged words that were too quiet for anyone else to hear. My father gave him a final grip on the arm before he released him for the last time. He walked past me, and with my mother and brother, they walked up the path to the castle, probably to give us some privacy.

Kingsnake and the others did the same, moving to their horses on the field and mounting them for the ride.

Aurelias stared at me.

I stared back.

It was quiet, so quiet I could hear the horses neigh and swish their tails. When they shifted their weight, their hooves tapped against the hard earth. The sunshine was bright on that cloudless day, even though it'd been overcast for the last week. It made his skin brighter than usual.

I didn't know what to say. How did you say farewell to the love of your life?

He clearly didn't know what to say either because his chin dropped momentarily.

I moved toward him.

His eyes watched me, taking a deep breath as I drew near.

I rose on my tiptoes, reached my fingers into his hair, and kissed him, so very softly.

His arms immediately hooked around my waist, and he pulled me close.

Tears wanted to escape my eyes, but I kept them locked away. I kissed him like it was the first time rather than the last, without heed or haste. These lips would belong to someone else someday. I would be another memory, just the way Renee was a memory to him. I just hoped it wouldn't bring him nearly as much pain.

I was the first to pull away.

His arms stayed on me like he didn't want to let me go. "Baby—"

"I love you." I didn't want to say more than that, to revisit the dreadful conversation that had no positive resolution. It was only painful for us both.

His eyes shifted back and forth between mine before he understood. "I love you."

I wouldn't say goodbye. Never.

He didn't say it either.

His arms left my waist, and he pulled away entirely.

I knew that he would never touch me again, that he was already a memory even as he stood directly before me.

He stepped back then turned away, his muscular back to me. He grabbed on to the horn of the saddle and pulled himself up and grabbed the reins. This was the moment he was supposed to dig his heels into the horse and take off, but he hesitated. He hesitated for a long time.

I prayed to the gods he would change his mind.

Please...

But then he dug in his heels...and left.

TWENTY-SEVEN
HARLOW
THREE WEEKS LATER

Winter arrived.

It was always cold this far south, but now that the season had arrived, the snow started to fall.

And it didn't stop.

The field where the battle had taken place was covered with the white powder, hiding all the bloodstains of those who'd given their lives. Peace had been restored to the Kingdoms, and Atticus began the daunting task of preparing everyone to travel through the snow and back to their homes.

Assuming they were still there.

I spent my time in the cottage in the village, wanting to be away from the prying eyes of my family. It hurt them to see me hurt, so it was best I just avoided them altogether. Lila visited me often, and we would go for a drink at the nearby pub or sit in front of the fireplace while the frost pressed up against the windows.

I spent most of my time at home, lying on the couch with a heavy blanket on top of me, rebuilding the fire over and over, making it burn constantly. I started to run low on firewood, but I didn't have the energy to purchase more from the lumberjacks in town.

I didn't have the energy to do anything.

Three weeks had come and gone, but it felt like Aurelias had just left yesterday.

I wondered if he'd made it back to his lands safely. It would be such a waste if he'd drowned on the way home.

A knock sounded on the door.

I was on the couch, and I almost didn't have the energy to stand up and answer it, but I forced myself up and across the room, wearing sweatpants and a long-sleeved shirt, my hair in an oily bun because I'd skipped the shower several days in a row.

The knock sounded again.

I opened the door without checking who was on the other side. "Father?" I hadn't seen him in a couple of weeks. They'd given me space and I hadn't had to ask for it, but it looked like their patience had worn out.

"I just had dinner with your uncle. Thought I would stop by." He held up the covered dish. "They had pot roast, so I thought you might like some."

"Oh, thanks." I took it from him and carried it to the counter. It was still hot like he'd come straight to my cottage after the pub.

He shut the door behind him and took a look around, his eyes settling on the empty rack next to the fireplace. "I'll grab you more firewood tomorrow. Looks like it's going to be a long winter."

"It's okay, Father," I said as I sat on the couch. "I can get it."

"It's no trouble." He moved to the armchair, wearing his casual clothes with his heavy fur coat on top. He looked at the stairs to the next landing where the bedroom was. "There're so many memories in this place…"

"Mother told me. She even told me about the time Grandmother poisoned you to take Mother away."

He rolled his eyes. "Not her finest hour."

"I'm surprised you forgave her."

"Didn't happen overnight." He stared at the fire.

"Mother told me this was your first home after you were married."

"It was."

"I like it here," I said. "It has a good energy."

A grin suddenly moved on to his lips. "Your mother caught me talking to Elora at the pub one night, not realizing she was my sister. When I walked in the door, your mother was so jealous, she stabbed me."

"*She stabbed you?*"

His grin widened. "Yep."

"Damn, she went full psycho."

"Yep." He said it with pride. "That's your mother."

My parents had been happy as newlyweds, and they were still happy as empty nesters. It made me feel lonelier, because I knew Aurelias and I would have been that way if we had stayed together.

My father must have felt the change in my energy because he asked, "How are you?"

I pulled the blanket to me and covered myself before I gave a shrug. "Same."

He stared at his joined hands. "I'm sorry."

"It's okay."

"It'll take some time, but it'll get easier."

"Yeah…"

"We can return to Delacroix when you're ready. I know you prefer the warm weather."

My eyes moved to the fire, remembering those long nights when the fire went out and we didn't even notice. The first time he told me he loved me, it was cold like it was now, so cold it took your breath away. I knew when I left, it would be a long time before I'd be able to return. "I don't mind it here."

TWENTY-EIGHT
AURELIAS

Our ships finally reached our shores, and our galleons docked. The horses were unloaded first, having stood idle for so long, and then everyone else came afterward, along with the slaves and the supplies.

I walked down the dock then stopped to look at the snowy mountains, the black castle visible against the contrast of white. The last time I'd looked at this place, I'd been a different person. Now I didn't recognize myself anymore.

Kingsnake came to my side. "Still how you remember it?"

"Yeah."

He clapped me on the back and continued to walk, Fang wrapped around his shoulders.

Now that I was King Aurelias, King of the Originals and King of Kingdoms, General Ashworth reported to me and asked for my orders every five minutes. My people turned to me and expected me to lead, something I was naturally good at after watching my father demonstrate his abilities all my life. It was a position I would have wanted in the past. But now that I had it only because I'd slain my own father, it didn't have the same meaning.

General Ashworth approached me. "Shall we stay in Crescent Falls or return to the Kingdoms?"

"Crescent Falls is fine."

Cobra came up to me next. "Viper is in the Kingdoms holding your position until your return. I'm going to ride there with Clara to check on things."

I nodded in agreement.

"You alright?"

"I'm fine," I said coldly.

Cobra regarded me like he didn't believe a word of that. "I forgot to mention...you're hung."

I turned my head his way in surprise.

"When I came to retrieve you after Father went all psycho on us, remember? You opened the door naked."

I continued to stare at him.

"Look, I'm not trying to be weird, but you looked like you needed to be cheered up, so..."

"And complimenting my dick is the way to do that?"

"Hey, who doesn't love a dick compliment?" He winked then walked off.

Clara came up behind him a moment later.

"Tell your husband to stop looking at my dick."

Both of her eyebrows rose at the comment.

I walked away before she could ask me about it.

It was nice to be on solid ground again. It took a day for the internal rocking to stop in my head. But now that the world was stable and there were no more distractions, I had nothing left to do but think.

Think about how miserable I was.

My old chambers felt like they belonged to someone else. Normally, I'd have a naked woman in the sheets by now, releasing all the pent-up frustration from the long sail across the sea, but my dick couldn't get hard for anything.

Well, except for one person.

I thought about her often. Not often...but all the time. I wondered how she was. If she had returned to Delacroix. If she'd already hooked up with someone else to replace me. How long it would be before she let someone else touch her the way I'd touched her.

Those thoughts were like poison, always bringing me to a state of misery that I couldn't escape. I drank, but that only made it worse. Going to sleep and waking up fresh seemed to be the only cure, but it was a weak one.

I sat at my father's desk, looking over his notes that made no sense, the words he'd scratched into the wood when he was bored. My mother's name had been engraved with his dagger. The mark was so deep and so clear, it was obvious that he traced it every single day, like freshening up the letters on an old tombstone.

A knock sounded before Kingsnake entered. "Received a message from Cobra." He set it on the desk for me to grab.

I didn't reach for it.

"He said the Kingdoms have been running smoothly in our absence. But Viper is cranky and ready to return home to resume his duties as general."

I continued to trace our mother's name with my forefinger.

"Are you listening?"

"Yes." I straightened and looked at him. "Heard what you said."

"Are you going to read it?"

"You just told me what he said."

Kingsnake stared at me for a few seconds before he sat in the armchair that faced the desk. "What happens now?"

"I guess I'll travel to the Kingdoms…"

"And rule as their king?"

"What did you think I was going to do?" I asked coldly. "Go shopping?"

"I just thought…since your politics have changed, you might not be interested in ruling over the humans like Father did."

I stared at my mother's name again. "Is that what you want?"

"I want to know what you want, Aurelias."

I wanted the one thing I couldn't have. "I don't really care, to be honest."

"Then what if we withdraw our government and allow the humans to appoint their own king. They can live separately from us. We can form a truce. We did usurp the throne from the Werewolf King, so they should hold no will toward us. It would be an opportunity for us to have the peace we've always wanted."

"And you don't think they'll want revenge for taking their throne?"

"I don't see why they would if we're the ones giving it to them."

My eyes went back to my mother's name.

"What do you keep staring at?"

I looked at him again. "I suppose. I can be the King of the Originals, and you and Cobra can resume your kingdoms. We can have an alliance with the humans."

"I think that would be best."

I sank back into the chair, waiting for him to walk out because the conversation was over.

But he stayed. And he stared. "You look like shit, man."

"You don't say..." My father was dead. My woman was gone.

"We can talk about it."

"Talk about what? That it's hard to sleep because I dream about killing my father or leaving my woman? Sometimes both?" My closed fist propped underneath my chin as my elbow rested on the armrest of the chair.

"I'm sorry."

"That I killed my fiancée and my father?"

"Those two aren't the same thing—"

"*Shut up, Kingsnake.*"

He didn't wince at my coldness. Took the beating because he cared more about me than his pride.

"My life had meaning. I fought to save their world from demons. I fought to protect the woman I love. Now I'm here...and I have nothing to live for." I would relinquish my title over the humans to live a quiet life in Crescent Falls, feeding on prey and fucking them during and afterward.

"Aurelias," he said gently. "You don't have to stay."

I ignored what he said.

"You didn't have to come back with us. You could have stayed a while longer—"

"The relationship had ended anyway. She ended it when I didn't give her what she wanted."

"But she tried to give you what you wanted."

My eyes focused on him.

"She came to me and asked me to turn her, but I said no."

If I'd had a beating heart, it would have stopped right then. "*She did what?*"

"You wouldn't turn her, so she asked me to do it."

"And you're telling me this now?"

"I knew your relationship was already tense as it was, didn't want to add fuel to the fire."

I dragged my palm across my mouth, annoyed that she'd pulled a stunt like that…but also unsurprised. "You did the right thing, Kingsnake."

"Did I?" he asked quietly. "She wants to be with you, no matter the cost, and you left anyway."

"It's not the right decision for her—"

"But it is her decision. You could be with her right now, but you denied her."

"Kingsnake, turning Larisa may have been the right decision for you, but it's not the right decision for us."

"I know you're afraid after what happened with Renee—"

"I warned you not to mention her again."

"Cobra or I could turn Harlow—"

"I would never let another man turn my wife, and if I can't do it myself, then I'm not man enough for her."

"Your wife?" he asked. "So, you would marry her if you could?"

My jaw clenched. "Obviously."

"Aurelias—"

"Just drop it."

"How?" he snapped. "How can I drop it when you're miserable?"

"I was miserable after Renee, and I got over it..."

"You never got over it. You still aren't over it. And it took you five hundred years before you loved someone else. We love Harlow—"

"Good for you."

"*Asshole, we love her for you.*"

I looked away.

"Turn her."

"No."

"Aurelias—"

"The answer is no. It'll always be no. Maybe someday I'll be smart enough to love a vampire instead of another human."

Kingsnake bowed his head in defeat.

I was glad he'd finally given up.

"And you aren't..." He took a deep breath like he didn't want to say what he was about to say. "You aren't willing to be mortal for her?"

In shock, I stared at him. "You'd want me to?"

"*No*," he said quickly. "But I'd want you to be happy."

Now I avoided his gaze for a different reason altogether.

"Now that I have Larisa, I know real happiness. I want that happiness for you. I'd be willing to give up my immortality for her if I had to."

"I'm not going to do that," I said quietly.

"So your solution is to...be miserable?"

"That's always been my solution." I'd been miserable a long time. The only interruption in that was my brief time with Harlow. Now I was back to my usual coldness.

Kingsnake turned quiet, his argument officially over.

I waited for him to leave my office so I could return to carving Mother's name in my father's stead.

My brother stood up and reached into his back pocket. "Harlow wanted me to give this to you." He set the folded-up piece of parchment on my desk. "She said when the time is right...but I guess the time will never be right." He left my office, the folded-up piece of parchment sitting where he'd left it.

I stared at it.

My fingers stopped tracing the name in the wood. The room was silent, the fire in the hearth suddenly quiet. The note could be anything. Could be a declaration of undying love...or could be filled with resentment for my departure. She wanted to be with me for the rest of her life, was willing to forsake her place in the afterlife just to have me, but I wouldn't allow it. I was the reason we weren't together.

Me.

I left the letter where it lay—and I had no intention of ever touching it.

The palace felt like a different place. Shadows lurked in the corners, and my father's potent presence somehow occupied the stone of the domain. I was King of the Originals, but I still felt dwarfed by his power.

Sleep was impossible. All I did was writhe in nightmares. My sword went through my father's neck, but I watched the whole thing, watched the blade sever the bone and then his head drop on the floor. I watched the light leave his eyes. Watched the blood pool on the stone and soak into the rug. Then his eyes grew animated, and he looked at me. "My firstborn...slew his own."

The nightmares were different every time, but more of the same. Now that peace resided in our continent, there was nothing to distract me. I would normally find a concubine who shared my same kinky desires and shack up with her, but I couldn't entertain the idea. I refused to allow myself to think of Harlow, but she was still the woman in my heart, still the woman who owned my body.

Once I fucked someone, it would really be over—and I wasn't ready for that harsh reality.

I was in the courtyard, standing under the open sky as the snow fell upon my shoulders. I breathed intentionally just to stare at the vapor as it escaped my nostrils. The cold was unbearable for humans, but for me, it was calming. The snow continued to pile upon my shoulders, and the world was silent. I wanted to walk to my father's grave to stare at the tombstone and ask for forgiveness, but his body was a world away.

Footsteps sounded behind me.

I knew it was Kingsnake.

He came to my side and looked up at the dark sky. "Storm is coming."

"I love it when it storms." I loved the howl of the wind, the flurry of snow as it rushed past the windows, the thunder as it echoed against the mountainside. Sunshine was overrated.

Kingsnake stood next to me in silence.

"Why are you in Crescent Falls?"

"We haven't talked in a while."

"I just saw you days ago."

Kingsnake turned to regard me, his eyes narrowed. "That was weeks ago, Aurelias."

It was? "That's what I meant to say..."

"You're drinking too much."

I was drunk right now. "It's not like it can kill me."

He turned quiet again.

I continued to stare at the courtyard, the stone benches covered in snow, the green leaves on the pines now white.

"You aren't okay."

"I killed Father. Of course I'm not fine—"

"*He deserved it.*"

I turned to look at him.

"His bitterness had poisoned his mind. His ambition was the only antidote to his misery and that ambition turned to obsession and that obsession to make others suffer as much as he had suffered was the only cure for his pain. He was a lost cause."

I looked at the courtyard again.

"I'm sorry you were the one who had to do it, but it would have been someone else at a later time. I wish it had been me...to spare you this pain."

"You wish you'd killed Father?" I asked quietly.

He hesitated. "You're my brother. I would do anything to shield your pain...including that."

"How touching..."

Kingsnake ignored my coldness. "Cut me down to protect your vulnerability. But that won't work forever, Aurelias. This pain won't go away until you face it head on."

"There's only one way to make it go away." Her palm on my cheek. The ache inside her chest, the ache she felt for my misery. Crystal-blue eyes that were both mischievous and so fucking pure. She was the only sheath to my blade, the only balm to my suffering.

"Then go back, Aurelias."

I could still picture her mind so clearly, even though it'd been two months since I'd said goodbye. She probably assumed I was already in bed with someone new…when I couldn't even entertain the idea. It felt like a betrayal even when I owed her nothing. "No."

"Turn her into one of us—"

"*Never*." I loved her too much to take her soul. Her pure, good soul.

"Did you read the letter?"

My silence was my answer.

"Why not?"

"I don't want to hear her voice in my head…"

"Aurelias—"

"Are you here to make me feel better or ride my ass?" I snapped.

He moved his hand into his pocket and pulled out the piece of parchment, probably having found it exactly where he'd left it on my desk and realizing I hadn't touched it. He opened it, read it in silence, and then started to read it aloud for me to hear. "Aurelias."

My eyes clenched shut.

"I can't predict the future, but I know for certain that the moment you read this, I'm just as miserable as the morning you left. I spend my nights alone and my afternoons avoiding the people I love. Solitude is the only tolerable friend in misery such as this..."

My eyes remained shut, listening to my brother's words but hearing Harlow's voice.

"There will always be a part of me that hopes you'll return. Whether that's in a few months...or a few years. Some may say I'm too young to know this, but I know our love was real. I know most people will never feel an ounce of it in their entire lives. I know most people will brush aside my words as childish infatuation because they can't even fathom a love like ours. They can say what they want. I know what I felt...what I still feel."

My eyes opened again, the ache inside my chest so much more painful now than it'd been a few minutes ago. It was unbearable, but I couldn't bring myself to silence him because I hung on every word she said...like always.

"If you ever decide to return, I'll be waiting for you. If I have a husband, I'll leave him for you. If I have children,

I'll share them with you. If you ever step back into my life, it'll be as if no time has passed. Even across the sea, my love for you will always endure...forever." Kingsnake folded the sheet and returned it to his pocket.

I stared at the snow, the heat deep behind my eyes, locked up in the vault that would never open.

Kingsnake took a breath as he stared at the courtyard with me. "There's nothing left for you here, brother."

The skies were cloudy, and there was fog in the air. The distant landscape was impossible to see through the thickness. It was exactly how I viewed my life, like it was nothing but opaque. "I have three brothers and two sisters...and a snake."

Kingsnake stared at the side of my face.

"All of whom I've treated like shit..."

"Forgive and forget, Aurelias."

I gave a subtle shake of my head. I had more to say, but it wouldn't come out.

"We'll always be your family. But you have another family across the sea now."

I couldn't look at him.

"It's where you belong...and you know it."

The ache became unbearable. "You'll lose me in the blink of an eye, Kingsnake."

"I can't pretend that doesn't hurt...because it does." He swallowed. "But I'd rather watch you smile in a single lifetime than be miserable for all of eternity."

I finally found the strength to look at him.

His eyes were pained, just like his heart. "It's okay."

"I think a mortal life is what I deserve, after I killed the man who blessed me with eternal life."

"No," he said. "This is how I see it. You lived fifteen hundred years to find Harlow. And now, you can live the mortal life you were supposed to have—just at a different time. And when this life is over, you can still be with her...in whatever comes after this."

The pain was worse than ever, but somehow, it felt right.

His hand moved to my shoulder. "This wasn't the right decision for Larisa and me. But I believe it's the right decision for you."

I realized a horrible truth, a horrible truth I'd known since the moment I'd arrived back here. "If I stay, I'll turn into him...Father. Bitter and angry and spiteful... I'll become withdrawn and unforgiving. My humanity will fade, and there will be nothing left but shadows and despair. I'll do terrible things...and feel nothing as I do them."

"The fact that you realize that on your own...is the reason you aren't him." His hand squeezed my shoulder before he let it go. "Let's figure this out and get you home."

"Kingsnake."

"Yes?"

A forced smile moved on to my lips. "Is this all a ploy to get rid of me? So you can take my place as King of Vampires?"

He stared for a second before a smile spread over his lips. "You caught me."

I took the lead, riding my stallion west, farther away from Crescent Falls and the rest of the Kingdoms. We'd never traveled this far west because it was only remote villages and mountains and other creatures.

It took several days to arrive in the small village, their buildings made of black stone and their main street made of dirt instead of cobblestone. My father had captured a witch and released her when she was of no use to him. She'd told us the name of her village, and that was where we headed.

When we arrived, we questioned the inhabitants until they told us about the cottage at the top of the hill. It was small, made of wood on top of a solid foundation, surrounded by willow trees. We took the path to the top and left our horses under the tree. It was sunset, so green fireflies were visible.

Kingsnake knocked on the door and waited for an answer.

Cobra came to my side. "You think you'll still be hung when you're human?"

I gave him a playful shove in the arm.

"You don't want Harlow to be disappointed, you know?" he asked. "If you come back to her with a small dick, she might not want you anymore. All I'm saying..."

"*Cobra.*" All Clara had to do was say his name, and he backed off like a well-behaved dog.

Larisa came to my side. "Your dick will be fine, Aurelias." She rubbed my arm. "Any second thoughts?"

"I'll always have second thoughts."

"You don't have to do this."

"I don't want to be human," I said simply. "But I want to be with her more than I don't want to be human. So, there's my answer."

Kingsnake spoke with the witch on the doorstep, and they remained in conversation for a while.

Fang left his pouch on the horse then slithered up my body, wrapping around my shoulders just the way he did with Kingsnake. ***I'll misss you.***

We'll see each other again, friend.

But we won't be able to ssspeak.

No...we won't.

I'm not sssorry that your father isss dead. But I'm sssorry for you.

I know, Fang.

They are all sssad that you're leaving. Asss am I.

This is the hardest thing I've ever had to do. Even harder than killing my father...

But asss much as it hurtsss, it'sss the right choice. I knew Larisssa was right for Kingsssnake. I know Harlow isss right for you. Ssshe'sss decent at cardsss.

That's how you approve people? If they're good at cards?

You can learn everything you need to know about sssomeone in cardsss. Ssshe'sss competitive, but she never cheatsss. Ssshe'sss not dissscouraged by her losssesss and keepsss trying. Ssshe'sss willing to play with me even when ssshe doesssn't want to, just to make me happy. Mosssst people are afraid of sssnakesss, but ssshe doesssn't judge a book by it'sss cover. Ssshe gave me a chance when

mossst people wouldn't. Her heart isss pure. I can sssee it.

Thank you for your approval, Fang.

The witch came over, dressed in billowing black robes, her hair as dark as midnight. She was young and attractive, but I knew witches could change their appearance on a whim. "Your father was deceptive and unkind. I didn't care for him, and I'm not sorry for your loss."

I didn't have anything to say to that.

"I would refuse to help you, but your brother tells me you do this for love. Is that true?"

I still couldn't believe I was about to do this. "Yes."

"You choose to spend one life with a human rather than spend an eternity with a vampire."

"Yes."

"For that reason alone, I will help you. Are you certain this is what you want?"

I looked around at my family members, all of whom would live for thousands of years after my death. I would be a memory to them, and then one day, they would probably forget what I looked like. The choice pained me, but it was the only choice I could make. "Yes, I'm certain."

The galleon was prepared for the voyage across the sea. I had a crew to escort me to the shore, leave me behind, and then return. The ship bobbed at the dock, the crew already on board, getting the ship ready to sail out of the cove. It was another cold day, the fog thick and heavy, but the experienced sailors would be able to get out to sea safely.

Kingsnake and the others stood on the dock, ready to say goodbye.

But no one said a word.

Neither did I.

I looked at all of them, words failing me. I knew this was what I wanted, but it was still the hardest thing I'd ever had to do. Now I actually wished Cobra would say something inappropriate to make this easier, but he didn't. He was dead serious, his expression hard. I couldn't feel their emotions like I used to, but I could tell they were all heartbroken. "I love you all." It was all I could muster myself to say.

Kingsnake made a slight nod before he gave me a hug.

I hugged him back, Fang wrapping around my neck to hug me with his body.

"I love you too," Kingsnake said to me as he clapped me on the back. He pulled away, his eyes slightly wet.

Larisa came next and hugged me around the neck. "I love you." She kissed me on the cheek before she stepped away.

Viper followed her, having the same stony expression I wore, locking his emotions behind iron gates better than the rest. "I love you, brother." He gave me a hug.

I patted him on the back then looked at Cobra.

"This really sucks…but I'm happy for you." He hugged me harder than all the others.

I gripped him back. "Thank you." I sniffed and let him go.

Clara came last, hesitant because she knew how I felt toward her kind.

But I let it go and hugged her. "Take care of my brother. You're the only person he listens to."

She relaxed in my hold and hugged me back. "I will. Take care, Aurelias." She moved away.

"Let us know when the wedding is," Kingsnake said. "We wouldn't miss it."

I nodded. "I will." I looked at them all again, knowing there was nothing else to do but get on the ship and sail away. "We'll visit. I promise."

"I know," Kingsnake said. "We'll visit too." He forced back his emotions as best as he could—not for himself, but for me. "Have a safe journey."

I turned away from my family, walked up the ramp to the deck of the ship, and then felt my body shift and rock with the waves that bobbed in the harbor. The crew removed the ropes that tied the ship to the dock, and the galleon immediately started to drift out to sea, the wind filling the black sails instantly.

I moved to the edge to see them standing on the dock, waving to me, forced smiles on their faces.

The heat seared the backs of my eyes, and when they were too far away to see the features of my face, I finally let the tears fall down my cheeks.

TWENTY-NINE
AURELIAS

After the ship took me to shore, I grabbed my horse and rode across the frozen landscape toward the passage that connected the bottom of the cliffs to the top. There was snow on the ground, and now the cold affected me far more than it did before. I rode hard, sticking to the shore where the snow was less deep, and then cut across the land once the cliffs were in sight.

The ramp was narrow with sharp turns, so I had to take this at a walk, but as I rose higher in elevation, I started to feel the change in temperature. It grew warmer the higher I rose, the cold now a distant memory.

When I reached the top, the castle of Delacroix was in sight. The grass was green, and the trees were in bloom. But the light was fading fast, and if I wanted to be there before dark, I'd have to ride hard down the path. It was the same place where Harlow and I had stood together and debated our next move. I'd wanted to take her to the docks so I could get a ship away from this land, but she'd tricked me into returning to Delacroix.

That trick was the reason I was there at that very moment.

I rode down the dirt path, passing merchants with carts as they hurried to get inside the gates of the city before dark. The gates were open, so I rode straight through them and handed my horse to the stable hand. Most of them recognized me and stared a little too hard, like they knew I had changed but couldn't determine how.

I walked into Delacroix, taking the long path up the hill toward the castle. Huntley and his family might still be in HeartHolme, but I suspected they had returned once the war was over to rebuild their other Kingdoms.

Once I would have known if Harlow were here because I would have been able to feel her mind. Now I felt nothing.

When I reached the gates, the guards let me enter without question, knowing exactly who I was.

I entered the castle, the grand stairs before me, the stone walls shielding me from the sunlight. But I realized it didn't burn anymore. It actually felt nice. I could head straight to Harlow's bedroom in the hope that she was there, reading on the couch or staring at the village from her open window.

But I turned to the right, heading to Huntley's study instead.

The door was cracked open, and he sat behind his desk, scribbling a note with a hurried hand. He finished it quickly then rolled up the parchment and dropped it into a copper tube to send to the aviary. He seemed distracted because he didn't notice me standing on the threshold. Or perhaps his guard was just down because the war was over and peace had returned to their lands.

I knocked on the open door.

Huntley's eyes immediately flicked up to mine, cold like he expected me to be a guard who had interrupted him. But when he realized it was me, his entire body went still, including his eyes. Several seconds passed of intense eye contact, and then all the muscles in his body relaxed in surprise.

He rose to his feet behind his desk and continued to look at me, his eyes quickly shifting over my body to identify the differences in my appearance, the change in my skin tone, the light in my eyes. Then a smile moved across his face, the biggest, grandest smile I'd ever seen him give.

The fist around my heart unclenched at his delight.

He came around the desk and moved straight to me, warm affection in his eyes, his joy infectious. His palms cupped my neck as he stared at me head on. "I knew you'd come back, son."

The heat burned behind my eyes, the emotion heavy in my chest. "You did?"

He nodded. "Welcome home."

THIRTY

HARLOW

I sat on the hillside in the shade of the sycamore, the castle walls far behind me. Little flowers had popped up in the grass, and I plucked one before I tucked it behind my ear. I wore a cream-colored dress, the air warm and humid on this beautiful day. I'd spent most of my time alone, and after months of Aurelias's absence, I'd come to accept that he wouldn't return.

But I was still as devastated as the moment he'd left.

I'd always been slender, but I'd lost weight from not eating, lost muscle mass from not being active. My parents tried to spend time with me, but I usually rebuffed their advances or made an excuse to avoid them.

"Mind if I join you?" My mother sat on the grass beside me, also in a dress, ditching her uniform and armor the second we'd returned to Delacroix. While I was miserable, everyone else was at peace now that the war was over.

"Sure." I picked another flower and handed it to her.

"Thanks, sweetheart." She tucked it behind her ear.

With my legs crossed, I sat and looked at the fields of Delacroix beyond, the dragons who napped in the area that we reserved just for them. Pyre was out there with Storm, the two of them balled together like they were cold.

"How are you?"

I was constantly asked that question, and my answer never changed. "Fine."

My mother didn't press me. "It'll get better."

I gave a quiet chuckle. "It'll never get better..."

"Time heals all wounds."

"Not when the wound is on the heart," I said. "I feel so stupid."

"Why?" Her hand moved to my back, gently rubbing me.

"I actually thought he would come back..." But he'd been gone for months, so he obviously preferred different women for the rest of his eternal life instead of one woman for one life. "I was willing to give up everything for him, but he wouldn't do the same for me. It wasn't a relationship...just a fling."

"A man doesn't give his life for a fling, sweetheart."

I knew I spoke out of anger, but that didn't stop my tantrum. "I offered to change for him, and he still didn't want me."

"Because he cared too much to let you. That's not a bad thing." She continued to rub my back. "I promise you, it will get easier."

I wondered if he'd slept with someone new yet. Or if he'd been sleeping with other people since the moment his ship docked. I hadn't even looked at anyone else, my heart so irrevocably broken. I didn't desire the things I used to, like a glass of wine at dinner, a chocolate-covered strawberry at the market, a good book. I didn't desire anything whatsoever, let alone another person.

A guard approached us on the grass. "Queen Rolfe, His Majesty wishes to speak with you."

Mother rose to her feet. "I'll be back, Harlow."

I was glad duty called her elsewhere. My mother was always my confidante, my best friend, the person I told everything to. But in this situation, she couldn't help me. No one could.

I sat there alone, the breeze moving through my hair, the sun continuing to set. Night would descend soon, and that was the hardest part of the day for me. It meant I was alone in a bedchamber, alone between the sheets, knowing other lovers in the world were cuddled close together in front of the fire. It was hard to imagine ever wanting that again, ever wanting that with someone besides Aurelias.

Footsteps sounded behind me. They were heavy, which meant it was my father to cheer me up after my mother had failed. They slowed as they came close then went quiet altogether.

I continued to look at the shadows from the trees, which were growing longer and longer with every passing minute. There was a chill in the air now, the kind that made bumps appear on my arms.

He moved to where I was on the grass and sat beside me. Black armor was visible on his legs.

My father hadn't worn armor since the last battle.

I turned to look at him, expecting to see dirty-blond hair and the blue eyes identical to mine. But eyes the color of the forest looked back at me. He had dark hair, so dark it looked like obsidian.

I stilled at his appearance and blinked, assuming my mind was playing tricks on me like it had in the past. But my eyes focused once again, and his appearance didn't change. His stare was intense, just the way it was in my memories.

Words left me because I couldn't speak. All I could do was breathe harder and harder. My throat grew hot and wet, and then my eyes started to ache as the tears coated the surface. "I..." I shook my head, my mind unable to string words together because I was shocked and happy and overwhelmed. He looked the same, but he also looked different. His face wasn't as pale anymore. There was a human aspect to his eyes now. I knew this was a different version of Aurelias from the one that had left.

He was human.

Finally, I was able to say something. "Aurelias..." Tears streaked down my cheeks as the emotion broke the surface.

His hand cupped my face, and he leaned in to kiss me, a soft embrace. It was gentle and slow, a kiss to heal our gaping wounds. Then he kissed my tears away before he looked at my face again. "I'm home, baby."

We entered the abandoned cottage where we were first together, the air stagnant from lack of use. It was dark because there were no candles or fire, but we knew the place like the backs of our hands, so we made it inside and upstairs to the bed that was last used by us.

Clothes dropped to the floor before we made it onto the bed, our mouths locked together in the most scorching embrace we'd ever shared. My back hit the sheets, and he moved between my thighs, his body hot for the first time. I could feel it when my palm touched his skin, feel the rushing blood underneath.

He kissed me as he rocked with me, his mouth devouring mine with purposeful kisses and heated breaths. His hand dug into my hair and fisted it.

The wait was killing me. I tugged on his back. "Get inside me," I said it between his lips, my words muffled with his tongue in my mouth.

He guided himself to my entrance then sank in with a moan.

My moan escaped as a quiet scream because it'd been so damn long. My nails clawed at his back, and we rocked together, both of us shaking because it felt better than it ever had. It felt different...more intimate...more potent.

"Baby..."

I'd had dreams where he called me that. Fantasies with his deep voice in my mind, my fingers down the front of my panties. It was real now, and it was so hard to accept, it nearly brought me to tears.

My orgasm was nearly instant, just a few minutes after he was buried inside me, his hot flesh warming the bed and the sheets around me. I squeezed him with my thighs as my center pulsed, as my eyes glistened with satisfied tears.

He was about to come. I could feel it. Feel it in his hardness, see it in the blotches of color on his skin.

But then he pulled out and released on my stomach, rocking his hips hard into me as he finished.

It was abrupt, and I hadn't anticipated it. He'd never done that before. And then I remembered he was human now…so his seed was fertile. He didn't ask if I'd been taking the herbs, and I hadn't because there had been no one since him.

But my disappointment was short-lived, because all that mattered was the man who was in my arms, who was over me that very moment, his cheeks red with blood, his skin sizzling hot.

"I can't wait until you can come inside me again."

His lips caught mine, and he kissed me hard, a sexy groan coming from his chest.

He started a fire for me in the hearth even though the sunrise was visible through the closed curtains. We'd been up all night, and even now, I wasn't tired. It was the first time the pain was gone from my chest, the first time I felt like me again.

My fingers touched his jawline, feeling the thick scruff that had grown through his journey. I continued to look at his face, unable to believe he was really there with me, that he had sacrificed eternity for a single life with me. "I didn't think you would come back."

He grabbed my thigh and hiked it over his leg, bringing us closer together. He smelled different now, still like sandalwood but with a heavier dose of manliness. "I didn't want to...but I was miserable."

My thumb brushed his bottom lip.

"And I knew I would always be miserable."

"Me too," I whispered.

"I knew I would turn into my father if I didn't come back to you. I would end up like him, bitter and angry, not caring who I hurt because I hurt. It was hard to leave my family, but they understood."

I couldn't imagine leaving my family. Choosing to live in a different place from my parents. Watching my father say goodbye to me. "I'm sorry."

"I can't feel your emotions anymore, but I know you mean that."

My fingers moved down to his chest, feeling the hard muscles that were as strong as I remembered. "How does it feel...to be human?"

"I don't love it, to be honest."

"Why?"

"The weakness is something I'll never get used to. My reflexes aren't as sharp. I'm more vulnerable to the temperature, whether it's hot or cold. I'm much hungrier than I used to be, needing to eat constantly."

"You should see what my father eats for breakfast."

"But it's all worth it...just for this moment." His arm circled my back, and he pulled me closer, both of our heads sharing the same pillow. The world began to stir outside the window as people got their days started, but we remained locked together in the little cabin, our bodies as one.

We spent the next few days together, retrieving food from the market and cooking in the cottage. We made the space our own, cleaning up the mess and changing the sheets. The curtains were pulled open to let the light fill the room, and the fireplace glowed when the nights turned cold.

It was a type of life we'd never had before. War was always in the back of our minds, but now there was only peace. We found new things to talk about, like our favorite dishes and flowers. I got to know him in a whole different way than I had before.

But he always had a tone of melancholy to him. When we were locked together in passion or conversation, it vanished, but the second he was left to his own devices, it returned. Storm clouds formed over him—and it poured.

He was trapped in one of those moments now, sitting on the couch looking out the window, the sun striking him in the face and highlighting the depths of his eyes.

"Aurelias?"

He stilled at his name and shifted his gaze to me.

I took the spot beside him, my hand moving to his arm. "What is it?"

"What is what?" he asked, his eyes hardening as he looked at me. Once his train of thought was disturbed, he became himself again, looking at me like I was the only flower in his garden. There was love in his eyes that hadn't been there before.

"The source of your despair…"

Now his eyes turned guarded.

"It's okay if you're sad…that you left."

He shifted his gaze to avoid mine. "That's not what it is."

"Because if it is, you can tell me. I know I would be sad if I'd left my family behind."

"Baby." His hand moved to mine. "I have no regrets. There's no way I could ever regret this…my only source of happiness."

He made me melt on the spot, made me weak at the knees.

"I just…" He kept his eyes averted. "I carry a lot of pain and guilt…about my father."

That had been my next guess. "I'm sorry."

"My brothers hold no ill will against me. Kingsnake even said he'd deserved it. In my heart, I know there was no other outcome to the situation. But nonetheless, it fucking hurts." He swallowed. "The only time it feels better is when I'm with you...and I'm not thinking about it."

"It's okay not to be okay, Aurelias. Even if your father wasn't a good man, it's okay to grieve for him." My hand squeezed his, feeling the heat from his flesh. It kept me warm at night, and that was a change that I loved. "It's okay to be sad."

He gave a subtle nod in understanding.

"You can always talk about it with me...if you want to."

"I know, baby." He finally looked at me again and pulled me close, brushing a kiss to my temple. "What are you making for dinner?"

"You're turning into a typical man," I said with a chuckle. "All you care about is food and sex."

"I didn't care about those things nearly as much before you."

THIRTY-ONE
AURELIAS

I walked into Huntley's study, finding Ivory reading on the couch, lying flat with her feet up on the opposite armrest. Huntley was working on something at his desk, wearing casual clothes because there was no reason to wear his bulky armor anymore. They were locked in comfortable silence and I didn't want to disturb them, so I walked away.

But Huntley heard me. "Aurelias."

I slowly turned back, slightly awkward that I hadn't seen him in days...because I had been with his daughter in a cabin for a week straight. I hadn't even seen Ivory until now.

But he regarded me with affection in his eyes as he rose from behind the desk.

Ivory set her book down and walked up to me, embracing me with a hug that reminded me of my mother's. It was warm with the perfect squeeze. When she pulled away, she grabbed both of my shoulders as she looked at me. "So glad you're home, Aurelias." She even kissed me on the cheek before she walked away.

Huntley watched her go before he shifted his gaze to me. "She must like you, because she doesn't kiss anybody but me." He turned to the bar and grabbed a bottle and a couple of glasses. "Let's have a drink to celebrate."

"What are we celebrating?"

He filled two glasses before he brought one to me and clanked his glass against mine. "Come on, Aurelias." He stared at me, a slight grin on his face.

I looked down at the glass, seeing the amber liquid that I'd drunk by the bottle when I'd been back in Crescent Falls. It had been the most depressing time of my life. I lifted my chin and looked at him again. "I have something to ask you."

"I know you do."

"Will you train me in the sword?"

Huntley's grin slowly disappeared. "That's not what I thought you would ask me."

"I'm not the fighter I used to be. It wouldn't be right to ask you for her hand if I can't protect her."

He stared at me for a moment longer before he set the glass down on the coffee table. "Aurelias." He took the glass out of my hand and put it down too. "Your skills haven't changed. There's nothing I can teach you that would be an improvement over your existing capabilities."

"But my skills are based on my previous abilities, which I no longer have. I need to learn skills based on what I can do. The weakness is prominent. I feel it in everything I do now. I miss it...deeply."

"Aurelias, you're still better than any soldier in this kingdom—whether as a human or a vampire."

"I'd still like you to train me. You fought well against the demons. Your kin did not."

His gaze hardened like that wasn't a compliment. "If that will make you feel better, then I'd be happy to."

"Thank you." I'd never thought I would ask a human for help, but my responsibilities toward Harlow were stronger than my pride.

"Aurelias."

My eyes had drifted away, so I looked at him again.

"You've earned my daughter. Now take her."

I released a heavy sigh because it felt wrong.

"You're being too hard on yourself." His hand moved to my shoulder. "Ask my daughter to marry you. You didn't sail across the ocean and forsake an immortal life to be anything less than husband and wife."

"You still give me your blessing?" I asked quietly.

His hand gave me a squeeze before he dropped his embrace. "I've dreaded this day since the moment she was born. And as she got older and I saw that she'd inherited my fierceness and her mother's no-nonsense attitude, I knew that she didn't need my blessing. I married my wife *against* my mother's wishes. She was the enemy to my people, and I did it anyway. Would do it all over again. So, while I appreciate that you asked, it's unnecessary. I trust her judgment. She knows what's best for her. And look who she's chosen." He gestured to me. "The hero who saved our Kingdoms from annihilation. She knows what she's doing. So, if you want to marry my daughter, go ahead and ask."

THIRTY-TWO
HARLOW

Aurelias walked in the door in his heavy armor, sweat on his forehead with his sword over his back. He'd just trained with my father, and whenever he returned, he was always starving like a bear.

He unclasped every piece of his armor and left it by the door, revealing his uniform underneath. It was still his old one, with the golden serpent on his chest, even though he was no longer an Original vampire. But it seemed to be important to him because he continued to wear it.

"How'd it go?"

He walked to me and gave me a quick kiss. "Your father doesn't go easy on me."

"Would you want him to?"

He gave me a smile and walked toward the stairs. "What's for dinner?"

"Why do you ask me?" I asked. "Do I look like a maid?"

His grin widened. "Want to have dinner at the pub?"

"Will we have sex in the alleyway afterward?"

"Of course."

"Then that sounds great."

He walked up the stairs and disappeared.

A few minutes later, a knock sounded on the door. I opened it to reveal my father on the other side, showered and cleaned up. "Hey, Father."

His eyes lit up when he saw me. "Sweetheart." He circled my body with a single arm and pressed a kiss to my temple before he let himself inside. "I haven't seen you in a while, so I thought I would stop by."

Time had flown by since Aurelias had returned. It'd been two weeks since I'd seen anyone else but him. "Sorry, ever since Aurelias has been back, I've just lost track of time." I used to have breakfast with my parents every morning and usually dinner. Now, I didn't see them at all.

"It's okay," he said quickly. "I'm happy for you." For the first time, he didn't look uncomfortable at the prospect of my having a man in my life. Didn't seem to care that I was basically living with a man who wasn't my husband. "I wanted to invite you to return to the castle. You don't have to stay out here in this little cottage. And we miss you."

My arms folded over my chest in discomfort. "I miss you too. But…I think I'd rather stay here with Aurelias." I didn't want to sneak back and forth. I didn't want us to be separated in two different buildings.

"This invitation extends to him as well."

"It does?" I asked in surprise.

"Of course. You're part of the royal family. You deserve all the amenities that your mother and I have at the castle." He glanced at the kitchen. "Instead of cooking your own meals and doing your laundry…and all those other things."

"I'll ask him what he thinks."

"Alright," he said, taking a look around at the small cottage, which contained old furniture and dusty rugs. "Would you like to join us for dinner?"

"I think Aurelias and I were going to have dinner at the pub tonight. But how about tomorrow?"

"Tomorrow it is," he said happily. "I'll see you then, sweetheart." He kissed me goodbye then left.

Aurelias came down the stairs moments later, dressed in trousers and a shirt, his muscular body stretching the fabric in the sexiest ways. His hair was still slightly damp, and his jawline had been smoothed with a good shave.

He smirked as he looked at me, as if he knew I was about to drool all over him. "Ready?" His arm snaked around my back, and he kissed me.

"I'm not going to be ready if you kiss me like that again."

His smirk grew before he grabbed my hand and walked me out.

We sat across from each other at the pub, both of us with tankards of ale and bowls of pot roast.

"This is my favorite," I said. "My father's too."

He took a couple bites, and when he didn't say anything, I knew he liked it because he just kept eating and eating, dipping his bread into the broth before shoveling more food down his throat.

I smirked. "I think it's your favorite too."

"It's good," he said, sitting over his bowl with his arms on the table.

"You eat like him too, like a bear."

He smirked. "Eating is exhausting."

"How often did you need to eat before?"

He shrugged. "Maybe once a week, depending on how active I was."

"Like a real snake, then..."

"I suppose." He continued to eat, wiping his bowl clean.

I remembered spotting him across the room and the way my thighs squeezed together at the sight of him. I'd wanted him right then and there, and I couldn't believe that I actually got him. He was mine forever.

When he finished his food, he grabbed his tankard and took a drink. "I admit, food tastes a lot better now that my body actually needs it. And there's much more variety to it. With blood...there's only so much variation."

I took a drink from my glass. "So, my father stopped by..."

"What did he say?"

"Well, I can tell he loves you, because he invited us both to live in the castle."

"Did he?"

"Said we deserve all the amenities as members of the royal family. Someone to cook for us, do our laundry, stuff like that." I knew Aurelias must have been used to that type of lifestyle as a prince in his lands, not that he would ever complain about our modest life in that little cottage. "What do you think?"

"Whatever you want, baby."

"I want to know how you actually feel."

"I'm happy to live in that cottage if you want privacy from your family. But if you want to be close to your family, I'm happy to do that too."

"Then I think I'd like to live in the castle, if that's okay."

"That's fine with me."

"We'll take one of the bigger chambers, not my old bedroom. Not enough space in there for both of us."

"I didn't realize we needed much space."

"You have no idea how many clothes I have…"

"You don't wear clothes around me, so I don't see why that matters." He smirked.

I smirked back. "I've never seen you smile the way you do now."

His smile slowly faded.

"I like it."

"I haven't been this happy in a very long time."

We walked home in the dark, the torches lighting up the main street and the alleyways. Hand in hand, we walked, both a little buzzed from all the ale we'd drunk. We walked in silence, and then Aurelias took us on a detour, down the small alleyways between the businesses and the homes.

My body burned in excitement because I knew what was coming.

When he found one completely deserted alley, he backed me up into the wall and kissed me, a possessive kiss as his hand fisted my hair. He grabbed my ass before his fingers snaked underneath my dress to hook his thumb inside my panties.

Wrapped in the darkness, I kissed him, anxious to have my panties off and his dick inside me.

He pulled them down my ass, and I raised my legs to step out of them before he shoved them into his pocket.

I undid his trousers and let his cock free before he hiked my leg over his hip and thrust inside me.

I moaned against his mouth when he entered me, sore from all the lovemaking we did every day but not enough to ask him to stop. He hadn't been inside me for all those months, and I never wanted him to leave. "Aurelias…"

Just like we were when we were clandestine lovers, we fucked in the alleyway, moaning and grinding while the world forgot we were there. I'd loved him then, loved him when I should have hated him, and now my love had deepened to such an intense level, it was indescribable. I wanted to birth his sons and daughters, to grow old with him and watch our children become adults, to appreciate every day together. I wanted to sneak into dark alleys to do things like this, no matter how old we were. "I love you…" I said it between our kisses, wishing he could feel how much I loved him. He knew how I'd felt long before I'd said it, and that was a gift that I missed.

He slowed his thrusts, his eyes on mine as if it was the first time I'd ever said that to him. He came to a complete standstill, looking at me in a way he never had before.

The heat was still there, but now there was a new tension added to it.

"Marry me."

I hadn't expected it, so the request floored me. I'd known he would ask me to be his wife someday, but I hadn't been sure if it would happen now or sometime in the future. But I also loved that he didn't ask me at all. He just told me.

Then he kissed me again, not waiting for an answer that he didn't need.

EPILOGUE
AURELIAS

I stood outside the temple and looked at the statue on top, the stone carved in detailed and masculine ways, showing the presence of the god Adeodatus, one of the gods the humans worshipped. The stone pillar rivaled the strength of the castle, the circular beams as big as a dragon's flank.

Kingsnake came to my side. "I've always found the human temples impressive, but this really is something." Fang was wrapped around his shoulders, and his head tilted back as he looked all the way up to the very top.

"Nervous?" Cobra appeared on my other side. "It's normal to be nervous."

"I'm not nervous," I said, my eyes on the large iron doors ahead.

"Good," Cobra said. "Because I wasn't nervous at all. Anxious, if anything."

"Can I speak to Aurelias for a moment?" Huntley appeared, dressed in his armor and uniform, his sword across his back.

My brothers scattered like scared fish.

Huntley stood beside me as he regarded the temple. "Did Harlow tell you her mother and I were married here?"

"Yes."

"I paid the priest to marry us despite my mother's objections. She wasn't happy."

"Well, I'm glad Harlow doesn't have to experience that."

He nodded. "Me too. Nervous?"

"No."

"When I married Ivory, I did it to save her life...but that was just an excuse."

I looked at him.

"Took a big gamble, but I won big." He grinned.

"How does this work?"

"The priest will bind your souls together forever. It's irreversible."

I continued to stare at him.

"So, if someone hates their wife someday...tough luck. You'll walk the heavens together, bickering then just as you did down here." He watched me. "Are you nervous now?"

My feelings hadn't changed. "No."

"Good," he said. "But there's something else you should know. I spoke to the priest, and with the way this magic works, it wouldn't be possible for you to turn back to a vampire someday...if you wanted to. This would make it ironclad, no going back."

I held his gaze.

"I should have given you some warning about that, but I didn't think about it at the time."

"It's okay."

"If you need more time, Harlow will understand—"

"The moment I decided to become human, I knew that was it. I've accepted this life fully. No going back."

He gave a nod. "Alright. I'm glad to hear that." His hand moved to my shoulder. "Time to get married, then."

We all entered the temple, the entryway fifty feet in the air. There was a fountain in the center with a statue, and the floor was a checkerboard pattern. We walked farther in, to the fire obelisk in the back where the priest waited for us.

Harlow was already there with her mother, wearing a white gown with flowers intricately woven into her hair.

I stopped when I saw her, never having seen her look so damn beautiful in my life. The dress had sleeves and stretched across the floor behind her. It was backless, and the material was thin and lacy, showing glimpses of her skin underneath. Her hair was in soft curls, white flowers tucked into the braids in different places.

I swallowed, unable to believe I was about to marry her.

Her eyes found mine, and instantly, there were tears.

I walked to her slowly, taking more breaths than I needed, and when I came close, she lifted her hands for me to take.

I took them like they were about to fall to the floor. I cupped the top of her hands with mine and brought them to my chest. A pain burned in my chest, an ache that wouldn't go away, a hurt so profound that it felt good. I squeezed her hands together as I looked at her, forgetting everyone else in the room who'd come to witness our eternal union.

Tears dripped down her beautiful face.

My hands left hers to wipe them away.

Then I realized she did the same to me, caught my own tears that I hadn't realized I shed.

My family and hers stood apart, giving us a moment to be together in silence.

The priest waited for us before he began. He started to read the rites from his text, but my eyes were on her and oblivious to everything else. I'd given up the most important gift in my life...my immortality. But now that I was with her, that life felt like a curse. This felt like the life I always should have had.

The priest finished then handed me the holy knife.

I brought it to my palm and sliced it across the flesh, drawing blood.

When it was Harlow's turn, she didn't hesitate to take the blade and nick herself.

I grabbed her hand with mine, squeezing our palms together, our blood coming together and dripping to the floor.

Then the priest spoke. "By the power of Adeodatus, your souls are forever bound. Death will part you in this life but not in the next. You'll walk through this world as husband and wife, and you will enter the afterlife as souls forever intertwined..."

I'm currently writing a dark fantasy romance that will release this spring. Sign up for my newsletter so you'll be ready to pounce on this epic romance. I'll also send you the first few chapters so you can meet The Death King and his mighty dragon Khazmuda. **Sign up for my newsletter here**

And if you want something new by me SOONER, I suggest you read my newest release **IT KILLS ME** under my contemporary dark romance alter ego ***Penelope Sky***. I'm offering a special preorder incentive to those who preorder the entire series. It's gonna be sooo much fun. **Grab your copy here**.

Printed in Great Britain
by Amazon